THE WATER CHILDREN

THE WATER CHILDREN

Anne Berry

**WINDSOR
PARAGON**

First published 2011
by Blue Door
This Large Print edition published 2011
by AudioGO Ltd
by arrangement with
HarperCollins*Publishers* Ltd

Hardcover ISBN: 978 1 445 85902 6
Softcover   ISBN: 978 1 445 85903 3

British Library Cataloguing in Publication Data available

Printed and bound in Great Britain by
MPG Books Group Limited

For Bez, my dear father-in-law, who never swam in the sea but chose to rest upon the changing tides.

1911–2010

'Give your will over to the flow of me. And let me take you with me to my mother, the sea. For there a bed has been made ready.'

The Water Children, Anne Berry

No water-babies, indeed? Why, wise men of old said that everything on earth had its double in the water; and you may see that that is, if not quite true, still quite as true as most other theories which you are likely to hear for many a day. There are land-babies then why not water-babies? Are there not water-rats, water-flies, water-crickets, water-crabs, water-tortoises, water-scorpions, water-tigers and water-hogs, water-cats and water-dogs, sea-lions and sea-bears, sea-horses and sea-elephants, sea-mice and sea-urchins, sea-razors and sea-pens, sea-combs and sea-fans; and of plants, are there not water-grass, and water-crowfoot, water-milfoil, and so on, without end?

The Water Babies, Charles Kingsley

1961

It is the recipe for a perfect day. The sun beats down from a cloudless blue sky. The air fizzes with heat and salt. The sea glitters and shifts and curls and breaks along the three-mile stretch of pale, gold, Devonshire sand—Saunton Sands. It somersaults over mossy rocks and tangled tresses of tide wrack. It sends the beach into a nervous, excited jitter. The sea-sawing cry of gulls rises to a crescendo with their swoops and nose-dives, then quiets as the curved beaks snap at darting fish. Apart from a few surfers riding the breakers, and sporadic clusters of people guiltily enjoying their mid-week leisure break, this coastal paradise is deserted. But then it is still early morning.

Like the day itself, the Abingdon family have all the right ingredients to be perfect. It only remains to see what happens when you blend them all together. They are stepping onto the beach now, arms full, trudging determinedly through the unresisting sand. There is the mother, Ruth, tall and willowy in build, and the father, Bill, prematurely balding, a couple of inches shorter than his wife and broad-chested as a weight-lifter. And then come the two children, a tousled, fair-haired, leggy boy of eight, Owen, pulling a sturdy little girl who is almost five after him, Sarah. Sarah is protesting, her plaintive whines muffled by her scrap of a comfort blanket, once pink, now greyed, frayed and faded with constant mouthing.

'Tell Sarah to walk properly,' Owen calls after his parents. Neither of them pause. This expedition to find the right spot, the precise one in this unfamiliar desert terrain, is a serious business. 'She's dragging her feet!' He gives his sister's tiny hand a shake, and pulls his brow down before rounding on her in his frustration. The sun is in his eyes so that he cannot see her face clearly. 'I can't carry you and the bag, now can I?' Sarah, who clearly doesn't see the logic of her brother's words, or chooses not to, sits down with a thump on the sand. Sighing with an exaggerated heave then slump of his slight shoulders, the way he has seen his mother do, Owen lets go of her hand.

'Mum, Sarah's being really naughty!' he cries out, but not very loudly, not nearly as loudly as he can, certainly not loudly enough to summon back his mother.

He pauses to see if his sister, fearing a reprimand, will rise to her feet, then make an effort to keep up. His life would be so much easier if only she would co-operate. But Sarah only grinds her little bottom deeper into the sand, and mutinously thrusts a thumb in her mouth. 'Do you have to be such a big baby?' Owen sets down his bag and drops to his knees. Hooding his eyes with a bent elbow, he can see that his sister's, a lighter shade of blue than his own, a radiant blue, and big and round, are wet-lashed, that her bottom lip is quivering. She reaches her needy arms up to him. Instantly he feels the tightness in his chest loosen, the irritation with this sister of his, this annoying millstone, fall away as if it never was. With one hand he strokes her loose curls, so pale they are almost white, so soft they feel like dust.

2

'Don't cry, Sarah, don't cry. It's all right. We'll go more slowly I promise.' He wants to hug her, to draw the stubborn pillow of her body close to his, but he feels a bit awkward out here in the open. At home cuddling her is fine, nice really, but maybe not in public. Least ways, his parents never hug outdoors, or indoors either now he thinks of it, definitely not in front of him anyway. Compromising, he moves to tickle her armpit. She gives a squeak of a giggle and rewards him with her special smile, the one warm enough to melt steel. He takes up his bag and they stand together, clasp hands, and move clumsily onwards, as if their legs are tied together in an obstacle race.

But ahead of him his mother has stopped. She is looking back at them and his father is striding towards him, so perhaps aid is on its way after all.

'Daddy!' exclaims Sarah in delight, and Owen's father moves straight past him to scoop his daughter right out of his son's grasp.

His father, Owen observes, as he watches him twirling Sarah about in his arms, is not dressed for the beach. Owen is wearing a white cotton shirt and tan shorts, his mother, a summer halterneck dress with a pattern of daisies on a turquoise background. Sarah is wearing a green and yellow skirt and a cotton blouse with frilly short sleeves. They all have their swimming costumes on underneath their clothes. They changed into them at the guesthouse, house before they left. But his father is wearing a long-sleeved shirt, a blazer and trousers, all grey, and his shoes are polished to the gleam of a conker. On his head sits a straw boater. He looks so silly, so absurdly formal that Owen wants to burst out laughing. It is as if he has gone to lots of trouble to

3

dress up for the beach, when most people are dressing down. He shakes his head when Owen asks if he will look after Sarah.

'Can't be done,' he says, setting Sarah down gently and planting a swift kiss on her head. 'On an important mission, son. Off to fetch some rocks to secure the beach mat. Got my orders and have to jump to it. You know the drill, old chap. Your mother's setting up camp,' he adds with a grin, gesturing in the direction of his wife. His Welsh accent is very faint. But Owen wishes even the trace of it would vanish. To him it sounds silly, vaguely comic, as if his father is a buffoon off a television comedy. Now Owen follows the direction of his stiff military hand, and sees that his mother is indeed setting up camp, that she seems to be unpacking so much they might be going to stay here for a week. 'Still, not much further to go now. Sarah, you be good for your big brother. Chin up, Owen. Forward ho, eh?'

And then he is gone, head down, marching determinedly, his arms moving like pistons. Owen sighs. He and his sister are wearing leather sandals. Following his father's gleaming shoes digging into the sand, the spray flying up behind him, Owen ponders that he would have taken a fair load on board by now, that each step must be uncomfortable. He grazes the corner of his mouth with his upper teeth, grasps Sarah's pudgy hand once more, and sets off after his mother. By the time he reaches her he is feeling hot and cross again, and rather wishing they had not come on this outing at all. It is supposed to be a treat, but it is beginning to feel more like torture.

He can see that his mother is itching to unpack, to

4

unroll the beach mat and declare ownership of their plot. The breeze keeps freeing wisps from her pony tail, and he can tell by that slight nervous tick in her cheek that she, too, is irritated. She satisfies herself by unrolling the windbreak, and with her son's assistance driving the wooden sticks into the sand. Sarah is sitting down on the bright beach towel their Mother has opened out for her, and babbling to herself in a musical baby talk that she alone understands. She fills her chubby fists with sand and drops it all very deliberately in the lap of her skirt, marvelling at how the material dips, at how heavy the slippery yellow stuff is.

Ruth looks at her dimpled daughter, plump as a dumpling, blonde-haired, blue-eyed, and the sight of her lifts her heavy heart and fills it with light. She scolds her, but her tone is at odds with her words, and her lips twitch upwards. She takes off Sarah's blouse and skirt and shakes the sand from them. Then she makes an arch of her hands over her brow, and scans the beach in search of her returning husband. But there is no sign of him. She clucks impatiently and starts to talk under her breath. Perhaps she thinks that Owen cannot hear her when she speaks like this, but he can. Sometimes he thinks that he is especially sensitive to these mutterings, as if he is tuned into their hissing sound waves, much like a wireless set.

'That'd be right. Just like your father. He can't pick up any old rocks. Oh no! He has to make a performance of choosing them, selecting them, hefting them over and over in his hands. How heavy are they? How smooth? How suitable for the task? As if anybody cares. As if anyone gives a damn. They're just rocks for goodness' sake, rocks to hold down the blessed mat, not the supporting columns of the Acropolis!'

As she speaks she unrolls a small portion of the mat, sets Sarah upon it, lifts and shakes out the towel and tucks it away again. She pulls a white sailor's hat from a bag, tugs it over her daughter's breeze-rumpled curls and slips off her sandals. And then she instructs Owen to sit with his sister.

'I'm going to find your father,' she says, swatting back the flying wisps of her own hair with a few slaps of her hand. 'You are to stay here with Sarah till I get back.' Owen is only half-listening. He is eyeing up the new beach ball they have brought with them. It is the blow-up kind, red and white, and he can just see it peeping out of the largest holdall between the clutter of buckets and spades. 'Do pay attention, Owen. You're to look after Sarah while I'm gone.' Owen gazes skywards. He envies the seagulls, he really does, screeching and flapping about any old how. At least they are free—not always being asked to mind pesky little sisters prone to getting into trouble. Sometimes he wishes that he has a brother in her place, a rough-and-tumble boy who adores him and trails obediently after him, like a puppy, doing everything Owen tells him to—and not a contrary, disobedient girl. Girls are trouble. They are so independent, such a handful. He will never manage to train Sarah.

'Owen, are you listening to me?' his mother says now.

'Yes, I heard,' he replies sulkily. He rolls his eyes. And when his mother gives him that look of hers, the one where she raises her eyebrows, tightens her mouth, and puts her head on one side, he speaks again. 'I'll watch her. I promise.' They are always

6

worrying about Sarah, he thinks dully. Never about him. Always Sarah, Sarah, Sarah! Oh, he doesn't mind really, it's only that sometimes he would like them to be interested in him, perhaps even a bit concerned if he grazes a knee or something. I mean, he isn't a cry baby like Sarah is, but it would be nice if they told him he was brave. Yes, that would be really nice.

His mother nods curtly, hesitates for a moment, then with another of those looks walks off in the direction that his father went. After a minute they can't even see her, not with the windbreak in the way.

'You're a brave boy, Owen!' He tries the words out for size and finds they fit very well. 'You're a brave boy, Owen!' he repeats, and the sentence feels as catchy as an advertising slogan. Sarah, by his side, glances up.

'Bwave boy,' she says.

She can't pronounce her 'Rs' yet, but he supposes it's quite cute really, and besides, she'll probably grow out of it eventually. He clambers onto his knees and walks forward on them. Still on the mat, he can just reach the deflated ball. He stretches out a hand and retrieves it. Now for a bit of magic that will really impress his sister. 'Watch this, Sarah,' he says, bringing the clear plastic nozzle to his lips. He blows and blows and slowly at first, then more rapidly, the ball swells, its glossy plastic skin growing taut. Sarah is delighted with the trick and claps her hands. 'See, see how clever your older brother is.'

'Owen, it's so lovely,' she gasps.

In one of those sudden impetuous moves of hers, Sarah throws her little arms around him. He took off his shirt while his mother was undressing his

7

sister, and now he feels the ligature of her limbs tightening on his bare skin, her face rubbing against his chest. It is one of those mysterious moments when everything seems much larger. He can feel her hair, like water, and the unbelievable softness of her lips, and even her eyelashes moving. They are like a butterfly's wings fluttering against him. The wind seems to be getting up a bit now, and although they can't feel it because of the windbreak, they can see how it is battering the canvas and making the segments billow like sails.

He closes his eyes and concentrates on the squeeze of Sarah, so light he can push her away with one shrug, and yet so strong it brings a blocked-up feeling to his throat. And this feeling, the way he imagines a corked, fizzy drink must feel, wanting to burst out but not being able to, well . . . it's gigantic. It's so gigantic, in fact, that there seems to be nothing more to him, just the squeeze of Sarah and the bursting feeling.

The tide is coming in and the waves seem to be getting bigger, not folding on the shore any more but smashing against it. Owen decides he will be a surfer one day, that he will ride the rollers in like a cowboy on a water horse. The dark shapes balancing on their boards look like hitherto unknown sea creatures, sweeping towards the shore. And when at last they tumble off and clutch the dripping surfboards in their arms, it's as if they are pushing giant sharks before them into the shallows, the upright boards, their fins. He bets it's fun, more fun than driving a car even.

'Do you want to watch me kick the ball?' he asks, glancing down at the white-gold curls and disproportionally large hump of head. 'Do you want

8

me to show you how good I am at football?'

He feels Sarah nod rather than hears her. 'Right then,' he says, pleased to be doing something. Disentangling himself from her, he springs up clutching the ball. 'Watch this.'

The mat lifts a bit when he gets off it, but he can see that Sarah's weight is still sufficient to partially anchor it down. He starts kicking the ball, just small taps at first, then running a few yards and kicking it back, as though there are two of him and not one. Sarah claps gratifyingly.

'Again,' she cries enraptured. 'Again, Owen.'

She isn't telling him he is brave, but . . . well, it is near enough. For a while he knees it. Then a sudden gust of wind grabs it and runs with it towards the sea, so that he has to give chase. Behind him he hears Sarah call.

'Owen! Owen! Owen, don't go!'

'I'm only getting the ball. I won't be a second,' he throws back over his shoulder.

'Don't leave me, Owen.'

When he catches up with it, he glances back, just to make sure that Sarah has stayed put. But he need not have worried, she is sitting exactly where he left her, prattling to herself, counting on her fingers, and staring around her, wide eyed. They are not beach dwellers. In fact he can only remember going to the seaside a couple of times before. No, this is definitely a holiday outing, and an unusual one at that. Home is Wantage in Oxfordshire. His parents seem much happier hiring a caravan or camping and sitting in a field of green grass, than coming into close proximity with the sea. Perhaps it is something to do with the fact that his father is a gardener, or that his mother doesn't like the sand.

She complains that it gets into everything—clothes, food, even your hair. She'll start complaining today, he's sure of it.

Owen hasn't learnt to swim yet. There has been talk at his school of taking the older classes to a pool, and giving them proper lessons. But nothing has come of it so far. His parents are always promising to teach him, but how can they if they are nowhere near the sea? He keeps pleading with his father to take him to the local swimming pool, so that he can learn there. Actually he has thought about this quite a lot. Having all that time alone with his father, with him showing Owen what to do, even touching him, putting his arms and legs into the right positions. He is looking forward to this more than he can say, because his father doesn't seem to like to touch him very much. He prefers to slap Owen on the back or shake his hand as if they are not related, as if Owen is an adult too. And even this physical contact makes him go all red and embarrassed. He knows what his father thinks, that embracing him is unmanly, that hugging your son is a soppy way to behave. So in those intimate moments he clears his throat, or starts talking about a new plant or taking cuttings or something. Though he isn't at all embarrassed about hugging Sarah, Owen notes. Of course his mother does put her arms around him and give him a peck on the cheek, pretty well every night. But it is sort of automatic, as if she isn't thinking about it. Whereas with Sarah all his mother's hugs, his father's too, really, are kind of whooshes, like the sudden flaring up of a flame.

In any case, his father always seems too busy to go to the swimming pool. They have been once or twice but he just seemed restless and bored, and

10

when Owen didn't take to the water the way a duckling would, he was impatient to go home again. And that impatience, that sense that his father knew he was going to fail, made it come true. It was like being cursed, him looking at the big clock-face on the wall and folding his arms. And the next thing Owen knew was that he was spluttering and choking, and feeling a belt of panic tightening about his belly, so that he really believed he might drown, right then and there, with his father watching. They hadn't got as far as learning the swimming strokes so there wasn't very much touching—well, hardly any at all, if Owen is truthful.

It is while he is thinking about this, while he is dribbling the ball and picturing his father holding him up in the water and saying encouraging things like, 'Well done, terrific, you're going to make a racing swimmer one day, my boy', that he notices his mother. She is a long way off up the beach, running towards him shouting something. But he cannot decipher it because the wind is making a whirring sound in his ears, and besides, she is too far away. Still, there is something about the untidy way she is moving that makes him stiffen, and feel a bit empty and sick inside. It is a sort of headlong fall, nearly tripping up in her haste every few steps, and even though she must be out of breath, shouting in sharp bursts, rather like the screeches of the seagulls.

And then a flint arrow lances his beating heart and turns it to ice. He remembers. Sarah. He spins round. The stripy windbreak seems miles away, and as small as a postage stamp. How can it be that he has come so far? What was he dreaming about? But then he knows that, doesn't he? And he can see the beach mat blowing away beyond it, bumping the sand and flapping, like a wounded bird. Surely, surely, oh please let it be true, Sarah is tucked up safe behind that buffeted stamp of canvas. Of course she is; she is sitting behind the windbreak happy as can be, precisely where he left her. Where he left her. The words clang in his head. Where he left her. 'Don't leave me, Owen.' Even though he is barely a few years older than his sister, he knows in some kind of dreadful, intuitive, grown-up way, that her plea will never leave him. He is as good as branded with it. 'Don't leave me, Owen.' This is the sinister dread that takes hold as he sprints. And because he is lighter and not sinking into the sand, he is much faster than his mother.

He is good at running. He even won the twenty-five yard sprint at his last school's sports day. He recalls how proud he felt, his chest heaving with it, as he neared that ribbon. Then breaking through it, and turning round breathlessly to look for his father in the crowd of parents. And the disappointment, like a paperweight sinking in his stomach. His father had wandered off to talk to the school caretaker. He could see him by the trees at the edge of the field leaning over a bush tweaking the leaves. He had missed it. He had missed Owen's victory.

But this is a different kind of race, a horrible race, one that you aren't sure whether you want to win or not. He can hear his mother's shrieks now, big ugly sounds, like the ones he hears in his head when the witches and monsters speak in stories. And he can hear the name too, screamed again and again.

'Sarah! Aargh! Aargh! Sarah! Sarah!'

And then he is rounding the windbreak and screaming her name too. But she isn't there, only the sailor's white hat without her in it. There is a small pile of sand, and he thinks he can detect the lines where Sarah has drawn in it with her stubby fingers. And her scrap of pink blanket is peeping out from under it too, that horrid smelly thing that seems to be impregnated with an incredible power, sending his sister into a serene trance each time she rubs it rhythmically over her lips. But though he peers hard at it, she doesn't appear. He keeps barking her name, as if in all likelihood she will suddenly rise up from under the sand. She will be like the sand creature in a book he has read, *Five Children and It*. And any moment she will spring up and shimmy the glittering grains off her, giggling at the great game.

Out of the corner of his eye he sees his mother streak past and hurtle down to the sea, and then straight into it with the waves breaking over her, and her behaving as if she cannot feel them. He rushes after her, rushes into the water, as far as he dares to go, knowing he is unable to swim. Then he runs up and down, the way he has seen dogs do sometimes when they are nervous of getting wet. And his mother keeps bobbing up like a seal, gasping out words as though a saw is grinding on her throat.

'Sarah! Sarah! I can't . . . can't find Sarah!' And Owen thinks stupidly, as salt spume strikes his eyes, making him wince, why is she searching for her there in the wide ocean, why is she trying to fish for Sarah? Then under again and up, a gulp of breath, another dive. A long beat and she explodes from the water, fixing Owen for a second, her brown eyes slitting with the salt bite, or is it something else? 'You stupid boy! You stupid, stupid boy!' Then

13

down again, and for the longest time, it seems to Owen, the stupid boy, darting to right and left as if blocking a goal. And up to spit out once more, 'I told you to watch her. I told you to stay with her. I told you, I told you, I told you, you idiot!' And her face all ghastly and coming apart like a mirror breaking, and her ribbon undone and the wet hair streaming over her eyes, and stuffed in her mouth.

Then suddenly his father thundering past him, like the charging rhinoceros he saw on his last birthday at London Zoo, only pausing to kick off those shiny shoes. The two of them now, both seals together, one, an arc of grey, one of yellow, white and turquoise, looping about each other. And his father's straw hat bobbing on the water, bobbing so gaily on the water that Owen wants to tear it to pieces. And finally his father bursting triumphantly from the waves with something in his arms, something that is Sarah. He dashes out of the breaking surf and Owen sees Sarah's head lolling over his arm, and the sunlight of her curls ironed straight with their load of water. He sees that her body is so white it is almost silver, that her eyes are sealed shut as though she is sleeping soundly. He sees the bright pink and yellow dots of her swimsuit, and that his father's comb-over is snarled with grit that glints like pinheads. He sees them arrange Sarah as if she is a display of flowers, sees her splayed out on the sand, sees his mother kneeling beside her, gripping the star of her hand. The shadow of his father slides over them. Then he distances himself from the dismal frieze, his blue eyes bulging with horror, so that Owen can see the red veins against the waterlogged whites.

'Bring her back!' hisses his mother in a voice more

14

dreadful than the ones he imagines in the fairy stories. It lacerates the air and consumes the gulls' cacophony whole. And the look she casts at her son is blacker than hate and darker than death.

Again his father steps forward reluctantly, bends his clumsy body, kneels slowly, awkwardly, the way Owen has seen him do in church. He takes hold of Sarah's brittle arms and gives them a jerk, as if urging her to stop this tomfoolery and get up. Nothing. His great hands span her motionless chest and he pats her ineffectually, like a dog. His eyes are swamped with panic, for this little Lazarus will not rise up and be well. All the while his sodden clothes dribble salty tears. And then it strikes Owen with the force of a sledgehammer: his father does not know what to do, he does not know how to bring Sarah back.

The surfer comes racing out of the water, hurling aside his board, barrelling into their grief. He shoves Owen's father out of the way, wipes the wet tendrils of hair from the blanched face, pulls back Sarah's head and hooks a finger in her mouth. Then he pinches her tiny nostrils between a graceful thumb and forefinger, and, as Owen looks on aghast, he kisses his sister. He is trying to kiss Sarah alive again, like the prince in *Sleeping Beauty*. His father hovers in the background, impotent, his drenched clothes drooping over his slumped frame. The kisses are light puffs of air that seem to oil the rusty hinges of Sarah's chopstick ribs. Owen gives a strangled whoop of joy as they swing. She is coming back after all. But the moment the surfer stops they stop, and are still again. Then he feels her chest, and finds the spot where the buried treasure is hidden. He starts to delve for it, digging with his

15

fingertips. And still no gleam of life, just the jagged pieces tumbling from his mother's face, making the portrait of it grow more and more indistinct.

People come and crowd about them. Someone shouts that they have called an ambulance. His mother rocks to-and-fro, and eerie noises emanate from the abyss inside her, making Owen want to block his ears. The surfer keeps trying, he keeps trying to raise Lazarus; right up to the moment the medics arrive with a stretcher he is trying. Then they try too, and afterwards they put Sarah on the stretcher and hurry off to the ambulance, to try some more, they say.

It is then, as they jog up the beach looking like something out of a Charlie Chaplin film, with his father stumbling behind them reaching for his car keys in the soggy envelopes of his pockets, that his mother collapses. She seems to be eating the sand where Sarah has lain, pasting it over her face and cramming it into her mouth. And the noise that comes from her then is an inhuman roar. It commands a sea of tears to cascade from Owen's eyes. The wind harvests them and sews them like seed diamonds in the sand. People bend over his mother and help her up as if she is an invalid. Propped between a tall man and a short woman, his rag-doll mother is dragged after his father and the ambulance men, and the stretcher with Sarah lying white as a cuttlefish and very still upon it.

The onlookers start to drift off, muttering in low voices to one another. He hears an elderly man say that he thinks they are too late, that the little girl is dead. No one seems to notice Owen. He stoops to extract Sarah's comfort blanket from the sand, presses it to his nose and breathes through it. And

16

there is the scent of his sister, lemony sweet and warm and sleepy. With her filling him up, he stumbles after them.

*　　　*　　　*

For Owen the best moment of the day was the very first, the glow of consciousness before he opened his eyes, before the images and sensations assailed him. But the trouble with the glow was that it ended almost before it had begun. And his bedroom was soon so crowded that there was hardly any room in it for him. It was like being on a film set, only not having a named role, just being an extra, a walk on, a bit part, absorbing the atmosphere, being careful not to upstage the real stars.

Sounds. The neat, brisk tap-tapping of footsteps in the hospital corridor, fast approaching. The pop of air rushing out of his mother when they told her. The grinding of his father's teeth that came again and again, as if he was trying to file them down into stumps. And the shout of silence from the empty back seat as they drove home in the Hillman Husky, the silence imploring them to go back, reminding them that they had forgotten something, that they had left someone behind.

Smells. The stink of the sea, salt and mineral and washed-up dead things slowly rotting. The bitter, mothball odour of his mother's breath for weeks afterwards, the air seeping stale and stagnant from the bleakness inside her. The fading scent of Sarah in every room of the house reminding him that she was gone, like a receding echo. The rich, heavy, fertile fragrance unleashed, of crumbling earth teeming with worms and maggots, undoing creation,

17

as the open grave reached for his sister.

Sights. Her blithely ignorant clothes busy preparing themselves for her return, swirling around in the belly of the washing machine, waving merrily at him from the washing line, piled patiently in the ironing basket. His mother's insistence that they be laundered, pressed, hung in her cupboard, folded neatly in her drawer. For what purpose? That they remain in readiness for Sarah's second coming? And toys looking all lost and forlorn, as if they were clockwork and their keys were missing. Her drawing of the family taped to the kitchen cupboard, a stick daddy and mummy and Owen and Sarah, all standing in front of a square house, with the sun sending its rays in straight, uncomplicated lines to illuminate all their days. A tiny, white coffin with a brass plaque on the lid that caught the light as they lowered it into the ground, and him imagining that it was Sarah's golden soul, that they were burying the dazzling hummingbird of Sarah's spirit, consigning it to eternal darkness. It did not seem much bigger than the shoebox he had buried his hamster in at the beginning of the Christmas holidays, the coffin that held the remains of Sarah.

Touch. The grip of his father's fingers digging into his shoulders at the funeral, the nails feeling like thumbtacks being driven into his flesh, the pain that made him want to be one never-ending scream. The fineness of the hairs he pulled from her brush and tucked in the pages of his bus-spotting journal, the sensation of rolling them gently between his fingers, and recalling the crowded touch of them against his bare chest that last day on the beach, almost a year ago. And the guilt, the great collar of guilt that he was yoked to, from the second he woke, with its load growing steadily heavier and heavier, until by the evening he felt like an old man who hardly had the strength to straighten up.

But today was different. He could tell straight away that he had not wet his bed, and surely this was a good sign. Just to make sure, he propped himself up on an elbow and explored under the covers with his free hand. Dry. He was dry. Perhaps today his mother would not suddenly cave in mid-sentence, imploding, deflating as if she was a punctured balloon, and groaning, that growling groan that he knew carried the cadence of death.

And all told it was not a bad day, that Saturday, not as bad as some that had gone before it. The groan did not crawl out of his mother's gaping mouth, not in his earshot anyway. His father took the afternoon off and helped Owen to make his model Airfix Spitfire. They sat at the dining-room table with layers of newspaper spread out before them. They did not talk, except to mutter the name of the next piece they would be assembling. The newspaper crackled quietly as they went methodically about their allotted tasks. They did not touch, except once when their fingers met, sliding the tube of glue between them. They focused all their attention on the fighter plane. Owen looked forward to painting it. When it was complete he had already decided to buy another one. He had been saving up his pocket money.

His father came to tuck him in at night now. His mother only put her head round the door and blew him a kiss. She shied away from physical interaction with her son, much as his father did, but for very different reasons, Owen thought. She was scared that she might show her revulsion for the stupid boy

19

who left Sarah alone to drown.

But then all was ruined, for that night the Merfolk came again for him. He woke and saw that his bed had become a raft, rapidly shrinking on a rough sea. He gripped the sheets, his palms damp with sweat, and felt his small craft pitch and toss under him. In his struggle there were times when the deck seemed virtually perpendicular, and he was fighting with all his might not to slide off the wall of it. At first he only glimpsed them, caught a flash of dishwater-grey, a sudden splash, the sound of hollow laughter rising like streams of bursting bubbles. He drew up his knees and pushed his face into the mattress. But even in the blackness their lantern eyes found him. When, panting for breath, he reared up and gulped in air, their webbed hands shot out of the water and grabbed at him. He gazed in horror as their spangled bodies humped and wheeled. It was as if a huge serpent was writhing about his boat bed. He peered into the depths and saw their merlocks waving like rubbery weeds in the murky swill. The water's surface was eaten up with their scissoring fish mouths, the worm stretch of their glistening lips, the precise bite of their piranha teeth.

'Tacka-tacka,' they went, 'tacka-tacka.' And they tempted him with their honeyed promises. 'Owen, come with us. We will teach you to swim. Ride us like sea horses. Gallop with us through an underwater world of neon blues and greens. We will juggle with sea anemones and starfish. We will dig in the silver sand for huge crabs, and trap barnacled lobsters in their lairs. We will net all day for fish and shrimp, and tie knots in the tails of slimy eels. We will surf the bow waves of blowing whales. And we will build coral castles, and play tag in gardens of

20

kite-tailed kelp. Only, only . . . come with us.'

And he stuffed his fingers in his ears and hid under the covers, refusing to listen to any more of their lies. They did not fool him. They forgot, he already knew they had stolen his sister, drawn the shining soul out of her limp body and kept it to light the black depths they skulked in. Would they never go? Would they haunt him forever? He turned on his bedside lamp and prayed, soaked in sweat, for the visions to fade. He did not call his father to witness his shameful cowardice. He did not call his mother, because she was no longer there. But he did look at the photograph in the ebony frame that stood on his bedside table.

His father had taken it last Christmas. It was a picture of him and his mother and the snowman they had made. His mother had her arms wrapped about him and he was holding a carrot to his nose, in a fair imitation of Pinocchio. Beside them was the most magnificent snowman Owen thought he had ever seen. His chest swelled with pride knowing they had built it together, just the two of them, his mother and him. As he stared at it, his memory fast forwarded a few days, and he saw himself looking at the same snowman, tears spilling from his eyes. The sun had come out, the barometer in the porch was reading 'Fair', and the snow was melting. Their snowman that they had worked so hard to build, was vanishing. Then his mother was beside him, asking him what was the matter. And when he told her she said an amazing thing to him. Not only did it stop him crying, but it also made him smile. And as he remembered her words, they made him smile again. She told him that locked in the big frozen body was a child, a child made out of water, a child

21

who pined to be free. Only when the snowman melted was the Water Child freed.

Owen's heart was still banging like a drum and his hands were still trembling. So he closed his eyes and began to paint the melting snowman in his head. He screwed up his face with effort. He concentrated until it ached, and at last he saw him, a cymbal crash of silver light as the snowmelt dripped into the puddle. And that is when he was born, a child cut from shivering silver light, a child his mother had breathed life into, the Water Child. When Owen opened his eyes he could see him clearly, a skipping luminescence on his bedroom walls. The Merfolk, who had risen up from the sludge at the bottom of the world, who came from the heavy mud of nightmares, from the nocturnal realm of monsters too hideous to face, melted away in his presence, just as the snowman had done months ago. And although Owen's lips remained too stiff to bend into a smile, his heart did slow and his hands became steady enough to build a model plane. And so at last he slept.

Owen didn't want to learn to swim any more. He didn't want his father to teach him. Swimming pools and lakes became lucid blue ogres waiting to ensnare him. As for the sea, it was a mighty pewter giant that feasted on children who wandered too near to its grimacing waves. The doctor gave a name to Owen's terror. He told his mother that her son was an aquaphobic. 'It is probably the result of some childhood trauma, a bad experience with the sea, perhaps? I shouldn't press him to conquer his fear just now. In time he's bound to grow out of it. The important thing is that there's nothing physically wrong with him. In the meantime, I'll write to his school asking that Owen be excused swimming lessons, for medical reasons.' Glancing up from his notes, he gave Owen his most reassuring smile. 'Plenty of opportunity to learn how to swim later, eh lad?'

2

1963

A 1940s house in Kingston, South-West London, its frontage pimpled with pebbledash and painted cream. Upstairs. The smallest bedroom of three. 7 a.m. Catherine has been awake for some time. She heard the milk float and the chink of bottles on the doorstep. It is the 17th of September, her ninth birthday, and she has a plan. She stayed up late the previous night working out the details. Now her tummy is alive with thumbnail butterflies. She pictures them fluttering about in there in jerky, bright colours. Light fingers its way doggedly through the gaps in the curtains. In their bedroom across the landing she can hear her parents stirring, her mother's high croaky voice, her father's acquiescent teddy bear growls.

Her plan begins with a prayer. Catherine has never been very good at praying, she admits to herself now. When she goes to church with her parents, she pretends. She moves her lips in a kind of mumble and counts things in her head. How many people wearing hats? How many lighted candles? How many empty pews? In any case, she knows her mother isn't praying properly either, she is far too preoccupied studying what the other women are wearing, making sure that she has outdone them all in, say, her new custard-yellow Orlon sweater dress, cinched in at the waist with a wide black belt, plus her matching kitten heels with the fashionable almond toes.

Deep down Catherine isn't really sure about God, about whether he truly exists. And if, just say he does, he is really bothered with her birthday. She has her doubts, grave doubts. She thinks about all the awful things that happen in the world, like murders and aeroplane crashes, and famines with thousands of babies swelling up like plums, and terrible storms that wash away whole towns. He doesn't do anything about them, does he? So why should he intervene on Catherine's behalf to ensure that her day goes smoothly? If he can't be bothered to sort out the most ghastly of life-and-death catastrophes, why on earth should he trouble himself with one girl, a shop-bought cake and a few games?

Still, she presumes that it is worth a try anyway, and it certainly won't hurt. So she takes a deep breath, and trying to be absolutely truthful, puts real words to her prayer. She feels a bit shy (although it is only her and God, and even he might not really be present at all), so she slides down under the sheet and blankets. She clasps her hands together in the fuzzy greyness, then begins to whisper:

'Dear God, please let today be exactly as I have imagined it. Don't let the bad thoughts ruin it. Let Mother come into my room in a minute with a real smile on her face, not the one she usually glues there, the one that looks fixed, like a painting. And don't let her lose her temper with me, or Father either, and

24

shout out in that screech of hers that makes me jump inside. And don't let him shuffle about looking all lost, making me feel embarrassed in front of my friends. Please make sure that Stephen doesn't forget about the motorbike ride. And also, could you see to it that I get all the presents I want, and that they let me win one turn of pass the parcel, and that Penny Rainbird is so jealous of me that her face goes all red and blotchy. Amen.'

Not bad for her first real prayer, is her assessment, not bad at all. And God really seems to listen because the day gets off to a very promising start. When Catherine comes down for breakfast, her hair brushed and her mouth tingling with toothpaste, there are two parcels waiting for her on the dining table, both with cards sitting on top of them. And there are other cards too that have arrived in the post, one all the way from America that she bets is from her cousins.

'Here she is, the birthday girl,' her father, Keith Hoyle, says, getting up from his seat to give her a kiss on the cheek.

'Hello, darling. Many happy returns of the day,' her mother chimes in perfunctorily, stooping to kiss a spot in the air somewhere past her head.

'Now, where to start, that's the dilemma,' he continues kindly, a twinkle in his faded blue eyes.

As he retakes his seat and Catherine sits down opposite him, her mother floats by. She is distracted by her reflection in the oval mirror. It is suspended from the picture rail above the sideboard by a brass chain. She pats her curls, then peers closer at her image, worrying that she may have spotted a couple of grey hairs tucked in among the red. Catherine, oblivious to her mother's preening, considers

25

grabbing the packages and ripping them open, careless of ruining the paper. But that will be wasteful and probably earn me a scolding, she cautions herself.

It is good manners to open the cards first, and besides she can't wait to read what Uncle Christopher and Aunt Amy have to say. She has heard whispers that the American Hoyles may be coming to spend Christmas in England. The idea of seeing Rosalyn again is so exciting that she is petrified to dwell on it, in case, like a wriggling fish, it slips away. She has a presentiment that if anyone realizes how much it means to her, even God, they will maliciously sabotage the trip.

She hasn't seen Rosalyn for, well . . . almost a year. She may have picked up an American accent by now. She wonders how they talk in Boston. And she wonders if they will recognize each other, or if they both will have altered too radically. She suspects that she is much the same. Grape-green eyes, an oval face, fine Titian hair cut short, worn with a side parting and secured with several grips. Will Rosalyn like her as much as she used to, or will a year living in America have changed her mind about her cousin, Catherine? She may find her dull now, or worse, annoying. Oh, but to spend Christmas with Rosalyn, to go to sleep with her on Christmas Eve and wake up with her on Christmas morning. She dares to believe that it is possible in a miraculous kind of way. There has definitely been talk about her family joining them, the English Hoyles joining the American Hoyles in the house they are considering renting in Sussex. To open their stockings together, and pull crackers and read the silly riddles to each other, and to sneak out for long walks, and share the secrets they have collected in the months they have been apart. Actually, Catherine can't remember any on the spot, but given time she's bound to come up with some. And if she does have to invent a few, Rosalyn will understand, she is certain of it.

She loves to listen to Rosalyn talk. She has a voice that is clear as glass, a voice which tings the way her mother's best crystal tumblers do when she flicks them with her long nails. She doesn't apologize for herself when she speaks. She isn't at all hesitant, or ready to concede the floor if no one wants to listen. She is accustomed to people paying attention. She has a confident air that clings to her, the way clouds do to mountain peaks. And she tells wonderful stories with beautiful descriptive words, draws them with the words, and then holds up the sketches with a smile that makes Catherine melt like butter on a hot crumpet. But this is too bad, she is already letting herself think about it as if it is as good as arranged. The consequence of this sort of thing will, of course, be that it is cancelled. So she pushes it out of her head with the brute force of her own will. As a penance she will open the other cards first, make herself wait to hear the news from America. Her father clears his throat and she looks up to see *his* expectant face, at least, is on her.

Grandma Stubbings has sent a crisp ten-shilling note, and a card that is really too young for her, with a picture of Miss Muffet on it and a big hairy spider. And there are a couple of other cards as well, one from the godmother who hasn't forgotten her. She has opened a savings account for Catherine and keeps telling her on birthdays and at Christmas time, that she has put in another pound. But

Catherine thinks, although generous, that this is very wearisome, because she can't take any money out until she is eighteen, which is a lifetime away. And there is a book token from her godfather who lives in Wales, and a prayer card from the lady who runs the Sunday school. Then at last she opens the one with the American stamp on it. Her Uncle Christopher and her Aunt Amy, and her cousins Rosalyn and Simon, have sent a postal order for one pound and ten shillings. Aunt Amy has written a note on the side of the card that doesn't have a printed message on it. Catherine reads it and her heart thumps loudly in her chest.

'Thirty shillings. That's generous of my brother. Isn't that kind of Christopher and Amy, Dinah?'

'Mm . . . very generous, I'm sure. We'll have to match it for Simon and Rosalyn, though,' remarks Catherine's mother, sounding less than pleased. Her brow scrunched, she picks at her hairs rather like a monkey.

'What do they say, Catherine?' Her father slips out his pipe to make room for the words, then plugs it back in and puffs contentedly. He will have to extinguish it in a minute, but he may as well enjoy it while this rare reprieve continues.

'That they haven't decided about Christmas yet. Uncle Christopher may not be able to take the time off with all the seasonal flights.' Her father wags his head to either side in that accepting way of his. But Catherine wants to scream, to beg him, no, to beseech him on her bended knees to force his brother to come, to make a long-distance 'phone call right now and insist on it. Even if it means cancelling all the flights, then that's what he should tell Uncle Christopher to do. Because otherwise she will die, she will simply curl up and die. But she mustn't say that, mustn't let on how vital it is, because then it will all be over. There won't be one grain of hope left in the empty sack of her life. *Yet, yet* . . . that is the word she must hold onto. They haven't decided *yet*.

With grim determination she swallows back her dismay. She will act like Elizabeth Taylor in *National Velvet*. She gathers up her money and postal orders now and makes a fan of them in her hand. She flutters them and pulls her lips into a smile. She is overwhelmed by her sudden wealth, but when her father questions her she has no clue what she will spend it all on. Such unexpected largesse and all those things in the shops to choose from. Her parents have given her one of the new Sindy dolls, with curly blonde hair and bold chalk-blue eyes. She is dressed in navy jeans and a red, white and blue stripy sweater. And she has two extra outfits, a glamorous pink dress for her dream dates, and an emergency ward nurse's uniform.

'Like it?' her father asks. Catherine nods. She would have preferred a bike, but she hooks up the corners of her smile valiantly. Keith Hoyle glances surreptitiously at his wife, then relights his pipe which has gone out, with the mother-of-pearl lighter he always keeps in his pocket. He settles back in his chair as if he is not in any hurry at all. 'Let's see her done up in all her glad rags then,' he requests. So, face radiant, Catherine dresses Sindy up in her party outfit and trots her round the crockery.

'She's really swinging now,' he says, when Sindy finally stops jigging by the sugar bowl. Truly he makes Catherine want to laugh. She lets her mind run on him for a while. It is inconceivable that her father will ever be really swinging. He is thin as a

29

beanpole, with a mournful, equine, lined face that appears sun-tanned. This is a bit of a conundrum because he is never in the sun long enough to catch its rays. His hair is very fine, the colour of a silver birch tree, clipped close around his ears and neck, parted to one side like Catherine's. He massages brilliantine into it before combing it down, which makes it appear as if there is even less of it. It has a funny whiff about it too, rather like an old tweed coat. Her father doesn't talk a lot either, but it isn't noticeable because her mother prattles enough for both of them.

Stephen, Catherine's older brother, has promised that he will call in later on, after the party. He has a job in a garage not far away. The owner lets him stay in one of the spare rooms above the business, so he returns home infrequently, and only to bring his washing or have a hot meal. Catherine thinks he resembles James Dean with his red BSA Bantam motorbike. He is saving for a Triumph Bonneville, and when he finally has enough money to buy it, he has said he will take her all the way to Brighton on it. But today, as it is her birthday, he has promised her a ride to Bushy Park and back instead. Honestly, she is more excited about this than her party, which she feels sure is bound to be a disaster.

Later, as Catherine trails through to the sitting-room to arrange her cards on the mantelpiece over the tiled fireplace, she considers her Uncle Christopher. He is a pilot, which is just about the most romantic thing in the world, she believes. He is handsome in a chiselled kind of way, while Aunt Amy has the grace of a model about her, with her wavy blonde hair, her clear skin, and her calm, low voice. There isn't a huge gap between Rosalyn and Simon either, not like her and Stephen. Rosalyn is ten and Simon is twelve. And they talk to each other about shared interests, and watch the same programmes on the television sitting side by side. In a way Catherine is a bit frightened of Stephen. After all, he is pretty nearly an adult, and besides there is a strong scent that hangs about him, under the smell of leather and oil. It makes her feel very shy, especially on the rare occasions when she is on his bike with her arms folded about his waist, and the thrumming, dizzying whizz of the machine between her legs.

As she starts up the stairs with her presents, her mother appears in the kitchen doorway, a cigarette in her mouth, a lighter halfway to her lips. Seeing her daughter, she slips it out and wafts it in her direction. 'You aren't wearing that dress for the party?' she calls after her. 'I told you that the pale pink velvet is best. It's hanging in the airing cupboard.'

As Catherine lifts it out, despising the fussy, lace neckline, she imagines what it must be like to be a pilot. Her father works in the city. He is a commuter with a hat, not a bowler hat but a hat anyway, and a briefcase. He trudges off to work in creased suits looking exhausted before he's even left. And he returns grey and even more exhausted, often long after dark. Sometimes when he blows his nose black stuff comes out, which Catherine thinks is revolting, as if he isn't just black on the outside but is slowly turning black on the inside too. He makes her think of Tom, the chimney sweep, in the book *The Water Babies*, as if he needs a good scrub to get the engrained dirt out of his pores. But Uncle

Christopher goes to work in a smart uniform, one fit for a general or a commander or a president. They are in the back of her mind all day, her aunt, her uncle, Simon, but mostly Rosalyn, though she is determined to make the best of her party.

*   *   *

It was Christmas. They were staying in the house in Sussex with the American Hoyles. And it was every bit as amazing as she had imagined it would be. The house was huge, nearly as tall as a castle, redbrick, rectangular and solid, with lots of windows that gleamed like dozens of golden, unblinking eyes in the winter sunshine. And there was a fire-engine red front door that had a brass knocker in the shape of a face with swept-back, wild hair. When you lifted it and banged it down a couple of times it boomed satisfyingly, like a cannon firing. There were lots of bedrooms upstairs and none of them were pokey like Catherine's. And there was an attic floor that had been converted into yet more rooms. The kitchen was massive, dominated by a milky blue Aga that crunched up scuttles full of coal every morning, while spewing out gusty exhalations of glistening dust.

The lounge was twice the size of theirs. It had wall-to-wall carpet, not just a lino floor with a rug thrown over it. There was a baronial fireplace, in which a real fire crackled and spat and hissed in the grate. It permeated the room with a homely, spicy fragrance, because of the pine logs they fed it, her uncle said. Even her mother, in a rare moment of enthusiasm engendered by the festive season, remarked that it was all rather jolly. Though she added that their built-in bar fire was definitely much cleaner, and probably a lot more efficient—cheaper too, when you considered the outrageous cost of fuel.

It was called 'Wood End', the stately house, the name painted on a sign at the bottom of the drive. Catherine's mother admitted grudgingly that it was a suitable name, because the property actually did back onto woods. Another bonus, woods to explore and have adventures in. When they had first approached it in the grey Ford Anglia, puttering along the meandering tree-lined drive, her mother kept reminding her father that the house was only rented, that anyone could afford a house like that for a few weeks.

The property stood in enormous gardens that ran all the way round the house, with no partition dividing the front from the back. There were sweeping lawns and clusters of shrubs and lots of trees. One of them, an ancient oak, with bark like deeply wrinkled skin, only crustier, had a magical tree-house wedged in its branches, with a ladder hanging down from it. There was a separate garage, with double doors, as large as an entire house all by itself, Catherine estimated. They had brought one of the suitcases they usually took on holiday with them, Catherine cleverly sandwiching jeans and jumpers in among the dresses she so hated wearing. She had been overcome with nerves by the time they arrived, she recalled. Dry-mouthed and feeling rather sick, she had climbed out of the car as the American Hoyles piled onto the porch to meet them. This was the moment fated to sully everything, the moment Rosalyn would materialize looking incredibly grown up and aloof, surveying her cousin Catherine with a head-to-toe sweep of her crystal-blue eyes, and turning away, pained.

But that wasn't what had happened at all. Catherine drooped there, looking frumpy in a patterned corduroy skirt and butterfly collared blouse, and making so many wishes that her head throbbed with them. To be taller, slimmer, to have black or blonde hair, to be dressed fashionably, to instantly shed her chipmunk cheeks, to have a different voice, different parents, to have arrived in a different car, oh, just to be somebody else and not Catherine Hoyle, that would do it, not Catherine the calamity, who didn't have a single interesting trait in her solid personality.

But a second later and Rosalyn was there, standing before her smiling that self-assured, relaxed smile with the mouth that had never known a quiver. The parents were embracing, voices rising up like startled birds on the crisp morning air. Simon, head tilted, fingers spearing his thick, blond fringe, was hanging back a little, not shyly, just making it clear that he wasn't up for any of this sloppy stuff. And Rosalyn, who Catherine noted in one stolen peep, had grown taller and even, astounding as it was, prettier, had stepped forward and was wrapping her arms around her and giving her cousin a hug of pure pleasure.

'Catherine! Oh, it's brilliant to see you. I've got so much to tell you. We're going to have the best Christmas ever.'

It was a decree. Rosalyn would accept nothing short of perfect. And Catherine felt like Atlas shedding the weighty globe from his bowed shoulders after an eternity of burden. It wasn't her responsibility if it went badly, not something for her to feel guilty about and to relive agonizingly in the months to come. And she needn't feel anxious anyway because Rosalyn was going to take care of it. It was going to be the best ever. And you couldn't jinx her, the way Catherine knew she could be jinxed. If you tried to put a hex on Rosalyn, unfazed, she would gather up the sticky skeins of doom, pat them into a neat ball, and hurl them straight back at you with that dauntless grin, and the sure aim of a girl who was top of the class in PE.

The next moment and she had been delivered into the arms of her aunt, whose embrace was just as genuine, just as sincere, and whose perfume wasn't sickly sweet like her mother's but had a subtle soapy aroma. Then her Uncle Christopher bent his tall frame for her to peck him on the cheek, and his skin smelt wonderful too, fresh and clean, not tainted with tobacco, as if bathed in the expanse of glacial blueness above them. Before Catherine knew where she was, Rosalyn had taken her by the hand and was running with her into the house.

'I want to show you where we're sleeping,' she cried excitedly. 'At the very top, in the attic. We've got it all to ourselves.' Behind her Catherine heard her mother beckon.

'Catherine. Don't just dash off, dear. Your father and I need a hand with the bags. Catherine!' Catherine hesitated at the bottom of the stairs, and her forehead slipped into its familiar groove.

'Oh never mind about that,' Rosalyn told her carelessly. 'They can manage fine. Daddy's there to help them, and Mummy, and even Simon.' She was on the third step, her daring blue eyes locked on Catherine's, still clasping her hand.

'But—'

She gave the hand a tug. 'Race you to the top.' And then she was off, bounding up the stairs two at a time. And Catherine was charging after her, breathless with laughter. She felt as if she was escaping, as if, as they scurried upwards towards the sky, freedom was rushing down to greet her.

'What do you think?' Rosalyn demanded, hands on hips, inside the attic bedroom. She was wearing tight jeans and a loose, long-sleeved T-shirt in navy blue, which emphasized her boyish slimness.

Catherine couldn't gasp as she stepped after her. It wouldn't have been enough, a paltry gasp in exchange for the sight that met her eyes. It simply would not do. There was a huge bed with an old-fashioned, carved, wooden headboard, and a deep mattress that looked perfect for bouncing on. Above was a large skylight with the morning brightness flooding through it. The floor was cosy with colourful blankets, the walls banked up with cushions and pillows.

'This is our den. Strictly private. I told Simon. Mummy let me take practically all the spare bedding and cushions for it. And at night we'll be able to lie in bed and look at the stars. We can tell each other stories about the people who live on the different planets, describe them to one another, make up names for them. It'll be terrific.' There was a long pause while Catherine just stared, floor to bed, bed to skylight, skylight to floor, floor to bed. She thought she might cry. But Rosalyn wasn't having any of that rubbish. 'Well, put me out of my agony. It took ages to get it just right. Do you like it?' she asked, giving Catherine a nudge with a swing of her bent arm. Catherine turned to her.

'I love it. It's better than perfect,' she breathed

36

solemnly, and then they were off giggling again.

'I think we should try out the bed,' Rosalyn suggested, her shoes already off. 'Check out the springs. See who can remember the most. I've got heaps of new American ones.'

It was a favourite game. They clambered onto the mattress, straightened up, holding onto each other like two fragile old ladies who'd had one tipple too many, and started to leap as high as they could, bumping frequently.

'A free glass. Yours for the price of Duz,' yelled Rosalyn, her hair flying across her face.

'Caramel Wafers by Gray Dunn, a crunchy treat for everyone,' retorted Catherine through her chuckles.

'Get that lovely, lively, Lyril feeling,' crooned Rosalyn into a make-believe microphone.

'Spirella, they'll like the way you look,' Catherine thundered back.

The words of the jingles kept pace with their jumps.

'You're never alone with a Strand.' Again her cousin mimed, only this time elegantly smoking.

'Diana—the big picture paper for girls!' sang back Catherine.

'Cadum for Madam. Cadum for Madam.' Now Rosalyn set about lathering up her face with an imaginary bar of soap.

'Rinso white, Rinso bright,' Catherine broke off to rub her hands. 'Happy little washday song!'

'Wake up your liver with Calomel,' panted Rosalyn.

Rosalyn won in the end, but Catherine didn't mind. She'd kept going for ages and had acquitted herself fairly well, she thought.

37

'You're getting really good,' complimented Rosalyn, not in a patronizing way either, and Catherine blushed at the compliment.

Eventually they fell over in a tangled heap, their heads still spinning, laughing hysterically until Catherine's tummy felt sore. And just when they were calming down, Rosalyn got them both going again, because she squealed that she was going to wet herself if they didn't stop. Then, as though attached at the hip, they rolled onto their backs and stretched out like stars. Rosalyn's arm lay across Catherine's chest. Catherine's leg lay over Rosalyn's thighs. They shared a sublime sigh. Catherine took stock of her cousin with a sideways glance. She was the same but different. Taller, yes, and she seemed to be growing into her athletic build: long legs, broad shoulders, her mother's classic facial bone structure. She had cut her black hair. It was a blue-black shade she had inherited from her father. As the light fell on it, the dark tresses shimmered with traces of purple, green and gold. It suited her, gave an impish, gamine quality to her face. And the blue eyes, well, they had grown more dazzling, more full of merriment, more mischievous.

Later on in the afternoon Stephen arrived on his motorbike. He roared up the drive looking more like James Dean than ever, and they rushed out to meet him. For ages, still sitting on his bike and rocking it to either side, then rolling it forward half a foot and back again, he held court. Simon was terribly impressed. He hunkered down, peered interestedly at the mechanics of the thing, and kept asking questions. Rosalyn and Catherine struck a haughty pose, their weight on one hip each, regarding Stephen coolly, until he offered to give them rides up and down the drive. Then in a second they lost all their contrived composure, and hopped about as though an electric current was pulsing through their veins.

As Rosalyn had ordered, all continued without a hitch. A walk in the woods, filling bags with snippets of prickly, dark-green holly studded with blood-red berries, collecting knobbly fir cones and spruce boughs that smelt of pine sap, to deck the house. Rosalyn storytelling in their tree-house retreat, which enchantingly had its own dear ceiling light. Tea of toad-in-the-hole, crispy batter pudding and sausages that were cooked just right. Television—a double episode of *Supercar*. A bubble bath, where they fashioned wigs and moustaches of sparkling soapsuds. And then, Catherine, not minding about her tartan ladybird pyjamas with the elasticized wristbands, because Rosalyn didn't even seem to see them as they lay in bed in the enchanted darkness, star gazing.

Rosalyn told Catherine all about America, her school and her friends, and how terrible the assassination of John Kennedy had been last month, in Dallas, Texas, and that everyone was dreadfully sad about it. And Catherine managed a short extempore speech about her own school, in which she made up a friend called Karen, who had her own horse which she rode on weekends.

Even Christmas Day, notorious for scenes in Catherine's experience, with her mother feeling so put upon, went well. Everyone lent a hand cheerfully, the seasonal songs tra-la-la-ing from the radio. The snow fell on Boxing Day and quilted the scenery in virgin white, so that it looked like a sparkling picture on a Christmas card. Catherine

39

wasn't sure whose idea it was to go for a walk, perhaps even find out if the pond that was too large for a pond and too small for a lake, had frozen over. They left their mothers nattering in the kitchen, peeling vegetables and preparing lunch, their fathers, in the lounge having a serious discussion about something called the Profumo affair, and debating whether or not a Labour government would get in next year, and Simon transfixed by Stephen tinkering with his motorbike in the garage.

For a while it felt like they just walked aimlessly. It had turned a good deal colder and they were both bundled up in coats, gloves and scarves, Rosalyn wearing a red beret that looked so dramatic against her shiny black hair. They found their way to the end of the drive, then to the end of the lane, pausing to throw snowballs at one another. They discussed making a snowman that very afternoon, getting the boys to help. Then Rosalyn mentioned the pond again and they set off more purposefully this time, pushing their way through the copse that bordered the lane, sending the canopy of snow scattering in little flurries. For a short distance the growth was fairly dense. Dry, frosty twigs snapped with sharp reports as they shouldered their way through. A robin looked on inquisitively when Catherine tripped into a hollow hidden by the lambent carpet. But she wasn't hurt and she was quick to assure Rosalyn of it, and to dismiss her suggestions that they turn back. The sky had a yellowish tint to it that possibly meant more snow. The low sun had not yet broken through the layers of clouds. The uneven ground they trudged over with its mounds and dips, looked like a lunar landscape with, here and there, a skeletal tree throwing up its bony branches in desolation.

It was very quiet. The snow seemed to soundproof the setting, so that they had that shut-off feeling Catherine had known when Stephen had taken her to a recording studio. They were a long way from the lane now, a long way from the house in its relatively deserted location, a long way from the main road, from cars, from people. Catherine was dimly aware of a shift in both of their demeanours. The casual wandering had become a determined trek, the destination they sought was the pond. It was unthinkable to them now that they should retrace their steps and abandon the mission. Like mountaineers seeking the summit of a challenging peak, or arctic explorers following a planned route in rigorous conditions, turning back was not an option. Their conversation had grown sporadic, then hiccupped into a quiet that neither wanted to break.

They were still, more or less, walking companionably side by side, one slipping down a small slope and then speedily clambering upright again, the other circumventing a split tree-trunk and bending to brush snow off her boots, then the two of them falling into step again. Neither felt cold because of the exercise. They watched each other's breaths misting the chilled air. The pond was screened by a thicket of saplings and bracken, so that when they finally fought their way through and came upon the winter oasis, they were both awed by the scene.

The hoop of vegetation stood out in dark relief against the pallid sky. The banks, blanketed in white, canted down to an iced mirror of frozen water, edged with hoary reeds. They could just glimpse dusky shapes looming up from the opaque depths.

'It's beautiful,' said Rosalyn, taking in the zinc-grey gleam.

'You were right, it's iced over,' said Catherine, wonder-struck.

'Our own private skating rink,' said Rosalyn covetously. Their eyes met, blue and green, and both alight with devilry. 'Can you skate?' Rosalyn wanted to know. She crouched down and started to make her descent, knees bent, gloved hands searching the snow for a hold of woody stems or sunken rocks.

'Of course,' said Catherine, following her. This was untrue, but then how complicated could it be? You slid your feet on the ice, skidded, skated. This would be much easier than trying to balance on real skates, the ones she had seen on television with flashing silver blades, the ones that cut the ice with a hiss, sending a fine spray flying up. She followed Rosalyn. When they arrived at the place where the ice began they both stopped and faced each other. Catherine thought Rosalyn had never looked lovelier. Her skin was very smooth and white, except on the rounds of her cheeks, which were flushed rosy red with the cold. Her mouth was leaning towards a smile. The irises of her vivid blue eyes were ringed in a velvety indigo. Her abundant glossy curls were such a contrast to the scarlet beret pulled down over them, each accentuating the vibrant colour of the other. Yes, she was truly lovely, Catherine thought. Then the sequential thought, that she should like to remember her just like this, a snapshot that she could carry in her head forever. She shivered involuntarily.

42

'Cold?' Rosalyn asked.

'No . . . no,' she answered a trifle hesitantly, because now they had stopped walking she did feel cold tentacles worming their way through her layers of clothing.

'Oh, come on. Last one on the ice is a rotten pig,' teased Rosalyn.

And then she was pushing off from the bank, rising to her feet until she was standing tall on the frozen platform. She slid forwards once again, flapped her boots against the ice to check that it was solid. Satisfied, she slid a few more steps. Now Catherine was on her feet too. Copying her cousin, she traced her silvery snail trails on the ice with her boots. Rosalyn was gaining in confidence, her feet arcing out as if she was on a real rink. She was putting all her weight on one foot as well, the other foot flicking up behind her. Catherine was nowhere near as adept as her cousin was. Rosalyn had actually skated on several rinks in America, she called over her shoulder. There was nothing to it. Of course, it would be much better if they had proper skates, but then they had their own rink, so they really couldn't complain. Catherine slid forward gingerly, but either the soles of her boots were not the slippery kind or she was plain hopeless; she suspected the latter.

Rosalyn was heading for the centre of the large pond, her progress as fluid as a boat bug. Catherine, who had only narrowly avoided falling over by flexing her knees just in time, and propping herself up, hands flat on the ice, arms braced, had just succeeded in standing up again. She was concentrating hard, but glimpsing up, saw how far Rosalyn had gone, that she was nearing the middle of the pond. She herself was still only a couple of yards from the bank. The red beret swooped before her eyes.

'So I've had a go with my hands behind my back. Now I'm going to imagine I've got a big, fur muff, bring my hands to the front and burrow inside it. I'm like one of those Victorian girls skating in a fur-trimmed coat.'

'Perhaps you'd better come back now, Rosalyn. You don't know if the ice is the same thickness everywhere,' Catherine cautioned, not liking to dash her exuberance, but feeling impelled to.

Rosalyn spun round to face her, one leg out, like a professional skater. She had a look of mild surprise on her face. 'You've hardly come any distance at all, Catherine. What's the matter? Do you want me to come and help you? We could skate in tandem if you like?'

'I'd *like* you to come back, that's what I'd *like*,' Catherine said a little tremulously.

'Oh Catherine, don't be such a scaredy-cat. It's perfectly safe,' Rosalyn assured her with that breezy smile of hers.

'Please, please,' Catherine said, now unable to keep the pleading note from her voice. She reached a hand towards her cousin, trying to keep her balance despite stretching as far as she could.

'You want me to help you?' Rosalyn asked, head to one side, not able to comprehend this sudden plummet from bliss to fear.

'Yes, yes, that's right, to help me,' Catherine shot back.

Rosalyn took three sliding steps. The sound when the ice cracked wasn't very loud at all. It seemed to sink as if in weariness, giving a series of muffled pops. Rosalyn's leading leg just disappeared into its

44

craggy mouth in one smooth movement. As her trunk hit the ice, fissures appeared, the way they sometimes do on a glass just before it shatters. She scrabbled with the other leg, trying to regain her footing, but now the tension of the ice was weakened. She felt the previously solid surface dip under her, like a pie crust that has lost its support. Another chunk crumbled away from her so that a few inches of her hips sagged beneath the water.

'Oh!' she said, more in bewilderment than consternation.

'Don't move. Just keep very still. I'll get you out.' Catherine took two tentative steps towards her, with terror starting to claw at her reason, then felt her own feet break through the deceptively stable surface. She kept on steadily sinking, the ice pop-popping and creaking about her. Her hips were half submerged when she contacted something immovable. Tree roots? The sloping bank itself? Perhaps the pool was relatively shallow.

'Oh!' Rosalyn said again. Freezing water was pooling around her bent leg as the ice dipped into a cracked water cradle.

'Look, don't worry. I can feel the bottom. I'll get out and . . . and . . . and I'll help you,' Catherine finished lamely. Rosalyn was really not that far from her, five yards, no more. Perhaps if she managed to climb out she might be able to reach her with a stick, pull her to safety. Under the water Catherine tried to lift her feet, to take an experimental step towards the bank. But already she was icy cold, her boots were full of water, her feet were numbing fast. Beneath her trousers she could feel the blood pumping painfully through her legs. Again she attempted to lift them, to take an underwater stride.

45

Her movements were performed in slow motion, her body unresponsive, her breathing constricted by the shock of the sudden severe chill. Her legs pedalled clumsily under her, making no progress at all.

'I'm freezing,' said Rosalyn, with a truthfulness rarely applied to the hyperbole. There still seemed to be a hint of faint amusement in her voice, as if their predicament was a practical joke. Her other leg had disappeared now, but the cot of fractured ice was still acting as a submerged raft, partially bearing it up. Ignoring Catherine's advice, she panicked and struggled to heft herself out, but as her hands pressed down on the ice surrounding her she felt it shift.

'No, I told you to keep still!' Catherine ordered. She'd never used such a schoolmarmish tone to Rosalyn before. She would have preferred not to, but again she had an idea it was necessary if she was to hold her attention. 'I will get you out, but you must listen to me.' A moment passed that might have been five seconds or might have been two minutes, while Catherine tried and failed to crest the ice herself.

'I'm very cold now,' said Rosalyn. She was in up to her waist and with her red beret looked strangely comical, like a cartoon figure. 'I can't feel my legs any more. Catherine, I can't feel my legs.' She was supporting her torso from the waist up with gentle pressure from her spread, sodden, gloved fingers. It was just dawning on her how difficult it would be to maintain her precarious position, that too much pressure and the ice would shatter and give way, too little and she would sink slowly but surely beneath it. Teetering on that point of balance was like

46

finding the biting point on a clutch, and attempting to hold it there forever with a foot fast losing feeling. It needed superhuman strength, the kind of strength the cold stripped you of in minutes.

'Don't worry,' said Catherine again.

The lightest snow powder, like a dusting of talc, was starting to fall. The sky had deepened so that they were no longer peering up through a yellow-tinted lens, but a green one, oppressive and malignant. The closed feeling that had been intimate before, lending a clandestine atmosphere to the outing, had begun to transmute. Catherine felt as if they were being sealed up in an alabaster tomb. She saw a blackbird hopping on the bank, head cocked, gleaming eyes swivelling curiously at the two creatures floundering in the frozen pond.

The revelation when it came was not the kind accompanied by a fanfare of trumpets, or a fall of biblically blinding light through which the sonorous pronouncement of a god boomed. It came quietly, a small voice in Catherine's ear, a tickle of prophetic truth. Rosalyn is going to die now. And so are you. You are both going to slip noiselessly under the ice, flail about for a moment, then die. It was as simple as that, she thought. One moment she was walking with her cousin in the snow and having a laugh, and it was the best Christmas ever, just as Rosalyn had ordered, and the next they were sliding under icy water readying themselves to drown.

In church they talked about the still small voice of calm. It was just like that, what she heard. Catherine found herself wondering if it sounded inside everyone's head the moment before the darkness came, before the light died. She could accept her own death. It was not that she wanted to

47

die. Oh, no; life, however problematic, was still preferable to death, Catherine realized. But that Rosalyn, her cousin, who was a beacon of life force, who drew you into her circumference and let you bask in the glow of her, who had never, not once, made Catherine feel she should be grateful that she was bothering with her—that she was about to die was unthinkable. It might have been the extreme cold—her teeth were chattering uncontrollably now—or fear unhinging her imagination, but that was the moment she saw the hooded man hunched on the far bank. She was going to call out to him, but when he looked up there was a blank where his face should be. In the same instant she saw Rosalyn's body being winched, stiff as a plank, from the gelid water. Her dripping hair clung to her face, her mouth was wide in a scream of terror, her blue eyes were those of a dead fish, glassy and lifeless, the whites bulging and bloodshot. The beret, heavy with water, sagged under her head. She thought about burying Rosalyn, the physical act of lowering her in a coffin into the hard winter earth. She wondered if her parents would want her grave to be in England or America.

'Catherine, I really am very cold now and sleepy too. Terribly sleepy. I want to close my eyes and just drift off. Only . . . only a minute but I . . . I must shut my eyes,' came the querulous voice from the ice maiden who was slowly being claimed by the pond. Then, dreadfully, as if she had been reading Catherine's thoughts, 'Am I going to die now?'

Catherine closed her eyes. There was a skewering pain in her head. No, she thought. She opened them. 'No,' she said. Her voice rattled out of her.

48

'Now pay attention, Rosalyn.' The schoolmarmish timbre was back, if a little ragged. 'I am going to call for help.' The red beret bobbed a nod. Then Catherine started to shout. She didn't shout anything particularly original. 'Help! Over here! Help us, please! We're stuck in the ice! Help!' But the extraordinary thing was how enormous her voice had become, as if it was magnified many times over, a great manly bellow that came from the base of her. At the outset Catherine was hopeful. Each time she paused to draw in another breath, she half expected to hear someone shout back, 'It's all right. We're coming.' But all that answered was a cathedral of silence. She had fooled Rosalyn, made her believe just for a moment that she could fix this, that she could outface death. With each cry, though, the light faded in her cousin's blue eyes, to be replaced with a terrible resignation.

'You might as well stop,' Rosalyn whispered the next time she gulped in air. 'There's no one out there. We're all alone.'

Catherine tried to rekindle her fight, but found herself suppressing dry, involuntary sobs. And she, too, was tired, so tired that defeat seemed almost welcome. So that when, a minute later, a small round face reared up from the side of the pond, her immediate thought was that it wasn't real. Her mind was playing tricks. Her eyesight could not be trusted. Then the head tipped to a quizzical angle. And a voice came from it.

'What are you doing in there?' it said.

Now she knew the ginger-haired boy was real, and that there was not a moment to waste. Although at the sound, Rosalyn had glanced up, she was sinking

49

fast. 'We're stuck, stuck in the ice. We fell through. You need to run for help. Quickly! Go quickly! There's no time to waste!' The boy hesitated. 'Hurry! Hurry!' Catherine screamed. And then he was off, streaking away like a snow hare. The instant he had gone a plague of doubts descended on her. What if he forgot or was distracted? What if he didn't understand how serious it was? What if he wasn't real after all, that she had dreamt the strange encounter in this bleached wonderland? Rosalyn's head lolled on her shoulders, so that all that was visible of her was the red beret, like a red full stop punctuating the ice. *Please*, Catherine prayed in her head, *please*. Without her having to say anything, she could feel Rosalyn's will sapping away. She had to keep her going until help came, she had to do that much.

'I can't feel my hands either. I think they're slipping,' sighed Rosalyn drowsily.

'No they're not!' snapped Catherine. 'Nonsense! Stop thinking about it! They're going to come and get us out, any second they'll be here.'

'I'm not sure I can—'

'Oh yes you can!' Catherine interrupted her. She took a shaky breath. The cold no longer hurt. It was a bad sign. 'I've got a story to tell you. It's very important that you listen to it, to all of it. You're always telling me stories, so it's only fair that you should listen to mine now.'

'All . . . all right,' Rosalyn said uncertainly, her own teeth clacking together. 'But I'm so tired.'

The story Catherine told made no sense at all. She had no talent for making things up the way Rosalyn could. The rambling plot and motley band of characters were fuelled by sheer panic. Suddenly

50

she could feel Rosalyn letting go, as if she was inside her body, as if they were connected. And that was when she screamed at her, when she stoked up a fire of rage.

'If you don't listen to the end I'll never forgive you, Rosalyn Hoyle! Not ever! I made it up, out of my head. Out of my head! Do you understand what I'm saying? You might find that easy but I don't, so there. And you may not think it's very good at the moment, but I promise you it's got the most fantastic end. And I'll hate you if you don't listen to it. I'll hate you! I will! I really will! Not just now but forever! You have no idea how much I'll hate you!' She was shrieking the way her mother did at her father sometimes after they went to bed, shrieking so loudly that her throat hurt.

'Okay, I'll try,' Rosalyn quavered. 'I'll try my hardest.'

When Catherine saw Stephen's face appear as he thrashed through the thicket, her father and Uncle Christopher on his heels, she could have fainted for sheer elation. At the sight of her own father, Rosalyn rallied a bit. Instantly Uncle Christopher took control. He'd brought a rope. Of course he had. He was a pilot. He was prepared for every eventuality. Hurriedly he fashioned a lasso with it, talking all the while in that soothing tone of command, the one Catherine expected he used when they encountered a bit of turbulence in his aeroplane. Nothing at all to worry about, ladies and gentlemen. Just stay in your seats and fasten your safety belts. We'll be through this in no time.

'Well, what on earth have you two girls been up to? Surely it's a bit cold for a dip, Rosalyn, even for you?' Rosalyn managed a suggestion of a smile from her paralysed blue lips. 'I know you're a school champion but this can't be much fun. Now, I'm just going to toss this rope over to you. What I want you to do is use one hand to slip it over your head and shoulders, then ease it down to your waist, and at the last minute pull your other hand through.' It took two goes and progress was painfully slow. Rosalyn's hands and arms had locked in the bitter chill. But her father's encouragement never wavered, his pace upbeat, almost jovial. The instant he saw that the rope was safely under both arms he sprang into action, though. Legs apart, knees bent, he put his back into it and began to heave.

Meanwhile, a short way from him, Stephen, his own legs gripped by his father in possibly the most intimate contact they had ever had in their lives, snaked over the ice, grasped Catherine's arms and pulled. He didn't say much but his eyes looked more animated than Catherine had ever seen them before. It was tricky manoeuvring her stiff body onto unbroken ice but he succeeded in jerks, levering her out in a side-to-side movement. Once she was lying on her stomach, no longer impeded by the lip of ice, it was comparatively easy to drag her to the safety of the bank. With Stephen, her gawky brother, folding his lanky limbs round her, Catherine raised her head to see Rosalyn being drawn steadily over the iced pond. She resembled a seal in her drenched clothes, a seal being slowly but surely reeled in by her father, the red beret still perched waggishly on her head.

After that Catherine seemed scarcely aware of her coat being pulled off, of her body being hoisted up into Stephen's arms, of the march back to where the car was parked in the lane. Rosalyn was also being carried by her father. Catherine caught a flash of his face, the expression no longer seemingly blithe, but one of entrenched concern. Her own father appeared occasionally at the edges of her field of vision, his arms full of their wet clothes. He looked absurdly like a photograph of a Sherpa she had seen when they were studying the Himalayas in geography at school. Also, he had the air, Catherine thought, of a non-relative, a man who didn't quite belong to their party, who had just tagged along, a hanger on, somehow unconnected to the tragic events.

The cousins were propped side by side on the back seat of the car, and staring down, Catherine found herself worrying in case the water that seemed to be leaking from them stained the upholstery. They were back at 'Wood End' within minutes, which seemed odd to both girls. Only moments earlier they had been on the brink of death. Now they were being set down in a steamy kitchen where saucepans bubbled on the stove, and where a discussion was blaring from the radio about Kenya and somebody they called the Burning Spear. And in this increasingly surreal world, Catherine's mother swung round and berated her for being so daft, before they were whisked away by Rosalyn's mother to have a bath.

Catherine was on the verge of protesting that she wasn't dirty, but it was clear from the set of her face that Aunt Amy would brook no argument. Modesty too seemed to have been abandoned in this curious dimension. Her aunt and her uncle were both in the crowded bathroom, and oblivious of proprieties, were jointly unbuttoning, unzipping and tugging off the girls' dripping clothes. Catherine stared at

53

Rosalyn, who stared back. Their bodies looked very white, deathly white, their flesh was tinged with blue here and there. Still more outlandish, the water, which Aunt Amy insisted was tepid, scalded Catherine the way she imagined having a kettle of boiling water poured over her nakedness might.

'Oh, oh, oh. It stings. It really stings!' she whimpered, trying to get out but being prevented by her uncle.

'It will, after the freezing temperatures you've endured. But it shouldn't last too long,' he insisted.

If Rosalyn was suffering, she was more stoical than Catherine was, allowing herself to be manhandled, to have her limbs rubbed vigorously by her father's big hands. Aunt Amy ministered to Catherine in much the same manner, cooing soothingly all the time. Then the bath that had nothing to do with soap was over, and they were being briskly towel dried, put into pyjamas still comfortingly warm from the airing cupboard, and bundled into blankets with hot-water bottles cunningly concealed in their folds. Once again they were borne aloft to the sitting-room and given mugs of warm, sweet cocoa, while Catherine's father banked up the fire. This was when the discomfort that she had thought was over, returned with a vengeance. Her entire body seemed to be tingling painfully now, as if it was gradually coming back to life, as if she was defrosting like something her mother took out of the freezer.

Intuitively she knew everything had changed. The atmosphere in 'Wood End' had grown unaccountably funereal, though neither of them had died. The radio was turned down, everyone talked in low voices as if they were in a doctor's waiting room, and Aunt Amy hardly spoke at all, which was completely out of character for her sociable nature. Catherine noticed that her eyes darted warily all about her, alert, on guard, as though possible threats lurked everywhere. Permission for walks were denied the pair of them, and even a suggested game in the garden and a quarter of an hour in the tree house had to be strictly supervised. But as Rosalyn didn't seem very keen on any activity at all, preferring to curl up on the settee or in their den, it didn't much matter that their antics were being rigidly curtailed.

When Catherine awoke the next day and the day after that, there was no hump that was Rosalyn on the other side of the bed, no black curls spread on the pillow. Seeing her emerge from her parents' bedroom on both occasions when she ventured downstairs, Catherine concluded that she had stolen into their bed some time during the night. Whether inside or out, Simon now shadowed Rosalyn protectively all day long, so that the privacy previously afforded them that Catherine had so relished, was entirely lost. She felt uncomfortable speaking to Rosalyn within his hearing, so their conversations lapsed into an uneasy silence.

Then Stephen took off on his motorbike, claiming he had to get back to work, that cars needed to be repaired and ready for their owners by the first week of January. Coupled with this unscheduled departure, Catherine's mother was more than usually irritable with her. And her voice began to ascend into that piercing register of hers that normally she reserved for behind their closed front door. Suddenly they were going too, packing the suitcase and bags and loading up the car. They had planned to stay for New Year's Eve, to see the New Year in, her mother had enigmatically said, as if the New Year was a person you let into the house in the middle of the night. But now it seemed her father had been summoned back to London.

'I'm so sorry, Amy, but he's required urgently. That was what that telephone call he had to make was all about. He was checking up on some problem he thought had been solved. But apparently things have worsened. And now there's another crisis. Very hush-hush, so I can't really say much more. Such a disappointment! So, darling, I'm afraid you mustn't try to stop us.'

Aunt Amy didn't. In fact she hurried away to cut sandwiches for their journey, and then assisted them with an alacrity Catherine read as eagerness, in ferrying their baggage out to the car. So there it was. They were going home. Although Aunt Amy had promised that Rosalyn was coming out to say goodbye, she did not appear, could not even be glimpsed in the hall through the front door which stood open like a shocked mouth.

'It can't be helped,' said her mother laconically, only just succeeding in keeping her tone level, and holding the car door open for Catherine to climb in.

But it could be helped, so Catherine dashed back into the house and galloped up the stairs to their attic room, where she found Rosalyn lying on the den floor sucking her thumb. She pulled it out the moment Catherine tore breathlessly into the room, and sat up as her cousin kneeled down.

'I was just coming to say goodbye. I'm sorry, I must have—'

But Catherine interrupted her. 'You'll always remember me as the cousin you almost drowned

56

with. That's how you'll think of me now. The feeling will be all black and bad.' She hadn't realized but she was crying, her cheeks were wet and her pitch was warlike. From downstairs she heard her mother's impatient call.

'Catherine, do come! We're all waiting for you.'

'Oh no, no, no!' appeased Rosalyn. She took Catherine by the shoulders and held her gaze for a long moment. Dinah Hoyle's imperious voice rose to them again.

'Catherine, do I have to come up there and get you?'

'I have to go,' said Catherine miserably, dashing away her tears.

'Because of you . . .' But Rosalyn could not go on. A deep intake of breath, and then most awful of all, the mouth that never had, wobbled. An unsure, childish wobble that brought more tears to Catherine's eyes.

'Catherine!' came her mother's furious shout.

Her cousin didn't say anything else. She looked as if the effort of speaking that much had utterly depleted her. Then she hugged Catherine hard and their cheeks touched. Rosalyn's felt very smooth and cold, like marble, against Catherine's hot, damp one. She drew back, stood, took one last long look at Rosalyn, into her frightened, uncertain blue eyes, and left.

3

The summer solstice. Stonehenge. 1965. The sun rising. The shared intake of breath. And the shadows lengthening on the scrubby grass. She'd been coming here for this since she was seventeen. It was what you did when you were a traveller. You followed the light. Now she was twenty-five. That meant she'd been roaming for eight years, falling in and out of company. Forever on the move. Naomi Seddon the nomad. She wondered what would happen if she stood still, if she gave the blackness inside her time to come bubbling to the surface. I am like one of those Russian dolls, she thought. If you pull me apart at the waist you will find another doll within, a black doll, Mara. She stared at the mysterious stone giants huddled in the middle of nowhere, like a gaggle of gods. Glancing about her, she could see that some of the onlookers were praying, and some were singing, and some were chanting. So she fell upon the words the priest had spoken to her when she arrived at the home, renaming her. They were all that remained of him under her skin.

'And she said unto them, "Call me not Naomi. Call me Mara; for the Almighty hath dealt very bitterly with me."'

She reached out a hand to the towers of rock. The feel of their solid flesh was chill and rough and lumpy under the pads of her fingers. She scratched them with her bitten nails and listened to the reassuring 'scrit, scrit' of their reply. And then suddenly she was aware of the tall man at her side, the unruly brown, shoulder-length hair tethered messily in a loose ponytail, the moustache that drooped down at the edges of his mouth in a way she thought delightfully old fashioned, like some romantic poet. The hint of sensual, full lips partially concealed under it. The dark-blue eyes perpetually

58

amused by some private joke, the irises sparkling as they reflected the rising sun. All set in the slightly hawkish, predatory face. He slung an arm casually about her shoulders as if he'd known her forever, as if they'd journeyed there together, as if they were an old married couple. Then he pulled her round to face him, bent, moulded his large frame to hers, and kissed her as if they were not an old married couple, as if they had only just met, as if the powerful animal attraction between them made words superfluous.

Later, when she wandered back to his van, after they drew the faded olive-and-yellow curtains, slipped out of their dew-damp clothes and fucked so sweetly that she wanted to weep, he took a huge breath and made a present to her of his speech. He dropped onto his back and rolled her over until she was on top, lifted her up into the saddle of him, his fingers almost meeting as he circled her narrow waist with his broad hands. And while his penis, still stiff and glistening, teased her open sex, he spoke.

'You have nice eyes. Different colours. I like that.' She could feel him begin to jut, feel him butting into her an inch or so, no more, then withdrawing, and again, until she felt her own thighs clenching, the greedy muscles contracting in welcome. 'I'm Walt,' he breathed, his moustache quivering. She gazed down at the geology of his body. Well built, a labourer's physique, the muscles—arms, abdomen (she glanced back over her shoulders), thighs—were hard, the contours clearly visible through the nut-brown hue of his flesh. There were springy curls of hair on his chest, legs, and around his groin and scrota, mingling with her own black bush. He was American, his voice a bass, luxurious and creamy, a voice that hugged you, that opened you up, that plundered you with an affable smile earning your groan of acquiescence.

'I'm Naomi.' He lifted her up, and as he did so eased himself in a few inches further, making her fit him. In response she emitted a sound that was more than a mew and less than a growl. He took another bellows-ful of breath, and through her half-shut eyes she saw the barrel of his chest heave. In unconscious mimicry she drew in the tincture of nicotine, oil, sweat, and the hint of fungal spores wafting from the rolled-back blankets.

'Naomi,' he said, all that breath of his spent recklessly on the three costly syllables. He pushed his way deep inside her, and deeper still. 'I can feel the end of you, Naomi,' he said, and she smiled because she doubted the truth of this, as she absorbed the tartness of his feral scent.

Now, four years on, he was still thrusting into her, satisfied that he had plumbed her depths, that he had found his way to the source of her rivers, that he had possessed her entirely. And why should she spoil the delusion? It was a good life that she had with him, travelling from city to city, through green fields, along open roads in his VW camper van, with the psychedelic flowers winding over the tricoloured bands of its paintwork. Red, white and blue, for the Stars and Stripes. She liked the large skies, the dialogue of the windswept trees. She liked the smell of rain, the feel of it on her skin, in her mouth, sliding down her throat. Its taste altered subtly, so that sometimes it was salty, oily, smoky, sometimes it smacked of industrial machinery, had that tang of metal about it, the bouquet of belching, tall, grey chimneys. She liked to step out of her clothes and let it sluice over her body, finding out her hidden places, a far better detective than Walt would ever be, she acknowledged privately to herself.

But she *loved* the sea, the slap of the icy, bleak, British sea—the only antidote she knew for the blackness. They sought out the sea weekly. Walt said that the salt was an antiseptic, that it did for a shower, that it was better any day than trying to wash your feet in the basin of a public convenience, then wipe your armpits and your groin on a scrap of dripping paper towel that was coming to pieces in your hand. He believed it even served as a mouthwash, that as you gargled it cleaned teeth and gums, both. But it was the dirty core of her that she wanted purified. Only the stinging assault of the North Sea, the Irish Sea, the English Channel, and the big brother of them all, the Atlantic Ocean, could cleanse her. The sea had knowledge of her that Walt lacked. It understood that chained within her there lurked a gothic monster.

While Walt wallowed like a hippo, or lay on his back and blew a fountain of brine up from his sodden moustache, while his penis shrivelled with the frozen caress to the nub of a rosebud, she opened herself up to an altogether more satisfying kind of intercourse. She would swim out a few yards, her stroke an unexpectedly athletic crawl for such a slight woman, her arms scything through the water in mathematically executed arcs. Then, very deliberately, she would open her thighs as wide as she could, letting the sea rush into her, and in its carnal exploration confirm what it already suspected, that that was not the end of her, just the beginning.

61

She could recite the names of the many places they met, like a woman naming the hotel rooms where she and her lover carried on their stormy, illicit affair. Durdle Door, Chesil Beach, Skegness, Saltburn-by-the-Sea, Fishguard, Tenby, Falmouth, Camber Sands, Eastbourne . . . On and on, they tripped off her tongue. No matter how far they wandered, eventually on this great island they encountered the sea. She didn't tell Walt how she felt. She kept her sea fever to herself. After an encounter, her skin felt chafed with salty friction, her body battered with cold, her eyes streamed and her vision was misted. But the filth had been strained out of her and she was shriven, a sanctified vessel. Their last swim in Studland Bay had left her with the flu, her temperature rising steeply, until she felt so dizzy she could not stand up. He said it was just a cold, insisted that once she got to the festival she'd soon recover. But she'd been adamant.

He'd removed the back seats of the van long ago. They slept wrapped up in blankets on a bit of blue-and-beige carpet he'd lifted off a skip. Now she huddled so deep into this, that all that was visible of her was her long black hair streaming out like a troll's—witch's hair, he liked to call it in jest. He tugged a strand, and for answer she gave a yowl that seemed to slash her raw throat like a knife. He lifted his hands in surrender and backed off, sulking with a joint in the corner of the field where they'd parked. Here, he attracted the interest of a herd of Friesian cows, their expansive nostrils huffing in the unusual aroma, their ears twanging off the flies, their soulful eyes rolling.

And so they missed the 1969 festival. She wasn't sorry. The music was more his thing. He'd introduced her to it. Though it was true she enjoyed the way that, similarly to the purge of the sea, sometimes it drowned out *her* voice, Mara's voice. But beyond this bonus, it was just background noise to her. You smoked, you floated, you made love or fucked as the mood took you, and it jangled away, shredding the air. She appreciated it with a kind of detachment. Not like him. He entered into it as a monk might renounce the world and vanish into a monastery. He submerged himself in it, was liberated, regenerated, reincarnated he would have claimed, in the waterfall of its undulating notes and chords, in the sweet, sour, salt, bitter psalms, in the penetrative shudder of it.

After hearing about Woodstock he was doubly determined that they make the 1970 festival. And just to ensure she did not jeopardize the trip, he kept the van steered well away from the coastline and the inclement sea. Once it was confirmed that Leonard Cohen would be performing, nothing would have prevented him from going. He set about it with the fervour a disciple might have dredged up to see the risen Jesus.

Naomi tried to share in his excitement, but her blood was dulled. Did he think she was an idiot? Mara was an all-seeing, unforgiving deity. 'Walt is tiring of you,' came Mara's voice now, her buried twin, her black inner doll. 'He is taking his pleasure elsewhere. You can smell the sex on him.' She scraped and worried and clawed at Naomi's scabs, until the wounds bled afresh. 'He's planning to leave you, did you guess? He's thinking about going home, going back to America, to San Francisco. Alone. He's going to offload you. He's made up his mind to jettison you like rubbish.'

The camper van had been playing up, so Walt insisted that they travel on foot to the Isle of Wight. They left it on a gypsy site nearby, taking with them rucksacks and a small blue tent they had picked up second hand. In truth, their fun bus was in a decline, like an elderly relative in poor health whose every day brings some fresh woe. The carburettor was blocked, a gasket had blown, the starter motor needed replacing, the exhaust was falling off, and the rust was so extensive that you could glimpse the road in a few places.

'All we need is for it to pack up and ruin things,' Walt said, screwing up his worried eyes, and drawing down his eyebrows at the prospect of such an unthinkable outcome. To end up tinkering with the van while a god was descending from his cloud onto the Isle of Wight, or more likely from a helicopter, well, it didn't even bear thinking about. After a heated dispute they left on the Saturday, finally managing to board the 3:45 p.m. ferry from Portsmouth, arriving at the Festival site at Afton Down two hours later.

'Well, we've missed Joni Mitchell,' Walt said, peeved. 'I told you we should have come on Thursday or Friday at the latest.' Naomi, who hadn't really felt like coming at all, chose to ignore him. They set up camp on Desolation Row, overlooking the stage.

'I feel like a pioneer,' Walt said, grinning. 'A pioneer building a log cabin on the great prairies. Only it's a tent.' He looked to Naomi to share the joke but she remained po-faced. 'We can enjoy the show from here for free. If we feel like it tomorrow we can get tickets, go into the arena and get up close and personal, eh?'

Naomi nodded. She gazed about her. The people just kept flocking in, as if a dam had burst, a dam of people cascading into the fields and onto the slopes until they were chock full with tents. They looked just like wooden building blocks spilled over the yellowing grass, blue and orange and green and red and white. The stage was a pale hump in the distance. The surrounding marquees provided hopelessly inadequate facilities for the hundreds of thousands of tired, hungry faithful, struggling with groundsheets and guy-ropes. The air was filled with the strains of music, with the collective murmur of the masses of jostling bodies, wreathed in beads and flowers and hats and scarves. And it was dense with the fragrance of incense and hash.

'The atmosphere is wild, just wild,' Walt told her, miming playing electric guitar. 'You can trip on this alone. Who needs drugs?' But despite his protestations it seemed he did. He produced some purple hearts, gave one to Naomi and took one himself. Discreetly she pocketed hers. They wandered about the canvas city letting the music possess them. Walt began chatting to some Americans, two men, Kelwin and Alan, and a young woman, Judy, she said her name was. They joined a queue, bought cups of soup, and sat cross-legged, companionably sipping it together. All but Naomi. She had lost her appetite.

She examined Judy with her contrasting eyes. In her blue scope she observed that she was pretty, a few inches taller than herself. She itemized her clothing. Leather stitched boots, purple tights, an A-line dress with a V-neck and fitted sleeves. The material was a colourful pattern of dotted ovals,

65

which looked vaguely like a frog spawn. Her brown scope took particular stock of her hair. Though mostly a golden yellow, it had lots of other shades in it, streaks of brown and strawberry blonde and red. It mantled her shoulders, hung down her back. The scarf tied round her head made her resemble an Indian, an Indian squaw. She wore a thick silver band on the middle finger of her left hand, and occasionally glanced down at a watch on her wrist.

Now Naomi felt Walt's eyes veering between them. 'He's comparing you,' Mara said. She looked down at her own boyish flares, her tight T-shirt. 'He's thinking that you have no tits, that Judy is shapely, feminine. He's thinking that she is young, unspoiled, and that you are old, used.'

They stayed together, all five of them, although their tents were pitched some distance apart. They strolled into the woods, climbed a huge tree and hung off its branches as if they were Christmas baubles. They made a campfire with a few sticks and sat around it talking. They smoked some hash, and the shorter of the men, Kelwin, with buck teeth and frizzy hair, offered round a bottle of red wine and some small white pills that he vouchsafed were good stuff, the finest. Naomi pretended to take one but she tucked it in her cleavage. When the bottle came round she mimed having a swig but hardly wet her lips. They were all too far gone to notice. Mara cautioned her that she needed to keep a clear head.

As the night drew in around them Naomi studied Walt, the way an artist might study a model. She saw him put his arm around Judy and murmur into her hair. Her different coloured eyes followed the stroke of his hands on her legs in their purple tights. Chin lifted, she saw him trace the lines of the ribbed cotton. When he found the zips on her boots and started rhythmically pulling them up and down, her eyes were riveted. She registered the tenderness with which he touched Judy's face. The brush of their lips scalded her own. She could feel the black tide of Mara rising up, as Walt pushed Judy back on the grass, and laid his head on her full breasts.

'I can hear your heart,' he said. 'Boom, boom, boom.' Far away the music played, and his head bounced as Judy giggled. 'You have the crisp unworn fragrance of brand-new clothes,' he said. Naomi scrutinized them through the pathetic little fire. Walt cupped one of Judy's breasts. 'Your nipples will be pastel pink, like sugared almonds. Kissing them will be like sucking on small, hard, sugared almonds,' he rhapsodized. Kelwin and Alan laughed raucously at this and exchanged lewd looks. Alan ran a hand down Naomi's spine, tried to make a nest for it on the swell of her buttocks. She sat like an ice sculpture and hexed him with her wild eyes. And he rose, rubbing his thighs awkwardly, as if they were soiled, and went to collect more firewood.

'I need to make love to you, Judy,' Walt said reasonably. Judy clasped her hands behind her head and sighed contentedly. Then they were holding onto each other as if they were cast adrift in an ocean and each was the other's lifebuoy. They stood. Again they kissed, long and lingeringly. When they headed off towards Judy's tent, Naomi tracked them. She waited, and when they re-emerged she joined them as they made their way down Desolation Row. They found a loose panel in the fencing and clambered through into the arena. They managed to fight their way right up to the stage, and The Doors played, and The Who, and Sly

67

and The Family Stone. Walt caressed her wiggling serpentine body. He toyed with her and petted her. Feet apart from them, Naomi gave off intense hatred like static. When they went back to Judy's tent she hastened after them, tripping over sprawled bodies, being sworn at, being kicked. She stayed outside until she had counted the stars, then snuck in. She squatted like a gargoyle in a corner and kept vigil while they slept. The music vibrated her ears, and Mara was a marble rolling in her head, muddling her thoughts. She was wide eyed when Judy sat up, stretched, yawned. Walt woke more slowly. He saw Judy beside him, her fair hair sleep-tumbled. A second later he started at the spectre of Naomi crouching at her feet. The tent was jade green, the morning light filtering through it creating the impression that they were all under the sea.

'Hello, Naomi,' Judy greeted her, as if there was nothing out of the ordinary in waking up to see a woman squatting like a gargoyle ogling you. 'I want to take Holy Communion. It's Sunday. There's a service by the marquee. Roman Catholic and Church of England. I saw a notice.' Judy whistled through her even white teeth into the watery greenness. She was naked and so was Walt. Blinking at her, he nodded. Naomi backed out of the tent on her hands and knees like a dog, leaving them to worm their way from their sleeping bag and into their clothes. They emerged from the tent, hands clasped, to find her still attending them. She did not look vengeful, or angry, or jealous, just blank, a blank page.

'Hello again,' Judy said, relaxed. And she leaned forward and kissed Naomi lightly on the cheek. Walt followed suit.

'Naomi, have you been with us all night?' Walt wanted to know. She nodded.

'Are you all right?' breathed Judy. She had her scarf in her hand and had begun folding it, running a thumb and forefinger along the fabric edge as if creasing paper to make a fan. She tied it around her head. Then, 'Do you want to take Communion? Come with us.' And she clasped Naomi's hand in hers and felt the rough nails scrabble against her palms.

When they got close enough, the priests—there were two of them speaking into a microphone in resonant sing-song tones—ushered them forwards. Judy looked very earnest as she took the silver chalice. She focused on her reflection in it before she took a swallow. Walt mimicked her example. He glanced round to locate Naomi and saw that she was frozen. Her arms were slung about her chest, hands plunged into her armpits. She was staring at one of the priests, her expression haunted. He was robed in satin, the dark material patterned with huge swirling flowers, wide white cuffs on his bell sleeves. He was elderly. A side parting navigated its way through untidy grey straggles of hair. Horn-rimmed glasses perched on a large nose, which was latticed with broken red veins. His head was down, one hand lifted stiffly in blessing over the plate of wafers.

The other priest, taller, less ostentatious in black, was pouring the wine into a second chalice. Suddenly Naomi spun on her heels, shoving her way through the communicants and fled. For a space she walked aimlessly. For a space she merged with a group who were all leaping like grasshoppers to bat about an enormous orange balloon, on the scale of a hot-air balloon but lacking the buoyancy.

'Man, this is great,' said one guy, his shoulder-length brown hair lashing about as he jumped. 'Don't you just want to do this forever?'

She realized, startled, that he was addressing her. She was standing on tiptoes and lowered herself carefully. She made no reply. She was tiring of the pointless game. 'I've won,' she said.

'Oh, far out! You're a riot.' She fixed him with her individual glare and he stopped springing about like Zebedee from *The Magic Roundabout*. 'Wow, your eyes are amazing. Like two separate women in one. Want to go somewhere?' he propositioned bluntly. She gave her hesitant mechanical blink and stalked off.

She joined a queue, shuffling forward patient as a cow, and was rewarded with a slice of melon, a hamburger, a pint of milk. She ate hungrily, drank thirstily, licked the cream off her top lip. Re-energized, she stepped into a wall of foam and leapt about, making believe she was inside a cloud. It was mildly amusing. It made her feel sexy, the foam on her skin and people looming out of the whiteness. She'd like to have fucked Walt with all that foam splitting and flaking around them. It would have been like screwing in a giant snow-globe.

'But then he's probably busy fucking sweet little Judy right now,' she mumbled under her breath.

She wasn't in the mood to trampoline on clouds after that, so she spent a period staring at a plantation of rubbish. It seemed to be burgeoning right before her, dividing, doubling, a cancer spreading. It stank, its rank odour permeating the air. She wondered if anyone else saw the astonishing beauty in this living monument to decay and death. Then it was the evening. She materialized out of the throng and sat beside Walt and Judy on the grass. They heard Donovan, Ralph McTell and the Moodies. She decided that she would never forget the Moodies, the music from that incredible Mellotron seeming to wrap around them. It came from everywhere and nowhere, reverberating off the slopes, bouncing off the canvas gables on Desolation Row. The huge darkness was pegged with stars, the air was a mêlée of scents, of grass and hash and dew and people, and yes, even here, garbage. She was a drop in an ocean of people, pulled by the currents of music.

'Judy, we were always meant to be together,' Walt declared. 'Come back to San Francisco with me?' And when she did not reply, only smiled, he asked her to give him her address, her phone number.

'You're a treasure,' she said as if he was an adorable puppy she didn't want to keep. Then, 'Goodbye.' She kissed him on the cheek and Naomi as well, and shimmered off, losing herself in the heaving mass. Walt's face cracked as if it was a nut split open in a nutcracker. He was hardly aware of Naomi, of the bottle she handed him.

'Jimi Hendrix,' she said.

'Foxy Lady,' he replied, gulping the drink she had handed him. He grimaced. 'What . . . what is it? It tastes like air freshener.' But such was his thirst that he drained the bottle anyway.

After a time she said, 'You're tired.'

As if she was a hypnotist and he was her subject, he nodded obediently. Instantly he was exhausted, worn ragged. He needed to sleep. Jimi Hendrix seemed far away, a blur of pink and orange, a flash

71

of silver around his neck. He wanted to hear the end but he hadn't the will to keep awake. Then Naomi was helping him back to the tent. 'I want to see . . . see . . . Je . . . Jethro, Jethro Tull. I want . . . want to see Joan Baez. Naomi? Naomi?' He waved his arm and stumbled. Distantly he knew he was losing co-ordination, control. 'Was there something . . . something in that drink?'

'Don't be silly.'

'Na . . . omi?' he slurred.

'Yes?' she said, a clear bell sounding through the fudge of his speech.

'Don't let me miss Leonard. Don't let me . . .' He broke off, remembering he had to breathe. 'Don't let me miss Leonard Cohen. I must . . . must hear Leonard.' Someone was turning the volume down on his voice. The effort of making himself understood was too great. 'Mm . . . mm . . . Na—'

'I hear you,' Mara, the black doll inside her, said. 'Don't worry, Walt, I'm going to take care of you.' Now she was helping him into their tent and he was falling on his sleeping bag. 'I'm going to make you comfortable.'

'You're . . . you're . . . you're . . .' She stroked his brow, drew her hand down his face, closing his eyelids as you might a dead man's. His mouth fell open and his body went slack. She made a tight roll of her sleeping bag, and then held it over his mouth and nose. Using all her strength, she pushed down for long minutes, until her knuckles were white as lard and her hands ached. She only removed it when she was absolutely sure that he was dead. She pressed her fingers into his neck and felt for the pulse in his carotid artery. None. Walt's blood was stagnating. Already his cells were breaking down,

72

decaying, until all that he would be fit for was to be buried in the rubbish plantation. She sat back on her heels and surveyed her handiwork for a couple more minutes. She was grinding her teeth, the pestle-and-mortar grating punctuated by small satisfied grunts. She listened to her own eulogy for a bit and reminisced about her life with Walt, good and bad. Then gradually the tent impinged on her mix of thoughts. She didn't like it, and he had been going to leave her alone in it while he lay with Judy.

She wished that they had brought the camper van. She felt safer in the van, shored up in the van. She could lock the doors and no one could get in. No one could pull her from her bunk in a sleep so deep that it felt like a trance, no one could grip her small hand in theirs, crush it between their strong adult fingers like a closing vice, and drag her through a forest of bunk beds where *The Blind Ones* slumbered. *The Blind Ones* chose to be sightless. Images played before their eyes, then vanished, never to be recalled. They were present, ever present, their eyes glowing but they witnessed nothing. Did you see? Did you see what happened? Mara wanted to scream at them, at their blank pudding faces. But she knew they would only turn their empty eyes on her and shake their heads. No, they did not see Father Peter creep past like a malignant ghoul in the thick darkness, Father Peter who in the daylight made them press their hands together and pray for forgiveness of their sins. In the sunshine with the sea breeze salty in their nostrils, he told them that they were miserable sinners, and that there was no health in them. Then in the black of night he came and drew Mara from the warmth of her bed. He took her to his small room, and told her as he lifted off her sleeping shift, that he needed to examine her, to seek out the marks of sin, to test her for evil. If she cried out the big hand was slapped over her mouth until she thought, just as Walt had, that she would suffocate. And when it was over the voice rasped that if she ever told anyone, she would go to hell, drown not once but for eternity, in a pit of molten flames.

And when she returned to her bunk, her skin bruised and crawling, the wet, musty smell of him on her, in her, she curled up in the dark forest and listened to the sounds of the others, *The Blind Ones*. The coughs and sighs and sniffles, the creaks of the wooden bunks as their occupants stirred, the rattle of windows, the thin whistle of the wind. She hugged her knees and imagined what it was like to be in hell forever, roasting in its fires. She imagined all of her, her organs, her flesh, licked with flames, consumed, until all that was left of her was the black crisp of her wicked heart.

On the third night after her ordeal she crept from her bunk, barefoot, holding the rough cotton of her shift between her legs to sop up the blood. She slipped through the doors like a shadow, and stumbled in the twilight. She trod grass and gravel, twigs and grit. She felt her way to the steep path that led down to the beach. She heard both her names spoken in the 'shush, shush' of the sea. Naomi. Mara. Naomi. Mara stepped onto a plain of cool grey sand, the pads of her feet sinking into it.

'And she said unto them, "Call me not Naomi. Call me Mara; for the Almighty hath dealt very bitterly with me."'

As she neared the sea it greeted her with a cheer. Raising her head, she saw something that made the charred lump of her heart leap—its long blue smile faintly lit by the push of dawn. And then she was running, peeling the bloodied shift off, over her head, and running heeled with exultation into the icy water.

4

Sixteen-year-old Owen has been set an essay for English homework, the topic 'Childhood Memories'. It begins rather well as he lists remembered sensations. Sucking milk so cold from gill-sized bottles through paper straws that the ice splinters pricked his tongue and raked his throat. Sitting in a wicker chair that creaked and pinched his thighs when he shifted position. Eating jam sandwiches that stuck to the roof of his mouth. Squashing a tomato in his hand and feeling the juice of it ooze from between his closed fingers, and the seeds plant themselves in his sticky palm. Smelling the manure that had just been dug into the earth at his father's allotment, as he stepped into the Cimmerian gloom of his rhubarb shed. He records his first sight of the blush-red rhubarb stalks poking up lewdly from the tangle of dowdy brown roots.

When he has finished the assignment he creeps into Sarah's bedroom and sits on the side of her bed, feeling as if he has stepped into a time warp. Nothing has been changed in here. The space, Sarah's space, is petrified in time. A clock stopped with Sarah's last breath. His mother never opens the bedroom window. She wants the air that her daughter inhaled, that inflated her small spongy lungs, sending oxygen

75

whizzing around her four-year-old body before she exhaled it, to remain trapped in the jar of this room. It is the reason that she slips speedily in and out, slamming the door with haste. Once inside the airtight hallowed place, she rations her own breathing, moves to new positions where she hopes that the air has not yet been recycled, and very slowly lets the snail of it slide into her. Look, this air, this air here, in the corner, inside the cupboard, at the back of the bottom drawer, this has not been tampered with. This is virgin. This is Sarah's. She scrabbles about on her knees, and her head and shoulders disappear inside an empty drawer, so that she looks as if she is sticking her head in an oven, as if she is attempting to gas herself.

Both Bill and Owen have seen her do this, and both have guessed her motive as she rolls about on the floor, buries her head under the rag rug, or stands on tiptoes on a chair, her respiration at a turtle's pace. Someone who was not there on the beach that day, someone who did not hear the words, 'Don't leave me, Owen,' someone who didn't see Sarah dredged up from the ocean bed, vampire white, eyes cemented shut, that someone would not have known. They would have surveyed Ruth Abingdon contorting her body into cramped gaps, or stretching giraffe-like to lick the ceiling, and they would have said, 'That woman is mad; she should be taken to a locked ward.' But Bill and his son Owen were there, and her behaviour does not seem so bizarre to them.

Owen glances about him, his gaze settling on the small, mahogany, free-standing bookcase. There are several titles of Noddy, a collection of fairytales with lovely illustrations that Sarah liked to trace with a chubby finger, while her father or her mother or her big brother read to her. His eyes rove the room and take inventory. The white enamel paintwork on the cupboards has yellowed with age. The curtains, a pink floral pattern, have been bleached long ago by the sun. The rag rug that his mother made for her daughter has faded too. Sarah's cuddly toys are piled up on the pillow, a small teddy, sunflower-yellow with a black button-nose and a balding head, a floppy rabbit, its long ears lined with peach felt, and a golliwog whose stuffing can be peeked through a splitting seam on his foot. The worn scrap of her comfort blanket is kept folded in a lacquer jewellery box on the bedside table. There are more toys in a box at the end of her bed.

The contents of the wardrobe he knows by heart. He is confident that he can faithfully reproduce every dress and skirt, every cardigan and jumper and coat, every blouse and vest and pair of pants, her dressing gown and folded pyjamas. The socks have a drawer all to themselves. They nestle there like rows of white mice, some with lacy cuffs, or bows, or motifs of lambs and baby chicks. The shoes are polished. That is something his father deals with under the heading of 'Caring for Sarah's Kit'. Everything must be ordered for a surprise inspection one morning, one fine morning when they will chance to open her door a crack and see the spill of Sarah's light-golden curls on the pillow. You can smell the polish when you fling wide the cupboard doors, and see the shoes standing to attention like soldiers on parade. They shine as his father's did that day on the beach, the day she died. And there are tiny wool slippers, and a small pair of

77

wellington boots, bottle green. Sarah's smell is still here too, though like the curtains and the rag rug, its hallmark lemony heat grows fainter by the week.

His mother comes in every day, religiously, as if attending a daily service. Owen has seen her coiled like a rope on the bed, her knees drawn up, her face pressed to the pillow, to the toys, sobbing dryly. She would prefer Owen not to enter Sarah's bedroom. She has not expressly banished him, but he has grasped this from the cross engraved on her brow, the downward pull of her mouth, the jump of the nervous tick in her cheek when he approaches the door. So he tries to resist the urge to spend time with Sarah, or at least to put it off until the need has become so strong that he cannot help but succumb to it—as he does now.

Sarah's last words to him are caged in his head. 'Don't leave me, Owen.' They clang like a heavy chain. 'Don't leave me, Owen.' They make his scalp feel tight and his brain throb. Sometimes it is only the prick of a needle trying to winkle out a splinter, a nagging pain that, although it makes him irritable, is just about tolerable. But sometimes it is an ice pick hacking away in his skull, over and over and over, until the agony of it is unendurable. 'Don't leave me, Owen! Don't leave me, Owen! Don't leave me, Owen!' When it is like this he is prepared to do anything to make it stop. He visualizes the ice pick driving into the sentence and cleaving the words apart. Owen. Don't. Me. Leave. Don't. Leave. Owen. Me. Leave. Owen. Don't. Me.

He drives the heels of his hands into his eye-sockets. But it is no good because after a second they begin to reassemble. The word worm wiggles and wiggles the shape of the sentence back again,

78

and then Sarah calls out even more loudly, enunciates ever more clearly, 'Don't leave me, Owen! Don't leave me, Owen! Don't leave me, Owen!' And it sounds as if Sarah is right here next to him. There is the stranglehold of her arms belting his waist, and the fairy-dust hair brushing his chest, and the feathery lashes tickling his flesh.

His attention is distracted by the apple-green candlewick bedspread. It is looking threadbare now, as if the moths have gorged themselves on it. Actually it is not the moths but his mother who is responsible for the damage. Her busy fingers have pulled the cotton cords from it so many times that it has developed chronic mange. He shuts his eyes again and this time he is besieged by an image of himself. A gangly limbed boy, his mussed sandy hair like a tangle of gold wires in the candle flames. He is swaying slightly on the balls of his feet, feeling suddenly dizzy, the burnt smell in his throat. He draws in his breath with wonder, hypnotized by the glistening crimson arms of the rhubarb stalks, the ruched crowns of buttery yellow and natal green, edging towards the light. The flames flicker as if stirred by his exhaled breath. Their grey felt shadows graze the rough shed walls, tall then short, short then tall again. He can see them etched on his eyelids, jostling one another in their struggle to escape the suffocating wooden womb. He inhales and takes the musty smoke-laced odour deep down into his lungs. He looks automatically to his left, a twin looking for his other half. But Sarah is not there. Wire-wool tears scour his eyes. He blinks them away, and then he sees the Water Child blazing in her place.

Owen is visited by another memory that he

79

omitted from his essay, the memory of a man who gave a brandy glow to his mother's brown eyes. His name was Ken Bascombe. He was their next-door neighbour's brother. He came to stay with his sister, Eileen Pope, one summer. He had sold his house in Surbiton and was emigrating to America.

'Just a few things to do, one or two bits and pieces to sew up and then I'm off,' he tells Bill, his deep, well-modulated voice bouncing over the garden fence.

Bill has been digging. He always seems to be digging, as if one day he thinks he might unearth something precious. He has soil particles clogging his scant hair, and brown flecks on the lenses of his National Health glasses. And he has a smear of mud on one cheek and a patch on the other, like tribal war paint. He is a primitive native emerging from the jungle, ill-equipped with his garden weaponry for this meeting with tall, suave, sophisticated, civilized man. Owen is wearing a secondary school uniform, grey flannel trousers, a white shirt. He is sitting on the kitchen doorstep in the sunshine pretending to read, but really he is observing, he is observing his father and Ken Bascombe.

'Oh yes,' says Ken, adjusting his tie and smoothing back his own abundant, crisp, blond hair. 'So many more opportunities to make money over there, set up new businesses, get things moving. No limits to what you can achieve in that brave new world.' Bill leans on his spade and nods. He rubs the inside of a wrist over one cheek, another brushstroke of earth paint.

'Sounds . . . sounds, well . . . super,' he manages eventually. He is stripped to the waist. His skin looks as unhealthy as the raw chicken's spread-eagled inelegantly on the chopping board in the kitchen, waiting patiently to be drawn and quartered. In contrast his nipples seem very pink. They look out of place, as if someone has stuck them on him, as if you could just pinch them off like milk bottle tops. He rolls his shoulders, uncomfortable in his plucked-poultry skin.

'I tell you, Bill, all those things you dreamt of having, over there in the Big Apple, you can really attain them. They encourage you. Not like here, eh? Slap you down just for trying over here.' As he talks he describes a big circle with his arms. Owen notices that his hands are shapely, graceful, long fingered, expressive as a musician's, with very clean, neatly filed nails. He has never scratched about in the dirt, you can tell. He appears to prod the ceiling of the sky, as if he can dip into heaven whenever it pleases him. He gives a chuckle and his magnetic eyes sparkle. Bill's answering chuckle is a mirthless, agitated cough that is gobbled back hurriedly.

Owen's eyes flick over the page of the book he is reading, *Gone with the Wind*, then back to the man. Ken Bascombe is wearing a suit. The fence cuts him in half but the portion he can see is very smart. A cream linen suit, a pressed, laundered shirt, a shiny, blue tie that matches the striking, frosty blue of his eyes. He is tall and handsome, and in his jacket he looks cooler than his father does with nothing on. Now he slides a hand in an inside pocket, produces a packet of cigarettes, and a gold lighter that catches the sun with a scintillating flash. He offers one to Bill who shakes his head. When he starts smoking, Owen squints at him and conjures Rhett Butler.

81

His mother comes out into the garden to take the washing down from the line. She crosses to the fence holding her empty basket in her arms, and chats easily to Ken Bascombe for a while. Her tone is such a low lisp that he cannot hear what she is saying. His father hangs back, looking oafish. After a few minutes his mother puts down the basket and rests her weight on one leg, the other leg bent back at the knee. She leans over the fence and smiles archly. She accepts the offer of a cigarette, although she knows her husband does not like her smoking. And Ken Bascombe, who will soon be travelling on a ship across the Atlantic Ocean to America, places her cigarette between his lips, holds his own to its tip, inhales deeply, and when it is lit hands it to her. Owen, thinking about how high the price of freedom was for the plantation slaves, notes that unusually his mother's hair is brushed and loose. She has abandoned her apron too, something unheard of when performing her household tasks, until today, that is. Her cotton-print dress flutters in the gentle breeze, so that her son becomes aware for the first time that his mother has a body, a slender waist, shapely hips, full round breasts. For the rest of the day his mother sings.

She is still singing weeks later. Now she takes rides in Ken Bascombe's Humber Super Snipe. The car has a top speed of nearly 80 m.p.h., she tells her son. It is a rich maroon colour, as if red wine has been sloshed all over the exterior, and it has real leather upholstery. Owen has sniffed the pungent animal scent of it. But he has declined the frequent invitations from Mr Bascombe, asking if he might like to take a spin in it. His mother's spins have become so frequent that Owen imagines her as one

82

of those twirling ballerinas. Round and round and round she goes. And he wonders if she will ever stop.

She arrives home later and later in the evenings still spinning, with her hair secured under her Liberty paisley scarf, newly bought sunglasses concealing her eyes, her cheeks flushed red as ripe strawberries. There is a funny smell that seems to cling to her too, a briny, fishy scent that reminds Owen unnervingly of the Merfolk. And her skin is pimpled all over as though she is cold. She sits in a dream on the staircase, slipping off her sunglasses to reveal dewy eyes, and easing the knot of her scarf with quaking fingers.

Then one night his father is in the kitchen scraping the vegetables for the tea that has now become a late supper. He has been listening for the door, ears pricked for his wife. Owen watches him carefully shave a potato, so that the peeling hangs unbroken, like a single muddy ringlet springing from a creamy white scalp. Then, while the pans are bubbling on the stove, Owen sees him fold the washing soporifically, smoothing out the wrinkles in the different fabrics. He stabs the potatoes with a fork, and deciding that the flesh is still resistant to the tines, busies himself guiding the carpet sweeper, push and pull, forward and back, as if he is practising a dance step. Owen, trailing him like a wan ghost from room to room, notes his brow slackening with the repetitive motion. His eyes have filmed over too as they trace the monotonous licking of the carpet pile, the ritual cleaning thorough as a mother cat washing her kitten.

The next day Owen comes home from school to find his father sitting at the kitchen table. He has fat, brown tears streaming down his face. He must have been rubbing it and the tears have mingled with earth, he realizes. His father is crying tears of clay, his nose dripping brown mucus, his quick, flighty breaths finding the grains of soil in his flaring nostrils and catapulting them out.

'Hello, Father,' Owen says.

He blinks his bloodshot eyes at his son in astonishment, as if having to remind himself that he did not drown as well that day on the beach. He seizes an onion from the sorry mound of vegetables by the chopping board, and brings it speedily to his eyes.

'Peeling onions,' he mumbles thickly. 'You mustn't mind me. I'm just a novice. I'm afraid your mother's the expert.' He takes a sudden desperate breath and then bites down, the way Owen has seen wounded soldiers do in war movies to stop from crying out in agony.

Owen's doubting eyes flick to the papery, copper skin of the uncut onion. He wants to ask where his mother is, although he knows. A series of fleeting images chase through his head. His mother sitting in the front seat of the Humber Super Snipe, windows down, the wind in her hair, eyes shining, screeching in exhilaration as the powerful car swings round a hairpin bend in the road. Then the same car parked near the Ridgeway, and his mother and Ken Bascombe walking up a sloping path, hand in hand. Lastly, his mother looking eerily beautiful, lying flat on her back following the drama of the swirling clouds. Her hair, threaded with wild daisies, speedwell and maiden pinks, is spread like an embroidered pillow on the green, green grass. Now she lifts herself up and folds her body over the man's

84

stretched out by her side. Light as dandelion seeds blown on a breath of wind, she bends to kiss his fair hair, the fine skin around the vivid eyes, the unlined forehead, then lets her lips brush his. The kiss deepens and his arms close about her, the two blurring into one another. Owen wants to ask where his mother is but he does not.

Instead he says to his father, 'Do you want any help?'

And his father shakes his head, the wisps of greying hair flying about making him look like a mad professor bending over his marvellous new invention, the onion. With an effort he straightens his shoulders and summons up a gritty smile, a tracery of fine, brown lines cracking his lips.

'I'll call you when . . . when tea's ready,' he assures his son in wavering tones. Then, as the boy creeps from the room, he adds robustly, 'We're having . . .' but he never finishes the sentence. As Owen mounts the stairs he hears him sob, and feels his own heart jerk in answer.

There is no tea that night. Owen sits upstairs in Sarah's room on the balding, apple-green coverlet, as the darkness digests the small house. He resists its advance, leaving on the bedside lamp. He will not give way to tiredness and close his eyes. And, as if he is plagued with vertigo crouching on the ledge of a skyscraper, he will not look down either. He does not have to peek to know they are there, reptiles writhing about his bed. Their shadows glide like blue-grey fish among the sweeping ferns of her flocked wallpaper. Sometime in the night, or perhaps it is the morning, he hears the Humber Super Snipe return, hears it revving outside the window. But still he does not move, just follows the

Merfolk as they weave and slide along the aquarium walls of Sarah's bedroom. Later, the click of the front door sounds very loud in the orphaned house, and the drone of the milk float that follows it, almost deafening.

When he ventures out of Sarah's room he finds his mother sitting on the stairs, a suitcase propped on her lap. He has to clamber over her and it is a tricky operation in the greyness. On a lower step he swivels round and, feet apart, legs braced, faces her. For a longest time their eyes lock. He wonders if, like him, she is thinking of the day they made the snowman together.

'Where are you going, Mother?' he asks in a small voice. He hears a noise and glancing over his shoulder sees his father, face crinkled like a used teabag, cheeks still stained with brown streaks, standing, hands in pockets in the lounge doorway. 'Are you leaving, Mother?'

But his mother does not answer. And then a moment, a moment when a diver is on the edge of a high board, when he sways forwards, feels for the point of balance, and holds himself there. Owen listens to the sound of his own breathing, light puffs, and his father's dragon breaths dragging painfully in and out. His mother inhales and expels air silently under her butter-yellow belted summer coat. The horn of the Humber Super Snipe shrills, and Owen and his father swing round to stare accusingly in its direction. After a pause it screeches again. The note seems more urgent now, more impatient.

When Owen looks back, his mother has risen and is clasping the suitcase. And the way she stares at the front door, is as if everything else in the cramped hall, the telephone table, the telephone, the coat stand, the man and the boy, are without any substance at all. One last time the car horn blares, and this, a long sustained beep that makes all their ears ring as if they have been roundly boxed. Owen steps aside so that she can pass by unimpeded. She treads down the stairs, crosses to the front door and rests her hand on the handle. He is still riveted to the spot where she sat and so he does not see her glance back, not at his father but at him. Slowly she turns and starts to heft the case back up the flight of stairs. Outside, the engine that has been idling, leaps into life with a bellicose roar. Then it is the purr of a contented cat. And finally it is no more than a mouse scampering away, the horn a distant squeak.

He blinks and a merman has slithered out of his nightmares. He is sitting on the same step that his mother sat on minutes earlier, his scaly tail flapping against the striped runner, briny puddles soaking into it. He shakes his head, and his brass-wire hair floats up like the mane of a jellyfish, to sting the white ceiling. The salty, dead-fish stink of him fills the air, making Owen want to gag. He turns and runs into the lounge, slamming the door behind him and very nearly tumbling over his father. Bill is on all fours harvesting the vegetables that are scattered all over the carpet, orange-coned carrots, copper-balled onions, sausage strings of Lincoln-green courgettes, cucumbers lying like sea slugs on the woollen pile, and dozens of cherry tomatoes. He is still dressed in yesterday's mud-stained gardening clothes, and Owen is still wearing his school uniform. He moves with purpose over the vegetable patch rug, uprooting the vegetables one after another, and placing them with care on the seat of the settee.

'I won't be long,' he mumbles, taking in his son with a swift upward glance. 'Just clear up this mess. Wouldn't want your mother finding it like this when she gets up, now would we?' He chortles with impish pluck. He raises his bushy eyebrows at Owen, hinting at the dire consequences that might be in store for them both if he does not complete his mission. 'I see you're all ready for school. Good chap. Just the ticket. Won't be a moment and then I'll go and start up the car.'

Owen nods and presses his spine with all his might into the lounge door, arms spread, palms flat, knowing what lurks behind it. He thinks of the Humber Super Snipe eating up the roads, heading for the coast and the waiting ship. And then he thinks of their Hillman Husky in its washed-out shade of grey, an old, mud-caked elephant. He recalls the grains of earth freed from the upholstery creases by his weight, the gritty sensation of them sticking to his bare thighs, the stacks of plant pots that fight for space at his feet. He folds his arms, and feels his diaphragm jig to the uneven metre of his phantom tears. And then the Water Child is there, drowning his demons in a flood of light.

Owen receives an 'A' for his essay on childhood memories. The Abingdon family he writes about is just like the Woodentops. The father works in an office, the mother is happy all the live-long day in the kitchen, and the son plays in the garden in the reliable sunshine. His English teacher, Miss Laye, asks him to read his essay aloud to the class. She tells the other students how accomplished it is, how vivid and descriptive. 'Owen has set a very high standard with this excellent piece,' she says, giving her student an approving smile. He wonders what mark he would have got if he told the truth. What would she have said to the waiting class then?

5

Sean Madigan is standing on Richmond Bridge staring down at the Thames. It is a glorious evening in early summer. Tyre tracks of pale cloud etch a ghostly path across the hyacinth-blue sky. The only hint of approaching night is the denser, more richly pigmented line of the distant horizon. The river is still busy, a thoroughfare of pleasure boats and smaller rowing boats. From where he stands he can see people strolling along the towpath or enjoying a drink outdoors in one of the riverside pubs, a mother pushing a double buggy, a man walking a dog, a family of ducks bobbing on the merry-go-round of the water.

In just under an hour he will be meeting Catherine. It is their third date and he is going to take her out to dinner at a pretty Italian restaurant on Richmond Hill. He has picked it mainly because of the views, the panoramic views over the river, though he has reconnoitred and glanced briefly at the menu. He knows she will like it. She isn't hard to please, not one of those women who are forever summing you up, what you wear, if you're mean or generous with your pennies, whether or not you take them somewhere besides the pub. Catherine appears content to be carried along with the current. As far as he can tell, and he admits that it is still early days, her nature is easy-going, self-contained, appreciative. She seems to enjoy listening to him talk, to his craic, to his jokes. And when he outlines his plans for setting up a business selling shampoo, her eyes follow his with interest. He recognizes that she is impressed. She sees he is a man with aspirations, that before long he will be making his mark. She has foresight, this English woman; she approves of his goals. She has the perception to look beyond an Irish navvy moving from one construction site to the next, to glimpse the man he will become. He is saving, puts by money each week, has worked out to the last detail what he will need to get his business up and running. He has sketched out his blueprint and she has encouraged him in his endeavours.

He met her at L'Auberge where she was waitressing. He liked the look of her straight away. Shoulder-length red hair tied back neatly with a velvet ribbon, and constrained green eyes that fluttered away from you and had to be coaxed back constantly. There was an immediate rapport between them. He didn't imagine it, because she smiled and accepted the note he passed her with his 'phone number scrawled on it. And then she rang him no more than a week later. On their first night out he took her to the pictures to see *The Poseidon Adventure*. He put his arm around her protectively in the darkness. But that was all. For some reason he didn't want to take advantage of this young woman, who dressed so demurely and who gave him licence to be whatever he wanted to be.

For their second date he suggested ice-skating and was surprised to see a flash of real anxiety light her otherwise placid eyes. So instead he took her shopping to Kensington Market, and out for lunch at a Beefeater. Catherine seemed delighted with that outing too, letting him choose an embroidered Indian smock for her, and a necklace of amber beads that stood out against her pale skin.

Her voice is very English, very posh. He hasn't met her family yet but he expects that they are quite highbrow. If he is correct in his assumption, it means that he is already moving in the right circles. Who can say where their relationship may lead? He has only kissed her once so far, on the lips but chastely, her mouth firm and unyielding under his. He doesn't mind. In fact he sort of approves in a masochistic way. She is a good girl, a virgin, he is sure of it. Ironically, she is just the sort his mother might select for him, except of course that she is English. He can wait. It will be all the more special when it comes. He will teach her the joy of lovemaking. But he will take it very gently, very slowly. After all, she is beginning to matter to him, so it is vital that he do things properly. When you stumble on a woman of Catherine's class, you don't want to go scaring her off.

The meal on Richmond Hill is a success. He has spaghetti and she has grilled trout with new potatoes. There is a long-stem red rose in a swirling clear-glass vase on the table, and the restaurant has cleverly used empty Chianti bottles as candle-holders. The flames reflected in the green glass are multiplied romantically, and the warm light gives their reed-wrapped bases a golden harvest hue. Afterwards they cross the road and search out an ideal spot to gaze down on the winding river. The yellow pools of lamplight illuminate the grassy banks, and make the towpath a glimmering snake.

The water looks forbidding, its sinister spirit only enlivened by the twinkling reflections that fracture then repair themselves on its sliding surface. Staring down at the Thames, his arm lying casually about Catherine's shoulder, he recalls that other river that held him in thrall—the hypnotic River Shannon.

Sunday afternoons, that was when he did it. Not because it was the best day for it, because it was special or anything like that, but because it was the only day that it was possible. Mass in the morning and *it* in the afternoon. That was the trouble with the farm, it took everything you had to give, that's why Sean hadn't stayed, that's why one day he had left. You see, he wasn't going to wake up middle-aged to discover he was spent, that the farm had used him all up. Besides, everyone acknowledged that the land was poor on the West Coast. No one got fat on these windswept acres. You could see the storms blowing in from the Atlantic, see the whorl of gales and torrential rain whipped up in the boiling ocean, rolling in towards the holdings that were scattered precariously over the hills. You could tally up the ruined crops, the injured cattle, the damage to the thatched farm and barn, the galvanized hay barn, before it had even happened. You could predict it with daunting accuracy.

But it wasn't all bad. There were things that Sean loved too. Roaming the woods close by, for instance, and munching up the hazelnuts he'd collected, or watching the squirrels scampering in the tree-tops making the leaves lash out at the sky, or spying the quaver of a rabbit's ears and then the twitch of whiskers as it stood on its hind legs, or the rustle of a mouse burrowing in dead leaves unloosing the smell of the earth's heart. And there was the ancient road also, he mustn't forget that, the one that ran adjacent to the farm. It was a raised road a good twelve feet wide, with deep ditches to either side. Overgrown now of course, but nevertheless he knew ways to burrow in. And once inside, oh, it was like being on another planet, it really was, secretive and strange. He would crouch among the bracken, close his eyes tight and imagine the soldiers marching along this very stretch, imagine their legs thundering past him.

He'd seen pictures of soldiers in books at school. The breastplates of their armour would glint metallic blue in the sun, and the wind would catch up the plumes of their helmets and make them swirl. And they would carry shields and weapons that clashed against each other thrillingly. The Irish hills on this outpost of the West coast would rebound with the drumming of their purposeful steps. They would be brave, these men, know how to fight, how to attack and defend themselves. Sean would like to be a soldier. Well, he'd like to be anything that had nothing to do with farming. He wasn't that choosy, just so long as he became rich.

Mixed dairy, twenty cattle grazed for milk and meat, and a pig kept for their own consumption, slaughtered annually. That was about all there was to 'West Point Farm'. You couldn't help but get accustomed to the poor pig, as it rootled and grunted its way through the passing months. And then inevitably would come the ritualistic killing. The throat slit, then the belly split wide, the still-steaming guts pulled out and the carcass hung from a huge hook protruding from a roof-beam in the barn, while the blood drained blackly into tin pails. Then it was divided into twelve cuts and buried in salt, preserved to feed the family throughout the year. They were self-sufficient, his father would tell him grandly. They grew everything they needed to survive: potatoes, vegetables, their own wheat, took it to the local mill to be ground into flour, even used the stalks from the rye corn to repair the thatching.

'What more could a man want?' he would declare with a sweep of those hands of his that were the size of spades.

Electricity and running water just for starters, Sean had wanted to bellow back. Nothing but candles and the occasional oil lamp to light the gloomy winter days, and it was hard to read by their flickering flames. The lamps smoked too, and the smell of burnt oil seemed to suffuse the air in every room of the house, not just the ones they were lit in. Sometimes Sean's eyes stung and the print would go all smeary. He'd probably need glasses before long, straining his eyes like that. As for the water, it was backbreaking work drawing it up from the well at the bottom of the hill, and loading the barrels onto the cart. Probably not much fun for the horse either, trudging back up the steep lane with that heavy load. The butts of rainwater only went so far. Besides, sometimes the lids came off and the cows drank from them, so you could only use them for washing.

Come to that, he wasn't exactly enamoured of the outside toilet, no more than a few wooden planks that served for a seat, and a shaft sunk into earth. He couldn't put a number on those dreaded nightly scampers but it must be in the thousands, he reckoned. He would put it off for as long as he dared, but eventually the need became so pressing that he would fly out of the warm fug of the kitchen with its cosy peat fire, and into an icy darkness thick with ghosts and beasties, with only seconds to spare before his bladder exploded.

No, the farm was not the future. Sean was certain of that. His younger brother, Emmet, could have it and welcome. He wanted to own a motor car one day, like the priest and the schoolteacher did. He wanted more than that crummy battery-run radio too. He wanted a television and a cooker and a fridge. And he wanted a city as well, with shops and people and bustle. This place was dead, no excitement at all. The nearest town was Labasheeda three miles away. And what was that? No more than a pub and a few houses. Kildysart was a wee bit more lively, he supposed, but then it was much further off. So what did his father have that made him feel so smug? Green fields sprouting from poor earth and for company, the nearest neighbours over half a mile away.

He found the book one Christmas Eve. His Aunt Regan, the schoolteacher from England, had been staying, and she'd brought a suitcase full of them. 'They're only old, I'm afraid. They were going to throw them out so I rescued them. I thought the boys might enjoy them,' she had said while his father staggered down the path with it. Sean had grown alert instantly. Books. He'd rather have a book any day than toys. Books showed him other places, told him stories of other people who did not live on a farm and have to drag themselves out of bed on freezing, grey mornings to milk the cows. And he learnt things from books too. He bet that there were books that showed you how to make money, not by breaking your back lugging hay about the place, but by running a business, by buying cheap and selling for a profit. So as soon as supper was done he slipped down from the table and crept away.

He loved Christmas, not for the right reasons, reasons that his mother would approve of, like attending special mass. And not because of the presents either, which were never what he wanted. But because of the candles, the Christmas candles. His mother cut holes in turnips and used them as candle-holders, and she set one on every windowsill in the house. It was magical. For those few festive days he did not have to move carefully from room to room, for the most part feeling his way, his own candle with its stuttering flame held tentatively before him. The single-storey building was laid out in an 'L' shape, and at Christmas he could charge down a tunnel of light, almost convincing himself that they did have electricity.

But that night he did not charge, he walked slowly and steadily, with purpose, to where he knew his aunt's suitcase lay at the bottom of her bed. He snapped the shiny clasps open and rifled through the contents, looking for that one title, that money-making volume with instructions on how to get rich. His heart had been beating loudly and he kept glancing back over his shoulder, fearful of discovery. He knew the books would be presented to them tomorrow with official ceremony, knew that his brother, Emmet would only pretend to be pleased, that he would be happy for Sean to have the lot. But even so, he couldn't wait. He had to see what there was now.

It seemed a pretty drab haul at first glance, a few Bibles, as if they hadn't seen enough of those already, and a load of hymn books and books on grammar, some volumes of poetry, and a couple of plays by William Shakespeare and someone called Richard Brinsley Sheridan. But as far as he could tell, nothing on setting up your own business. He was about to shut the case when he caught sight of a grey triangle peeping out from under the stack of poetry books. He delved and pulled out a small, cloth-bound book, frayed in places. He looked for the title, but finding none, thumbed through it. There were as many pictures as there were printed pages. It took him a minute to work out what they were of. Pen and ink drawings of a man taking up different positions. He was only wearing bathing trunks and a cap. You had to turn the upright pages sideways to see more clearly what it was. They were stage-by-stage diagrams of how his body moved through different swimming strokes. Towards the end of the book there were chapters that dealt exclusively with life-saving, how to rescue someone who was drowning. Sean felt like he was drowning most days. He would like someone to rescue him, he decided. He was so engrossed that he did not hear the footsteps behind him.

'What are you doing?' The tone was accusatory.

He swung round to see his brother, Emmet, peering down at him.

'I wanted to look at the books, that's all,' he said, trying not to seem flustered. If he showed that he felt guilty or afraid, his brother would be bound to tell his father and then he would be whipped, Christmas or not, he guaranteed it.

'Oh,' sighed Emmet. He sounded disappointed. He angled for a better view inside the suitcase, and what he saw seemed to confirm his suspicions. 'Nothing but boring books. You'd think she'd bring us something more interesting, like a football or roller skates.' He shrugged and shuffled despondently to the door, pausing to ask Sean if he was coming.

'Mother wants to sing some carols. She sent me to fetch you,' he said sulkily. Sean hid a smile. He did not think that a few hours spent lustily singing Christmas carols was his eight-year-old brother's idea of entertainment either.

'I'll just put this back, then join you,' Sean said. He nearly pleaded with his brother not to tell their parents what he'd seen, but Emmet had already gone. Looking after him, Sean thought it was a safe bet though that he wouldn't bother. Not out of loyalty. Oh no, that had nothing to do with it. If Emmet could possibly gain from tattling, he would. But in this circumstance, as the only reward he was likely to reap were books, *boring books*, it seemed unlikely.

It was odd them being brothers, when they looked so different. Emmet was black haired and thick set, with his father's broad shoulders. His features were coarse: fleshy lips, his jaw set in an overbite, his nose large, his iron-grey eyes too close together, his complexion tanned as leather. Whereas Sean had a hint of ginger in his fine corn-coloured hair. Depending on the weather, his smiling eyes could look blue as the sky or green as the river. His mouth was finely drawn. His nose was straight. His fair eyelashes and eyebrows gave a slightly vulnerable, nude look to his face. His skin was pale and dusted over the bridge of his nose with light freckles. And he was taller and slim in build. Their voices were octaves apart too, Emmet's gruff and surly, Sean's soft and lilting. His hands were those of an artist, not a labourer. Side by side it was hard to believe that they were related.

He took in the reflected flames and shadows moving like figures on the canvas of the whitewashed walls. They made Sean feel as if he was in a room crowded with people, instead of kneeling alone by a suitcase packed with words. Sean's hand, poised to tuck the book under the pile of verses, hesitated. In a second he had slipped it underneath his jumper. Then, quietly, he refastened the case and stole after his unlikely sibling.

His aunt never noticed it was missing and the book presentation went off without a hitch, with Emmet hardly paying any attention at all, let alone informing on his elder brother. The grey book became Sean's constant friend, no day passing without him studying it. A bold plan was forming in his head. He would teach himself to swim. He was ten years old, nearly eleven. He wanted to learn how to swim. No one knew how to swim round here. The farmers and their families viewed the sea with suspicion, and the nearby tidal River Shannon in much the same light. The sea brought the storms that ruined the harvest, that smashed up the fishing boats, that sucked hardened men with fit bodies of brawn and muscle to their deaths.

The Shannon was no more than three quarters of a mile away. Barely six months ago a girl from Labasheeda, Iona O'Neill, had drowned in its waters. They had been taking livestock from one of the little islands across the river to the mainland and she had fallen in. Sean had overheard the men talking about her in lowered voices outside the pub. Gap-toothed Finn, the fishmonger, claimed that he'd seen her ghost skipping over the dark-green waters and wailing eerily, her long black hair all wild and whipping about in the wind. The men had listened goggle-eyed and stroked their beards, and muttered that it was a bad business, that the lass should have steered clear of the greedy waters, for they brought no man, or woman either, it had to be said, any good at all.

But Sean did not want to steer clear of the Shannon. Despite his mother's ominous warnings, he wanted to make her acquaintance, to slip off his clothes and let her slither, cold and bracing and fresh, over his skin. He wanted to take hold of her fluid body and bend it to serve him, he wanted to dominate her, he wanted to have the taste of her on his tongue. He was patient, he waited through the long winter months, waited for the ice slide they had made on the hill road to melt, and for the snow to turn to slush and run away in muddy rivulets. He waited for the sound of birdsong to return, and for the insistent press of life to show itself in bright-green shoots and buds. He waited for a spring day, a Sunday, when the Kerry Mountains were wreathed in mists, for if you could see them clear as glass then sure enough, rain was coming. He tucked a small towel and his precious book under his jacket. With mass still ringing in his head, along with the names of those the priest had shamed for cutting hay on the Sabbath, he rode off down the hill on his bike.

He found his way to a spot he knew where a stand of trees gave shelter and privacy from inquisitive eyes, and where the bank of sand, pebbles and silt shelved gently into the green wonder of the estuary river. For a moment he gazed about him. Here, she spanned at least three miles across. The shadows of the clouds scurried over the face of the gliding waters, as if trying to keep pace with them. The flow shifted and stretched out its vitreous limbs, veined with diaphanous golden browns. The sun, emerging from behind a fan of feathery clouds, emptied rays full of gold nuggets on the gleaming highway. Birds swooped from the dark cordon of trees that fringed the banks, dipping their beaks in the shallows. In the distance, Sean could see the silhouette of a barge slipping silently by with its cargo of goods, destined for Limerick, he guessed. And he could just detect the low rumble of a Flying Boat that would land further up river.

Quickly, not allowing time for his resolve to weaken, he took off his clothes. He folded them in a neat pile and laid them by the side of his bike, which was propped against a tree. He took one last look at the first diagram in the book, and hopped naked down to the water's edge. Stepping into it, he braced himself for the shock of cold, which when it came was more icy than he had expected. He waded out until he estimated that the water was roughly two foot deep, sat down fast, astonished by how the drop in temperature and sudden immersion seemed to heighten his sensations. He could feel his buttocks pressing into the grit, feel a pebble, smooth and flat, near the base of his spine, feel silt being piped between the gaps in his toes. He was shivering, and his breathing suddenly felt conscious, as if he had to remember to do it. All in one speedy move he stretched his legs and rolled, arms before him straight as sticks, hands groping for the bottom. And it was there. No tricks. The sandy flesh of his green mistress was firm.

So now he was facing downwards, chin sitting on the shelf of the water, legs out behind him. He

101

began to kick. Immediately he liked the sucking row, the pother of it. He was starting to warm up. Then, slowly, he began to pull himself forwards, walking his arms under the water. He must look like a giant newt, he thought, laughing and taking a mouthful of liquid. He spat, concentrated, picked up speed. Forward and back, crablike, he went, covering a stretch of about twenty foot each time. Naturally it was easier going with the flow of the river, more difficult opposing it. After half an hour, his confidence growing, he went a little deeper, was even courageous enough to lift both hands up and paddle them a couple of times. Oh, he sank, but as the water was only a few feet deep he hadn't far to go, and had soon righted himself.

It was the elongating shadows that reminded him it was growing late, that it was time to go, and not the gathering cold. He had discovered that as long as he kept thrashing, kept dragging himself along, he did not feel the invasive chill. But when, with some reluctance, he clambered out, the evening breeze chopped like a blade against his wet body. Briskly he towelled himself dry, paying particular attention to his hair. He did not want to arouse his brother's curiosity, for he had no illusions. Unlike the books, this latest pursuit of his was far from boring. Introducing Emmet to such a dangerous pastime would earn him the severest of reprimands.

That summer learning to swim became Sean's chief occupation. At night by candlelight he pored over the by now tatty book, committed its drawings to memory, practised the positions on dry land before ever entering the river. And something he hadn't planned on was occurring too: the Shannon was schooling him. He had not expected this but she was, there was no doubt about it. It had only been his second lesson, the one in which he took the plunge and had dunked his head under the water, when she showed him how air could assist him in her realm. Before putting his head under the surface he had automatically taken a deep breath. To his astonishment, with his lungs full to bursting he found that sinking was nigh on an impossibility. The lungs were like inflated balloons, in fact rather like the floats that buoyed up the flying boats, enabling them to skim on the fluid runway.

Armed with this information, he rapidly grew more intrepid, swimming in water waist deep, because that was what he was doing, he now admitted to himself, flushing with pride at his own achievement. He was swimming. Sean Madigan had taught himself to swim. He had lost his fear, the fear inculcated by his family, by his friends, by the superstitious farming community. He had mastered two swimming strokes by now, the crawl and the breast stroke. He was getting faster too, venturing a few yards further out into the river each Sunday. By the start of August he had begun jumping and diving off the rocky promontory that jutted out into much deeper waters. The sense of elation he experienced as his body bulleted through the crystal depths was second to none. The sensual rewards of heaving the water aside were infinite. He kept his eyes wide open, had done so from that initial bathing. There was not sufficient salt to hurt, and he was enraptured by the bleary glimmer of his vision in this new environment. Most wondrous of all was looking up from beneath the water into sky above. It underwent a metamorphosis too. The light was a glitter, a chandelier of trembling planes, so that it took on the

103

appearance of another river, only a river of radiance, a river that merged with his beloved Shannon, that fused with it, that penetrated it, in the way he knew that man penetrated the inner softness of a woman.

And she didn't lie to him either. When he crept up to her, peered into her mirrored surface, the reflection that she sent back to him was true. She understood that he was a breed apart, a rogue seed that had planted itself in his mother's belly, defying the strictures of her world from the second of conception. Confirmation of this, although none was needed, came in the rare guarded looks his mother gave him. How seldom did those sharp dark eyes meet the yearning greenish-blue of his own. But when they did, he knew she was searching for something of herself, for her genetic imprint in her oldest son. She had teased apart the strands of him, hoping to find that instantly recognizable line that ran back to the years of famine and strife, the line plainly visible in the faded sepia photographs that stared out at her from the frames hung on the whitewashed walls.

But time and again as she had watched him grow, he sensed the ache of her disappointment. He was a foreigner even to his own mother, a cuckoo in her nest. And because she did not understand him, she was afraid of him. But the Shannon locked his image in the deep green of her. She adopted him as if he were her very own water child.

It was the final week of August when someone saw him. It was Brandon Connolly, that nosy man from the creamery down the road, who spotted him plunging into the water from his diving-board rocks. Right away he set off to inform his mother of her aberrant son's mischief. She told his father, and

Sean was whipped, not just once but several times. The brass-studded leather belt his father used raised huge welts on his back, his buttocks, and his thighs, welts that wept pus and took months to heal. He felt as if the bites of them were ingrained on his soul.

His mother told him he was disobedient, that given half a chance the water would kill him the way it had the little girl from Labasheeda, poor Iona O'Neill. His father told him that if he ever so much as paddled in the River Shannon again he would save it the trouble, and wring his son's neck himself. He demanded he say sorry for doing such an irresponsible thing, sorry to his father who needed him on the farm, sorry to his mother who, God help her, valued his useless hide, sorry to his younger brother who had seen him set such a bad example. Emmet smirked and asked to finger his wounds when they were fresh from his beltings. Sean saw that he liked the feel of the warm, sticky ooze between his podgy fingertips, liked the salty smell of his brother's pain.

But Sean did not apologize because he was not sorry. He was defiant. He loved the water, loved the education it had given him. The Shannon's catechism was that nothing was impossible. She instructed her disciple that if he had a will to do something, then a way could be found. He liked to sit in the twilight at the very top of the hill, from where he could look down at the view, at the farm he so hated, and at the green braid of the river he so loved. He knew she was waiting for him, that one day she would welcome him back into her heavy arms, and then, then it would be as if he had never left her embrace.

At fourteen his state education was over. There was no money for the church school. And besides, it was time to be a man, to take up his role working the farm beside his father. But Sean preferred his books, the books that promised him there was another life he could lead. He did not shoulder his share of the chores. He idled away the hours reading. What's more, he was too big to beat now, and though his father berated him and his mother wailed and prayed, he ignored them both, preferring to listen to the seductive voice of the river instead. Finally in despair they packed him off on an aeroplane to live with his Aunt Regan in a house in Twickenham, England, where she still worked as a teacher. There were rivers enough there, he found. He went to London and watched the Thames flow grey and sluggish under Waterloo Bridge. But his heart belonged to the Shannon and the pull of her was ever near.

He still has the threadbare book, keeps it under his pillow. And at night just before he drifts off to sleep, he hears the whisper of her telling him that anything is possible, telling him she is waiting, just like him, for the moment when they will be reunited.

6

1975

Catherine is wearing one of those medical shifts that tie at the back. She has done her best to draw the heavy white cotton flaps together, to leave no gaps. But she does not think that she has succeeded.

She feels that there is a ruler of bare flesh sliding from the nape of her neck, down her back, to the cleft between her pale buttocks and on to her clenched thighs. Under the shift she is naked. There is in fact only this single layer of fabric shielding her from the world. Oddly, nothing makes her feel more vulnerable than her bare feet. There are goose-bumps on her skin, and she is so cold that intermittently she twitches involuntarily.

She surveys the small room. Carpet tiles in dirty brown. A divan bed with a dark-blue cover. 'It crackles when you sit on it,' she mutters to herself. She established this when she hunched on a corner of it, chewing a painful hangnail. She pushed back the bedcover and saw the thick plastic sheet, then hastily drew it back again, as if she was nosing around in someone's private bedroom, as if at any moment they might come in and catch her snooping. There is a wardrobe too, painted in maroon gloss, where she hung her clothes. A tartan skirt, a jumper, woollen tights, boots. She visualizes the dark interior of the wardrobe and her clothes hanging up waiting for her to return, for her to inhabit and animate them again. She visualizes the other white shifts waiting for the other women to file through. There is a chunky wooden chair with a red plastic seat. Her white handbag squats in the centre of it, like a PVC cat. The room is lit from above, a hanging bulb in a smoky-glass shade. There are venetian blinds at the window. They were closed when she came in. She tried to open them but they seemed to have jammed. Still, she supposes it doesn't really matter. It is a cold grey November afternoon, a day in which the low winter sun barely seems to have the strength to crest the horizon, before starting its descent into the frosty darkness of another night.

Soon she will come for her, the nurse. Although she has said there will be a delay, that the earlier patient was late. 'Some of these young girls just don't think.' She snorted cynically when she said this, her eyes flicking over Catherine, appraising her condition, judging how far gone she was. 'Doctor's time is money.' She gave a disapproving sniff and her large nostrils flared, reminding Catherine of a pig's. 'Anyway, it's had a knock-on effect, so I'm afraid that he's running a bit behind. Nothing to worry about, though. He'll get to you before you know it. In the meantime, enjoy the rest. That's what I say.'

Catherine misheard, thinking she said 'get at you', and she tightened inside, as if bracing herself for his assault. She was understandably apprehensive. But she need not be. All she was saying was that there was a queue. Catherine was in line but must wait her turn. Nevertheless, she had taken an instant dislike to this woman, Miss Janney, two days ago when they first met, with her cropped greasy black hair, her shrivelled-apple skin, her cunning, small, grey eyes, and her foreshortened arms. She looked butch, muscled. Catherine suspects that Miss Janney isn't a nurse at all, despite the green overall she is wearing. It could be a cleaning uniform for all she knows. Didn't she keep telling Catherine, when she arrived, how clean the doctor was, how hygienic. She wonders if she means that he doesn't pick his nose, or that he washes his hands thoroughly after going to the toilet. But then the *nurse* added with a meaningful lift of her brows, that he kept his instruments sterile, not like some she could mention. No risk of infection here. And again, perhaps it was because it all felt a bit surreal, an image of the doctor polishing a trumpet had interrupted her chain of thought.

Miss Janney probably isn't qualified in anything except taking your money. Granted, she had been very good at that, though. Exceptional, actually. 'Only cash is acceptable, the full amount, mind, up front. Small denominations but no coins. Fivers are best. If you come without it the operation will be cancelled. You've been warned,' she told her when she rang, her earlier tones of consolation and reassurance falling away to be replaced by a hard, unyielding wall of terms.

Catherine's thighs are rigid now, so that she imagines the doctor having to jimmy them open with a crowbar. There is a funny smell in the air, a smell something like throat lozenges mingled with bad breath. It makes her want to gag. She gulps in air and controls her exhalation in one steady stream. And as she does so she attempts to gather up the wayward ends of her thoughts, and set about plaiting them together, making good.

She is here for an abortion. These days it is a common enough procedure, nothing to make a fuss about. She is a modern woman, and this is what modern women do when they discover they are pregnant and they do not want a baby. The nurse said that most women had one, some time or another. 'It doesn't always happen when it's convenient, does it? You've got to get things right. You owe it to yourself, don't you?'

You've got to get things right. That phrase leapt out at Catherine. Because she hasn't got things right, not ever. Only wrong, dreadfully wrong. And it seems to her that every decision she takes is like another step out on the fragile ice, another wrong turn in a maze. She has lost her bearings. The farther she goes the less likely it is that she will make it back.

'I won't lie to you. It isn't pleasant. But so long as you catch it early enough, it's no worse than having a tooth extracted.' Catherine hasn't had a tooth out yet, so this comparison, even if it is apt, is somewhat wasted on her. When Miss Janney said this, Catherine wanted to ask if she was talking from personal experience, if she'd had an abortion herself. But the prickly manner dissuaded her.

The *turn* in which she had walked up to the altar and said 'I do' to Sean Madigan, had been a monumental disaster. She hadn't loved him then, doesn't love him now, for God's sake. Is she an imbecile? Why does she think you get married? This she can answer readily enough, though. To escape, to flee the mother who yanks on the strings of your life, until you feel as if you don't have any control over it at all. Secretarial college in Twickenham? What had she been doing there? She doesn't want to be a typist. She doesn't want to type up the notes from someone else's life, from a man's life. She wants her own, her own life, her own notes, thank you very much.

Her thoughts wing back to their first meeting, hers and Sean's, the way people talked sentimentally about this fateful collision. Well, if it was fate, kismet, call it what you will, then it was a contrary branch of it. Not only are they star crossed, their families are a sea apart, literally—the Irish Sea. What's more, the pair of them are dismally lacking when it comes to explosive chemistry betwixt the sheets. There is, she broods meditatively, something to be said for sex before marriage. She should have tried it. The litmus test to check if you are compatible, and so avoid years of misery if you aren't.

She was waitressing at L'Auberge in Richmond to earn some spending money of her own. He came in for a meal with friends. He was very polite and his eyes—were they blue or were they green? Even now she couldn't make up her mind. But they were kind. His eyes were kind. Besides, she liked his soft Irish accent, his come-to-bed tones, even if when you got there it was a dreadful anticlimax. It was easy on the ear, his voice. It calmed her, made her feel safe.

She sits on the edge of the bed now and feels the plastic buckle noisily under her bottom. She expects that they have plastic covers because of the blood. Otherwise the mattress would be stained. And a stained mattress is sordid, a chilling taster of what's to come. It could put ladies off, ladies less decided than she was. This way they can pop the cover into a washing machine, give the plastic protector a wipe-over with a bit of disinfectant, and it will be as good as new. It's sensible really.

Sean doesn't know, not about the baby, not about the abortion. But she thinks he has guessed the other part, the heartless part. Because without it things don't work. They don't work with it, either, sometimes. But at least you stand a reasonable chance. Her mother and her father are ignorant too. If they knew where she was this minute . . . There had been a weak moment when she thought she might tell her brother, Stephen. But she changed her mind. She realized they would all try to stop her going through with it, not for her sake, but

111

for themselves.

Her mother would dote on a grandchild in a way she couldn't do with her own daughter. She would indoctrinate it, until one day Catherine's child would see her through her mother's eyes. And then it, too, would despise her. For Sean, it would be a better cure-all than brandy, for a short while anyway. A baby to fix things, to tether them together, to make them a family, to make him a fairytale father. She had a hunch that her brother would convince himself that she was only frightened, and would intervene. And then he would go away and leave her to it, feeling like a great guy, a brother who looked out for his kid sister. Selfish motives, all of them, really.

If she lets the baby come it will bind her fast to this nightmare existence, to Sean, the dreamer, the drinker, the womanizer, the man with big ideas that evaporate with the coming of dawn and the arrival of the hangover. Was it only two months ago that they married? It seems like a lifetime. She closes her eyes and sees herself on the big day. And she very nearly gasps because she looks so young, like a little girl who has been let loose with a dressing-up box, a girl trying on her mother's outgrown ball-gown. She does not look like a woman in a wedding dress, radiant on her wedding day. She had dropped a dress size in a matter of weeks. She was lost in flounces and frills of white satin, lost in the snowy maze of a winter's day where every turn brought her closer to the perilous ice. The tightly gathered crinoline skirt, fitted bodice, puffed sleeves, designed to emphasize such feminine attributes as a neat waist, shapely hips and an alluring bust, sagged on her drooping frame. Even her red hair, gathered optimistically into tortuous loops and curls, was rebelling. Wisps had defied the industrial hairspray, applied so copiously by her mother that Catherine, choking, thought she might pass out. They gathered in single-strand corkscrews at her hairline and shadowed her eyes, giving her the vague appearance of a pampered poodle before a dog show. She was slumped on the uncomfortable leather-effect settee. Her mother's earlier admonition that she must remain standing so as to avoid creasing, at least until her father arrived to collect her, being patently ignored.

'Otherwise you'll look all crumpled, darling. You wouldn't want that.' Catherine, eyes down, made no response to this. She battled back the tears that threatened to finish off the job started by her hair, and devastate her makeup as well. Shortly after this her mother departed for the church. Her father had rung to say he was leaving her brother's garage. This very minute he was sputtering his way towards the Kingston house in the polished, beribboned Austin Seven, with her brother, Stephen, the chipper chauffeur for the day, at the driving wheel. And despite the cloud she was engulfed in seeming impenetrable, it did have a lining that was considerably better than the hackneyed silver one. White gold, Catherine decided, her green eyes lifting to lock with Rosalyn's.

Yes, the American Hoyles were over for the wedding. Better still, Rosalyn was her unofficial bridesmaid—unofficial because she would not suffer her to wear a hideous garment on a par with her own. She was bridesmaid in title only. In fact, Rosalyn in a laurel-green silk trouser suit, with a scarf dappled in beiges and purples looped at her

113

graceful neck, was a feast for the famished. Her shoulder-length black hair fell in thick layered waves. She wore a chipped fringe that gave a quirky, mischievous slant to her pretty face. In addition, she had another accoutrement that filled Catherine with envy. In her lap was a camera, a Rolleiflex. Rosalyn was a freelance photographer, and although it was early in a career that promised to be successful, her work had already been remarked upon. It was garnering attention in the right quarters because, exactly like Rosalyn herself, it was unique and original. Today though, she would probably face the greatest challenge ever to her burgeoning skills—how to make a desolate bride look ecstatic. She narrowed her eyes and peered into the viewfinder, sighting her cousin, and adjusted the focus. Catherine flinched. Snap. A crystallized second. Photograph one. Frightened young bride swamped in ill-fitting wedding dress. She lowered the camera.

'Catherine?' she said. 'Catherine?'

Catherine sniffed and there was something pathetic in the sorry little inhalation. Her lips quivered and she pursed them tightly. Not now, don't cry now, she told herself. The voice of reason whipped back, 'If not now, then when, Catherine, when?' She dismissed it and spoke up instead.

'My mother says this was the happiest day of her life.' She delivered the line with the aplomb of an actress off an old black-and-white film, terribly correct and English. 'She says that she felt like a princess, that everyone treated her like a princess. She says the day passed in a swirl of dancing and champagne and presents.' She picked disconsolately at a seed pearl sewn into her dress. Rosalyn contributed nothing, knowing when to keep silent. Catherine took a huge breath, as if her next words would be a physical feat, as if, like a runner primed for the starter gun, she needed extra oxygen to get clean away from the blocks. 'The last time I saw you was at granny's funeral.' A barely perceptible nod from Rosalyn. She kept mum, her little finger stroking the barrel of the lens. A pause that thinned gradually with the beginning of a sentence. 'Ah . . . ah . . . mm . . . I was happier on that day than I am now.' Their eyes met again and held.

'She was a tartar, Granny Hoyle. Do you remember how she used to charge out of the house, a tea towel flapping in both hands, to scare the starlings off the bird feeder? Black vermin, that's what she called them.' Rosalyn sprang up and moved effortlessly into mimicry. 'Shoo, shoo, you nasty things. Vermin! Flying vermin! No better than rats. If I had a rifle I'd shoot the lot of you, pick you off one by one. Shoo! Shoo! Shoo!' Catherine laughed in spite of herself. Rosalyn took a bow and sank back into her seat.

'She was like a gunfighter with those tea towels. Deadly aim. Remember how she used to hit Grandpa with them? "Out of my kitchen, now. You're getting under my feet. How can I be expected to cook with you shambling about?"' Her imitation was a poor cousin of Rosalyn's, but then, she felt like she was a poor cousin. 'I bet . . . I bet . . . oh never mind—'

'No, go on,' urged Rosalyn, sitting forward.

'It's stupid.' For a moment she had forgotten and it was good, but she remembered now.

'Go on,' persuaded Rosalyn.

'No, it's . . . it's just that I imagine she's still doing

115

it in heaven.'

'What?'

'Shooing starlings off the pearly gates.' A giggle from Rosalyn. 'I told you it was daft.'

'Only,' said Rosalyn, ignoring this rider, 'only she's more than likely using her own wings to do it these days.' They lapsed into another silence. They could hear a car revving its engine. 'He'll be here in a minute, your father.' The gold clock on the stone-effect mantelpiece was electric. It did not tick, but there was a metal pendulum wheel that spun at its base, on view through the glass-dome case. Forward and back it went, forward and back.

'I don't love him,' Catherine mumbled, eyes cast down. The tiny pearl hung by a thread. She raised her eyes to her cousin. 'I don't love Sean.'

'Oh Catherine!' said Rosalyn. Then, 'Why?'

'Because—' Her lips were numb and she broke off to collect herself, started again. 'Because I hated secretarial college. Because I hated living at home. Because it was like a prison. I had no free will. I thought this was a way out.'

Rosalyn slipped the camera strap around her neck and got up. Catherine stared at her. She was tall and elegant, beautiful, a woman full of passion for her art. She had matured while Catherine felt her growth was stunted. 'We'll call it off,' said Rosalyn courageously, her high cheeks flushing in empathy.

'I can't,' Catherine uttered wanly.

'I'll do it for you. I'll explain everything. It will be absolutely fine.'

'I can't.'

Then she was sitting beside Catherine, a big sister taking control. 'You absolutely mustn't go through with it. You made a mistake, that's all. Lots of

116

women do it. The important thing is that we stop this whole rigmarole before it goes any further.' They heard a noise on the porch. Catherine's heart lurched. 'It's okay. You stay here. I'll go out. I'll explain.'

As she rose, Catherine caught hold of her hand. 'Do you think about it?' she asked in an urgent whisper.

A suspenseful pause, then quickly, 'Yes.' As if the line of telepathy established that long-ago day was still intact, she had no need to query what her cousin meant.

The front door shuddered open. 'Catherine,' boomed her brother from the hall. 'Are we allowed into the bride's presence yet?'

'Just a minute,' called back Rosalyn, then she immediately dropped her voice. 'I think about the ice every day.' Their handhold tightened.

'We almost died,' whispered Catherine.

'I almost died,' corrected Rosalyn. With her other hand she pushed back her cousin's corkscrew impromptu fringe.

'Catherine!' The father of the bride was importuning her now. 'Any longer and we'll be unfashionably late, sweetheart.'

'Please, let me speak to them?' begged Rosalyn.

Catherine's 'No' was simply a flick of her eyes. She rose to her feet. 'In this damn dress I feel as cumbersome as a pregnant cow,' she murmured. They were both on the verge of tears; the pain of holding them back was not shared but doubled. 'My veil, if you please,' Catherine forced, sounding a rickety note. It was displayed on the coffee table, draped over its edges and corners so that it resembled an iced cake. Rosalyn obliged, and with dexterity fitted it on Catherine's head. She looked steadfastly into her drained green eyes.

'It's not too late,' she mouthed.

'There was a second when it all changed, a second when we realized it wasn't a game. Buried by bricks of ice in the freezing water.'

Rosalyn nodded. 'Catherine?'

'No. How do I look?'

'Lovely. You look lovely.'

Catherine gave a soulless smile and instinctively, Rosalyn looked down into the viewfinder through the impartial lens. Snap. Photograph two. Resignation under a veil. Then a slight rise of her chin. She was ready. Rosalyn went to open the hall door, to let the men in. There was the proud paternal gasp as Keith Hoyle surveyed his daughter.

For Catherine there was but one way to survive this. She became the child who, having raided the dressing-up box, now made up the play. As she went through the motions her thoughts ran on:

'In this part I am a woman desperately trying to grasp every second of this, her most jubilant day. I am riding in an Austin Seven, ribbons and roses on its gleaming bonnet, with my father and my brother and my best friend, Rosalyn. People passing in the streets peep in to see the beautiful bride. I am arriving at St Andrew's Church in Ham, stepping out of the car, treading under the covered gate, walking up the path. It is a summer's day. The leaves on the trees glisten as if they have just been dipped in green paint. Sunlight and shade pattern the sky above and the land below. The gravestones and tombs stand erect and peaceful. I clutch my bouquet of white roses more tightly and wonder how long it will be before the blossoms wilt. My chauffeur winks at me.

Rosalyn goes before me, taking her photographs. Snap, wind the hand crank, snap.

'As I move into the church the music strikes up—"Mendelssohn's Wedding March". And I think, is it me? Am I really the bride? Is this how a bride feels? A sea of heads bob. My eyes rove and take in their costumes and disguises, posh frocks, smart suits, beards, moustaches, glasses, blonde, brunette, red and grey wigs too. The air is a playground of coloured shafts of light. There is a smell of dust and wood, a glint of silver, a flutter of candle flame. I can see my mother. She is scrutinizing her reflection in her compact mirror, still looking for those stubborn grey hairs. My heels click on stone. There are huge displays of flowers, their fragrance scenting the air, and more flowers and ribbons at the end of the pews.

'The vicar is waiting for me, arms outstretched. And someone is standing in front of him in a pearly grey suit. I see his fair hair lifting against his collar. I wonder, will he turn, this bridegroom, turn to see his bride? He doesn't. When I am next to him he steals a peek, gives the hint of a smile, takes my hand. His is trembling but mine is quite steady. It strikes me that he is nervous, and suddenly I find this hilarious. But I mustn't laugh. It is as essential not to laugh now, as it was not to cry before. I pinch my waist as a preventative measure and find it is not there any more, only satin slips between my thumb and forefinger.'

Then, 'Do you, Catherine Hoyle . . .' In the hush she understood suddenly that the vicar was addressing her, and that she wasn't starring in a play, but in her own catastrophic life. 'Snap' went the camera. Photograph three. Catherine praying.

'Should I marry Sean Madigan?' His fingers felt frozen and hard in hers, like the ice closing in.

'I do,' she said. And they were man and wife.

Her wedding vows were a sham. Her wedding night was a sham. She is a sham. Of course she understood the mechanics of it, of what was expected of him and of her. But the truth was that she entered her marriage bed a virgin. Sean was very attentive and patient, but it made no difference. When the rip came she cried out with pain and outrage and humiliation—but not with any pleasure, never that. She does not love him. She does not love this Irish man. She does not even fancy him. He is not repulsive to her, but by the same token he does not remotely attract her either. She feels about him the way you might do about someone you happened to be stuck in a lift with. There is no getting away from them, and to pass the time it is sensible to be pleasant. But that is all. She has married him but she does not love him.

She revisits the night of her deflowering, spies on the newly married couple. There she was, the bride, Catherine, or at least there were her legs splayed, her arms outstretched, her hands gripping the sheets. If she kept her neck at that angle for long she would have a terrible crick in it by morning. There was the groom, Sean, heaving into her, panting and gasping, his face grim with effort. Her light-green eyes were just visible. As if in some sort of meditative state her gaze was trained on the bumps on the ceiling, on the futile progress of a feathery moth colliding repeatedly with the sage-green lightshade, on its distorted shadows wavering on the woodchip. Finally he rolled off her, spent, replete, sat up and swung his legs over the edge of the bed.

'Are you okay, Catherine?' he asked his bride. The chord struck was that of a politely solicitous inquiry—the *good morning, how are you?* delivered habitually to virtual strangers. Feeling, she imagined, rather like a rape victim, it struck her as pure bathos.

'I'm fine,' came her retort, much in the same vein. If this was a farce, she considered, it would be rather funny.

'It wasn't very good for you.' This last was the understatement that brought the house down. 'I'm sorry. But it'll get better, you know. You'll start to enjoy it. Oh God!'

A sudden rise in pitch indicating alarm. 'What?'

'I think the damn thing's split.' Was he talking about her? She certainly felt as if she had been cleaved in two with an axe, as if the bloody core of her had been exposed, as if only stitches and plenty of them could sew her together again. But then came clarification: 'The condom. Damn! Oh damn!' He rose and she watched his pale body retreating into the bathroom. 'I shouldn't worry, Catherine. Your first time. You won't fall, darlin',' he called out in the deliberately careless tone that in a comedy was inevitably the forerunner of impending doom. 'I'm sure you won't fall, so. We'll be more careful from now on, eh?'

Her heart imploded. She would be doing this again, enduring this again. That was what she siphoned out of his words. Then an echo in her head. *Fall.* Whatever did he mean, pondered Catherine, grown addled with weariness, pulling the blankets up to cover her nakedness. Comprehension arrived like a light bulb being switched on in her

121

head. He meant fall pregnant. As if what she had been through wasn't bad enough, she ran the risk of becoming pregnant because the condom had split. It seemed she was in a nightmare of bottomless horrors, all trying to outdo each other. He was back, sitting on his side of the bed, facing away from her. He reached for the hip flask on the bedside table. This was a prop she was unfamiliar with, but it was destined to become so ubiquitous in the scenes of her married life that soon she would effectively be blind to it. He leant back and, ever courteous, offered her the first sip.

'No, thanks.'

'Sure?'

'Quite sure.'

His took several swigs himself and showed his teeth to the drab decor. 'Just this once you won't be caught. Trust me, my darlin',' he reassured, as if he was God and to conceive or not was in his gift. But she was caught already. She didn't need a test tube to confirm it. There was no escape from her predicament. He drained the flask, clambered back into bed, kissed her on the forehead and switched off the light. She wound herself up in a tight ball and wept soundlessly.

I am still trapped in the ice, she reflects now, as the plastic sheet grumbles beneath her. Hot tears trickle down her cheeks. They wet her lips and she licks them off, tasting warm salt. She has held all these years to the conviction that it is Rosalyn who was irreparably damaged by their encounter in the iced pond, that it is Rosalyn who will never fully recover from the ordeal, Rosalyn who will pay the price for their tussle with death as surely as if she was horribly scarred that winter's day. But no, it is

122

her, she is the damaged cousin. Rosalyn has thrived. She is now a successful photographer, she is at the helm of her life, master of her ship, navigating safe passage. Whereas Catherine is shipwrecked, slowly but steadily being devoured by the icy teeth that still grip her. The baby is an anchor pulling her down and she must cut herself free or drown.

Now she hears approaching footsteps in the corridor and wonders if Miss Janney is coming to fetch her. Suddenly she badly wants to spend a penny, the way she did as a child every time nerves got the better of her. A door leads off her room into a cubicle where there is a toilet and a basin. She dashes in to relieve herself as the footsteps recede. She is rinsing her hands under the ice-cold water that gushes from both taps, when her mind drifts back to the occasion of her ninth birthday.

To begin with it had gone very well. The sun stayed out so they had games in the garden. And she blew out all nine candles on the cake in one go. Can she recall what she'd wished for? That's easy, she'd wished to stop feeling so *nothingish*. More than ever that day she felt like one of those magic painting books they sold in the newsagents. And today she is still waiting for someone to bring her to life, to colour her in, someone like Rosalyn. When her birthday tea was over they had all taken turns to see how long they could bounce on her pogo stick. Afterwards they all had a go with the Magic 8-Ball someone had brought along. They piled indoors and sat in a circle on the lounge floor, taking turns to ask it questions. Her mother had closed the curtains so there were great blocks of shadow and streaky wands of light on the floor.

But when her go arrived everything changed and

went sour. Her jaw locked and her ribs hurt so that it was a struggle to breathe. Everyone stared at her, and suddenly a horrible sensation of being hot and cold all at the same time travelled over her skin. And then she felt the blood rushing to her face and her cheeks burned. She knew it was stupid but she disliked everyone looking at her. She felt self-conscious and embarrassed, the way she did when a teacher asked her to stand up in class. She had a horrid taste in her mouth as well. If she didn't concentrate she was certain that she would be sick. At last she managed to clear her throat and speak in a little voice. 'Is it possible that my aunt and uncle and my cousins will come for Christmas, and that we will spend it together in a big house in Sussex?'

She had been careful not to mention Rosalyn by name, acutely aware of her mother's crafty green eyes blinking at her. She was leaning back on the wall by the door, arms folded critically. She was sure if her mother found out how badly she wanted to see her cousin, out of spite she would cancel it. She inhaled slowly, straightened out her shoulders, and repeated the question more loudly this time.

'Is it possible that the American Hoyles will come to England for Christmas?' She shook the ball, imagining it was a huge dice, held it upside down and rubbed the bottom of it vigorously with her thumb pad. Her eyes were riveted on the dark space, waiting for the message to appear. And they carried on holding for long seconds, hoping that there had been an error, that the spidery grey words would fade and reform. But they didn't.

'My . . . my reply is . . . is no,' she faltered at her friends' prompting, her voice squashed flat with disappointment.

124

There were a few consoling murmurs. But they didn't seem to help. It was so awful because Catherine knew that she was going to cry, really cry. Her throat contracted until it was narrow as a pencil, her nose itched, and her lips grew swollen. After that the day had sagged, like one of her mother's sponge cakes that hadn't risen properly in the middle. Catherine longed for them all to leave, then she could go upstairs and crawl into bed. Wanting to cry and not being able to was the most hateful thing she had ever experienced, her nine-year-old self decided as she fought back tears. She had been so afraid that someone would look into her and unlock the pain inside. Only, when it happened, she knew that it wouldn't be like emptying a cupboard until it was bare, it would just keep flowing out, forever.

By the time they all went and Stephen showed up revving his bike outside the house, Catherine didn't feel like a ride any more. Nothing he said could chivvy her into the mood either. Her father was concerned that it was too dark anyway, so her brother slouched off with a shrug of his well-built shoulders.

'Well, that's that for another year,' her mother commented tightly when she came to say goodnight to her daughter. 'Do you like your Sindy doll?'

'Yes, it's nice. Thank you,' Catherine replied levelly, eyeing Sindy who was doing the splits at that moment on her pillow. 'She's very pretty.'

'Your father said you'd like a bike, but I told him that was silly. The one you've got will do very well for another year.'

Catherine was ashamed of her bike. It had been second-hand when they bought it. Her mother kept mentioning the solid rubber wheels as if they were a selling point, reminding her that they wouldn't puncture. The trouble was, every jolt and bump went right through her, rattling her bones. Besides, it was painted black and white, the blobs and bubbles convincing her that the job had been done by a clumsy child. And really, she had wanted a bike that was red or blue or possibly purple; a Raleigh would have been nice. Her mother stood, patted her on the head, gave a quick sigh and tripped off. Later, when her parents assumed that she was asleep, she listened to them talking.

'I suppose that went off all right,' her mother sighed. 'Though Catherine didn't seem to appreciate it very much. Really, I don't know why I bother sometimes.'

'Oh, I think she did enjoy it,' her father placated good naturedly. 'She's like me, she struggles to show her feelings.'

'Well, she's certainly not like me!' her mother exclaimed on an indignant rising inflexion. 'God, I didn't want to be bothering with all this now. You were careless, Keith. She was an unfortunate accident.'

'An accident we wouldn't be without, Dinah,' her father asserted, to which her mother made no response.

Catherine meditated on this for a while. An accident. Like a bad fall, that was an accident, wasn't it? Or a car crash, or an electric shock, or slipping with a knife while you are cutting up vegetables and slicing off your finger by mistake. They usually meant lots of blood and pain, and sometimes operations and stitches, accidents. Even the little ones could leave a mark, and the big ones could scar you for life, or cripple you, or even paralyse you. A bad burn, say, or slipping on broken glass, or being crushed under a horse? However you viewed them, they weren't nice things, they were unwelcome, circumstances you would prefer never to have happened. It hadn't been a pleasant thought to slide into sleep with, Catherine remembers, so she'd visualized Rosalyn's face instead, the bluest of eyes, the mouth that had never learnt to wobble, the nose that was neat and straight, a nose that hadn't been rubbed into anything horrid.

Her hands are freezing so she turns off the tap now, dries them and returns to her perch on the bed. She ponders what misty pronouncement the Magic 8-Ball would have made on her decision to marry Sean Madigan? What wise oracle would have risen from its murky interior? *Better not tell you now* or *Outlook not so good* or even *Very doubtful.* And if she'd shed a single tear of the squall that her itching eyes had heralded, they would have kept on coming. Once begun, she would never have been able to empty the cupboard of her misery. Well, it *is* the worst feeling in the world, wanting to cry, to sob her heart out, and not being able to. Her nine-year-old self had concluded this on that wretched birthday, and her twenty-one-year-old self could confirm the childhood hypothesis this winter's day.

The door opens, startling her from her reverie. 'Doctor's ready for you now, Mrs Madigan,' Miss Janney says, her desiccated face assembling in a quick smile. And she steps into the room and stands back, holding the door wide open for Catherine to pass through. Catherine pushes off the bed, and lands on legs that have dissolved. She straightens them with the sheer force of her will, knitting together sinew and muscle with resolve. This is a private abortion because she has to keep it a secret. She concedes that it would probably have been safer to go to a hospital, but then there would have been all those questions. Isn't this something she should discuss with her husband? He really ought to know, to have a say in the decision. If she is married, what's the problem? Often women are a little dismayed when they discover they are expecting, but generally this negativity soon passes, to be replaced with delight. She plays through the imagined consultations over and over in her head. No, best to avoid hospitals, and get the thing dealt with swiftly and efficiently, before the trap is sprung.

She trots after the nurse feeling scared, hoping it will soon be over, wanting to miss the bit in between. Afterwards she will recall only the sketchiest of details. Bright lamps concentrated on a medical trolley. This mattress covered in a paper cloth that reminds her of the disposable tablecloths her mother used for her messy birthday party teas. A tray of what, in a speedy glance, looks like cutlery. Black curtains falling in grimly funereal folds at the windows, blocking every arrow of light. A looped tube attached to a tank. Stirrups in the air so that you can ride upside down. And the doctor, whose white tunic is spattered in blood, whose hair is tucked away in a skullcap, who wears plastic gloves. His mask, hooked over one ear, is hanging down so that she can see his mouth.

'Hello, Mrs Madigan. Sorry to keep you waiting. Just hop up here and we'll soon have you feeling nice and relaxed.'

And, perhaps because of the nurse's earlier simile, comparing an abortion to a dental extraction, what strikes her suddenly is the most absurd thing. His two front teeth, nothing else about his appearance but his two big furred front teeth, rat's teeth. Worrisomely, they are off centre, so that the line of symmetry she mentally draws from his capped brow, down the large bony ridge of his nose, and on to divide his mouth, suddenly comes adrift in the yellowing enamel. It is as though his face has a kink in it.

'Mrs Madigan, are you all right? You look a little unwell? I can assure you that there is no need to be alarmed.'

What can she say to this? *I am alarmed because you are out of kilter, Doctor. Crooked.* Better not. So she doesn't say anything. She just briskly retraces her steps and grabs her clothes, making a dash for the front door. She finishes dressing in the stairwell of the building, with the parting words of Miss Janney ringing in her ears.

'You can't have a refund. I told you, no refunds. If you change your mind, that's your affair. But we don't give refunds.'

And then? Why then comes the slamming of the door, the jarring impact seeming to pass straight through her, making her eyes snap shut. And when she reopens them she winces as another fracture makes its jagged way across the ice floor.

1976

Summer. Britain is in the grip of a heat wave. Drought conditions prevail. Anxious farmers squint at fields of atrophying crops. The rays of a milky sun, magnified through the starch-blue glass of the sky, scorch down mercilessly on both town and country alike. Cars have transformed into motorized ovens. People loll like panting tongues from open-mouthed windows. They crowd the air-conditioned cinemas where *The Omen* and *The Man Who Fell to Earth* are screening. Forests appear to spontaneously combust, the dry tinder of the trees bursting into flames. Humps of torched, blackened heath patch the hillsides. Low rivers thirstily suck back meandering streams. There is a rush on the diamond sparkle of water, a sudden lust for its many facets. Feverish residents huddle round standpipes, determinedly filling their bottles and pails. In the cities, dust, dirt, exhaust fumes, sweat and decay, all merge in the shimmering heat. Reservoirs gape with sinking watermarks. Placid temperaments are in meltdown, distilling into a collective swill of suppressed rage. Surges of uncontrollable anger test the seams of society until they burst.

A basement market in the centre of London. The fluorescent ceiling lights emit a flickering subterranean radiance. Here, if possible, it is even hotter than above ground. The music blares out from loudspeakers, the bass rhythm sounding the gonging heartbeat of this warren of trade. The merchandise, souvenir plates and cups, costume jewellery, watches, clothes, bags, belts and buckles, glitter like the treasure trove in an Aladdin's cave. And the market people, sweat-slicked, grubby and old before their time, fan themselves with sticky hands, and swear disgruntled oaths. High noon, and they subside into lassitude, for once both depleted and defeated. The sales patter fogs in their fuddled brains, and sticks in their dry throats. They splash bottles of mineral water over their heads to keep cool. The victims, the tourists, their garish clothing tight against bulges of damp flesh, have grown rebellious in the close heat. They pick over the displays, point and scowl at the shoddy workmanship, gripe to each other at the exorbitant prices. Dry lips are licked. Soufflé hairdos collapse, makeup melts and colours blur. Beads of perspiration freckle brows, noses and upper lips. Plump thighs wedged in short skirts rub together until skin reddens and burns with prickly heat. Wilting banknotes stay snug in warm wallets, refusing to be peeled apart. London is holding its breath. If release does not come soon, if the rains do not fall, how long before markets, roads, traffic, buildings, people, Uncle Tom Cobley and all, will expire with heatstroke?

Only ten minutes earlier, Owen returned from the toilets, face wet, hair dripping, hands washed and mercifully clean for a space. Already his broiled flesh is crying out for another dunking, though. He is working the Irishman's stall, Sean's pitch, Sean Madigan. He has been here for only three weeks, although it feels like three years. He has come to London to reinvent himself. He plans to model his personality on Rhett Butler, a man who does not give a damn, not about the present, not about the future, and most crucially, not about the past. Looking young for his age, his age being twenty-three, is undoubtedly a disadvantage in this process. Fair hair, diffident blue eyes, virtually a stubble-free chin, is not an asset when you are aiming for hard-man status—but he determines to get there, to achieve the emotional lobotomy he craves. In his favour, he is tall, broad-shouldered, with the effortlessly well-toned build that some are lucky enough to inherit. Observing himself in the mirrored counter of the stall, Owen accepts that he looks more like a Romeo than a Tybalt.

Naomi Seddon, Sean's girlfriend, as distinct from Sean's wife, and his stall manager, has gone to buy them iced teas. She has promised extra mint and sugar, because it cools, she says. Owen is suffering with a bad headache. It feels as if his brain is alternately expanding and contracting inside his skull. He closes his eyes and backtracks. How is it that a lad from a council house in Wantage comes to be in the bustle of a London market enduring some of the highest temperatures since records began? Mentally he counts off the years.

Exams, university, dropping out, loafing about the house, sitting in Sarah's room for hour after hour waiting for something to happen. Then the ad in the paper that grabbed his attention. *Actors wanted for the Punchinello Children's Theatre Company, a small innovative theatrical company, bringing theatre in education to schools.* And subsequently the high-voltage enthusiasm that came from nowhere as he rehearsed his audition piece, Jimmy Porter, from John Osborne's play *Look Back in Anger*. The thrill of getting the job, of acquiring the much-coveted

Equity card. The sudden recognition that here was a craft he was good at—a craft, unbeknownst to him, he had been practising for most of his life—the art of pretence. And the idea, gradually taking hold, that acting could transport him away from the sepulchre of their home, where Sarah's ghost took up so much room that there was none left for him to occupy.

The slip of paper with the scribbled telephone number of Sean Madigan that a fellow actor had given him, on learning his plans to relocate to London. It came with the prospect of casual work, cash in hand, for those annoying periods all seasoned actors have to deal with when they were 'resting'—a euphemism thespians use for the long idle stretches when no employment can be found. Dialling the number from a callbox in Twickenham, where he had stayed with an old school friend temporarily. The conversation resulting in an *on the spot offer of employment* in a London market. He would be covering the busy tourist season. Time off for auditions as and when required? No problem. His new employer believed flexibility was a two-way street.

So there it is, a series of random events that transported him from Wantage to London, and ultimately delivered him here on what feels like the hottest day so far this summer. Sean's Covent Garden flat, as of yesterday, Thursday, June 10th, officially became his home. Owen had been looking for a more central place to stay, a base from which he could attend auditions and interviews with agents, as well as somewhere within easy access of work. It made sense, especially considering the expense of train and tube fares. Within minutes of mentioning his dilemma to Sean, the solution had been hatched. He would flat share with Naomi, pay a nominal rent, and in return keep her company when Sean was away. This would be no hardship, he was sure.

He likes Naomi. Her most distinctive feature is her unique eyes. Her right eye is a pale powdery blue, the left is a rich brown. Her short blonde hair, dyed he thinks, is all awry as if permanently windblown. Her delicate nose and wide sensual mouth are set in a heart-shaped face. Of medium height and slim, he guesses that she is considerably older than him. It is hard to tell by exactly how much under that heavy make-up she wears, but he estimates that she is well into her thirties. Her undoubted experience, her confident dallying, her overt sexuality, all fascinate him. She makes him feel alive and manly. He's had a few girlfriends, but none of the relationships were particularly successful. He finds young women difficult to talk to. They don't seem content with his sporadic, trivial conversation. They all, without exception, arrive at the same conclusion, that he needs 'bringing out of himself'. And when they come up against his Houdini-proof doors, they quickly lose interest. But so far, Naomi has not grilled him. She is, he is certain, far less interested in him, than he is in her. The prospect of having her all to himself some nights, of having those bewitching eyes focus entirely on him, is appealing to his young male ego.

To hear Sean talk, the flat is of the penthouse variety, a prime residence in a prime location. And Owen was duly impressed, he has to admit, until he saw it. Situated on the third floor of a ramshackle building, it is not much bigger than a large

134

cupboard. A cramped hall, two tiny bedrooms, a bathroom with leaky bath taps, a small lounge-cum-diner, and a galley kitchen. He tries to marry this up with Sean's initial description, but fails. It seems that his employer is also fond of pretence. And yet he cannot help but warm to this man. Apart from anything else he is affable, exudes easy Irish charm, and has his countrymen's gift of fluency. He is of average height and thin, but not fit, if Owen is any judge. And he reckons that he too is in his thirties. Although his smoker's cough is still in its infancy, there is a pallor about his face, an edginess in his jaundiced eyes, that suggests a lifestyle toll. Initially he thought that Sean was fair haired, like himself. But in the sunlight he has detected more than a hint of a gingery red in his shade.

One significant detail is that he has a patch of rough, inflamed, flaking skin on his neck, about the size of a thumbprint. If his collar is buttoned up, you may miss it. But the sun is loosening everything, collars included, exposing previously hidden flaws. Owen has noted his habit of scratching at it, and has seen that the resulting relief is merely temporary, that the irritation when it returns has only been exacerbated.

Actors must be observant, memorizing people's idiosyncrasies to use at a later date when character building. He has read this. The market is an ideal source for a novice actor like him. Already it is making him into something of a sleuth. He is collecting intelligence, collating facts. As the mercury rises in thermometers in the capital, and the fetor of unwashed bodies crowds claustrophobically around him, he concentrates on putting together the puzzle. He selects one detail,

135

picks it up like a jigsaw piece, examines the colour, the texture, the shape, gauges where it might fit in. Gradually he is starting to discern the picture. He keeps thinking that now, like Rolf Harris, he can tell what it is. But then he scrutinizes it from another angle, and it breaks on him that he is no nearer the truth.

Nevertheless, he thinks he has got an approximation of the arrangement now. Sean has set up his mistress, Naomi, in his rented flat. He stays over three nights, sometimes four, whenever he can get away, in fact. Get away from what? From a wife, Catherine, and from a new baby, he learns, a girl, who was born only days before Owen started work. He knows their names. He has overheard them. Catherine and Bria. He would almost prefer to be in ignorance. In his imagination they are becoming flesh and blood, a mother and baby surviving an unhappy situation, something he can relate to. They are giving his life the very quality he is fleeing from, the ring of reality.

At the close of his first week, Naomi and Sean asked him back for supper. He was flattered at the invitation. A fuss was being made of him, a welcome dinner. But when it came to it, the evening was hijacked by another, another complication, another adjustment in his perception. As far as he could tell, Enrico had not been formally invited. He was an audacious gatecrasher, slouching about drinking beer and leering at Naomi. He is the Italian who owns the first stall you come to when you descend the market stairs. Sean's sobriquet for him, 'a trashy dago', did not bode particularly well for a harmonious evening, Owen decided. He soon grasped that far from being the honoured guest, he was as invisible here as he is at home.

They ate pasta, drank some wine that sent his head into a spin and caused his stomach to somersault, and smoked some dope that sliced into his throat like a scalpel and turned his limbs to steam. The lounge they sat in was so hot that it felt as if the foundations of the city, baked in the kiln of the day, were making a sauna of the night. Through the fuddled miasma that subsumed him, he watched. He watched as Sean drank, tossing back a succession of brandies like fruit juice, while his waxy skin freckled with clammy sweat, and his bloodshot eyes ogled Naomi, and fixed Enrico with lethal intent.

'Tell us about the drowned village,' Naomi said into the sudden ringing silence. 'Tell us about the village that lies at the bottom of the lake.' She was crouching down expectantly, her hands, with their bitten nails, resting on his parted knees. Their eyes, his granite grey, inscrutable, hers of two distinctive shades, locked. The silence climbed a scale or two until it screamed. Feeling a vein pulse at his temple, Owen balked. This was the last topic he could wish to discuss. Unable to help himself, he imagined that they were all under this fabled lake, that funnels of muddy green light were filtering down from the surface penetrating the gloom that engulfed them. His dope-fuelled fantasy conjured ghosts of the drowned flitting past them to skulk in the sunken houses. Sarah's ghost, her blonde curls water-tousled, still wearing her spotted swimsuit, was among them. Naomi wetted her lips with the sharpened point of her tongue. 'Tell us about Teodora. Tell us about the woman who sat combing her long dark hair and staring into the fire, while

137

her husband froze to death on the mountain.' With a heavy heart, Owen realized she was as insistent as an eager child wanting to hear a favourite oft-told bedtime story.

Without breaking her gaze, Enrico strummed a few chords on the guitar slung in his lap. They shared a smile and she drummed her fingers on his knees, while the plucked cat gut reverberated in the hollow wooden belly. Owen took stock of the tall Italian, of his sprawled rangy limbs, of his olive skin and his distracting orange string beard. Before such a blatant show of masculinity, Naomi looked feminine and petite. As for Owen, he perched beside the bare-chested musician feeling as uncomfortable as a schoolboy in a staff-room. If it were not for the fretboard of the instrument pinning him back, he would have been tempted to flee discourteously into the night's obscurity.

Sean loured in the tatty spoon-back armchair, seeming no keener than Owen to let Enrico take centre stage. It was a poor throne, with its shabby green velvet upholstery. He was staring morosely into his tumbler of brandy, as if transfixed by something he saw there. His face was drawn, his sea-coloured eyes red-rimmed and underscored with livid smudges. Despite the heat he was still wearing his swordfish-grey trousers. His suit jacket did sleeve his chair-back though, so that the toxic purple lining was visible. He was sweating profusely. And the patches mapped on his white shirt were fast spreading, like oceans reclaiming the land, Owen reflected dismally. His tie, a dizzying pattern of interlocking diamonds in eye-watering shades, had been loosened. His shirt collar was undone, revealing the postage stamp of flaky, inflamed skin.

Owen thought that he resembled a condemned man wearing a noose, waiting for the hangman to pull the lever.

'Tell us about the drowned village, Enrico,' Naomi persisted, her tone silky and seductive.

Sean mumbled sourly into his drink. 'Not that fuckin' nonsense again. It's late. Perhaps we should call it a night. Some of us have work to do in the morning.' His genteel Irish brogue sounded as if it had been roughed up in a bare-knuckle fight. Enrico, damned not with faint praise but this well-aimed brickbat, seemed blithely unconcerned. He arched his neck, fingered his golden medallion and swooned over his guitar. Owen felt the restraining pressure on his diaphragm. Naomi clambered up, using the Italian's substantial knees for leverage. In the galley kitchen she opened another bottle of Mateus Rosé and topped up hers and Enrico's glasses—though not Owen's. He covered his and shook his head. He was unused to alcoholic beverages. The blur of a Hendrix and a Dylan poster, the lava lamp, the blow-up plastic chair, all revolved giddily about him. With each fresh heave of his stomach he earnestly wished everything were bolted down, him included. Naomi raised her glass to Enrico, sipped and then crossed to the record player on a corner shelf. She stooped to a wire rack on the floor, lifted up a single, removed its cover and whistled the dust from it.

'"Suzanne". Leonard Cohen. This is my song. He sings it for me, you see. Because I'm the lady of the lake, the lady of the sea,' she crooned and swayed, briefly closing her eyes. 'Mm . . . lady of the lake . . . lady of the sea.' Her eyelids jumped, but it was a moment before they came unstuck and flew open.

She put the record on and whirled round. She reached out her arms to Enrico. 'Dance with me,' she coaxed with a wiggle of her narrow hips. 'Dance with me, Enrico.' Obligingly he extricated himself from his guitar, as gently, Owen thought, as if he was climbing out of bed, trying not to disturb a sleeping lover. The music started. He moved close. They clasped each other.

Sean glowered at them over the rim of his glass. His eyes lingered on Naomi, on her snaking arms, her circling buttocks, on the page of flesh that gaped from her hipsters to her sleeveless shirt, which was knotted under her small breasts. Draining his drink, he jerked to his feet. He shouldered his way past the gyrating couple, and into the galley kitchen. There he poured himself another drink. Although the guitar, propped up against the settee, was no longer an impediment to escape, Owen stayed seated. He felt stiff as a cardboard cut-out. Covertly he glanced about at the remains of the dinner party, plates smeared red with pasta sauce, scattered breadcrumbs, dregs of wine, melting butter. There was a mess of dirty cutlery too, looking as if murder had been done, or perhaps was about to be enacted. The flat is a lot pokier than Sean had initially let him believe, a lot shabbier. That night, his introduction to it, he was taken aback by the discrepancy between his employer's earlier description and the reality that met him. Tiredness had fled now, to be replaced with the kind of itch that came when a wound was trying to repair itself.

Back in his chair nursing his drink, Sean's sullen eyes resettled on the dancing partners. Naomi's mouth was open, her tongue feeling its way along the serrated edges of her teeth. Owen detected the creak of Enrico's leather waistcoat in the drone of music. His eyes followed the ripple of his dragon tattoo as he flexed his biceps, and the swish of his dark ponytail as he circled his head. The ants must really have been biting that evening because Jack rocketed out of his box again. Sean's heels cracked on the wooden floor. The empty glass fell from his hand and bowled along a floorboard before coming to rest. Only Owen seemed to pay attention, sitting up a little straighter. The song finished. The record continued revolving on its turntable. The needle scratched rhythmically. Without haste or embarrassment the melded bodies divided.

Naomi blearily focused on Enrico's medallion, St Christopher, patron saint of travellers, gleaming against a few curls of dark moist chest hair. She leaned in and kissed it. 'I'm your lady of the lake,' she muttered, then took a pace or two backwards. She put her palms together in a gesture of prayer, bowed her head, raised her eyes to Enrico's, and giggled. He winked back, then tossed himself down on the settee. Naomi snuggled between him and Owen, then like *déjà vu* she said, 'Tell us about Italy, about the village under the lake. Tell us about your home, Vagli Sotto, which overlooked the reservoir. Tell us about the woman who drowned in her cottage when they flooded the valley.' And all Owen's hopes that the taboo subject had been forgotten were dashed.

Enrico made himself comfortable, a far-off look stealing into his grey eyes. 'Teodora was very young and beautiful. Big dark eyes. Thick black hair. She was in love with a boy from a nearby village. But he was poor.' He shrugged and gave a half-smile. 'Her

141

father disapproved of the match and forced her to marry Anselmo. He was old and ugly,' he continued, accompanying his narrative with an insolent grin and a sly nod of his head at his reluctant Irish host. 'But he was rich.' Sean sighed in irritation at the intended slight. Naomi was absorbed. But Owen was full of mute dread. 'One freezing winter's day, Anselmo went to collect firewood on the slopes. He strayed and lost track of the time. He missed his footing on the icy rocks, fell and broke his leg. He knew that if they did not come for him he would freeze to death overnight. But he consoled himself that his anxious wife was sure to raise the alarm. Soon they would rescue him.'

Naomi reached forward and playfully flicked the beads knotted into Enrico's tassel beard. They jiggled and caught the light. She traced the metronome arc of them and whispered, 'What happened then?' Her bare arms were all gooseflesh with anticipation. Glimpsing Sean's clenched fists, Owen gained the impression that he would quite like to punch Enrico's teeth out. As if telepathic, the object of his rage bared his large, gleaming, white teeth—intact, every one.

Then, 'Teodora sat by the fire and recalled her wedding night. She was filled with disgust at the memory. As the hours crawled by she glanced at the mantle-clock. But she stayed put, cosy by the fire, until daybreak. Only then did she raise the alarm. They bore his frozen body home late that afternoon and laid it out inside the church. And when Teodora came they eyed her fearfully, and called her a witch and a murderess.'

Naomi leapt to her feet. 'Anyone would have done the same.'

Enrico raised his dark eyebrows sardonically. 'She cursed them all. And when they dammed the Edron river and flooded the valley, the legend has it she stayed in her cottage and drowned with the village of Fabbriche di Careggine. It is still there, you know. In times of drought you can see the church tower poke up from the depths of the lake. And they say if you squint at the water, you can see Teodora swimming like a mermaid under the surface.'

'What a load of gobshite!' Sean exclaimed, on his feet for a third time. 'I'm going to bed.' He stomped from the room, tangling briefly and bad temperedly in the doorway's bead curtain. The entire flat seemed to shake.

Enrico dragged himself up, gave a leisurely yawn, stretched and retrieved his guitar. 'Perhaps I'd better go,' he said, a remark that fell into the sudden stillness like an overdue library book. He leant over Naomi and spoke into her dishevelled hair, 'Would you like to go? Would you like to see the lady in the lake for yourself?' For a second their eyes held, and then her gaze slipped past him. Next that hesitant blink of hers that Owen was getting used to, and the spell was broken. She rose, pushing him away, and shooed him off into the torrid night.

'Oh, it's hot as Africa here,' she grumbled, fanning herself with a record sleeve. Her extraordinary eyes came to rest on Owen. 'I'm sorry. I forgot about you.' He looked up like a startled rabbit. She touched his arm, then took hold of his hand. 'What's wrong?' she asked.

'Nothing. It's . . . it's . . . late, that's all. I'm overtired.'

'Of course.' She pulled him to his feet. 'Let me

143

show you your bed. I have made it up with clean sheets.'

'Thanks,' he murmured back. But he had not heard her. He was miles away, high up in the Tuscan mountains, where a dead village lay sprawled at the bottom of a lake. It was Teodora and not Naomi he saw leading the way. And she was not taking him to bed but to his watery grave.

Since then, he has had an unhealthy preoccupation with the lake and the submerged village. Now as he spots Naomi descending the stairs in a shaft of sunlight, he is reminded of his thirst. She pauses to flirt with Enrico, tiring of the sport suddenly and striding towards him. Sean is absent, utilizing the flexible two-way street to the full. He is often away and gives no explanations of his frequent comings and goings. A fat balding man rifles through a tray of belt buckles with sausage fingers. Owen polices him with his savvy eyes, giving fair warning that already he is wise to shoplifters. But he stays perched on the stool, hostage to his lethargy. Why waste the effort? This man won't buy, he can see it in his mean, closed expression. He will fiddle with the buckles, then say he doesn't like any of them. After a minute, as he surmised, the fat man waddles off with an impatient shrug.

Owen fixes on the large paper cups of iced tea clasped in Naomi's hands, thinks of her bitten nails digging into the cold condensation. His own throat is cardboard dry. He tries to swallow but can't. Droplets of sweat trickle down from under his armpits, along the ridges of his spine, collect in the bends of his knees. His cheeks burn and his eyes itch. Then she is beside him.

'Why so serious?' she asks with a giggle.

144

His shoulders cave in. 'It's the heat,' he pants. Her amazing eyes crinkle at the corners. He can see the swell of her breasts above the white vest top as she breathes in, breathes out. She sets the cups down on the mirrored counter, then ruffles his hair. The gesture has the element of surprise about it, of intimacy. Her fingers, still cool from their contact with the cups, feel like sprinkles of cologne on his scalp, the sensation making the roots of his hair tingle. Now she takes the lid off his tea and picks out an ice cube. Pinching it between thumb and forefinger, she circles his face, draws it down his brow, along the bridge of his nose, over the tip, brings it to rest on his slightly parted lips. He can feel the scald of the ice trail. The cube is melting. He sucks in the cold moisture, feels a gelid slick soaking into his cardboard throat so that it spasms in thirsty anticipation. In a blink he summons the vast basin of Lake Vagli, with moonlit serpents flickering over its shivering surface. His hands are faintly trembling. He cannot hear the Abba lyrics, only the eerily bewitching song of Teodora, luring him into the chill marbled waters. Her eyes lock on his.

'Better?' she says.

He nods. And she pops the melting cube into her mouth and crunches it up.

8

The crying baby is keeping Naomi awake, that and the heat, the interminable heat. The thin reedy wail bores like a screwdriver into her head. Why doesn't

145

Sean do something? It's his baby, isn't it? Bria? Only, this isn't Bria. This is the baby growing inside *her*, the ball of cells dividing and sub-dividing, getting bigger every day. And already, nestled in the red blanket of her womb, as hot and sleepless as she is, it has begun its endless mewling. She turns to Sean, but Sean is drunk. Sean is wallowing in oblivion. His breaths are so shallow he might as well be dead. She must take care of it herself, be Mother to it, rock it to sleep. Because that's what mothers do, they comfort their crying babies, when they are sad they make them happy again.

Her own mother died, and that was very careless of her because it meant that when she was sad there was no one to make her happy again. And when she cried, there was no one to comfort her. Soon she would be a mother herself. She wondered if she would know what to do, how to dry up the tears. This baby is hers, hers and Sean's. Or is it hers and Enrico's? Enrico's baby? She doesn't know, doesn't care. She only wants it to be quiet. She will do anything for silence, anything at all. She squeezes her eyes shut, wishing herself away, somewhere quiet, somewhere she can be solitary. But when she reopens them time has played its customary trick on her. It has drawn her back through the veil of years, unmade the woman until she is a girl again, an unwanted child, one among many, inconvenient, abandoned, orphaned, wakeful in the unending night. On and on and on it goes, the crying baby in the cot by her bed. It no longer knows for what it cries, just that it has needs, needs that no one will fulfil. Why doesn't the house mother come and shut it up? Why doesn't she make it stop? It will not let her rest, the screaming baby.

146

She kicks back the sheet and still she is too hot, sliding about in her own sweat. So she tears off her sleeping shift and stands in the thin grey moonlight, reviving her body with her fluttering hands. If *The Blind Ones* hear Baby howling, if they peek through the narrowed slits of their eyelids and see her out of bed, they also choose to be deaf and dumb. Both sash windows are stuck fast. Using all her might, she manages to lift one an inch, lowers her face to the warm draught, gulps in air. But the other will not budge at all. She reported it to Miss Elstob, told her they were stuck, that she needed to get Mr Plinge to come and mend them. But nothing was done. Nothing is ever fixed here. And still the baby cries, wailing and wailing into the suffocating gloom. She treads softly, reaches the cot, sees Baby, the sickly scrap, rigid and purple, eyes bulging, face wet with tears and snot, night shift sodden and stinking. She can smell piss, piss and puke. She reaches down and feels the forehead. It has a fever. Miss Elstob should give it a bath, a cool bath to bring the temperature down.

Someone should put the poor hot baby in a tub of cold water and wash all the hotness away. Now she grabs one of the waving arms, grips the tiny forearm so tightly that the infant gives a piercing yell, making her eardrums itch. The door immediately flies open, as if the house mother has been waiting behind it, and the light blinks on. And there she is, Miss Elstob, in a stained dressing gown, her wide-set mud-coloured eyes screwed up, her broom-brush hair awry, the large black mole on her knobbly nose quivering with each indignant inhalation.

'Mara! What are you doing? Why are you naked?

Have you no shame, girl? You're a whore, like your dead mother was. All filth, that's what you are. I told you not to touch the baby, never to touch the baby again. Your job is to clean the shoes and make the beds.' She speaks in a voice that is dreadfully kind and mushy. 'Do you remember what I said? If I saw you near the baby again I'd have to punish you.' And *The Blind Ones* hunch their necks into their tortoiseshell shoulders, and fist their sheets more tightly. They push their sightless faces into their mattresses. 'You need to be taught not to behave like a savage.'

She begins to advance. But Mara stands her ground. She pulls herself up so that although she is small, she feels as if she is growing tall as a giant. And Miss Elstob must also see the giant for a second, because she pauses, her eyes running all over her nakedness. 'The baby . . . the baby won't stop crying.' Between the wooden slats of its cot, Naomi sees bubbling spit frothing at the baby's open mouth. It fights for breath, making ghastly grinding choking noises. 'I took my shift off because I am hot, too hot. The windows won't open. I told you they wouldn't. And I am hot, hot as fire.' The baby takes a sudden gasp, then a beat, followed by a howl that makes Mara's blood curdle.

In one stride Miss Elstob is at her, slapping her face, her chest, punching her in the belly, kicking her legs out from under her. She has a hold of Mara's wrist, and each time she strikes her and the child flies backwards, she tugs her in again. Then she drags her kicking and screaming downstairs, in passing seizing up her cane, where it lies propped in a corner. They are in the kitchen, the homely room with the big table that all the children sit round to take their meals. She grabs a fistful of Mara's long black hair as she wields the cane. She can hear it whistling through the air, feel it biting rabidly into her buttocks. But she will not cry out, she will never cry out. Her hair is being torn from the roots, her beautiful black hair, but still she makes no sound.

Now her nails are driving into her shoulders, pinching so tightly that it feels as if they are being hammered through her bones. And she is being pulled across the room, through the doorway and down the corridor. She smells Miss Elstob's bad breath, foul as a sewer drain, and with it she sniffs the acrid buried scent of coal. Then she is being thrown into the coal cupboard with such force that her head strikes the wall with a crack, so that she thinks her skull may have broken open like an egg. The door slams shut and the key turns in the lock. 'Don't,' she whimpers quietly. 'Don't . . . Miss Elstob.' But the next second the line of light, the line of hope, under it is gone, and she is plunged into absolute darkness.

She is sprawled on a heap of coal. She can feel ragged lumps and points of it digging into her battered body. And there is the taste of salt metal on her lips. She licks it and savours her own blood. The heat in the coffin-like space is so intense that it is as though she is being cooked alive. But she does not cry out. And this, not because she is brave, not now. Now she would holler all night, and beat upon the door until her fists are worn to tattered stumps of bleeding flesh. She does not cry now because, just as the baby will soon discover, it is senseless. No one will come to rescue her.

She is breathing in the soot. It is choking her lungs, clogging her pores. With each painful move

149

the coal possesses more of her, blacks up her white skin, fills her nostrils and her mouth with peppery dust. By daybreak she will be a chimney sweep, the soot so ingrained in her that she will not be able to wash it off. She will be branded with its sooty mark. And the crust of fear in her stomach is a living thing, a black spider with a hundred tangled legs spinning fur balls inside her. Her bladder is full and suddenly she feels the stinging warmth of her own urine as it empties. If she dies this second it will be okay. She rests her head against the bricks, lets them bruise her cheeks with their rough touch.

The black is only a seed behind her eyes when it is born—a dot, a speck, no more. But it propagates. A bright jet bead that sends out a million inky shoots to dye every cell in her body. And with this black dawn comes rage, a murderous, unwieldy, uncompromising tidal wave sweeping through her. She scrambles to her knees and the sharp spears of coal stab agonizingly at her kneecaps. She grits her teeth and feels for the door. She knows it is painted in sky-blue enamel gloss. With the black wind at her back she carves her name. She uses all her fingers, all her nails, chipping at the paintwork, digging them deep into the wood. In the stillness the scratching seems loud, deafening. A splinter jabs under one nail, two, then three. She pauses, listens to the 'huff, huff' of her rapid breathing, feels in the dark for the needles of wood, and carefully picks them out. When next she carves her fingertips are bloody. She cannot see it, will not see it till morning, but her blood has stained the pale wood, coloured the engraving. 'Mara' is inscribed in red. She speaks with the little breath she has left. 'I am Mara,' she hisses. 'I am Mara.' Then she sinks back on her bed of coal. In her overheated dreams she becomes a mermaid. As she darts through the healing coolness of water, the blackness dissolves to reveal the spangle of her platinum scales.

*   *   *

Owen's second night in the flat. They share a salad. It is too hot to eat. And they drink chilled white wine. Naomi plays records, Bob Dylan, The Eagles, then later, when they are all mellow, Johnny Cash. She knows her music and Owen wonders about that. If they ate little, Sean ate nothing. But he drinks as if he has an unquenchable thirst. Owen, tracing the falling level in the brandy bottle, marvels at his appearance of sobriety, at his steady hand and clear speech. He goes to bed before them, wary that he may be intruding, pleading exhaustion. He lies back on the divan, among the towers of cardboard boxes full of stock for the stall. For once there are no visitations from the Merfolk, or from Sarah either. He takes this as a good sign. He dozes for a time and wakes to the sounds of Sean and Naomi making love. In spite of feeling like a guilty voyeur, he listens intently, hardly daring to breathe. With only a stud wall between them, their mounting tension is his, the rock and roll of their tussle, the ascending scale of their groans and gasps, the shudder of Sean's pleasure, the shriek of Naomi's orgasm. Afterwards he becomes aware of the leaking bath taps hissing. Sean keeps promising to replace the washers, but for now it is an unending chorus of laryngitic croaks. It is as though they are having a conversation, as though there are spirits locked in the pipes.

151

'Haaa . . .'

'Ahhh . . .'

Sometimes they stutter or give a wheezy cough. He nods off again listening to their ghoulish dialogue. When his eyes open next, apart from the taps all appears peaceful, so that he ponders what must have disturbed him. Then a scraping noise, or is it scratching? He sits up and pays heed. Is there someone moving outside his room? The scratching noise resumes. He turns on the light, rises, creeps to the door and opens it a few inches. The rest of the flat is in darkness. He passes a hand across his brow and wipes off sweat. He sleeps in boxer shorts and has no dressing gown. He contemplates pulling on his jeans, and then decides he is being foolish. In all likelihood it is nothing, night nonsense, the creaks and whines of old buildings expanding in the heat. And even if it is Sean or Naomi, he is decent.

He does not switch on the corridor light. He has no desire to attract attention to himself. They may feel it is peculiar, their new lodger prowling about in the middle of the night, on the pretext that he was disturbed by scuffling sounds. He steals past the bathroom where the taps whine like the wind, then moves stealthily through the bead curtain and into the lounge. The sash windows are still open, and a warm breeze, tainted with the residue of exhaust fumes, reaches his nostrils. A mix of moonlight and lamplight filters through them. Far off a door slams. He picks out the bulky shapes of furniture, not yet familiar to him. He glances to his right at the galley kitchen. All clear. He is about to go, to return to bed, when he hears the noise again, much louder now, very close, here in the room with him. His heartbeat is instantly racing. Perhaps they have

152

mice, says the voice of reason. He stands very still, his eyes raking the semi-darkness.

He spots her knees then, her knees capped in moonlight. In a few steps he rounds the end of the settee and sees her, quite naked, curled up in the space between the settee end and the corner of the room. Her head is resting against the wall, and her fingers are scrabbling over it. Her silvered body takes him unawares so that he staggers back a pace. Her nipples appear black, and to his surprise so do the curls that cover her sex.

'Naomi?' He keeps his volume low, his tone reassuring and steady, though all this while his heart bangs in his ear. 'Naomi? Are you all right?' She makes no response—none at all. Her eyes are glazed over, unseeing. The blue is luminous, picked out in the nocturnal rays. The brown is one huge black pupil. He thinks that she may be sleepwalking, knows that it is dangerous to rouse someone too quickly from this hypnotic state. Snatching up a throw from the settee and crouching down, he cloaks her nudity with it. Her lips are moving but he cannot decipher any words. 'It's Owen, Naomi. Did you have a bad dream? Shall I take you back to bed?'

'The baby won't stop crying,' she whimpers. 'Someone make it stop.' She must still be dreaming, Owen concludes. 'It's sick. Has a temperature. Needs a cool bath. I need a cool bath.'

'Shall I take you to the bathroom? I can wet a flannel to cool you down.'

She seems not to hear him. 'Look at me. Look at me.' Her hands fall, palms outwards, inviting inspection. She might be reciting a nursery rhyme. Her tone is sing-song, a childish chant. It unnerves

153

Owen because there are traces of Sarah in it. It has the cadence of need. 'I'm all black, all filthy, just like she said. And I want to wash it away but I can't.' It is definitely a nightmare. He will have to be very careful not to startle her awake. There is no knowing what she might do as a result of such trauma. He considers fetching Sean, and then thinks about how much brandy he has consumed and decides not to. He attempts to lift her to her feet, but she resists.

'No, no, I won't go with you. I want to stay in my bunk. I want to stay with *The Blind Ones*.' Now she is humming, a nasal hum interspersed with a few lyrics. He recognizes the song. Leonard Cohen's 'Suzanne'. The record she put on the night he came for dinner, the night she danced with Enrico, the night the Italian described the drowned village that lay at the bottom of Lake Vagli. He has begun to feel the pull of it, of the ghost village where once the stone buildings breathed the mountain air. Today no sky opens up above the hamlet. It is buried in water, icy dark water. 'Walt? Walt? Is it you?'

'It's Owen, Naomi. Come on. It's Owen. You're safe with me. Let me take you back to bed.'

'Walt, you shouldn't have left me and gone with Judy. You shouldn't have made me angry.'

This time when he gently pulls her up she is compliant, allowing herself to be meekly led. He hesitates before hers and Sean's door, cautious of waking him. But he need not be. Sean is in his own drink-induced stupor, and does not stir. Owen helps her into the free side of the double bed, and tucks her in as if she is a child. Before he leaves he hears her mutter something. Back in his room he runs the sentence over again.

'Walt, you shouldn't have left me and gone with her. You shouldn't have made me angry.' A past boyfriend who had been unfaithful? Possibly even a husband? He mulls it over for several minutes. If he is correct, it is ironic. After all, isn't Naomi stealing Catherine's husband now? He thinks of his own mother, of Ken Bascombe, of America. She stayed, but she might as well have gone for all the difference it made. He wonders idly where Walt is this very second, and if he ever thinks of Naomi, of his one-time love with the spell-binding eyes.

9

Sean stares at a plug of chewing gum on the floor of the carriage as the train shuttles him back to Hounslow, reliving his exchange of barely an hour ago with Naomi.

'I don't want it.' He did not have to think about it. His reaction was instant. She continued speaking as if she had not heard him, prattling on so that he wanted to hit her, to stop up her mouth.

'It wasn't planned. I know. But we can make it work. I'm sure we can. I'm not saying that it's going to be easy. But it will be worth it. You know, Sean, I can't quite believe it. I am going to be a mother. A mother! For you it's different. You don't have to tell me. I understand. You're already a father. You know what to expect.' She was moving restlessly about the bedroom, as if, he mused, she was in a cage, as if they both were. He was lying on the bed, elbows bent, clasped hands cushioning his head. The

155

sash window was pushed up as far as it would go. They had a view onto a brick wall. The bleat of traffic, ever audible in London, filled the pauses. And there had been many so far. The hot weather was doing his rash no favours. It itched like crazy now, so that it took every ounce of his willpower to resist the urge to scratch it.

'I don't show at all, do I?' she asked, halting to display her concave belly to him. 'It's incredible to think that there is a baby growing in there. I've been choosing names. Is that foolish?' He did not answer. She studied his face, searching for an indication of how he was receiving this news. But his eyes were poker straight, his gaze on her steady. 'For a boy, Ashley? Too effeminate?' She wrinkled her nose, gave her slow, hesitant blink. 'You're right. We don't want him to be teased at school.'

On the move again, she crossed to the window. She sat on the sill and rested her head on the glass. 'When will the rain come?' she sighed. 'God, I hope it's soon.' In a glance he saw that her hair was matted to her forehead. The black roots were plainly visible. She needed to dye it again. She was dressed in a cream blouse, muslin cotton, tied under her breasts. A single crystal gem of sweat wavered on her collar bone, broke free and trickled into her cleavage. She was not wearing a bra. She seldom did. He could see her nipples outlined clearly under the paper-thin cotton. Her pale-blue denim shorts, sitting low on her hips, were frayed about her thighs. She was barefoot. Her heavy make-up gave her features the immobile look of a ventriloquist's dummy. She leant across the bedside table, took a cigarette from his packet of Camels, scooped up his lighter and shook it. It was almost empty, so it took her several goes to light up. She inhaled deeply then held the cigarette away from her, examining it carefully. Absently she picked a speck of tobacco from her tongue.

'I suppose now I'm expecting, I should really give these up.' He made no comment. He did not care what she did. He fucked her, enjoyed ownership of her, but that was the full extent of his investment. His shirt sleeves were rolled up. His trousers were polyester and it felt as though his legs were sheathed in plastic. But he refused to give in to the heat, though. In the market more and more flesh was on show, sometimes white, flaccid and not very appealing. Sean maintained that the impression you created was very important. If you let standards slip, before long you looked like a bum. And then it was only a matter of time before you began behaving like one. If you wanted respect, you had to earn it. But in these temperatures he gladly admitted it was proving a struggle. The Shannon called to him then, tempted him with the memory of the crisp green cling of her against his naked body.

'What about Daisy for a girl?' Naomi pushed her luck. She took another slow drag on her cigarette, then gnawed at a nail, chewing it to the quick. Her fingers were trembling. Some part of his brain registered television noise, music, *Top of the Pops*, he guessed. His hip flask was in his trouser pocket. He slid it out, sat on the side of the bed, unscrewed the top, took a mouthful, then another and swilled this second like mouthwash before swallowing. He hauled himself to his feet, flask still in hand. He had slipped off his shoes, was still wearing his socks, and now he pushed his feet back into them.

'Where are you going?' Her voice was shrill. He

157

grabbed the packet of Camels, the lighter, but did not look at her.

'Home,' he said.

And now he is being thrown about on the Piccadilly Line, feeling like he is sitting in a dustbin. It is so bloody hot that he thinks he might really kill for an ice-cold lager. The other passengers in the carriage look as dejected as he feels. He broods on the conspiracy there is against him, the snare that has been set for him. He is fed up of fighting. Like the salmon swimming up the Shannon to spawn, it seems that everything, everyone, is contriving to thwart him. Nothing in his life will stay where he has put it. It is all spinning out of control.

He married Catherine because she was a nice girl, from a well-to-do family, a family who didn't scrape a living on a wind-blown farm in Ireland. He'd hoped that some of their wealth would rub off on him, still does. He wanted to make his Mam proud, his brother Emmet jealous, to demonstrate to his Da, where he lay in his early grave, how smart men attained success. You did not have to get up at 4 a.m. and break ice on a tub of water to splash your tired face. You did not have to go to bed by candlelight, with calloused hands and a crippled back. You did not have to quake with superstitious fear each time the wind changed direction, or the priest frowned at you. But his Mam was tight-lipped after meeting Catherine. As always, she couldn't see the bigger picture, how advantageous the marriage could be. 'She isn't of the faith. She isn't Roman Catholic, Sean,' she finally told him, her expression horrified. She said it the way you might say someone wasn't human, that they were an abomination in the sight of God. 'And she's

158

English,' she continued in the same vein. 'Whatever are you thinking of, bringing a lass like her into the family? It will only lead to trouble.' It hurt, but her criticism just made him more determined to have her. He would show them all, he had simmered, small-minded bigots every one of them. His father had whipped him when he swam in the Shannon. But he had not broken his spirit or dashed his dreams.

Some days, though, he wonders if she might have been correct, if he has reached too high, been too ambitious. Still, he has not abandoned his plans altogether. One day he will start up his own business. He's had a few setbacks, but what successful man hasn't? The market stall that seemed such a profit-making concern, through an alcoholic blur minutes before the closing bell was sounded in a pub, is hardly breaking even. True, at the height of the tourist season there's a profit to be made, but how long will it last? And Catherine, too, has done her best to jeopardize his future. She went and got herself pregnant, on their wedding night, most like. Oh, he knows it wasn't her fault, the condom splitting and so on. But did she have to conceive? A virgin. Her first time. What were the chances of that?

He loves Bria, but now is not the season for her to be born. This should happen later, when they are settled, and he's bought a house and got a bit of capital behind him. Catherine's parents think as much. They look down their snooty noses at him, at the mess he is making of things. They deplore their daughter's judgement. They earnestly wish she had not interrupted her typing course for a good-for-nothing Irish farm lad. But if they are disappointed, well, so is he. Catherine has changed, or maybe it is just that at last he is seeing an honest image of her, not as he wants her to be, but as she really is. They have nothing in common. Why he hadn't spotted it from the outset he cannot figure. Perhaps they were both projecting qualities onto each other that simply weren't there. In any case, it isn't working out. Bed is a disaster. His wife is frigid. He made an effort not to put pressure on her in the early months, understanding she was innocent, inexperienced. He needn't have bothered. Once the pregnancy was confirmed she claimed she'd had a threatened miscarriage, and they'd given up the whole wretched business altogether. But he is a man with a man's needs, and that was where Naomi entered his life.

She was a whore he'd met trawling King's Cross late one night. The sex had been great, every time, and he liked her too. When he was with her he felt good, powerful—up until recently, that is. He should have kept to their original arrangement—two, three times a week, no obligations, no expectations. But the thought of her going with other men bothered him. He wanted her all for himself. So he set her up in the flat and got her running the stall. And it had all seemed perfect, for a while. He hadn't minded about his marriage, hadn't worried so much about the baby coming early, or the business being put on hold. His life had equilibrium. Then, before he knew it, the scales had tipped up. Enrico had muscled in, rolling up to the flat whenever he felt like it, drinking his booze, and fucking his woman when he wasn't there, he had no doubt. Taking Owen in as a lodger had been a masterstroke, his very own watchdog. He thought the game was won, but it was only that hand. Naomi's next cards have brought it all tumbling down. So she is pregnant, talking as if she is going to have the kid, as if they are going to play at happy families. Well, he already has a family. It may not be very happy, but he sure as hell doesn't need another one. The kid probably isn't even his.

'I've told you, I'm not hungry,' he flares up, confronted by that other baby, his legitimate daughter.

'All right. You don't have to bite my head off.'

Catherine has offered to make him something to eat twice now, when he has made it clear that he has no appetite. He glowers at her. She looks dreadful, wandering about in a shapeless towelling robe stained in baby vomit. Her hair, that glorious red hair that had attracted him like a copper crown, looks unwashed and limp. She is red-eyed, a sign that she has been crying, a common occurrence these days. This is not how it is meant to be. He wants her to look pretty, to wear expensive clothes, to be tastefully made up, hair clean and brushed, exuding the fragrance of costly French perfume when he comes home. They are in the lounge of the scruffy rented terrace, her pacing, a distressed Bria wriggling at her shoulder, him in the armchair with the sagging bottom, the one he had thought such a bargain from a second-hand furniture shop in town. He knows she hates this place, but it's all he can stretch to at present. No posh Kingston houses for them, not yet anyhow.

'Sean . . .' She hesitates, then fishes in the pocket of her robe, produces a slip of paper and puts it on the table next to his drink. He glances down and

161

recognizes what it is. A gambling chit. 'You told me you'd stopped,' she says, her tone flat. Music thumps through the wall from next door. Wherever he is, that bloody music seems to find him. The market, the flat, and now here.

'Are you going through my pockets now, Catherine? Is that what you're after doing?' His tone is low, baleful. He does not look at her but at the note, fuming that she has resorted to frisking his clothes.

'We can't afford it,' she says, her stance defiant.

'Why don't you let me be the judge of that?' he counters swiftly, his suppressed rage loosed suddenly, so that she flinches back. He is fast becoming the bully his father was, he thinks miserably.

'I'm worried, Sean.' She has begun jigging as she speaks, rubbing Bria on her back. Far from calmed, this gesture seems to add to their daughter's discomfort and she gives several piercing cries of protest.

He takes a gulp of his drink, neat brandy purchased from the off-licence on his way home. 'Don't be. It's all in hand,' he tells her shortly. His eyes slide up to meet with hers. After a moment she breaks the gaze.

'I don't know what the matter is with Bria. She's like this almost every night,' she frets.

'All babies cry, Catherine. It's only natural.'

'Not like this. If you were here more often you'd understand,' she accuses, her green eyes hostile.

'Catherine, I'm sorry. But you know how it is,' he says wearily. 'Some nights I have to stay in London. I've told you, I've got a couple of things on the go that I need to see to.'

She shoots him a resentful look that says she knows there is another woman, that he is keeping another woman. He elects to ignore this, tops up his drink instead, and brazens it out. Bria is grizzling now, a persistent breathy whining that, like a swinging pendulum, seems to have its own indefatigable momentum. 'Is she after being fed?' he inquires.

'No, of course she isn't,' Catherine snaps. 'She's not wet either, or dirty. And for your information I've taken her to the doctor but he says there's nothing wrong.' She gives a despairing sigh.

'So, there you are then. Why don't you just put her down for a sleep? She's probably tired.'

'I don't know if she's tired, but I am. I don't remember when I last slept. Most days I feel like a zombie. Do you realize, Sean, that most days I feel like the living dead?' She closes on a rising inflexion that makes him grimace and startles the baby.

'Motherhood is hard, love,' he pacifies. 'I know. But it'll get easier, as she grows. I promise.'

'I need a break. If I don't get some sleep soon, I don't know what I'll do.' She is shouting now. Her hysteria is transmitted instantly to Bria, who whoops in a breath and, face empurpled, yells angrily.

'What about your own mother? Couldn't she give you a hand?'

Catherine flashes him a withering look. 'You know what she's like. She'll only make things worse.'

On the farm, babies were the preserve of women. Men did not get involved. But Catherine has a kernel of the new woman in her, the one that is coming, the woman who wants more, the woman who dares to consider the impossible—equality. Sean senses this 'coming woman' emerging from

163

the worn-out tatters of his wife, and he feels the floor of his world tip a little more. With a snort he ponders how long it will be before he concedes defeat and slides off. He drains his glass. 'Give her to me. Go to bed. I'll look after her, so.'

She hands her to him, gratefully, and hurries upstairs. He cradles the child in his arms, strokes her head. Her wisps of damp fair hair are tinted with a hint of red in the evening sunshine. She smells of baby talc and milk. He observes a pulsing fontanel, a soft spot on Bria's skull where the cranial bones have not yet fused. The crying abruptly ceases. The aftermath of her storm, hiccups, sends powerful shudders through the small body that seem to surprise her. They have the same eyes, Sean observes suddenly. Identical. Bluish green, greenish blue, a hard one to call. Tonight they are decidedly blue. She is cocooned in a yellow wool blanket and looks red-faced and boiling.

'You're hot, aren't you, my darlin'?' says Sean, unwrapping the bundle. Under it she wears a light-green baby-grow. He undoes three of the top poppers, and opens the neck up, exposing the miniature chest. 'Is that more like it? There you are. What say we take a walk round the estate and a peek at the stars?' Bria blinks, and with a jerk of her head sucks in air. 'Is that a yes?' She yawns pinkly at him. He stares down at this wonder, this perturbing wonder, his daughter. He climbs to his feet and makes his way to the kitchen and out of the back door. The garden is a patch of lawn bordered by a leaning fence. But this is level with Sean's head, so that however small, there is a sense of privacy in this outdoor space. 'No stars yet for you, my darlin'.' It is a suburban sunset. The sky is streaked with pink and orange. A baseline of lavender blue is creeping very gradually upwards. Rotating, he sees a panorama of rooftops, chimneys, aerials. The main road thunders round them. He remembers the wide spaces of Ireland, the lush greens that quenched your sight. He listens for the silences, for the calm inner strength of the Shannon. Bria is peaceful, her eyes very wide and alert now.

There is a concrete patio, with a couple of steps down to the grass. He sits at the top of these, his daughter propped on his knees, her back to his chest. 'It's not much, is it? But it's only temporary, you know. Till your father gets on his feet.' He is riding the brandy now, a distance still from the stampede that will trample his brain into blackout. 'Don't be after telling your mother, but I've got a few deals going down that will make all the difference. I've made a connection with a man who has influence, a man who can alter the course of our lives—yours, mine, your mother's. He's loaned me a bit of money and in return I'm running a few errands for him. Couldn't be simpler. I can turn this all round, you wait and see. One day your daddy's going to be rich. What would you like, my darlin'? Take your pick from the sweetie shop of life. Anything you want an' it's yours. No idea? I was like that once myself. Not sure what I wanted, only, that whatever it was, I needed money to get it. I tell you what, I'll decide for you. A great big house, with a garden you can run round in, and a pretty dress for every day of the year. How's that? And what about a swimming pool? I'll teach you to swim, Bria. I'll take you to the Shannon, and together we'll dive off the rocks. And no one will stop us, no one will tell us that the river is evil. I know her

165

secrets and now I'll tell you. Because you're a water baby, my darlin'. My very own water baby.'

10

Owen is increasingly reluctant to contact his parents. When he does, he works hard to describe a reflection quite unlike the one that stares back at him from the bathroom mirror. His father listens avidly to this Nicholas Nickleby son, to his daring exploits, to tales of his dashing days spent in the company of other actors. They do not discuss the infant phenomenon. The subject is taboo. Instead, they resort to that great British tradition and debate the weather, the oppressive heat, water rationing, plants suffering, reservoirs drying up, the desperate need for rain. That done, Owen improvises. He has told them that he has a job now in the box office of the Palace Theatre, where the extravaganza *Jesus Christ Superstar* is showing. He has offered to get complimentary tickets for them. He has even jauntily hummed a few tunes. His father has said that it's a date.

What Owen does not tell them is that all attempts at securing an agent have failed, and the few open auditions he stumbled on in the magazine *The Stage* wanted trained dancers and singers. But Owen isn't the least anxious that his charade will soon be discovered. He knows that his parents will never visit him. So he carries on describing the glamorous West End, the crowd of artistic, flamboyant friends he has made, how he is out every night hobnobbing with directors and producers. They receive the news

166

that he has relocated to the heart of London with a mixture of awe and detachment. His father is awed. His mother is detached.

Owen only rings on the rare occasions when he is alone in the flat. They have a 'phone set on a small occasional table, just inside the lounge door. Sean actively encourages him to use it.

'Family's important, Owen. Your roots, so. Where you came from.' Owen thinks of the beach in Devon, of the sand and the sky, of the cold indifferent sea, of his mother eating the sand, and of Sarah's scrap of comfort blanket in the box on her bedside table. He breathes essence of Sarah, a bittersweet fragrance if ever there was one. That's where he came from. He would give his soul to sever his roots, to cut the kite strings attaching him to his past and fly free. 'You need to keep in touch. Your Mam might worry otherwise.' The irony of Sean's directive, as he lounges in a flat with his mistress, his own wife and baby home alone, seems to elude him.

Increasingly Owen's calls are triumphs of invention. He always manages to impart some fresh titbit that signposts his path to fame. And, as if by tacit consent, his parents keep up their part in this apple-pie conspiracy. Neither of them refer to the night before he left home, to the stark red blood spattered on the lino floor. Entering the kitchen after supper, he saw his mother standing with her back to him, in front of the sink. Above her head on a wooden drying rack was a thick, white, china plate. The clusters of soapsuds were still sliding off it, drifting like light snow flurries into the sink. Behind his mother, to one side, hovered his father. He was whistling 'My Bonnie Lies Over the Ocean',

167

stooping and fumbling with a red-and-white checked tea towel. The glint of metal in its folds caught Owen's eye. Brows deeply scored, he was bringing all his concentration to bear on the task of drying cutlery, as methodical with this as he was in cleaning Sarah's shoes.

Suddenly his mother stretched her dripping wet hands upwards, in a gesture uncannily redolent of an act of worship. She plucked the pale china moon from its rack in the sky, wheeled round, and brought it crashing down on her husband's bent head. A thud and a crack melded together. His shiny pate, criss-crossed with a few judiciously arranged grey hairs, juddered forwards, then dropped a foot or so. The segments of gleaming moon, rimmed in bright blood, clattered down, then rocked and seesawed on the tiled floor. The tea towel fluttered after them, cutlery spilling out of it. His father staggered back. He raised a shaky hand to his head in stupefaction, and stroked it over the dome of his skull. When he lowered it he saw, as did Owen, that there was blood on it, a shockingly vivid scarlet slash of it standing out bathed in bald white light. For a second they all froze, as if none of them really believed what had just happened. Then his mother fell to her knees and began gathering up slices of the moon, trying to piece the night back together. Owen took control. He helped his father into a chair, gave him a clean tea towel and told him to hold it against his head. Next he joined his mother on the floor.

'Leave that, Mother,' he told her, prising a wedge of china from her hands. 'You might cut yourself. The edges are sharp.' He spoke in the sort of tone you would use to address a timid child. He managed to raise her to her feet, and assisted her into the chair next to his father's. And there the two of them sat staring straight ahead, like one of those famous medieval paintings of married couples. A worm of blood, only small, but a heart-stopping shade of pillar box red, made its way out from under the tea towel and slithered down his father's forehead. It paused briefly on the shelf of his brow, gathering in the grey tangle of his father's right eyebrow, before curling under it to skulk in the cave of his eye socket. He took his father to the hospital, clutching the now sodden tea towel to his gory head. It wasn't fractured. They sewed up the gash with luminous purple stitches.

His last sighting of his father was on the railway platform at Didcot Station, next day, looking like a bewildered Frankenstein. His mother waved him off from their front door. Just before he climbed into the car he turned back, the sudden desire to run to her, to hug her, overwhelming him. But she had gone inside, and closed the door on him already. The Doctor prescribed his mother Valium for her nerves, and suggested she take a sabbatical from her work as a dinner lady in the local comprehensive. Probably just as well, considering how many plates she handled in her job, Owen ruminated.

Now he learns that his mother is well, extremely well actually, planning to return to work any day. She has gained so much weight that some of her skirts no longer fit. And not to be outdone, his father has been awarded a grant to buy gardening equipment, and is helping to plan the gardens for the new hotel they are building outside Wantage. In short, they are the iconic British family, as perfect as the Janet and John model who taught Owen to read in school—only, with a few significant differences.

See Father, see. See Mother, see. See John playing. John is playing ball. See the red and white ball. See it bounce high. See Janet splash, splash in the sea. Look, Mother, look. See Janet drowning. Look Father, look. See John playing. See John playing while Janet is drowning. See Mother running. See John running. See Father running. See him fishing Janet from the sea. See Janet on the sand, see Janet dying. Look John, look. Janet is dead. Janet has drowned.

Owen omits as much from their shared past, as he does from his present, in these telephone conversations. He does not tell his parents about his middle-of-night encounters with Naomi, or that when he scrutinized the patch of wallpaper she has been scratching at, he was certain he could faintly decipher a name. Mara. Nor does he report that one night, *en route* to the kitchen to fetch a glass of water, he found Sean sitting at the dining-room table drinking alone, gabbling away to himself.

'What's up, Sean?' No response. 'Can't you sleep? Sean, are you okay?' Still no response. He sat down opposite him at the table. The windows were open, a slight breeze periodically making the half-lowered rattan blinds rattle. Sean swallowed and breathed fire, then looked straight through him.

'Labasheeda,' he mumbled. 'Labasheeda.' The lava lamp on the telephone table was the only light turned on, the orange globules bouncing up and down in slow motion like excited egg yolks. The room was untidy, streaked with light and shadow. 'My mistress, my green mistress.' The words hardly

170

stirred his lips, and they were muddied so Owen had to strain them from the slurry. 'Gap-toothed Finn saw her, saw little Iona O'Neil's ghost jigging away on the water, tossing her long black hair. A chit of a girl swallowed by the hungry green lady, sucked down, they said.' Owen felt his hair stand up on the back of his neck. 'She fell from the boat, see. Taking the livestock over. The lass couldn't swim. Mind, none of us could. Because, you see, the water's bad, a jinx, a curse. They said there were devils lurking there. But that's not what I found when I dived into her.'

'Sean, do you want me to get Naomi?'

He gave an open-mouthed, mournful sigh. His breath smelt fetid and sour, and Owen fought the impulse to recoil. He was still dressed, crumpled shirt, creased trousers, the sharp odour of sweat. 'Fuckin' Brandon Connolly. He diddled my Da every week at the creamery, but the bloody fool didn't see it. He didn't have a head for numbers, my Da, not like me. He wasn't clever. There was evil in the outhouse. It waited for me there, you know, lurking in the dark and the cold, so. They said that it came from the river, but they lied. It was in their own fields, in their milking sheds and barns, in their sick heads.' Another pull on his drink, the glass hovering halfway to the table, returning to his lips. He drained it through a mouth burnt with booze. 'He made me strip, stand naked and shivering before him. Emmet watched through a peephole in the wood. I stared at the ball of his eye framed in a knot of wood, stared and stared at it as the belt bit into my back, my buttocks, my thighs. I didn't cry out. I was a rock for her. And all the while the thick blood from the pig carcass dripped into the tin pail,

171

the sickly sweet smell of it filling my nostrils, and the leather whistled, and the brass studs crucified me. But not one tear did I shed for their delight. I was her brave warrior, brave as the warriors who marched through my dreams.' Eventually Sean dragged himself to his feet and lurched off to bed, leaving Owen with little Iona O'Neil's ghost tap dancing on the water.

Nor did he confide to his parents that on the nights when Sean returned to his wife and baby, bizarre sounds in the flat made him start awake. Oh, not the whistling taps, they were a constant, a crackling radio that never tuned in. He was fast becoming immune to them. No, what made him wake with a start were the creeping footsteps outside his bedroom door. Indistinct conversations reaching him through the wall separating his and Naomi's room. He did not say, Mother, I am frightened by what I have witnessed and heard. The time when nightmares could be scotched in a moment in her arms was long dead.

'Owen, Owen, what's the matter? It was a bad dream, that's all. I'm here now. Mummy's here. Nothing can hurt you now.' He remembered how she would climb into his bed, and coat his shaking body with the heat of her own. Her kettle-drum heartbeat was strong enough for the two of them. The smooth flow of her breaths made him tranquil. But now all he sees in her brown eyes is the loathsome image of himself.

Meanwhile, the underground kingdom is steadily becoming more intoxicating to him. He is discovering that the incessant beat of those endless disco numbers stirs the blood as effectively as tribal drums are purported to. In this mole's tunnel there is a razzle-dazzle, an alchemy, which makes the over-ground world seem dull by comparison. Goods, that Owen suspects will look cheap and tasteless dragged up into the glare of the sun, are transformed down here into something rich and glorious. Colours are subtly altered as well, as if enhanced by the pink glow of a theatrical lighting gel.

In fact his new environment is not unlike a buried theatre, subtly lit to obscure defects and exaggerate good features. It entertains and diverts with the entrance and exits of lively street cameos; illegal immigrants escaping the steaming kitchens; working girls more comfortable browsing in the half-light; hapless tourists drawn like moths to the motley bazaar; teenagers smelling of sex and exuding restless energy as they scuttle about. Words uttered in the market take on a value they can never achieve in the busy city. Far above Big Ben chimes out the hours, governments rise and fall, and all the while the exhaust-belching traffic-dragon writhes and slumps, slumps and writhes. Up there, Owen contemplates a sky full of shitting pigeons and streaking aeroplanes, where the hot polluted air dulls emotion. But in the market the basest feelings metamorphose, bread and water change into ambrosia.

As removed from her sleepwalking incarnation as Dr Jekyll was from Mr Hyde, the wide-awake Naomi draws him into the aureate orbit of her affections. Throughout the day she pulls him close, pets him, rests her head on his shoulder, kisses him on both cheeks, on his lips, on his brow. She links arms with him, runs a finger over his open palm, holds his hand, as if all this is the most natural behaviour in the world. He reacts as only an untouchable can, with desperate gratitude. One morning, Enrico waylays Owen as he returns to the stall with tea and rolls.

'So you like it here now?' he says, one arm impeding his progress.

'Yeah, sure.' Owen's eyes are already scanning for Naomi.

With the pad of a thumb Enrico rubs a small mole on his cheek thoughtfully. 'And your manager,' he continues smiling, 'Naomi, your manager, you are good friends with her now—flatmates, hmm?' She has seen them. She smiles, beckoning Owen over, patting her stomach as if to demonstrate how ravenous she is.

'That's right. I'm staying temporarily. Enrico, we're friends, just friends. That's all,' he says with emphasis. Enrico nods, accepting this. 'Look, I've got to go.' Still his arm obstructs Owen.

'You need to take care. The market can be a funny place. It attracts all sorts.'

'Yes, yes, of course I will,' he retorts a touch impatiently. Again his eyes vacillate. The short man covered in Elvis tattoos is back, fingering the hanging rows of belts. Naomi giggles over his head. 'The teas are getting cold.' He attempts to extricate himself but Enrico moves again to block him. 'Enrico!' he complains. He comes closer until the plastic cups are almost crushed between them. Owen feels their steam rising against his chest, and smells spices, garlic and just the hint of a vinegary, animal scent. He is level with his tassel beard, with the knotted purple beads.

'Sean is mixing with bad people.' His voice is low. Owen looks up and their eyes hold for a moment.

'I know. I've tried to tell him but it's no good.'

Enrico shakes his head. The plaited orange tail arcs distractingly. Owen can feel his breath on his face. 'I'd keep your distance from them, if I were you.'

'Thanks for the advice.' Enrico shrugs and stands aside. He has only voiced his own growing concerns, and his sense of impotence. He has failed to warn Sean off Blue, the notorious thug who haunts the market. Enrico has not been back to the flat since Owen's first night there. They had words and Sean told him that he was not welcome any more. He suspects, though, that it will only be a matter of time before the brash Italian breaks the embargo. But far from improving Sean and Naomi's relationship, over the last few days it seems more strained than usual. So far what he has observed of them has been both passionate and volatile. But now he senses a darker element to their affair, something more malignant than erotic.

It is with this in mind that he chooses to take a leisurely stroll to the corner shop in the evening, to give the two of them an hour alone together, bridge making. July, and it is still unbearably hot, with temperatures in the mid thirties. The sky, mottled with blotches of shell-pink and rose red, dulls in the teal gleam of the Thames. The images of the buildings ripple on the moving water. Height becomes width. On the way home, weighed down with his groceries, he dodges commuters hurrying to Waterloo Station. Scooters and bikes have become a common sight, zipping along the London roads, dodging traffic. The wind whips up twists of litter. Exhaust fumes, soot and the many odours of the river percolate through the dusty air.

Being on the third and topmost floor, he is out of breath by the time he reaches the front door. As he fumbles for his key, raised voices reach him. Hesitantly he lets himself in, and sets his bags of shopping down in the narrow hallway. He takes a moment to stretch and ease his throbbing fingers, letting the blood re-circulate where the plastic handles of the carrier bags have dug into them. Through the screen of the beaded curtain the argument suddenly becomes more strident.

'I want to keep it.'

'We've already talked about this, Naomi. If you think I'm stupid enough to pay for Enrico's bastard, you'd better think again.' Sean's pitch is rusty with controlled rage, then the two sounding together like a clash of cymbals.

'I told you, I never slept with him. He's just a friend. But you're so paranoid, you distort it all in your head. Perhaps if you didn't drink so much—'

'All right, Naomi, you go ahead. You have this brat. But I'm nobody's fool. You won't get a penny out of me.'

There is a shriek followed by a crash, then strangled words. 'What is the difference between my baby and Catherine's? You . . . tell . . . me that, Sean!'

'No. It's not the same. She's my wife.'

'Oh, and I'm what? Your whore? Is that what you mean to say, Sean?'

'No, of course not. But I told you, I'm not supporting a child that isn't mine. Go to him, why don't you. Perhaps he'll be more sympathetic. Though somehow I doubt it.' Then a cry of frustration from Naomi. 'Look, it's not my fault

176

you're pregnant. I told you that I was happy to deal with that side of things, but you said you'd take care of it—so take care of it . . . or clear off!' His accent has become more entrenched with his rising ire.

'So you're happy to fuck me, but not to deal with the consequences. Why's that, Sean? Am I so different from your sainted wife who, let's face it, can't be that hot, or why would you come sniffing round me?'

'Shut up! Don't talk about Catherine like that.' This last is delivered in a vicious hiss. But Owen can still discern every word lifting to him on the nip of the consonants. 'I'm not debating this any more. If you don't take care of it, I want you out of this flat. And I don't want you working at the market any more either. Not on my stall, anyway. Of course, I can't speak for your Italian lover boy.'

'You can't throw me out of my own home.' The passion is gone from her timbre now, only a frosty vitriol remains.

'Have you forgotten who pays the rent, my darlin'? Who pays the bills?'

Then the sounds of a struggle. Something drops on the floor. Sean swears.

Owen pushes through the curtain and sees them both standing in the middle of the room squaring up to one another like a pair of prize fighters. A chair lies on its side, and there are pieces of a broken china cup on the floor before the fireplace. The record rack has been knocked over, and records have fallen out and partially slipped their colourful sleeves. Cushions too are strewn about, and the sheepskin rug is rucked up in a corner of the room, exposing bare floorboards.

'Naomi! Sean! Stop this!' he begs, but neither of

177

them pay him any heed. She has her back to him, but Sean's normally passive face is puce. In that second his hand sings through the air, striking her face such a blow that she stumbles backwards. One leg buckles under her, and for a moment she looks like a wild animal that has been darted with some powerful sedative. She starts to overbalance, then rallies and regains her footing. 'What have you done, Sean?' Owen steps to assist her. But she forestalls him with a raised hand. Then in two quick strides she is at her lover, lashing out, her ragged nails raking his cheek.

'I despise you!' She hawks the words out, bunches her own cheeks then arrows a gob of spit into one of his eyes. He flinches back a pace. For a brief instant there is a hush, then the rasp of Naomi's panting breaths. She is flushed with exertion and fury, her eyes shrunk to jewelled dots. Owen gropes the air, trying to crank up his voice from the shaft it has sunk in. Sean's mouth gapes open. One hand gingerly probes his cheek where bright beads of crimson blood are threading together. He exhales a breath slowly from his lungs, lowers his hand disbelievingly and stares at the red smears.

'See to it, Naomi.' This, a low monotone that trembles from his lips. For long seconds their eyes hold. Then he glances briefly at Owen, his Adam's apple working as he swallows. The expression he wears is one of profound regret. The next moment, he storms out of the flat, sending the bead curtain swinging, slamming the door behind him. For a shocked second Owen stares after him, unable to believe what he has seen and heard. Turning slowly, his gaze rests on Naomi and he is jogged into speech.

'Are you hurt?' he asks, hesitantly touching her arm. Without looking round she shakes her head. 'Sit down. I'll make some tea.' She sinks down, her face now impassive. Glancing at her as he prepares the tea, he sees that she is focusing on the Bob Dylan poster pinned to the wall next to the one of Hendrix. 'The Free Wheelin'' Bob and his girlfriend, pictured walking down a road in Greenwich Village, New York, a VW camper van in the background. He spoons extra sugar into her tea. It is really too warm for hot drinks. But then, sweet tea is recommended for trauma, he knows. He recollects making it for his parents the night the moon dropped out of the sky. He sits beside her, hands her the mug of tea, waits, hoping that she will speak first. 'I'm sorry,' he dredges up eventually. 'I'm sorry about the . . . the baby.' She clasps the mug close to her face. Little curls of steam veil her face. 'What are you going to do?' She volunteers nothing, hunched on the settee, her beguiling eyes still on the poster.

A woman would probably have known what to say, but he is hampered by embarrassment. He pats her back awkwardly, tries to make the gesture more sympathetic than hearty. Although he has experienced a tragedy, the physical brutality he has just witnessed is entirely alien to him. Unwittingly he is becoming embroiled in circumstances that are ugly, and far too real for comfort. It makes him want to run, and if this is cowardly then perhaps he is a coward. But he is also decent, and walking out on Naomi in this crisis seems a desertion so callous as to be unthinkable.

Finally she sets down her mug on the occasional table and turns to him. The cardinal-red impression of Sean's hand on her cheek is clear as print on a page now. She does not wait for him to make a move towards her, but impetuously winds her arms about his waist, and burrows deep. The sensation recaptures the memory of Sarah's last embrace, jarring so agonizingly that it is as though he has been winded. Naomi feels matchstick thin, breakable. He touches her cropped hair, smoothes it. Then his hands meet behind her back, move up and down, feeling the separate nodules of her pronounced spine. Her natural hair colour is growing out fast. Her roots are black as a witch's hat.

'Shall I get you something to eat?' he offers.

'I'm not hungry,' she mumbles into his stomach.

Her features pastry cut into him. The elfin chin, the straight nose, the warmth of her lips. He imagines what it would be like if he was not wearing his shirt. Would it be similar to Sarah's face pressing into the mould of his flesh? Would he feel her butterfly-wing eyelashes brush against his skin?

'What about your parents? Might they help?' he asks quietly. 'Your mother?'

'My mother's dead,' she mumbles. Her breath seems to pass through the cotton, to burn his skin.

'Oh, I'm sorry.' She shrugs. 'Your father?'

'No.' He closes his eyes and pauses to summon courage. 'Enrico?' Will she spit and claw him like an angry cat? But no, all the choler in her seems to have died. She gives a dry, wistful laugh, and he reopens his eyes. Then she replies as he expected. 'No, not him.' They both know that in the real world, if married men do not want to be burdened with illegitimate babies, neither do the irresponsible, pleasure-seeking Lotharios. Owen cannot see an alternative to a termination of the pregnancy. But he has the sense to stand back, to let her make her own decision.

'Don't leave me, Owen,' Naomi says in an eerie echo of Sarah's last plea to him. And so they sit like this in the feverish heat, as the light ebbs away and the room is infused with darkness. Finally he pours her a brandy (Sean has left his customary bottle) and helps her to bed. 'Stay with me for a while? Stay with me, Owen, until I fall asleep?' she requests. He nods and sits on the bedside. Her fingers worry incessantly at the satin trim of the blanket. A chunk of light from the corridor weighs in through the open door. She wars with sleep. At last her tense body slackens, a rhythm is imposed on her flighty breathing, and her eyelids droop, flutter, close. He gets up, goes to the lounge and rings Sean. Catherine answers.

'Hello.'

'Hello, is that Catherine?'

'Yes, who is this?'

'It's Owen. I work the stall with your husband. Is he at home?'

'Yes.'

'Can I have a brief word? It's nothing important. Just business.'

'Oh, okay.' A pause. He hears the thin, distant wail of the baby.

Next, Sean's voice. 'Owen?'

'Yes. Look, I need to take a few days off, to be with Naomi.'

'Fine.' Another pause. He wonders if Sean will offer to accompany her to the doctor, if he will see her through her ordeal. Surely this is the very least he owes her. Then, not much more than a whisper,

181

'If she needs money, tell her, tell her I'll pay.'

'Okay.' Suddenly the baby's crying is much louder, as if Catherine has brought her into the room. 'I'll ring when . . . when it's . . . it's over.'

In the morning he accompanies her to the family planning clinic. He remains in the waiting room while she is examined. Half an hour passes. For much of it he studies his shoes, brown leather loafers that could do with a polish. The doctor judges her to be eight weeks pregnant. The abortion is carried out a couple of days later. Owen waits for her to be wheeled back to the hospital ward. Standing by her bed, he takes her hand in his. It is feather light and clammy, and the sight of her uneven nails makes the breath stutter at the back of his throat. Her eyelids flicker, stick, in that manner he has grown so accustomed to, and spring open. Her hand slips from his and moves beneath the sheet. Then her eyes widen as if in surprise. When he leans close, her cracked lips crawl in unsteady speech.

'It . . . it doesn't matter.' She repeats it. 'It doesn't matter.' She is still woozy from the anaesthetic. She neither looks at him, nor seems to know him. It doesn't matter, she has said. But it does. It matters more than Owen will ever know. Again, he is not sure what to expect, but he braces himself for a couple of rough weeks. The first few days he insists on staying with her, leaving Sean to cope by himself. She lies curled up in bed staring at a spot on the wall, only stirring very occasionally to visit the bathroom. He brings her cups of tea and coffee, a bowl of soup, bread and butter, a boiled egg. It isn't the most appetizing of fare, but he seems to remember his mother arriving with a tray bearing

182

just this sort of food when he was ill. In any case, she doesn't eat anything. His attempts at conversation are stonewalled, so that he soon gives up. An unfamiliar, heavy, muddy odour lingers throughout the flat. He tries not to speculate as to its origins, though deep down he suspects it is blood.

On the second day he pulls the spoon-back armchair up to a lounge window, for her to sit in. He lines it with cushions like a luxurious throne. Without discussion he takes her hand and leads her to it. She goes with him and reclines into them. Somehow or other she has found her way to his wardrobe. She is dressed in one of his shirts, green and far too big for her. 'Why not sit here and watch the world go by? Perhaps tomorrow you'll feel well enough to go for a stroll in the park, get some fresh air, put the roses back into your cheeks,' he persuades, his hand resting on her shoulder. She gives a small shrug of resignation.

On Monday morning he returns to work. Naomi seems a bit brighter, and assures him that she is feeling much improved. He tunnels down into the welcome fug of the market. To Enrico's inquiries as to the whereabouts of Naomi, he manages some bright chatter about a stomach bug. Throughout the morning he takes money, gives change, and trots out superlatives about swinging London to round-eyed customers. And all the while Sean's eyes are pinned on him, until, choosing a lull in trade, he finally speaks up.

'I'm sorry that you got involved in all of this. It's unfortunate, you know.' When he makes no reply, Sean touches his arm diffidently. Owen is polishing one of the bags, buffing the black leather until it shines like liquorice. He shakes the hand off and

183

carries on rubbing.

'It's one of those things. Forget it,' he mutters.

'You probably feel I behaved very badly. I know it must look that way.'

'It's nothing to do with me, really. Let's not talk about it, eh?'

'It is not as clear cut as you might think,' Sean says. Owen takes a breath, is going to say more and then changes his mind. 'What?'

'Nothing.' He is reluctant to meet Sean's eyes.

'Oh, c'mon now, Owen. What are you thinking?' Gingerly, Sean fingers his rash. It appears to be spreading, and Owen can see that a cluster of minute yellow blisters have formed there.

'I don't know . . . only that perhaps you should have been there.'

'Christ, I don't even know if it was mine,' Sean mutters under his breath.

'Does that really matter?' And suddenly Owen is angry. This was his mess and he should have cleared it up. 'If I hadn't gone with her she would have been all alone. That's pretty awful.' He lets the bag drop and wrings out the duster as if it is a wet flannel. Then the glitz of the stalls diverts his gaze.

'You're right. But I'll make it up to her. And I'm sure she'll forget about it in no time.'

At this, Owen nods grudgingly. The entire episode has filled him with distaste and unease. He doesn't want to be any part of it. But he cannot simply abandon Naomi, at least not immediately. When it has all calmed down, he thinks he will probably move on. He is here to escape tragedy, not greet it. He grew up in its shadow, and now he wants to emerge, to tackle a comic role that skims the surface of life. For the remainder of the day he is grateful

184

that they hardly converse at all. Trade picks up and is brisk. The constant stream of customers robs them of the opportunity for any more confidences. Arriving at the flat, he lets himself in. Calling out her name, he feels like an actor in the opening scene of an Alan Ayckbourn play.

'Naomi? Naomi? I'm home. Where are you?'

A malevolent hush surges back at him, devoid of humorous undertones. The only noise he can detect is the rasping of the taps. No more than a minute, that's how long it takes to check the shoebox space, the empty lounge, to register the unoccupied chair by the window, to view the bedrooms with their vacant beds, unclothed and slovenly as *louche* women. Then he is outside the bathroom's closed door, unaccountably afraid, his voice querulous.

'Na . . . Naomi?'

The stillness is oppressive. He snatches a breath, depresses the handle and pushes. The door swings wide. He expels air on a long, horrified sigh. It is a scene of carnage. Naomi wears nothing more than bikini pants, black lace, and looks inappropriately sexy. She lies in a foetal position on the tiled floor. Her arms, elbows bent, are level with her head. Blood is smeared everywhere. It stains her pale body, streaks her blonde hair and oozes from her slashed wrists. Even her cheeks are rouged with it.

'Oh my God!' he gasps, dropping to his knees, taking hold of her shoulders. Her eyes are closed. He thinks she is dead. Don't leave me, Owen. That's what she said. But like Sarah, he left her, failed her. And now she is dead too? 'Naomi! Naomi!' He is shaking her frantically. Her eyelids twitch for a second before opening. Her lashes are wet; her tears are crimson. And her striking eyes stare

185

vacantly beyond the gleam of a razor blade, held loosely between her fingertips. 'Oh, Christ! Please, no! Naomi, what have you done to yourself?'

Panic seizes him and he acts instinctively, grabbing up towels, slipping the blade from her hand, using it to shred them, then lashing the strips round her bleeding wrists. He races to her bedroom, yanks the blanket off the bed, charges back with it. She does not resist as he lifts her to her feet, bundles her up, carries her through to the lounge and lays her down on the settee. But when his hand reaches for the 'phone to call an ambulance, hers whips out to stay it.

'What are you doing?' she asks. Owen looks at her in frank amazement, at her impossibly bright eyes peering out at him from a face sponged with blood.

'I'm calling an ambulance. What do you think I'm doing?'

'No.' The hand, tacky with fast-drying blood, grabs his. Her grip is surprisingly strong.

'What do you mean, no? You could have died. You've lost a lot of blood.' When she shakes her head, Owen erupts. 'Don't be stupid!' He tugs free, and still holding the receiver, starts dialling. But again she prevents him, bringing her closed fist down on the cradle and disconnecting the line.

'I am not going to die,' she announces calmly. 'Don't be so irrational. You must compose yourself, Owen.' The reproach makes him mistrust his own senses. She has just tried to commit suicide by cutting her wrists, and yet here she is, telling him to moderate his behaviour. He flings down the receiver and it hits the wooden floorboards with a clatter.

'For fuck's sake, this is insanity! You need to go to hospital,' he shouts, his arms spiralling about him

186

in vexation.

'If I go to a hospital, do you know what will happen?' she says coolly.

'They'll stop the bleeding and make sure you're okay,' he fires back.

'I'm fine now. Listen to me, Owen. If I go to hospital they will want me to see someone, a psychiatrist probably. They will think I am not well and—'

'Well, you aren't,' he mumbles, his mouth as unwieldy as wet clay. An image of his mother flashes into his mind, of the plate crashing down over his father's bent head, of the blood that slowly soaked into his tea-towel turban.

'No, Owen. They will think I am not well in here,' she retorts. She taps her head with a bloodied index finger. 'And they'll try to fix me, to lock me up. I couldn't stand that.'

'All right, all right,' he rejoins tersely, 'but you have to see a doctor.' She sighs with exasperation. 'I mean it. I'm not arguing about this.'

For a moment she considers, then acquiesces with an ungracious shrug. 'Very well. But a private doctor and they must come here.' He agrees quickly. At least he will have peace of mind knowing that she has been examined by a physician. After this has been decided he washes off as much of the blood as he can, careful to keep her bandaged wrists dry. While she is tucked up in bed, he succeeds in tracking down a private doctor who is prepared to make a house call. He mops the bathroom floor as he waits.

Doctor Laidlaw is a man of imposing stature, a Scot with a neatly trimmed, battleship-grey moustache and beard. He appears unruffled when he emerges from her bedroom. He follows Owen through to the lounge, the expression on his face phlegmatic.

'Your . . . um—'

'Flatmate,' Owen chips in.

'Ah yes, well, your flatmate should be fine,' he tells him in his practised bedside manner. 'I've bandaged up her wrists. The main thing is to keep them dry for a few days.'

Owen rams his hands deep into his trouser pockets. A feeling of unreality has persisted ever since his grim homecoming earlier this evening. 'But won't they need stitching or something?' he asks, astonished, unable to believe such a potentially serious injury can be dealt with so simply.

'Goodness, no! The cuts weren't really very deep and they were nowhere near the main arteries. I think it was more a cry for help than anything else. They'll heal well enough on their own.' He exudes an aroma of tobacco and spicy male cologne, and there is a kind of permanence in his solid stature which reassures Owen more than any platitudes can do. 'She's a wee bit depressed after the termination,' he goes on. 'A common reaction. These things take a while to get over.' He shoots him a shrewd look, and it strikes Owen with something of a shock that he probably assumes the baby was his. 'It's just a question of time. I've left some spare bandages, but I should think a sticking plaster will do well enough in a day or two.'

11

Naomi has dragging pains in her belly. She sits in the spoon-back armchair unconscious of the passing hours. Some days are eked out for a year. On others, Owen leaves for the market, and in a blink he is back. He fusses, asks questions, makes her eat and drink. He doesn't realize what she is concealing, though. Fantastic colours, mixed up in the palette deep inside her, are seeping through her flesh, dyeing her skin. Blues, purples, greys, yellows, greens and . . . black, chimney-sweep black. Oh, she is saturated in black. No one notices except *The Blind Ones*. And they won't tell, not ever. No reason to.

Miss Elstob was precise with her punches, only landing them where the light didn't shine. When she arrived at Fulwood Cottage Homes, Naomi was five. By the time she ran away she was fifteen. In the reception room they stole her clothes and gave her new ones, so that she looked like everyone else. And they stole her name too. Father Peter bent down and peered into her strange eyes.

'And she said unto them, "Call me not Naomi, call me Mara: for the Almighty hath dealt very bitterly with me."' He put his hands on her head and twirled strands of her silky black hair between his thick fingers, as he spoke these words. Then, 'I christen you, Mara,' he said. 'This is your new home. And Mara is your new name.' She wanted to tell him that she didn't like the name, that she preferred Naomi. They said she had nits. But she knew that already. She liked to pop them between

189

her fingertips. They took her to the assembly hall and chopped off all her hair. Then they rubbed something that smelled oily and fiery into it. There were lots of stone houses that all looked identical, and a patch of grass, with more stone houses the other side of it. They brought her to one, cottage number 3, full of children. They told her she would be sharing a bedroom with five other girls. There was another bedroom full of boys, and a room where the house mother, Miss Elstob, slept. She was just like the old woman who lived in a shoe, and who had so many children she didn't know what to do.

When she wet the bed, the Mother made her wrap the sodden sheet about her, then shoved her in a corner, shoved her so hard that her head banged against the wall. The others came and jeered, and held their noses, and pulled ugly faces. They sent her to lots of different schools. She hadn't been to school before. She didn't like it there either. They called her *one of them fresh air kids*, and spat at her in the playground. The teachers smacked her with rulers, and reading and sums were so difficult that her brain fizzed. She had to travel to and fro on buses, and they gave her tokens to pay for the tickets. All day her tummy rumbled, and sometimes in the night as well, because it was continuously empty. They made her do sewing and knitting. She pricked her fingers so often that they bled into the material, and she kept dropping stitches, and pulling the tension of the wool too tight. Miss clipped her round the ears for that, and chided her for being so clumsy. Then she made her stand on a chair. She was still there long after *The Blind Ones* had gone to bed. Eventually she became so tired that she fell off, and only then was she permitted to crawl upstairs to sleep.

She had to attend chapel too. Father Peter was there and he made her skin creep. He had a shaggy beard and moustache, so you couldn't see his face properly, and his nose was large and red and sore looking. The things she liked were the snow, when it was deep and smooth and it made everything clean. And sledging down the steep pasture next to Blackbrook Road. She liked playing on the slide and the swing. And when she was flying high up in the air, she could see all across the Mayfield Valley. She liked picking blackberries from the hedgerows, and bilberries on the moors, and eating them until her stomach ached, and her lips and tongue turned dark purple. She liked it when the bus drivers overtook each other on the Redmires Road, and all the children screamed with excitement. And she liked seeing the films in the big hall, Charlie Chaplin, Buster Keaton, The Keystone Kops, and sitting round the Yorkshire range, listening to music on the radio, singing along. She liked taking her token to buy sweets from the stores, as a Friday treat. Sometimes she was sent to the office to collect ice cream for pudding. When she spooned it into her mouth it felt so good, the cold creamy sweetness, that she tingled all over.

But there were more of the things she hated, much more. She hated cleaning the dirt off the wet shoes when they got back from school, and polishing them until she could see her face in them, and making all the beds that she'd stripped in the mornings. She hated scrubbing the floors with red carbolic soap, until her hands stung. She hated how her head throbbed when Miss Elstob whacked it too

191

hard, and she hated the baby coming and being put in a cot beside her bed. It squeaked like chalk on a blackboard and then began to cry, and when she put her finger to Baby's mouth and shushed it, it only yelled louder. She hated having her ears and neck inspected, and the smack she got if they were grubby. She hated her legs being chapped with the cold, and having chilblains on her hands and feet. She hated when she was struck with the broom handle, and she hated being locked in the coal cupboard, so that it felt like she was nailed in a coffin and would die there.

What she learnt was that you can hate something so terribly that it put a fire in your chest, and made you want to pull your toes and fingers back into your body. And at the very same time you could love it, love it so that your heart became a giant's heart and you kept floating up in the air, having to concentrate to keep yourself on the ground. The hate was what she felt when Father Peter's face loomed up in her dreams, and he peeled her from her bunk bed. He took her off to the small room at the far end of the hut, and then peeled more layers off her. And it was as though he wanted to eat her up, poking himself into her, and sucking his fingers ravenously. And the love was what she felt when she stumbled onto the beach, and the sea sighed at the sight of her, and stretched out its salty arms to pull her in. Marske-By-The-Sea, the wooden huts, slipping out of her body and watching what Father Peter was doing to her from the ceiling, the need to wash, the dew-damp grass, the steep cliff path, the sea, the astringent sea.

Mara is sitting on her hands now, plumped on a chair in the kitchen. Can't talk. Mustn't talk. If she talks, Miss says she'll cut out her tongue. 'Snip, snap,' she says, making her hands into scissors, opening and closing her lumpy fingers. And Mara knows she's not lying. The big sewing scissors are in the drawer, sharp and ready. So she sits on her fingers, and her hands feel all numb. *The Blind Ones* do the same. Listening to the radio, squashing their fingers under their bottoms.

Miss is smoking, huffing and puffing and coughing and hacking. Mara pretends that her own lips are pasted together. 'Cos that way she can keep the words tied up. The evenings are slow-slow time, sat there on her hands. But she doesn't want to go to bed. When Miss Elstob turns the light off, that's when the baby starts up her caterwauling, howling and yowling, so that she can't stand to listen, so that she has to stick her fingers in her ears. But still the screaming comes, like pins, hundreds of red-hot pins pushed in her pincushion eardrums, pop, pop, pop. *The Blind Ones* pull the sheets over their heads and shrink, until they are far away, out of earshot. She can't do that. She's tried. But the baby's noise slides in, no matter what.

She told *The Blind Ones*. But they only laughed at her. 'Don't be daft, Mara,' they said. 'The baby's dead. Don't you remember? They came and took it to the sick bay. It had a fever.' And then they said, 'You shouldn't have put it in the cold bath. Miss said that's what did it, what's gone and killed her. The cot's empty, see.' And they showed her the cot with the stained mattress and the dents in it, said it was proof, and that she was a loony. 'The baby don't make no noise now, 'cos it's dead.' And some of them followed her about and whispered that she was a murderer, with her funny eyes and her heavy

193

blink. They did it for weeks.

And then one day the black tide rolled up from her toes, and she wheeled about and ran after them. She caught one of them. And by then the blackness was gushing out of her, so that she couldn't stop punching and slapping and kicking, like Miss did to her. And they all came and gathered round. The superintendent hemmed and hawed, and Miss Elstob screeched and hopped about like a chicken, and the children whooped and jeered. And their faces stretched, and their mouths fell open. But she carried on. She couldn't have stopped if she'd wanted to. So they had to pull her off. Even then she fought the air, pounding at it. And they dragged her by her collar and hurled her in the cupboard again. Only this time it wasn't hot, it was cold, and the coal was like black ice. Her fingers were numb when she wrote the name they had given her, the same as when she sat on them. She got a big splinter under her nail, but she didn't feel it, so she left it there till they let her out.

After that *The Blind Ones* were frightened of her. They mumbled and jerked their heads in her direction. But if she stared them down, they soon scurried off. Miss Elstob pulled her lips off her stained brown teeth, and told her that she was a very bad girl. She said that her real mother had lived in Sheffield, that she'd sold sex for money, and had come to a bad end. She said that was why Mara had been brought here, to Fulwood Cottage Homes, 'cos her mother was dead and she didn't have a father.

When she ran into the sea in the grey sludge of dawn, she expected to drown. By then she didn't mind. It was worth it to be washed clean, to have the sea draw the blackness from her, like pus from an infected wound. But as the icy weight of it closed in, her body began to move, to swim. Her fingers closed into paddles. Her arms circled. Her legs kicked. The salt water lifted her up. She could swim! Shadow memories jostled in her head. Days at the beach. Her mother, head thrown back, a throaty giggle. Sunglasses, a dark-pink bathing costume, long black hair tussled by the salty wind. Perfume that smelt of pear drops. Shiny red nails. Lipstick on the tips of her two front teeth. And ice cream cones from the kiosk on the promenade. Someone holding her up in the water while she thrashed her limbs. The tickle of sand. The abrasive kiss of the surf.

She was not afraid of the vortex she was in. She did not resist. She let it toy with her, carry her, pull and push her, tease and comfort her. It ransacked her for hurts, chilled and purified. She took a breath, held it, pushed down, and although it stung, forced open her eyes. She gathered handfuls of sand and waved them about her, so that she was engulfed in a sparkling cloud. She found pebbles, small as boiled sweets, and ground them together in her clenched fists. She listened to the chords of the brine, high and low, let them peal through her. And the sea leached the black coal dust out of her, diluted it so that it was no more than a droplet in the wide, wide ocean. And when she clambered out, teeth chattering, briskly rubbing her shivering body, she was no longer Mara, but Naomi once again.

Miss Elstob said that if she was lucky, when she left she would get a job in service in one of the nice houses in Ranmoor or Sheffield. And failing that, there was always the factories, ever on the lookout

195

for reliable girls, for Fulwood girls. But she didn't want to be in service, or to toil on a production line listening to *Workers' Playtime*, half-sick for the sea. She thought that she would like her liberty, then she could journey from town to town. She thought she might enjoy travelling. When she escaped she reverted to her former self, Naomi. She gazed out of bus and train windows and saw England flash by. If she had looked to her left she would have spotted Mara sitting beside her, and Baby too, the dead baby who wouldn't stop crying.

12

London has become an insufferable furnace. Owen studies the sky, searching for rain clouds, and is sobered by the unvarying blue. The sun is gradually beating city dwellers into submission. Where once they marched the streets like soldiers, now they loll idly outside pubs, frosted glasses in hand. It is over a fortnight since the abortion and much to Owen's alarm, Naomi continues to be depressed, taciturn, lethargic. She has no appetite, no zest for life. She does not bathe. Her hair looks flat and greasy. Her face is puffy and there are give-away dark smudges under her eyes, indications, if Owen needed any, of her insomnia. As far as he can see, she sits in the chair by the window all day, would probably sit there all night, too, if he did not steer her to bed. He does not know what to do for the best. He does not have the maturity or experience to guide him. She shows no inclination to return to work either. And Sean has not come to the flat since the night of their bitter fray. They seem, all three, to be in something of a stalemate.

Besides this, the remission from his nightmares is over. The Merfolk are back. Sarah ghosts him constantly, her hair wet and streaming. And when he quickens his strides to escape her, she reappears ahead of him. She smiles as the gap between them closes. 'Don't leave me, Owen,' she says. She chants this until the words muddle up, and it feels as if he is going mad, has gone mad.

This evening he sits with Naomi on the settee. They hug mugs of coffee, and talk to each other between sips. They are listening to a Jimi Hendrix record, *Are You Experienced* to the track 'Foxy Lady'.

'In a previous life, I lived in a camper van travelling from concert to concert, chasing the music,' she says suddenly, unexpectedly. Her unique eyes look into the middle distance, as his light up with interest. 'I saw Jimi Hendrix perform this live.'

'Where?' Owen wants to know.

'The Isle of Wight Festival, 1970.'

'You were there?'

She nods. '31st of August. He wore this psychedelic pant suit. Orange, pink, yellow. Very bright. Flares. Big sleeves.'

'Wow.' He is trying to place her there, Naomi, among the crowds of people, dancing, as Hendrix gyrates on the stage, as he makes love to his electric guitar. 'Who did you go with?'

She does not answer this. 'You know, he was dead only weeks later,' she says enigmatically.

'Who was?'

'Jimi Hendrix.' He has had enough of death. The magic has gone. She sets down her mug, crosses to the open window and leans out. Today she is dressed. Jeans. A smocked blouse. She pulls at the neckline. 'It's scorching,' she says.

'I shouldn't lean out so far,' he cautions, rising from the settee and moving towards her. Naomi, braced on her straightened arms, hands gripping the base of the sill, cuckoos out her head still further, and peers downwards. 'We're three floors up, remember. Please don't!'

At his imploring tone she pulls back, straightens up, and fixes him with her perturbing eyes. 'What's the matter, Owen? Are you frightened of heights?'

'No . . . no, not of heights,' he falters, taking an involuntary step back.

'Then of what?' she smiles encouragingly. 'Of something, yes?'

'Of something, yes.' Owen echoes dully. He wraps his arms protectively about his torso. She nears him, pauses. A long beat. 'Of water. I'm frightened of water,' he confesses quickly, wanting to get it over with, like pulling off a plaster.

'Of water?' she quizzes, her tone high with disbelief.

'Of lots of water. Of the sea. Of swimming pools.' There is a quaver in his voice, and his heart is jumping. Although his stomach is empty he wants to retch. And because his legs are going to crumple under him any second, he goes to the settee and sits down heavily. 'I can't swim.'

'Oh, is that all,' she laughs. She is beside him now, putting an arm about his shoulder. 'I love swimming. I will teach you, Owen. And then we will go to the coast and swim like a pair of dolphins in the sea.' He rears back, then leaps up, shaking his head violently.

'No. No, Naomi. I can't even bear to talk about

this any more,' he says. 'Please, can we just forget it?' He is breathless, panting. He can feel the pinpricks of sweat dewing his brow. She is bemused, but does not argue. Nor does she argue when, a little later, he opts for an early night.

Asleep or awake, he is not certain which, when the image sharpens into focus before him. A dark mass. An orange glow. There is something, someone, in his room with him. A sideways glance and his alarm clock confirms it is 3 a.m. He leans over and switches on his sidelight. Naomi is sitting on the floor, back against the wall, knees bent, feet planted apart. She is wearing a baggy shirt, long sleeves rolled up, not one of his this time. She is smoking a cigarette and staring at him. She is framed like a painting by two pillars of cardboard boxes, the striped shadow of the taller seeming to sever her face in two, one side lit, one side dark. The curtains, a thick weave in dirty green, billow in the hot draught from the open window.

'Can't you sleep, Naomi?' he asks in a voice throaty with slumber. His heart is drumming and his skin is slippery with sweat.

'You were having a bad dream. I heard you whimpering,' she whispers. Tiny circles of reflected lamplight jewel her eyes. 'I came and you cried out the name, *Sarah*, in your sleep. Who is Sarah, Owen? Is she a girlfriend?'

His mind is all confused, and her tone is so soothing and caring. But he does not like to see her mouth close on his sister's name. 'It was a long—' He breaks off to give a heartfelt sigh. 'I really don't want to talk about it. I'm sorry if I disturbed your night.' He sits up in bed and pulls the sheet over his bare chest. He is in his customary nightwear of

199

boxer shorts, and feeling her eyes on his partial nakedness, he has the self-conscious desire to cover up.

'Don't worry. I was awake as well, Owen.' There is a pause. Into the silence comes the light 'tick-tack, tick-tack, tick-tack' of his clock. He glances at the framed photograph on his bedside table, the one of him with his mother standing proudly beside their snowman. He thinks about the Water Child imprisoned inside the frozen white flesh. She draws deeply on her cigarette, funnels her mouth and blows the smoke out in one steady stream. 'We both have secrets, don't we, Owen?' He says nothing. A papery 'phut' as she sucks again on her cigarette. It has burnt down almost to the filter. She laughs softly and grinds the stub of it out in a saucer by her side. The acrid smell, heightened by the sensory deprivation of the night, bites at the back of his own throat. He traces the last fraying tail of flint-grey smoke.

'My sister drowned,' he tells her. He stares at the boxes piled one on top of the other, like a brick tower. He traces the writing on one of them, an obscure code printed in red. 'She was four, nearly five. I was supposed to be minding her. I . . . I wandered off. It was my fault.'

She keeps very still as she listens. Then she climbs to her feet and comes to his bed. She leans over him and draws him to her. After a second she pulls back and smoothes his hair off his forehead. 'You weren't to blame. You were only a little boy yourself. It was an accident, a tragic accident.' He wants to believe her. But it is not her that he seeks forgiveness from.

'Thanks.' He says this not because he means it, but because he feels that he ought to. She gives a fleeting smile. 'Perhaps we should get some sleep.'

'Are you sure you're okay?' she asks.

'I'm fine.'

At length she gets up and goes to the door. 'And that's why you're frightened of the water? You think that you'll drown too?'

'Something like that,' he mutters.

'We should help each other,' she remarks cryptically. Then, before he can question what she means, 'Goodnight, Owen.'

13

'Owen, I wonder, would you be after running a little errand for me?'

The day had got off to a bad start with Sean disappearing for an hour with no explanation, while Owen was hounded by a disgruntled shopper. Red-faced and livid, the man was clasping the bag his wife had bought the previous day. The buckle was broken, and the stitching on one of the straps had come away. Owen had to refund nearly double the money to appease him. Now, with Sean's reappearance, he is hot and feeling cross. Naomi's unpredictable behaviour is unnerving him. Another thing setting the worry beads clicking in his head, is the procession of unsavoury characters calling in to see his boss. Today the noise and the cheap showiness of the market is proving too much. 'Yes, that would be fine,' he readily agrees, without waiting to be told what the errand is.

'We're short-handed. We need Naomi back at work,' Sean grumbles.

'I don't think she's ready yet,' Owen says, realigning a display of wallets.

'She's had nearly three weeks,' Sean complains. 'Surely that's ample.'

Owen decides that he is looking gaunt lately. He has bruised half moons under his reddened eyes, and lines that he has not noticed before are criss-crossing his brow, and drawing his smiling mouth down. He has not mentioned Naomi's suicide attempt. But now something in Sean's resentful attitude acts as a catalyst. His head comes up. 'She's really not been well, Sean. The other night when I got back to the flat, I found her lying on the bathroom floor. She'd cut her wrists.'

'Oh, Jesus!' Sean exclaims softly, his eyes darkening with concern. But the emotion is fleeting. A second later and there is a glint of scepticism in his expression. 'She went to the hospital?'

Owen hesitates before answering. 'Well, no. I wanted her to go but she wouldn't. She was frightened they'd lock her up, that they would think she was barmy because she'd tried to kill herself.' Sean gives an ironic bark of laughter.

'So . . . why didn't she bleed to death?' he asks steadily. Owen avoids his direct gaze. 'She slashed her wrists. Isn't that what you said?'

'Yes, that's what I said,' he mutters, wishing that he'd never embarked on this course. 'I stopped the bleeding and bandaged her wrists. I called a doctor. He came to the flat.'

'Oh yes. And what did this doctor say?' Owen presses his lips firmly together. 'What did the doctor say?' Sean repeats.

Then, 'She was lucky. She missed the main artery,' he reports tightly.

The Irish man's eyes narrow shrewdly. 'On . . . on both wrists she managed to avoid cutting into a main artery? That was lucky, wasn't it, so?' Owen sucks a breath in through his clenched teeth. Unfairly, he feels as foolish as a hysterical girl. 'She did it for attention,' Sean continues, more to himself than addressing Owen. 'That's how it was.'

'You haven't been with her. You don't know how it's affected her. I don't think you can expect her just to come back to work. Maybe she needs a proper break. Look, I don't know anything about this kind of thing, but my guess is that she should get right away for a bit, give herself a real chance to get over it.'

Sean shrugs. 'If that's what it takes, I'm not preventing her. A week in Majorca. Fine by me. Though frankly, Iceland's more appealing at present. I'm not a brute. She wants a holiday. She can go with my blessing. You tell her so.' Owen nods and screws his eyes shut. He feels the blood pulsing at his temple, the tick of it in his ears. 'I want you to go and collect a package for me,' Sean says now, seizing his advantage.

'Where from?'

'From my place in Hounslow. Catherine's in. She knows you're coming. She'll have it ready.'

'Why can't you go?'

'I'm meeting some people here, you know. One or two things to sort out.'

As if on cue, Owen notices two men heading towards the stall. He has seen them before. These are the scum that Enrico warned him to give a wide berth. They look like a comedy duo, one short and skeletal as a whippet, one tall and rock-solid, a great slab of a man. The whippet is boss, known as Blue.

The features of his face are delicate, almost effeminate. A cupid mouth, a snub nose, blue eyes, fringed with pale lashes, a thick mop of butterscotch curls. The slab has a square flat face, pockmarked skin and heavy-lidded close-set eyes. His hair, dun coloured at the roots and carroty at the tips, is slicked back. Both are smart, dark trousers, short-sleeved shirts. Blue's is open-necked, but the slab wears a dark tie. Seeing them approach, Sean rummages in his pocket and gives Owen a slip of paper.

'The address in Hounslow. Off you go.'

Owen does not need to be told twice. The types Sean has been mixing with recently fill him with foreboding. He has no wish to be sucked into any dealings between them.

Tube travel is intolerable in the heat. As the train clatters out of central London and the carriage thins, he finds a seat. He stares bleakly at his reflection in the window, at the neglected back gardens of terraced houses, patches of grass that look as if they have been browned under a grill. It is fast becoming apparent that Sean is not the business entrepreneur he pretended to be. He is much closer to the rambling alcoholic, chasing rainbows. Really, he is doing little more than surviving. The stall is hardly a profit-making concern, more a juggling act to keep ahead of costs. Owen has noticed that he likes a flutter too, a flutter on the horses, or the dogs, or anything else he can bet on. His guess is that he is fast accumulating debts. However, it is not Sean who preoccupies his mind for most of the sweltering journey, but his wife, his baby. What an unlikely husband and father his Irish employer is. He is no rock to build a family on, more shifting sands. He is curious, wondering what the third member of this *ménage à trois* is like. Is she tall or short, or average height perhaps? What colour is her hair? What length? How does she wear it? Is she plump or thin? Her eyes—what shade are they? Does she know about Naomi? Does she mind? He stares at his own reflection in the tube train window, the terraced houses rushing by, and he ponders. Is she lonely? Is Catherine lonely—too?

14

Catherine is absurdly nervous at the prospect of having a visitor. She knows that all she has to do is open the front door a crack, and pass the package through, that this is all that is required of her. And yet she has had a shower, shampooed her hair, got dressed. She is exhausted, because she was up most of the night with the baby. She cannot recall when she last had a decent night's sleep. Now, Bria has dropped off, but she daren't risk closing her eyes, not with Owen coming. She might miss him. Is she that desperate for company, she ponders desolately. Is she that lonely?

She has been thinking about swimming. Swimming was the best part of being pregnant, of having to attend the antenatal checks at the West Middlesex Hospital. Travelling in the bus to her first appointment, she spotted it, Isleworth Pool—well, its grey, concrete carapace, the dour building in which it was housed, anyway. It looked deceptively like something you might encounter in the heart of communist Russia after the revolution.

Who would have thought that enclosed in that dreadfully dull safe there nestled such a priceless sapphire? She smelt the tantalizing whiff of chlorine drifting towards her through the top vent of the bus window, gliding on the moist autumnal air, or maybe she only imagined it. But imagined or not, it triggered memories of her class being coached once a week to a pool to learn to swim. That small hour, that sacred sixty minutes, trimmed away from the fat of her school days, was revelatory.

It was a communion with the water that she had, no less, a communion that left her reeling. The allure of the luminous, azure liquid. The thunderous, reverberating clap of it as it received her body. A sky of water and Catherine, a cloud, borne aloft on its surface. The autonomy of her breaths. The taint of bodies wafting from a fog of bleach. It was so utterly in tune with her moods, the water, calm when she was calm, restless when she was restless. Theirs was a symbiotic relationship. They were interdependent.

Returning home from that first antenatal appointment, feeling as defiled as the victim of a sexual assault, she alighted at the bus stop nearest Isleworth Pool. Chin up, she squared her shoulders, determined to forget the slithery gel leaking slowly out of her, making her feel that she had wet herself, and walked back to the entrance. Then she had gone inside, checked the opening times, asked if she could see *it*, with a reverence that might have been reserved for begging to be ushered into the presence of a deity. How could you explain to someone who wasn't a Water Child how it made you feel, that glimmering expanse? It spoke to her, the lucid stillness. It was magnetic.

206

Unfortunately the schools were often in when she was there, but this turned out not to be such a disadvantage. They swam in the shallow end, flapping and paddling like a flotilla of fluffy goslings, while their teachers strutted alongside on the pool's edge quacking orders. Occasionally shrill whistles bounced off the gleaming tiles, prompting a mass of small bodies to hurl themselves like lemmings into the water.

For the most part she swam widths. The rhythm lulled her, absorbed her, as nothing in her life had ever done before. Afterwards it left a shimmering deposit at the centre of her. Gradually it pulsed into her veins, making her blood glow Kingfisher blue, as if irradiated. And it gave a cotton-wool blur to her eyesight that she carried with her into the coldness, or the sunshine, or the rain.

As the months passed she had to swap her navy Speedo for a maternity swimsuit, the green of new grass, and sprigged with small white flowers. It came in two pieces. The bottom, pants that fit snugly over her bump, with an elastic panel designed for the inevitable expansion. The top, very like a baby-doll nighty, gathered under the bust and flaring outwards over her hips. It was, she reflected wearily, almost as much of an encumbrance as being pregnant. When she climbed into the water, carefully grasping the rungs of the ladder, no longer able to jump or dive without doing a painful belly flop, the ugly garment flowered around her. By then she was so hampered by her swollen body, that she seemed to rock through the water, like a squat rowing boat with an uneven load.

An unfortunate event as she embarked on the

lumbering exterior and acidic interior of month eight, robbed her one day of this last blue pleasure. She arrived at the pool, put on her swimsuit in the ladies' changing-room, secured her clothes and her belongings in the locker provided and, despite her bulk, strode out to the poolside with brave abandon. At the far end, the shallow end, a group of boys huddled shivering at the pool's brink. Their small ribcages stood out like pairs of miniature abacuses under their albumen skins, their hovering hands battling the strong, self-preserving instinct to cup their shrivelled genitals, their goggles sitting on their foreheads like a second pair of bug eyes.

She was about to dismiss them and begin her cumbersome descent into the water, when she saw that they were no longer cupping their genitals, but their mouths. They were laughing uproariously, nudging and whispering to each other, and then pointing rudely at her. The boys continued smirking and sniggering even when she was in the pool, ignoring the teacher's reprimands. She became so embarrassed, having each of their four eyes trained upon her, that her swim was utterly spoilt. More diabolical, she did not have the courage to emerge, while in full view of these Peeping Toms. She ended up wallowing like an unhappy hippo, her flesh tessellating with tiny misty-purple capillaries as the cold seeped into her bones. It was only after the last boy was shepherded into the changing-room, that she risked heaving herself out, the water sheeting off her. She scuttled with as much grace as she could muster, into the sanctuary of her own changing-room. Pulling off her swimsuit, she soon discovered the reason for the children's cruel mirth. She was still wearing her lace-edged nylon slip, the elastic waistband sitting below her bulge. She had not espied it under the mound of her pregnancy. But the schoolboys would have. They must have seen it hanging like a lewd dripping cobweb around her legs, titillating their young male minds. After that she did not go swimming again.

She was not able to go through with the abortion. And, of course, she does not regret this now, not now Bria is here. But she was right, the baby has chained her forever to this unhappy marriage. She sits in the depressing lounge. The wallpaper is black with large pink and cream flowers on it. There are grey mildew patches both on this and the Anaglypta ceiling. The skirting board has buckled and the wood looks rotten. The carpet, cream zigzags on a mustard background, is stained. The room smells musty and damp, not the kind of home to bring a new baby to. The settee, like all the rest of the furniture, is second-hand, an asparagus-green synthetic fabric, with brown and white stripes running downwards, towards the floor. She fingers the package in her lap. She has not opened it, but something about the way it crackles when she squeezes it, makes her sure that it contains money. She leaps up when she hears the knocking, and runs to the door. It seems so loud, reverberating through the empty house. She flings wide the front door. There is a man on her doorstep, tall, young, blond-haired, blue-eyed, wearing jeans and a black T-shirt with a picture of Mick Jagger on it. He shuffles his feet and looks self-conscious.

'Hello. I hope this is the right house. I couldn't see a number. I'm looking for a Mrs Madigan.'

'Hello. I'm Catherine Madigan. Catherine.' She holds her hand out. He takes it. She bites her lip.

His hand feels dry; his grip firm.

'I'm Owen. Sean said you would be expecting me. I've come to pick up a package.' He says this as though it is a question, as though he is not really terribly sure why he is here, standing in the sunshine.

'Yes, that's right. Sean said to expect you. I've got it ready.' A lengthy gap. More shuffling of feet. In this aberrant England the sun is beaming unrepentantly into Catherine's face. She screws her green eyes back at it and is temporarily blinded. Owen is a furry, dark-purple blob. She feels dizzy. Cars, vans, buses, all roll on by. Drivers and passengers are draped out of windows, swigging from cans and bottles. People walk the pavements, ill at ease in their draughty cottons, missing the buttoned-up feeling of their coats, anoraks, scarves, hats, gloves and boots. Catherine is distracted by the gleam of Owen's white teeth in the purple haze.

'The package?' he prompts.

For a moment she is at a loss. Then she remembers. 'Won't you come in?' she invites, standing back, sounding the epitome of an English lady ushering a guest into her country home.

'I don't want to put you to any inconvenience,' he says. 'You must be very busy—what with the baby.'

'She's sleeping. Bria's sleeping. And it's so hot. Wouldn't you like a cool drink? I think I have some ice too.' She is annoyed that she sounds a needy note.

More pearly white. He is grinning now. 'Well, if you're sure.' She nods. She shows him through to the lounge. 'Have a seat.' He sits down on the armchair with a sagging bottom, and glances at the package lying on the settee seat. She does not want to confirm that yes, it is the one he has been sent to collect, just in case he immediately seizes it and rushes off. 'Lemon squash all right?'

'Perfect.'

The ice chinks in the glasses as she brings them in. He gets up to take his. 'Thank you,' sits down again. She sits opposite him on the settee. Together they take a sip, and breathe their relief. Catherine can feel the cold liquid moving down her throat and into her tummy. She holds the glass against her forehead and rolls it back and forth. She eyes Owen shyly through it. He is no longer purple. The colours of him have calmed down and arranged themselves in a handsome face. There is a vulnerability in his blue fair-fringed eyes, and a sadness too, a grown-up sadness at odds with his youth. She lowers the glass. 'I didn't realize how thirsty I was. I can't recall it ever being this hot before.'

'Me neither.' She smoothes the skirt of her buttercup-print dress. 'How do you like working at the market?' she inquires.

'It's great,' he replies, a little too enthusiastically.

'I expect it's dreadfully stuffy down there.'

'An oven.'

'Sean says that you've moved into the flat in Covent Garden.'

He takes another drink. 'That's right. It's very kind of him to let me stay. And it's so convenient for work.'

'So I suppose you know Naomi?'

He hesitates before answering. 'Yes.'

'She lives there, doesn't she?'

A pause. 'Yes.'

'And works on the stall too?' Their eyes hold for a long, telling moment.

211

'Yes.'

'I've never met her. I probably won't. Staff for the market come and go.'

'Yes, I should think they do.' He finishes his drink.

'I expect you'll move on, before too long. Where's home?'

'Home?' He says this as if he does not understand the word.

She smiles a touch wanly. A chord is struck. She tucks a strand of hair behind her ear. 'I mean, where your parents are?'

'Oh,' he says in understanding. 'Wantage. Oxfordshire.'

'Is it nice?'

He hesitates, shrugs.

'Are you from a large family? Do you have dozens of brothers and sisters?'

His gaze drops to the floor. 'No. There's just me.'

'It can be a bit lonely, can't it?' His brow puckers. 'Being an only child,' she elucidates, speaking quickly. 'Actually I have a brother, an older brother. But he's nearly ten years older, so I've always felt as if I was by myself.'

He swallows. 'Mm, yes. I suppose it can be.' Another pause.

'Perhaps I'd better be on my way,' he says, glancing at the package.

'Oh no, please don't go yet.' Then, embarrassed, she says, 'It's . . . it's nice to have a chat.' Her eyes rake the room. She has been growing steadily more immune to its lack of charm, but now every dingy corner glares back at her. 'This place is awful, isn't it?' She can see that he doesn't know what to say, that he is fighting to be polite.

'It needs a bit of decorating, that's all.'

She laughs. 'It needs to be demolished.' He laughs, puts his glass down on the table beside him. 'I bet Sean talked it up so that you thought you were coming to a mansion. He certainly did to me before he brought me here. He's like that.' A cry from upstairs. 'Oh, that's Bria. Actually I can't believe she slept all this while. She doesn't sleep well, you see. I bet all new mothers wish that they had a bit more sleep.'

'It must be difficult, especially with . . . with Sean away so often.'

'It is.' She stands up, sets down her own glass. 'Anyway, that's the package.' She nods at it. 'I expect that you have to get back,' she says, her voice coloured with regret.

He has risen too. Then, 'I'd like to see her, to see the baby.'

She is pleased and her pale cheeks pink with pleasure. 'Would you really? You're not just being well mannered?'

'No,' he laughs. 'I've heard so much about her.'

'Have you?' She is genuinely surprised.

He shoves his hands in his jeans' pockets. 'Oh yes, Sean talks about her all the time. He's very proud of her, you know.' She blinks quickly because she is on the verge of tears. She feels them rising at the back of her eyes, and the tightness threatening to break in her chest.

'I'll fetch her then.' In a minute she is back with Bria. Her daughter is wearing a white vest. Minute legs and arms poke out from it. She is moulded to her mother's shoulder. Catherine sits down and cradles her in her lap. Owen sits next to her. The baby blinks her startled blue-green eyes up at him.

213

He laughs out a breath.

'She has Sean's eyes. The exact shade. I've given up trying to decide if they are blue or green, because they're both.' She nods in agreement.

'I know. Would you . . . like . . . like to hold her?'

'Can I?' Another nod. Bria changes hands. 'She's beautiful,' he says with absolute sincerity. 'She has a hint of red in her hair. Not as dark as yours, though.' Bria is sucking on a tiny fist, looking as if she is determined to eat it. Her other hand is curled around Owen's finger. He tests the strength of her grip, pulling upwards. 'She's so strong.'

'Well, she certainly has stamina. She can go for days without sleeping.' The windows onto the small garden are open, and a puff of warm air ruffles the faded curtains. 'Sean's gambling,' Catherine mumbles under her breath. They both stare at the baby. 'I'm worried, Owen. We can't afford to lose.'

'I know.'

'The package . . . well, I think it's money. I think he may be getting himself into some trouble.' She is blinking again. 'I'm not sure what to do. He won't listen to me.'

'I'll have a word. But I don't expect he'll listen to me either.'

The atmosphere in the room is suddenly very busy, busy with patterns, wallpaper, carpet, curtains, so that Catherine wants to close her eyes and cover her ears. She sniffs in air and smells soap, shampoo, clean perspiration and the acidity of the slices of lemon she put in their drinks. Through her blurred vision she glimpses down at her dress and feels foolish for making such an effort for a stranger. She decides that she must appear ridiculous to him, the abandoned wife isolated with her baby at the end of

214

the Piccadilly Line. The oppressive heat is ironing all the energy out of her, all the spirit. You can no more stop her tears now than turn back the tide. They pour silently down her cheeks. Her shoulders shake them out of her. Gently, her guest lays Bria in a corner of the settee and puts his arms around her. The baby kicks her toes, and catches at dust motes sparked gold by the sun. Catherine turns into him and gives him her unhappiness. The sensation of his lips moving against her hair, of his breath on her scalp, temporarily arrests her weeping. He is her whisperer. His utterance is so hushed that all she detects is sibilance, a soft sibilant whistle above the beating of his heart. She strains it for words and what she is left with is this: 'Don't cry, Sarah. Don't cry. It's all right.'

15

It is late afternoon by the time Owen arrives back at the market with Sean's package.

'Oh, well done,' he thanks him, sliding it quickly into his trouser pocket. 'You met Catherine?'

'Yes. She's nice.' Owen recalls the dazzle of her red hair in the sunlight, the uncertainty of her pale-green eyes, his heart beating against the press of her head. 'And the baby, as well, I saw her too.'

'She's a darlin', isn't she so?'

'Mm . . . yes, she's lovely. She's got your eyes.'

'She has,' he crows. The market is winding down for the day. Stallholders are packing away stock, putting up their wooden shutters. A few disparate shoppers wander the aisles, resentfully watching as their choices are limited.

'What did those men want earlier?' Owen asks casually.

'What men?' Sean dodges. 'It's been a good day. We took a small fortune.' He unzips the purse in his money belt, rifles inside it and produces a twenty-pound note. 'That should cover your fares to Hounslow, Owen. And a bit of a bonus besides.'

'Thanks. But you don't have to. I was happy to go.' Sean is leaning back against the counter, eyes unfocused. Owen stands beside him, beset by needling anxieties. 'It was Blue, wasn't it? That's what they call him. And one of his minders? They were here this morning, wanting to talk to you. What's going on, Sean?' He is careful to keep his tone mild, his posture relaxed.

Sean shrugs. 'A bit of business, you know. They're influential, good connections to have, altogether.'

Owen sighs. 'I don't think you should get mixed up with them.'

'Oh Jesus, the kid's giving me advice now,' he laughs wryly, landing a mock punch on Owen's shoulder. 'Well, thank you for that, but I think I can handle myself,' he adds, striking a sour note.

'It's nothing to do with me, I know. Everyone enjoys a flutter occasionally, but you don't want to end up in debt, having to borrow off some loan shark.'

'What the fuck are you on about now?'

Owen refuses to meet his eyes. He is stepping onto unstable ground. He takes a deep breath. 'Gambling. Aren't you gambling? So long as it doesn't get out of hand.' Sean's pale face suffuses with an angry red.

216

'If I were you, I'd shut the fuck up!' His hand finds the sore on his neck and he picks it viciously.

'I'm concerned, that's all.' Owen begins clearing the counter. 'No offence intended.'

'How old are you, Owen?' Owen is on his knees now, pushing bags into the shadowy recesses of the under-counter cupboard.

'Twenty-three.'

'Half your life, half your life, Owen. That's how much older I am than you. Don't you be after lecturing me. Don't you dare lecture me. You know shit. D'you hear me, Owen? You know shit.' He is leaning over him, spitting the words out. Owen waits, counts in his head, clambers to his feet slowly and turns.

'I told you, I didn't mean to offend.' As they eyeball each other the music suddenly stops. They finish up without conversation, both observing the enforced silence. Owen is late leaving.

Enrico is at the flat when he gets back. He pushes through the bead curtain and there he is, lying on the settee, beer bottle in hand, propped on his chest. The sausage waft of pot hangs on the stagnant air. If the music has ceased in the market, it is in full swing here. The record is spinning on the turntable. The guitar is strumming to the easy slide of Bob Dylan's drawl. 'Tangled Up in Blue'. Owen glances down at the album cover slung on the floor. *Blood on the Tracks*. Bob, in profile, dark glasses, mass of curly hair, fuzzy focus. In the kitchen Naomi is also drinking beer. She is wearing skimpy black shorts and a coral and camel-brown bikini top. A small mother-of-pearl star is threaded on a maroon choker at her neck. Barefoot, she moves her body in serpentine waves. One hand is flat, pressing on

217

her once more concave belly. When she sees him she halts, and with the other raises her bottle. Her smile is loose and he judges that this is not her first drink of the day.

'Owen, come and join us. Would you like a beer?' she cries. Without waiting for a reply, she starts burrowing in the fridge. A second later and the cap comes off with a *sizz*. Bottle in each hand, she goes to the settee, then jerks her chin up at Enrico. Lazily, he lifts his feet from the seat and swings into an upright position. He is wearing worn grey jeans, Jesus sandals, no shirt, his belt unbuckled. The top metal stud of his jeans is undone. His belly is flat, toned. Over it, wisps of dark hair glisten with sweat.

'Come and sit with us,' Naomi says, perching next to him.

'Actually, I thought I'd take a bath, a cold bath.'

'Do you want company?' Naomi flirts tipsily.

'Another time,' Owen parries, smiling at her easy coquetry. He is thinking that if Sean finds out about Enrico being here it will cause more aggravation.

'Sit down. Have your beer first,' Enrico insists. 'We have something to talk over with you.'

Owen lowers himself onto the settee arm, accepts the beer and sips it gratefully. The icy bite of it on his parched throat is sheer heaven. Naomi seems much brighter, and yet he senses that her shift of mood is ethereal. The record has moved on. The track 'You're a Big Girl Now' is playing. 'Enrico has had an idea,' she opens. 'He thinks we should take a holiday.'

'We?' Owen queries. Who does she mean? Her and Enrico? Or all three of them? Perhaps, he hazards, the surreal impinging on his thoughts after the tension of the day, the invitation includes Sean,

218

Catherine, and even baby Bria.

'You and me,' she qualifies.

Enrico lounges back, beer in one hand, the other curling about Naomi's shoulder. He plucks at the shoulder strap of her bikini top. 'She's not been well. She told me. A virus. She needs to recuperate. I can't get the time off at the moment, but you two could go.'

'It's the peak of the tourist season,' Owen protests. 'We can't just drop everything and leave Sean in the lurch.'

'He'll be fine,' Naomi pouts. 'It will do him good to put in some solid hours at the market.' She rolls her eyes. 'You never know, it might keep him out of mischief.'

Enrico takes a couple of gulps of his drink and wags his head. His orange rat's tail jiggles impudently. 'I'll see he's okay. If necessary, I have some cousins over here this summer. They can lend a hand.' He puts his empty bottle on the floor and thumps his chest with a closed fist, suppressing a belch.

'You'd like a holiday, wouldn't you, Owen?' Naomi pleads, her eyes imploring.

It is unlikely, Owen broods, that Sean will want his rival's support, so he stalls. 'Well, yes, of course. But what about the cost? I've a little saved, but not much, not enough for an expensive holiday.'

He sees her and Enrico exchange a conspiratorial look. 'That's just it, Owen. It won't cost you anything, except petrol. Naomi says that you mentioned you had a car?'

Visualizing his Triumph Spitfire, under wraps in the garage at home, Owen nods. Naomi blows into the neck of her beer and it gives a ghostly whistle. 'Enrico says we can go to his village in Tuscany, Vagli

219

Sotto. We can stay in the cottage his father and his brother have renovated, for free. We'll see the lake where the other village was drowned,' she entices. Owen flinches and drains his beer.

'I've spoken to my father. The cottage is not let for the next few weeks. He is happy for you to go.' Enrico gets up and pads off to fetch another bottle.

'I want to see it so much. I've pictured it in my head often.' She flicks a finger playfully on Owen's bare arm.

'I don't know—'

'Why not? What's stopping us?' Her eyes shine with impetuosity, while her bitten nails pinch his arm. 'It'll be so much fun.'

He lowers his voice, humiliated. 'Naomi, I'm . . . I'm nervous around water.'

She leans closer to him. 'I'll be with you,' she flutes. He scratches his head, rakes back his hair. 'Only one week. That's all. We can go to Florence. I really need this, Owen.'

Enrico is crouched over her record collection, selecting the next album to play. '*Moondance*, Van Morrison?' he murmurs.

'Do you really think it would make a difference?' Owen's head is close to hers now. 'Would it help you to . . . to recover?'

'Yes,' she says decisively.

He conjures cypress trees, tall and swarthy, tickling a sky streaked with violet. He sees fields felted with scarlet corn poppies, and sucks in air clotted with spiky, black and cream, swallow-tailed butterflies. He sees villas stained the colour of the ochre earth, hugged by lemon trees. The soporific scents of rosemary and wild thyme assail him, along with the lulling drone of drowsy bumblebees. He

220

does not see the sunlight diluted in the gloom of Lake Vagli, dappling the moss-cloaked walls of the drowned village.

'All right. I'll speak to Sean, square it with him.'

She is on her feet, stooping, sliding her hands behind his neck. The palms and fingers are wet and cold from the beer bottle. 'Thank you.'

'*Crisis? What Crisis?* Supertramp?' Enrico says over his shoulder.

'If you like,' she agrees, her hypnotic lapidary eyes fixed on Owen's.

'Is it all settled then?' Enrico wants to know, lifting the record out of its sleeve and fanning himself with it.

'Yes,' replies Naomi. And her lips as they brush Owen's cheek are cool and determined.

16

Owen's parents give him and Naomi a cautious greeting when they arrive. More than once he looks at his mother to find her eyeing this woman her son has in tow, with an expression not far removed from suspicion. He is visited by a sudden uncomfortable awareness of how short her white skirt is, how much cleavage her low-cut top reveals, the diaphanous fabric virtually see-through. For the most part his mother keeps a low profile, saying little. But if he is not mistaken, she listens astutely to Naomi's conversation, as if searching for a key to her character in it. His father seems perturbed by the sudden news of their holiday plans. He corners him in the hall, and asks how the box office will cope without him.

'Isn't this their busiest season? Tourists flooding the capital, all wanting to catch a show in the West End.'

It takes a second for Owen to recall his elaborate deception, then he is quick with his explanation. 'Well, actually, Father, this heat wave is leading to a drop in takings. It's too hot to sit in a theatre. The city's dead. So really, before this weather breaks it's the ideal time to go.'

His father nods, accepting this reasoning without qualms. 'Oh, the weather! It's causing havoc everywhere, it seems. What I wouldn't give for a little drop of rain.'

'You and me, both,' Owen empathizes.

After this there is no more talk of theatre. Instead, his father embarks on an animated monologue on the trials of gardening in drought conditions. In the midst of the unusual flurry of activity, Sarah's room alone remains conspicuously silent, as if it has taken umbrage at all the irreverent chatter, and is sulking. A bed is made up for Naomi on the battered chintz settee.

'I hope you'll be comfortable here,' his father tells her anxiously. And she smiles and assures him that she will. Dinner over, he leads her out into the garden, to examine the pathetic casualties of the freak desert conditions. Owen and his mother are momentarily by themselves in the kitchen. She sits at the small Formica table stirring a cup of tea. Having dried up the dinner things, he finishes off putting them away.

'How have you been, Mother?'

'Oh, you know. Up and down.'

'Not back at work yet?'

'Summer holidays.'

An intake of breath, then 'Of course.'

'I'll go back at the start of the winter term.'

'Probably do you good to have a break.'

'Owen?'

He turns round at her lift of tone. His mother is sitting staring directly at him, unusual in itself. 'Yes?'

'So Naomi, she's a lodger in the flat you're living in?'

'Mm . . . yes. Where do I put this?' It is a new salad bowl and he is unsure where it lives.

'In the middle cupboard, bottom shelf.' As he is fitting it in she speaks again. 'How well do you know her?'

'Only since going to London.' He wonders if his mother, like the doctor, thinks that they are having a relationship and adds hurriedly, 'She has a boyfriend.' He joins her, pulling out the chair next to hers.

'But you're going on holiday together.' It is a statement of fact.

He looks into his mother's brown eyes, taken aback by this interrogation. 'He couldn't get the time off work. The boyfriend. Pity, actually. So she just wanted a bit of company, that's all.' He pauses. 'She hasn't been very well.'

'Oh? What's the matter?' She takes a sip of tea and waits, head to one side.

'Ah, some . . . some nasty tummy bug. She's over the worst of it now.'

'Really?'

'Yes, it dragged on and she's a bit low.' He strokes a hand over his cheek, clears his throat. 'The trip will do her good.'

223

'Italy. The Tuscan mountains. Sounds very nice.' She is on her feet.

'Hopefully. We're staying in her friend's house, an old stone cottage. You and Father should have a holiday.' He says this without thinking, then bites his thumb. She rubs the back of her neck and drops her gaze. He recalls the holiday in Devon, the sun, sea and sand, and the funeral that followed it.

'You know, I really am awfully sorry. Would you mind very much if I go and lie down? I've a bit of a headache. Half-an-hour. That should perk me up.' Her hair hangs limply around her face, and her eyelids are heavy.

'Of course not,' he says, when he would give almost anything for her to stay.

'I'm the most dreadful bore. Why don't you go and join them in the garden?'

'Shall I bring you up an aspirin?'

'No thank you. I'll be fine.'

After she has gone he sits at the table in the sun-filled kitchen wondering what she feels for him now, his mother, if anything. And wondering, too, at the interest she showed in Naomi. He is not surprised when she doesn't reappear. Later, after his father has also retired to bed, Naomi pesters Owen to show him the hidden interior of Sarah's room. He stammers out excuses.

'My . . . my mother prefers to keep . . . keep it private. Anyway, I'm sure the door is locked, and I don't know where the key is. Besides, we might disturb my parents, who are very light sleepers.'

But she persists, curious as Bluebeard's wife. She must see the box bedroom, must open it up and rouse the little ghost, Sarah. So Owen relents, and lets this Fatima have her heart's desire. He looks on

224

uneasily, arms folded, leaning against the wall by the door, as she explores. He feels as if he has ushered a gawking seeker of cheap thrills into his dead sister's tomb. He imagines Sarah's somnolent ghost disturbed by the intrusion, her bleached spectre levitating from the pillow, and staring reproachfully at him with her stark, enamel-blue eyes. When, after investigating Sarah's cupboard and remarking on the rows of socks bundled into fat white cocoons, and her pairs of polished shoes, she seems suddenly to lose interest, Owen is relieved. Downstairs once more, and she questions him about the day itself, the day Sarah drowned.

'I told you what happened.' He is unusually abrupt.

'Not the details. Tell me again,' she begs, undeterred. 'You ought to talk about it, not keep it all bottled up inside you.' But he will not be drawn. 'Can you really not swim, Owen?' she asks, changing tack. She sits on her makeshift bed, wings her legs up and hugs her knees. Owen shakes his head. 'Not a single stroke?' Her tone is one of disbelief.

Owen feels as though an infected tooth is being probed. 'No, not a single stroke,' he rejoins stiffly. He is at the lounge door, his back to her, his eyes tracing a dribble of black gloss paint. Then, 'Shall I turn the light off?'

'I find that hard to believe. So . . . if you fall into a swimming pool, or off a boat into the sea, or . . . or into a lake, you . . . you would sink like a stone?'

The nerves in Owen's shoulder muscles give an involuntary spasm. 'I would drown.' His voice is barely perceptible. 'Like my sister did. Goodnight, Naomi.' He is sure that the nightmares will come the moment he shuts his eyes. But the Water Child

225

is ready for them and sees him safe asleep. The next day they drive into the breaking pastel pink of dawn. The Triumph Spitfire, none the worse for its sojourn in a darkened garage, sputters valiantly through France and across a spur of Switzerland. They break their journey at Dijon and Geneva, then take the Mont Blanc Tunnel, cutting through the Alps to Italy. After a night spent in a quaint hotel in Varazze, they set out for Lucca and the peaks of Garfagnana.

As they near their destination, 600 metres above sea level, among the steep wooded slopes of sweet chestnut, hornbeam and beech, Catherine ambushes his thoughts. Where her cheek brushed his chest, it felt soft as lint. She has a slight overlap of her front teeth. There is a tiny white dash above one eyebrow, a childhood scar. Her hair is red at the tips and at the roots. Then, swinging round the tight bends of the mountain roads, there is Vagli Sotto, built on a headland jutting out into a huge reservoir. Then he remembers the drowned village haunted by its own siren, Teodora. In all other respects it is enchanting, a clutch of stone cottages and whitewashed houses, and the square tower of an old church rising up from a grassy hillock. It is set against a vista of awe-inspiring, charcoal-grey summits, festooned with streamers of glistening snow, the Apuan peaks. At once he is reassured by these curmudgeonly, humpbacked, ancient gods. They preside in grandeur over the ruinous doings of men, while the trails of their pipe-smoke swag the world's roof.

They have phoned ahead and Lorenzo Gallo, their landlord's son, Enrico's elder brother, is waiting for them. He directs them to a small patch of rugged ground on the outskirts of the town, where he says they can park the car, explaining that the narrow paths are unsuitable for traffic. They scramble out, stretching their cramped limbs after the long journey, and genially he gathers up their luggage. As they make their introductions, his eyes, shying away from Owen, dawdle on Naomi.

'Come, follow. I will take you to the cottage. Then later you will join us for a meal, homemade cheese and sausage and wine, then grappa.'

Scampering ahead of him like a mountain goat, Naomi glances back at Owen, then at the lake. Fear has planted its stake in Owen's heart. But as he trudges after them, the little village of Vagli Sotto draws the pessimism from him. He follows the sweep of banks matted with an entire palette of greens, the rich moss-green velvet of lush grass, the citrus green of the regimented rows of cultivated crops, the tawny green of scrub and bracken, the silver green of olive trees, the grey green of flinty rocks cloaked with sparse growth, and the lacy darker greens of the tall majestic pines, some of which are near black in their coloration. And here and there daubs of brilliance capture his attention, pinks and whites and reds, a cockerel proudly strutting about displaying his comb and wattle, a cluster of crimson-faced poppies, a pig scratching its pastel-pink rump contentedly on a dry-stone wall, the snowy blaze of a goat's beard.

He lifts his eyes once again to the peaks, then lets his gaze drift over the blue ceiling of sky, where the clouds are as diverse as the greenery mapped beneath them. Some are just ghostly scribbles, some no more than a hazy dove's wing, some are swollen milky pillows with pregnant mousy underbellies,

227

and some, sheets stretched taut until they are torn asunder. There is nothing dormant about this celestial arena. It is an endlessly changing display buttressed by the craggy mountains. Storms will brew fast up here, he judges, as the hot air glissades up the cant of blue-grey rock, cooling rapidly.

He drinks in a breath heady as wine and pauses for a moment to let Vagli Sotto take his measure. He pulls his eyes back from the slide down to the lake. There, skating on its polished rink will be the clouds. The shoulders of the mountains will thrust themselves up from its ebony depths. The green slopes, the winding stone-paved paths, the huddle of buildings that make up the village, they will all be wallowing in the water. Even the inky pines will seem to dip their branches in the mere, waving gently like mammoth ropes of seaweed. And if he looks closely enough, leans over the rough-hewn wooden fence that borders the incline, and cranes his neck, he knows he will meet the face of that other Owen, already possessed by them. Oh, he is wise to the baffling mirage, the phantasm of air and life and vibrancy, where there is only another Atlantis sealed in a water-logged womb. Suddenly dizzy, he feels the drag of the Merfolk, hears them serenading him, calling his name. He covers his ears with the flat of his hands, and catches up with Naomi.

The three-storey stone dwelling that is to be their home for a fortnight, nestles into the shoulder of the hillside. There is a kitchen and dining-room on the first floor, a living-room on the second, and a bedroom on the third. And there is a small paved patio, where a solitary mulberry tree provides partial shade for a table and two deck chairs. From here and from every window in the property, spectacular views of the mountains are afforded, and of the lake too, lying like a mammoth oil slick below them. The rooms are furnished simply with heavy wooden furniture, decorated with primitive paintings of flowers in bold colours. They smell of permanence, of pine resin and lavender and clay. Like most of the buildings in the village, the property seems as much a part of this landscape as the vegetation and rocks rooted round about it.

'It dates back to medieval times,' Lorenzo explains with pride. 'What do you think? We undertook the renovation project ourselves. Harder work than my brother, Enrico, has ever done, let me tell you.' He hands Owen the heavy iron key, leaving him astounded at the weight of it. 'Vagli Sotto is lovely, yes?' They nod. There is no denying it. The village is bewitching, soaked in the salmon-pink glow of early evening. The dramatic, remote setting ploughs its rugged beauty into the newcomers. There is something intoxicating about the isolation, Owen reflects. If only it wasn't for the lake . . .

Lorenzo's grey eyes flick over him with interest. 'Now we have a smart holiday cottage, rich tourists can come here, spend lots of money and enjoy it as well,' he adds, stroking his chin in a miserly gesture. Not so very unlike his brother then, Owen ruminates, except that his stall is set up closer to heaven than hell. His eyes dart to the few straggling black wisps sprouting from Lorenzo's chin—a poor imitation of Enrico's stunning orange tassel. Naomi seems energized by it all, dashing here and there, admiring the rustic furniture, exclaiming one moment, and firing questions the next. Through the open front door, Owen scans the steep precipices, and traces the looped script of winding road written into the slopes. He would like to leap back into his car and race down them, away from the lake, the lake that is visible from every window, from every walkway. Lorenzo follows his sightline and nods with approval. 'You like our lake in the mountains. We are another Lombardy up here. They have Lake Como, Maggiore, Lugano, Orta and Garda. We have Lake Vagli. Man-made but even more beautiful, I think. The dam was built to provide hydroelectric power for the mountain people living in Garfagnana. There was a village in the valley, but they flooded it in 1953. Fabbriche di Careggine. The residents relocated but the buildings are still there, under the water, the cottages, the church. Boating, swimming. Yes? I think the tourists will love it.'

Owen gives a weak smile in response and closes the door. They make their way up to the second-floor bedroom, the Italian's well-built frame dwarfing the narrow passage. Once there, his eyes glide suggestively towards the twin beds, and then back to where his two guests stand before a huge wardrobe. Naomi throws the doors wide, pulls out drawers, and runs her fingers over the smooth dark wood. She is transfixed by the slide of supple skin across the intractable, polished oak.

'This is the only bedroom,' Lorenzo says slowly. 'It's not a problem?'

'We'll manage,' Owen replies briskly.

Lorenzo winks cheekily. 'You can always make up the settee downstairs if you prefer it.'

Naomi rotates slowly, taking it all in. 'I love it,' she pronounces. She tugs at a fingernail with her canine teeth, and then with the back of a hand

230

smoothes her neck. She chatters happily to Lorenzo about Florence and Pisa, the places she wants to visit. Owen feels excluded. For a moment he becomes the adolescent version of himself, sitting on the back step in the sunshine. His eyes had vacillated between the book in his lap, and his mother talking to Ken Bascombe. He can see her now, leaning on the fence, smoking a cigarette, her cheeks glowing, his mother looking so beautiful and distant. The anguish that parted them has grown up like thorny briars, become increasingly intimidating and impenetrable. Seeing her is more dreadful than not seeing her. Her eyes hold nothing but punishment for him, and a truth so terrible that it must never be told. But he lives with the heavy knowledge. It is simply this: if he had died that day, if it had been him who drowned and not Sarah, his mother could have borne it. She could have buried him and gone on living. His teeth ache with needing her. He is half-made, incomplete, alone on an empty beach with the remote grey tide coming in.

A succession of tinny squeaks rouses him to the present. Naomi is bouncing on her bed, testing the metal springs. 'In the mountains,' she says softly, her white teeth snipping crisply around the words, 'I expect it gets very cold at night.' And her lips redden with pleasure. She blinks her gummy blink. Suddenly she jumps up and crosses to the window. Lorenzo follows and they stand side by side. Their arms are touching. She pinches back a corner of the closed ecru and mauve cretonne curtains, and peeps out. Leaning over her, he throws them wide. The rings skid along the metal rod with a sharp discord, and instantly the room is floodlit. Owen joins them, flanking

231

her right side, her devious blue-eyed profile. Lorenzo lifts the latch and eases open the window. All three survey the lake. Owen sways on his feet, the vertiginous sensation nearly toppling him. He imagines Teodora sealed under the lid of impermeable black water.

'When they dammed up the Edron River, they say a village woman stayed in her cottage, that she drowned. Teodora, her name was. They say she haunts the lake still, that if you see her you, too, will drown,' Lorenzo says with evident relish. 'Do you believe in ghosts?'

Owen gives a nervous splutter of laughter. Naomi smiles at Lorenzo, entranced. 'Yes, Enrico told us. We will keep our eyes peeled for the phantom of the lake and let you know.'

'It certainly makes an excellent story for you to . . . to embellish for your . . . your tourist guests,' Owen falters. Lorenzo chortles, undaunted by Owen's seeming cynicism.

After he has gone, while Naomi is getting ready for their evening out, Owen stands at the lounge window. He eyes the lake as if it is an invading army and he is a lookout on the battlements of a fortress. Then he scans the mountainous panorama. Night falls fast here. He can see it coming, inexorably blotting out the day. He has a vision. Teodora sitting in her stone cottage combing out her silky black hair, as the water gushes in under the door, then through the windows, and finally rushes down the chimney. In his mind the level rises like a running bath, until her mouth gapes and the torrent rushes in.

At Nerio Gallo's house that evening, Naomi gets drunk on grappa, and flirts with Lorenzo, and with

232

his bearded father. Owen reddens, because they are not in the market, where the lights are low and cheap things have guile. As they weave their way the few steps home, she slides her arm through his.

'It's so quiet here. Aren't you glad we came?' Her speech is thick, carrying to him on her alcohol-sodden breath. When he makes no reply she digs her heels in and they stumble to a stop. 'Did you hear me?' she slurs from a corner of her mouth. Looking down on her, he nods and thins his lips in a weak smile. The blades of brilliant stars stab the navy-blue arras of the night sky. A biscuit-gold harvest moon finds its double in the lake. The mountains are splashed in party silvers, greys and purples. The salty sausage and the grappa have given Owen a fierce thirst. The planes and hollows of Naomi's face, exaggerated by the dim light, appear unsettlingly skeletal to him. Her eyes blaze out from cadaverous sockets. Her mascara and eyeliner has smudged, giving a gothic look to her angular face. And her mussed hair, hatted in moonlight, looks white as a barrister's wig. 'Well?' she breathes.

'Naomi, you're drunk,' he observes, aiming for carelessness, but striking a pious chord. 'We'll talk in the morning.'

'But you are pleased we came, that it's all so pretty?'

'Yes, yes. I'm pleased,' he lies.

In bed, Naomi, sinks into boozy slumber instantly. But Owen is wakeful. He sits on the window seat and listens to the window trembling in the breeze. A ray of moonshine, refracted by the glass, shimmies on the ceiling. Lake Vagli glitters under the harvest moon like a slumbering mythical monster. He lifts his eyes and imagines he can see Teodora, a black mermaid beached on the gritty concrete bank. She is a chantress warbling honeyed notes that bring the tears to his eyes. And the wave of her voice rolls away across a universe blistered with uncounted sun, seeded with marbled planets, to break on some unknown shore, sending a ripple through the continuous circle of time.

*   *   *

Sunday morning. They are sitting sunning themselves on two deck chairs outside the cottage. Naomi leans forward and pulls off the tunic she is wearing. The fabric, magenta voile, is light as gossamer. She reclines again. Now she is wearing no more than a skimpy black bikini. Her eyes are closed. She has kicked off her sandals, and Owen studies her toes curling against the baked flagstones, relaxing, then curling again, like a contented cat. Each time, the balls of her feet rise a few inches. Her body is open, letting tongues of sunlight lick her flesh. Her only concession to the harmful rays is a pair of sunglasses. Owen, dressed in fawn shorts and a short-sleeved pale-blue shirt, has an engaging Enid Blyton innocence about him. His sandals are firmly strapped on and he is wearing a half-brim cap, but no glasses.

He has just applied sun lotion and there are streaks of it on his arms. One of his eyes itches and without thinking he rubs it. The lotion, still on his fingers, makes his eye water copiously. The same second the sun, reflecting off one of the gold hinges of her sunglasses, temporarily blinds him. Re-focusing, his vision is indistinct. He squints and makes out what looks like three Lilliputian priests. Then he realizes they are not men but boys, young boys, and there are not three but five, all wearing black cassocks and white surplices. Two of them carry flags, the third, spearheading the little group, a cross. Owen tries to sit up but the canvas back of the deck chair makes it difficult, and he flounders like a beetle on its back.

Following at their heels are the men of the village, most middle-aged, some bent-backed and grey-haired. Many wear suits, ties and even hats. All have made considerable efforts with their appearance. As they pass by their eyes stray to where the newcomers are sunbathing. Naomi's body holds them for a second but their expressions remain impassive. Owen prods her. She gives a small blissful sigh and wriggles away from him. The flash of a silver lantern draws him back. Now he sees that the life-size priests have arrived, three of them, dressed in long white robes, with short red capes tied at their necks. They form a semi-circle, at its centre a stooped, shrunken, old bishop, carrying a gilded crook. Owen has managed to hoist himself up and he nudges her again.

'Naomi, sit up. Put your tunic on,' he hisses. 'I think it's some kind of religious festival.' She sighs, shifts in her chair languidly, lowers her sunglasses and peers over the rim. She looks mildly intrigued but she makes no move towards modesty. He is about to speak again when several more men bearing a plinth round the corner. Crowning it, seated on a silver throne, is the statue of another bishop. Again Owen pushes her. When she does not stir, he retrieves her tunic from the ground and attempts to cloak her spread-eagled body. Only when the band arrives does she rouse herself, a

235

crowd mainly of youngsters dressed in black trousers, blue shirts and military-style caps. They all carry instruments, trumpets, drums and clarinets, and they are playing a solemn processional march.

She swings herself forward on the deck chair and climbs to her feet, the movement executed with considerably more grace than he could muster. The tunic floats off her. She is standing barefoot in her brief bikini. As Owen rises, she takes a couple of steps forwards and casually leans over the wooden railing, gazing at the spectacle on the climbing path. She claps her hands as they pass by, as if the ceremony has been arranged for her benefit alone. And this is how they find her, the women of the village, as they round the bend, bringing up the rear of the parade. One of them, a stout matron wearing a long-sleeved, dark-blue dress, the substantial shelf of her breasts adorned with a plain gold cross and chain, breaks away from the crowd. She strides purposefully up to them. Naomi turns to face her, raises her sunglasses now and smiles unabashed. Owen intercepts, stepping between them.

'Can I help you?' he asks, wrapping his own arms uncomfortably about his waist.

'Your washing,' says the woman. She has the gimlet-glare of a hawk.

'I'm sorry?' he queries, not understanding her meaning. Naomi, leaning back on the railings, lowers her sunglasses and gives a high, mocking laugh.

'Your washing, it is in full view,' the woman reiterates with a jut of her chin, looking beyond his shoulder.

He turns and sees their laundry spread out on a

wooden rack to dry. There are a few T-shirts but mostly it is a display of Naomi's lacy pants and a few bras. He feels his cheeks grow hot. Naomi raises her eyes, annoyed. 'Oh, of course. I'm so sorry, but we didn't realize,' he apologizes hastily. 'We'll clear them away. Naomi, give me a hand.' She looks at him rebelliously and lounges further back on the rails. 'Naomi!' he presses again through gritted teeth. He starts plucking clothing and underwear off the rack. When he glances up the woman has not budged. She is locked on the indecently clad visitor, her expression transparently hostile. Naomi takes off her sunglasses and meets her withering gaze levelly. The villager seems to wince slightly at the cloven-coloured eyes. Then, like a petulant adolescent, Naomi stoops, retrieves her tunic and slips it on. And all the while the other women, children at their skirts, troop by staring in their direction.

'I don't know what all the fuss is about,' she mutters. She lets her head drop back on her shoulders and scans the sky. Finally she shrugs, pushes off from the railing, skirts her challenger and stalks off into the cottage.

'I . . . I'm sorry,' Owen falters. The woman gives a grudging nod. 'I . . . we never meant to cause offence. We didn't know it was a . . . a . . .' He dries up, his mouth arid as ancient bones. For a second she does not move, just holds him in her percipient stare. Then the stern aspect of her face fades suddenly and she nods, appeased. She turns on her heels, head held high, hurrying to catch up with her neighbours. With his bundle of damp washing he hastens after Naomi.

Monday. After a breakfast Owen has lost his appetite for, they drive to Lucca and hire bikes. They pedal around the ancient city walls, enjoying their commanding prospect over the surrounding countryside. Half-way round they stop and clamber off to appreciate the panoramic views. The lacy leaves of the plane trees stir in the warm breeze. A horse and cart, loaded with market produce, clops by. Other cyclists pedal past. An elderly couple stroll hand in hand. Proud parents walk their young son between them. Owen and Naomi gaze out over meadows, clusters of dark trees, a sea of brick-red tiled roofs from which towers rise imposingly, and beyond these, as far as the eye can see, a vista of dusky majestic mountains.

'It's quite something,' Owen says. 'The kind of landscape an artist would want to paint.'

'You know, I can't forgive him.'

For a second he is disorientated by her remark, and then the wretched circumstances of this seemingly endless summer break on him. 'You say that now, but in time—' he opens hopefully, but she cuts him off smoothly.

'No, never. I have nothing but contempt for Sean now, for the cruel way he treated me.' She does not look at him but keeps staring outwards, her voice expressionless. 'He murdered our baby. He didn't even consider an alternative.'

Owen sighs softly. 'Naomi, you must see that it was difficult for all concerned.' He lays a hand on her arm and exerts a light pressure with his fingers.

She brings her other hand to her mouth and absently flicks a thumbnail and fingernail together.

'You wouldn't have behaved like that.' She casts him a sideways look, her tantalizing eyes suddenly shy. When he reserves comment, she makes it a direct question. 'Well, would you?'

'That's different,' he dodges.

'Why?'

'I'm not married,' he tells her with a shrug.

'I don't believe that you would have acted so callously even if you were,' she maintains.

'Who can predict what I would have done?'

She faces him now and their eyes meet. 'I . . . think . . . I . . . can.' She pays her words out slowly, making each one count.

He lifts his hand from her arm, opens both out to her, his gesture beseeching. 'Look, I don't pretend to understand how appalling this must have been for you. But it's done, finished with. You ought to try and put it behind you. Going over it will only make it worse.'

'Why shouldn't I be part of a family?' she asks unblinkingly. And Owen feels uneasily as if she is assaying his soul, testing the true mettle of him.

'No reason at all.' He takes a breath, attempts to frame a sentence, and fails. 'You are . . . you . . . are—'

'What am I, Owen?' She grabs his hand and holds it in hers.

'You are a lovely woman and one day you're bound to meet a man, marry, have children. It'll work out for you, I'm sure. Have a little patience, that's all.' She smiles broadly then, as if he has given her the correct answer in a competition, as if he has won the prize. 'You are such a gentleman!' she exclaims, clapping her hands, and she pecks him on the cheek.

They finish their ride, return the bikes, and wander the old town. There are so many churches, almost too many to count. Naomi keeps suggesting that they push open the heavy doors of one and explore the gloomy interior. But Owen is reluctant. They are not dressed for church. His attire, jeans and a T-shirt, is marginally more suitable than hers. The burgundy skirt she is wearing sits so low on her hips that her belly button is exposed. Without a bra, her breasts are clearly outlined in her tight, powder-grey, sleeveless shirt. He warns her that they are not suitably apparelled each time she runs up a flight of entrance steps, or pauses outside the massive medieval doors.

'I really don't think we should go in,' he advises as he surveys the trickle of locals entering and leaving the basilicas. The women wear long-sleeved, calf-length dresses, their covered heads lowered respectfully; the men, long trousers and shirts buttoned to the collar.

'Don't be so silly,' she admonishes. 'Why shouldn't we?'

'Naomi, there'll be people praying in there.'

She shakes him off, then huffs out her breath impatiently, making the wisps of hair that overhang her brow stir. 'I want to pray too,' she insists obdurately. Before he can stop her, she has grasped the heavy, iron ring-handle of the door she faces. In an instant she has disappeared inside. He hesitates long enough to stand aside for a woman who is leaving. She is fingering a rosary and still mumbling her prayers. Their eyes meet for a second, and Owen has a stab of compunction on Naomi's behalf.

On entering the huge space, pleasantly cool after

240

the hot streets, the reverential hush is punctured by the smart click, click of Naomi's heels on the stone floor. He is stealing along a dark corridor to one side of the pews. She is tottering down the central aisle, momentarily illuminated in a shaft of indigo light angling through a stained-glass window. It is late afternoon. There are several people either sitting quietly, or kneeling, hands clasped, lips moving in fervent prayer. He pauses by a tray of tiny cream candles, and watches a man light one with a taper, push a coin in a box, genuflect, and make the sign of the cross. He recalls Catherine and the dampness of her tears on his shirt, and is thinking that he would like to light a candle for her, for her and Bria, when he hears Naomi exclaim:

'Oh, look at that!'

He sees the bent heads come up fast. Stepping quietly, he hurries forwards, reaching the altar rail in time to see and hear a man reprimand her. The irate gentleman taps her on the shoulder, places a finger to his lips signifying that she should be quiet, then growls something in Italian.

Naomi gives an apologetic shake of her head. 'So sorry, I forgot where I was.'

Hastily Owen steps in, nods at the scowling man, and pulls her to one side. He bows his head as he retakes his seat. 'We should go,' Owen urges, drawing her away. But for the second time that day she gives him the slip, jogging his hand off her arm with a jab of her elbow.

'I want you to look at this first,' she urges, moderating her tone, now back at the altar rail and leaning forward to peer at something.

He would far prefer to scurry away, but knowing if he does not relent she may create even more of a disturbance, reluctantly he sidles up to her. With a pointed finger she directs his gaze. He stares with macabre curiosity at a glass coffin lying on a low table a few feet from them. Inside is what looks like the embalmed remains of a body. The skin is brownish-yellow, hugging the ridges and dips of the skull. It is impossible to tell if the figure is male or female. It is swathed in a long, flowing robe, and wearing some sort of religious headdress, like an elaborate egg cosy. Its hands resemble the bony talons of some huge bird. They clutch at a gem-encrusted, silver cross. There are other ornaments scattered about the remains, rings and chains and bracelets, as well as a few bones. They glitter in the conical radiance which issues from an overhead spotlight. Looped through these are garlands of silk flowers, their vivid hues long since bled away to the dusty beiges of dead leaves. The thin lips, like buff piping, are parted to reveal a few grey teeth. The eyes are mercifully closed. But the dark nostrils are stretched so wide they create the illusion that they are flaring open, that the preserved corpse is inhaling the dead air it lies in. He senses Naomi studying him.

'Is it real, do you think?' she asks in an awed whisper, transfixed by the grotesque spectacle.

He shudders and nods. 'Mm, it looks like it.' He feels suddenly claustrophobic. 'It's probably the remains of a saint or a bishop. Come on, Naomi. Let's go.'

'It is weirdly beautiful, don't you think?' She scans his horrified face and smothers a giggle. 'Oh, Owen, why must you take everything so seriously?' Out of the corner of his eye, he sees the man in the front pew rising to his feet again, his complexion flushing fig purple. She must have noticed him too, because as he moves towards them she drops to her knees on a hassock at the foot of the altar rail. Dramatically she makes the sign of the cross and raises her hands high in prayer. Owen is speechless, as is the angry Italian, whose mouth drops, then snaps shut. Hands thrown up, he turns and leaves. Owen retreats into the shadows, his own prayer that she will be swift. Finally she rises, pivots slowly, and pauses theatrically for a moment on the altar steps. With astonishment he sees that her eyes are welling up. She gives that idiosyncratic blink of hers, and first one crystal drop, then another, falls on a ruled line down her cheek. As if some sort of miraculous conversion has taken place, she drifts dewy-eyed from the church. She genuflects one last time as he waits for her, the great door jammed open with his foot. Outside in the blazing sun once more, Owen strides ahead. He is annoyed and embarrassed. His companion has made an exhibition of herself in a place of worship, a church where decorum and respect, in deference to the locals, should be axiomatic. Naomi catches up with him. She clutches his hand. She embeds her bitten nails in his palm possessively. 'It was wonderful, wasn't it?' When he doesn't respond she continues. 'What's the matter? We've had such a lovely day. And you're upset.'

'No, I'm fine,' he lies.

They stop at a street café and sit outside. They order beers and sip them slowly in the quiet of the afternoon. On a nearby table a young couple bill and coo like doves. A girder of light slants under the café awning. He notices that Naomi's foundation has been pasted on too thickly. It has sunk into the map of her face, accentuating the fine lines and creases, like a brass rubbing. Her eyeshadow is that shimmering shade of turquoise that makes a harlot of a sweet-faced girl, and converts a mature woman into a fairground attraction. Her eyeliner has run and her mascara has made spiders' legs of her lashes. She wears that old-fashioned shade of lipstick, a vivid carmine. It has bled in the heat of the day, fixing the corners of her mouth in a droop, as if she has palsy. He can see the dark roots of her hair advancing on the bleached ends, giving up on the charade. And in a stale waft of nicotine he detects her faint but distinctive scent, the gamey odour of high meat. He looks across at the lovebirds.

'Owen?' A pause.

'Yes?'

'You are so kind, bringing me here, looking after me. Most men would have walked out. But you stayed.'

He shrugs. 'I couldn't leave you like that.'

'Because you're decent and good.' A second pause.

'Naomi, when we get back . . .' He trails off, his courage failing him. He wants to tell her that his mind is made up, that he is going to move on. A week or two in the market, no more, and he will be gone. Not back home, not permanently anyhow. He's heading for the open road, where he will have no identity, where he will be able to reinvent himself weekly. He has managed to save a modest amount, sufficient to set him on his way. And when that runs out he will work his passage. 'Naomi, the thing is that . . . that when we get back . . .' His stammering speech sticks again.

'Yes? What is it?' she prompts, amused.

'Oh nothing,' he demurs. 'God, it seems hotter here than it was in London, if that's possible.' The rim of her glass is smudged with lipstick. She rests her head on his shoulder. For some obscure reason, it strikes him suddenly that Catherine has the scent of summer rain. The couple opposite them kiss. His eyes linger on the lovers consumed in their embrace, as Naomi snuggles closer.

At nightfall he asks her what she was praying for. She switches off the lamp, and stands in a spire of moonlight, surveying him, where he lies supine on his bed. She has taken to sleeping in his T-shirts. This one, plain white, swamps her like a nightgown. She looks eerily alien and inhuman, the more so because she is smoking. The floorboards creak as she crosses to the window. It is open and the curtains are tied back. She kneels on the seat, her body corkscrewing back to him. With her every move the lighted tip of her cigarette draws electric orange lines that linger in the air, the way the trail of a sparkler does.

'Owen?'

'Yes?' He rolls on his side towards her.

As she sucks on her cigarette the tip flares to crimson, then dulls again. It seems an age till she tunnels out the smoke. 'Sometimes I think about Catherine, about Catherine and her baby, Bria. I imagine what she looks like, if she's a blonde or a brunette.'

'She's a redhead.' He speaks without thought, an automatic response, regretting his indiscretion immediately. The resulting stillness is voluble.

Then, her voice suddenly very small, 'How do you know?' He cannot see her expression. Subtly lit by the glow of the street-lamp below, her features are

245

in shadow. He curses himself inwardly for his doltishness.

'I met her,' he tells her lightly.

'When?' she asks in the same constrained tone. She takes another drag on her cigarette. The smoke is tinted sulphur by the mango-yellow radiance. 'When did you do that, Owen?'

He bites down on his bottom lip before replying. 'Oh, I don't know. A couple of weeks ago. Sean wanted me to collect something from his house in Hounslow. I was only there a minute or so.'

She turns away from him and gazes out of the window. 'You didn't mention it,' she says.

'Well, no . . . no. I didn't think it was important,' he explains haltingly.

'Was it only that once? Or have you seen her before?'

'Naomi, I said. Just that meeting. That's all. In fact, you can hardly call it a meeting. We can't have exchanged more than a couple of sentences.' He does not fully understand why, and yet it seems imperative that he lies about this, that he protects Catherine and Bria. Though from what, he cannot say.

'What is she like?'

'Ooh, honestly, I . . . I don't recall,' he hedges.

'You recalled the colour of her hair,' she counters crisply. She stretches out her arm and flicks the ash into the night.

He pulls the wrinkles from his linen sheet edgily. 'Only because it was such an unusual colour.'

'Is she pretty?'

'Naomi, what is this? I went and fetched a package for Sean. I knocked on the door. She opened it, gave me what I'd come for, and I left.'

'You didn't go in?' She circles her head, and massages the back of her neck.

A second's hesitation and then he answers. 'No, of course not. Why would I?'

'She didn't ask you in?'

He sighs and sits up in bed, his head banging on the headboard. 'No!' There is an impatience in his tone, disguising his guilt.

'Is she pretty?' she repeats.

'I don't know what to say. She was . . . ordinary,' he replies, thinking that she was the antithesis to this.

'Ordinary but with red hair,' comes Naomi's instant rejoinder. He can hear her breathing the smoke in, pushing it out. It wafts back into the room, tainting the mountain air.

'Look, it's the only thing I registered about her.'

'Did you see the baby?'

He is instantly alert. 'No, why should I have?'

As she swivels back to him she spins her still-lit cigarette out of the window.

'I don't think that's a good idea.' He is up and beside her in a trice. 'Forest fires. You don't want to be responsible for starting one of those.' Glancing down, a broken whisker of smoke betrays its location on the stone patio to Owen. 'I'll go and get it.' Her hand latches onto his arm, preventing him.

'Why should she get to keep her baby?' she says coldly. 'Why should she have it all?' She pulls him down until he is perched on the seat next to her, her eyes finding his. Hers seem to smoulder with animosity, he thinks.

'Oh, Naomi, you know why.'

'Why?' she demands, unappeased.

247

'Because . . . because she is Sean's wife.' Her hands grip his upper arms so tightly that it hurts. She cranes her neck. Her rasping voice on his ear feels warped and covetous.

'In the church, Owen, I prayed for my baby, for my dead baby, that God would stop the crying in my head. And I prayed for Sarah, for you and Sarah, your poor drowned sister.' Her lipstick tongue outlines her open mouth. Owen tenses. If he could he would snatch back his tragedy. Too late, he realizes that it is not safe in her hands.

'You must give yourself time to grieve,' he says stiltedly.

She redirects her focus to the mirrored lake. 'I wonder if that old legend is true? What sort of a woman could shut herself up in her cottage while they flooded the valley? Think of it, Owen, sitting there and watching the level of the water steadily rising. Seeing your things floating on it, sinking in it, and knowing that very soon you were going to join them. It must have been horrible.'

'Let's not talk about it.' There is a quaver in Owen's voice. When next he speaks his cadence is consciously emphatic to rid himself of it. 'I'm shattered, Naomi. It must be all the fresh air.' He pulls away from her giving a stage yawn, grabs his jeans from a chair, and yanks them on over his boxer shorts. 'I'll dash down and check that your cigarette has gone out. It would be mad to run the risk of a fire.'

*   *   *

It is not until the middle of the week that they explore the village, ambling their way up the

248

intersecting paths. They stop by a tap, where icy mountain water runs continuously into a stone trough. Naomi makes a bowl of her hands and bends over to drink. The air screams with heat, and Owen's throat feels seared to ashes. The sight of her lapping fills him with an acute thirst. As he leans in, she springs back and throws the palmed water into his face. Soon they are shaking with laughter, gulping and splashing all at once. He swallows and splutters, exquisitely aware of the freezing finger sliding down his throat, prodding at his belly. By the time they have slaked their thirst, the legs of his jeans are damp, his T-shirt has a soaked bib, and his arms and face are freckled with round droplets. Her clothes are saturated too, the calico cotton of her drawstring blouse clinging to her body. She drops her head and shakes it, sending spray flying, like a dog drying its coat after a swim.

They meander higher and higher up the incline. In one of the small fenced gardens an Alsatian barks furiously at them. A short plump woman is taking down washing, a baby tied in a sling at her back. Owen greets her but she snubs him. A little further on and they pass a wizened man sitting on his doorstep, smoking. He raises the cigarette to his lips with shaking leathery fingers, sucking on it, then coughing, before sucking again. He touches the rim of his cap to them as they walk by.

After a while they come to a tall, rusty, wrought-iron gate. It squeals in protest when they push it open. They step into the tiny square cemetery. It is no more than a patch of wind-crushed grass and a few crosses, leaning tipsily. Naomi investigates a row of family tombs, like a road of exclusive holiday homes, bordering one low stone wall. As with everything else in the village, he has realized that this graveyard overlooks the reservoir. He decides that there can be few more isolated places for the dead to rest than up here, with only the snow-peaked giants for company.

Night is drawing in now, a grey rag rug unrolling over the peaks and barrelling towards them. Owen can hear the baying of the wind, feel the scissor-snap of its jaws through his damp clothes. Anselmo, Teodora's husband, hobbles out of the past. He pictures him hunching over to gather up fallen branches, stowing them in the basket strapped to his back, unaware at first that the mountain leviathans are stirring, raining their icy gales over him. Bent on his task, to start with he is not awake to the worsening weather, the drain of light, the blast knifing into him, the snow with its sand bite on his face, the frozen grains clinging tenaciously to his rough, woollen cloak.

Suddenly realizing the danger he is in, Anselmo starts to hurry down the slopes. But he is not a young man and the frozen ground has become lethal. His heart chatters in his chest. Each painful inhalation scrapes the scant warmth from him. His muscles lock with the effort of the descent. He slips, his load pulling him off balance. He skids down a wall of rock shellacked with ice, twisting to try to brake his descent. He lands badly on a heap of snaggle-toothed stones, and feels the matchstick snap of one leg under him. In that same second he knows, he knows he will die out here, alone in this desolate landscape, his body packed with snow. Owen envisages that death, the long hours surrendering inch after inch of his numb flesh, his slack-necked, tortoise face filmed with agony.

250

Then Anselmo fades to be replaced by another, his wife, Teodora, sitting cosy by her fireside. The blusher of peppery flames dapples her full cheeks. She is combing her streaming hair, and it gleams like black marble in the flickering light. The shrewish wind screams and nags at her window. She pauses, lifts her head and gazes through the glass pane at the maelstrom outside. She thinks of her decrepit husband now, of his sagging muscles and rumpled flesh, of the unmade bed of his face, of his greying gums and his missing teeth, of his rough whiskers and matted beard, of the wheeze of his dusty, stale breath, of how she sets like plaster as he pokes himself between her hot thighs. When next she casts her eyes deep into the hollow heart of the fire, she is smiling.

'I'm freezing. Let's go, Naomi,' he says in a rush.

But she clambers over the low wall on the far side of the cemetery, sitting herself down in the scrub. 'Come on, Owen. The view over the lake is spectacular. You must look,' she beckons with a scoop of her arm. He is crippled with fright, limping to sit beside her. She can feel the quake of him as the lake leers up at them.

'It's funny to think of the village under the water,' she says. 'When I walked around it with Lorenzo he showed me shrines . . . evenly spaced, with photographs of all the people who have drowned there. Those faces peering out at you from the grave . . .' She breaks off and looks closely at him. 'You really are very scared,' she ponders. 'Can you not swim at all?' He shakes his head. She snakes an arm across his tensed shoulders.

That night there is a storm. It begins with distant jags of lightning slicing at the black peaks. Each

251

blink torches bolsters of cloud as they bowl towards them. Naomi sits smoking on the window seat in the darkness, impatient for it to arrive. They hear the yawl of the wind plunge to a chesty roar. Then come the cracks of thunder that give a terrier tug to the earth. Curtains of pewter-grey rain sweep in. The trees grow unruly, their dripping branches scourges. Somewhere a bell jangles as the wind flings it. Each lurid flutter sets the lake alight. Twice Owen tells Naomi to close the windows. But she protests, not wanting to miss a single moment of it. He traces the tattered illumination of her face. She is rapt. Only when the rain has saturated the seat cushion, does she reluctantly turn her back on it.

Their last day. The weather is glorious. The sun polishes everything to a citrus gleam. The sky is a cloudless blue. From the moment she rises, Naomi seems to be in a state of heightened excitement, as if it is her birthday and a party is to be held in her honour. Determined to make the most of it, they drive into the mountains and chance upon a deserted village. Here lizards bask on the sun-kissed rocks, and the song of the cicadas pulses in the shimmering heat. They journey on to a town where the streets are hung with bright banners and coloured lanterns. The church square is filled with dancers and the sultry air swells with music. The women, in flower-print bodices adorned with spider-web collars, trill their tongues. They lift their full skirts to show their flounced petticoats, and twirl and skip and jump. Men in white stockings and shirts and black pantaloons tip their hats and hook their thumbs in their waistcoat pockets. Sure footed, they guide and stamp, lift, catch and spin their breathless partners. A huge man with a handlebar moustache trips his fingers lightly over the buttons of an accordion, deft as a lace-maker juggling her bobbins. And all the while, slick-haired guitarists pluck their strings, roll their lovesick eyes, and croon the songs of their forefathers.

Then they eat pizza slices and drink ice-cold Asti Spumante, sitting on the edge of a village fountain. About them the pigeons splash clumsily in the water, and from their swelling, feather-boa necks come a whole score of deep-throated coos. In the late afternoon they return to Vagli Sotto and begin packing their bags. Relief is Owen's overriding emotion. The week is over. Tomorrow they are leaving the sleepy town of Vagli Sotto, and the lake hemmed in by the towering wall of the reservoir. Soon, the ghostly clink-clink of the bells tied at the necks of the few wandering goats, the distant muted clucking of chickens, the mewling of the wind that comes and goes without warning, and the resonant clanging of the church bells calling the faithful to their prayers, will be merely a memory. He will walk out on this second life as he did his first—a life that promised escape, but has delivered yet another disturbing slant on reality. Sean's weakness for gambling, his drinking, his infidelity, his descent into the underworld of the city, Naomi's abortion, her attempt at self-harm, her disturbing sleep-walking, even Catherine's misery, all these he will leave far behind. Of course he is concerned for Catherine, for Bria. But she is not his wife and Bria is not his baby. Even if he wanted to, there is nothing he can do to alter their plight.

They choose to dine on this, their last night in Tuscany, in the nearby town of Castelnuovo. Owen's mood is upbeat, buoyant. They share a bottle of wine with their meal. On their way back, Naomi suggests that they pull in at the lakeside bar, and have a last drink to mark the end of their Italian interlude. Owen, light headed and feeling invincible, assents. They share another bottle, a Montepulciano, an expensive red wine, and chase it with liqueur glasses of grappa. By then the world, though a trifle unsteady on its axis, has rearranged itself into a benign paradise. It has become a utopia where little girls are sitting on the sand, waiting with ear-to-ear smiles when their brothers round the stripy windbreak that conceals them. Here, mothers have hearts roomy enough to forgive and forget. Here, if their daughters drown, their sons are their salvation.

'Let's walk back,' Naomi suggests. 'We can leave the car and collect it in the morning.' And when he hesitates she insists, telling him that in any case he is drunk and cannot drive. 'Let's take the lakeside path,' she adds. 'It is so beautiful bathed in moonlight.' And this other Owen finds himself agreeing. He has a misty recollection of a double with aquaphobia who could not be prevailed upon to go down to the water's edge for anything. But tonight this is his shadow. And he can think of nothing he would prefer than visiting a picturesque lake romantically lit. They link arms as they weave down the track that intersects with the path.

The moon is so bright that it makes its own silver day. The trees stand out in black relief against this pale wash. The silhouette of Vagli Sotto village rises up before them, lights twinkling, like a children's illustration. To their left the concrete bank shelves steeply down to the water. Close up, through his alcoholic haze, the lake looks deceptively still. It really is a mirror, Owen muses, a solid silver plate inscribed with mountains, stars and moon, the bridge across it seemingly a near circle. The air is spiked with the scent of water, soft and pure, and pine sap, and summer grasses. He floats along, fire in his veins, his feet not seeming to connect with the ground. For a time they do not speak. The shrines to the drowned that they pass have ceased to be sober reminders of the dangers of deep water. Intermittently they sprout like gleaming stalks. The plastic flowers twined about them are silver gilt. The photographs in their cellophane sleeves are no more than a blur to Owen. Both, as if by mutual consent, now slow to a halt.

'I've been here all this while but I haven't swum,' Naomi says wonderingly, tugging on Owen's arm. 'I want to wash myself in the water. Unzip me,' she commands. She turns her back on him.

He traces a finger up her spine, along the teeth of her dress zip. Her hair has lengthened considerably, so that he has to lift it up to find the metal tab. Her ivory flesh reveals itself as he pulls. He stands back swaying slightly on his feet as she steps out of it. Her hands reach behind her back and she unhooks her bra, wriggles off her pants and slips off her sandals.

She turns to face him, smiling, holding her hands out to him. 'Swim with me, Owen,' she pleads. There is a buzz in his head, a bustle confusing him, making him forget that he cannot swim, that swimming to him is drowning. He bends to pull off his shoes, to peel off his shirt and trousers. *You cannot swim, you cannot swim, you cannot swim,* comes the mantra in his head. Suddenly uncertain, he shakes his head and backs a pace. She laughs. Then she is stepping like a skier down the concrete incline. 'What are you afraid of?' she taunts, toeing the water. A spray of pearls scatter and melt back into the mirror. She stretches up her arms and shuts her eyes.

'Naomi, be careful!' he cries, as if remembering something, someone. But her knees are bent and the next moment she is arcing through the air, and disappearing like a flying fish into the water. The explosive splash, the concentric ripples, all still in seconds. His eyes rove the mirror seeking the spot where the water will split into jagged shards, and she will emerge. But it remains perfectly smooth, polished, nothing stirring beneath its surface. He begins counting the seconds in his head, trying to gauge how long she can safely hold her breath. He reaches twenty with no sign of her. He grips the sandpaper bank with the soles of his feet, and pigeon walks down to the water's edge. He side steps back and forth, shading his eyes from the dazzling moon, straining them in the shining, unsure what to do. It is fifty seconds, when, far out in the lake, she rockets up.

'Naomi! Naomi, are you okay? I thought something had happened.' She is swimming towards him, moving sleek as a shark through the black and silver fluid. He watches her approach with envy, wishing it was him, that he could glide over the ghost village and not be paralysed with terror.

'Owen, it's fantastic. Come on in,' she beckons, waving a hand.

'I can't swim,' he tells her. Then, 'I can't swim,' he tells himself.

'Put your arms around my neck and we'll ride over the lake,' she pleads. 'You have nothing to be scared of. I'll look after you.' She is by the bank now, making grabs for his feet.

'No, no, I'm not ready,' he pulls back.

'What's the matter, Owen? Don't you trust me?' she asks. She keeps slipping under the mirror, her head popping up again.

'It's not that. I just can't.' He sits down and draws his knees up to his chest. 'I'll watch you swim. I'll enjoy that.' She sculls the water for a bit so that she appears to be pinned in position. 'I can't change your mind?' He shakes his head and she shrugs. Then she is off playing like a dolphin, rolling and flipping and kicking. He knows that if he was sober he could not be doing this, that seeing her water tricks would bring his krakens lumbering to the surface. Only the numbness makes it possible.

'You'll have to help me to get out,' she calls ten minutes later. 'It's too steep.' He gets up, goes forward, bends from the waist and offers her his hand. She grasps it and he heaves her up. She clasps him, her body cold and sleek and shaking with exhilarated laughter. 'It was so good, so very good!' she breathes, this Teodora, who has swum up from the ghost village to find her lover. 'You should have joined me. I'd have kept you safe. Because I am the lady of the lake, the lady of the lake.' Her voice is husky, musical, the siren's song. He surrenders to its unbearable harmonies. And then they are kissing and he can taste mountain water in her mouth, trickling down her neck, varnishing her breasts. They stagger back, still entwined, up the bank and to a patch of grass. She wraps her dripping thighs about him, and as he sinks into her, gasping for air, his is the surprise of the drowning man.

He wakes with a jolt. His head is thumping. The interior of his mouth feels like flour. The previous day unrolls before his sore eyes. The abandoned

257

village. The country dancers. Sitting by the fountain. The meal in Castelnuovo. The lakeside bar. Naomi swimming. And then . . . Owen swipes a hand over his mouth as if trying to rid himself of a bad taste in it. He turns his head on the pillow to see Naomi sitting up, staring back down at him. She has pushed the twin beds together.

'Good morning,' she says. She bends and kisses the crown of his head. 'Did you sleep well?'

'Mm . . . like . . . a rock,' he stutters.

'Hung over?'

'Just a bit,' he winces.

'We've a long day ahead.' She has not taken off last night's make-up. The foundation is blotchy, the mascara has clumped, and her breath is sour. Her hair is a mess. She looks old, overnight old, her paint peeling.

He is full of remorse and regret. He was drunk. He thinks about the lake and his stomach heaves. Then he thinks about the sex and he is filled with revulsion and self-loathing, and a dreadful sense of the irrevocable. 'I'll make some coffee. Why don't you take a shower, get dress—'

'We could shower together,' she interrupts him with a lascivious giggle.

'No,' he says too vehemently. Christ, how is he going to tell her that it was a mistake, that it should never have happened? Her brow creases in displeasure. 'I mean, we've too much to do.' He is about to leap out of bed when he realizes he is stark naked under the sheet. Perhaps it was naive to assume that if he accompanied Naomi to Italy their relationship would stay platonic. He'd been a fool. He should have kept his wits about him, instead of letting himself get roaring drunk. But after all, she

258

was broken and grieving. He knew that she needed friendship, support, though surely not sex?

'Okay. Plenty of time,' she smiles suggestively, bouncing out of bed and running to the shower.

They thank their landlord and bid farewell to Lorenzo, promising to remember him to his brother, Enrico. Owen's relief at their departure is apparently shared by the handful of villagers who come to see them off, their expressions collectively surly. With every mile he puts between him and the lake with its drowned village full of ghosts, the sinister atmosphere seems to dissipate. They drive with the top down. And as the Spitfire picks up speed, zig-zagging the mountain roads, the air gusts into their flushed faces, cooling them. By the time they pull into a roadside café for lunch, he is less downhearted. It still remains for him to broach the subject of last night's unwise liaison. But he sees no reason why it should be such a trial to explain away, to extricate himself from what was, after all, a brief drunken episode. In fact, describing it as an episode at all is really according it a gravitas it does not merit. Truly, if his somewhat fragmented memory serves him right, the entire encounter was more like a few camera frames flashing by unnoticed.

He likes Naomi, and he has to confess, thought her attractive initially. But it was more curiosity than lust. He sees that now. Her maturity and experience, her blatant sexuality, her confidence, her tactility, even her mystifying past, these are all magnets that would naturally attract a young man. But in hindsight, they have nothing whatsoever in common. The tracks of their diverse lives have crossed one another, that is all. And now they will continue their journeys separately. Apart from anything else, there is the discrepancy in their ages. He concedes that this is not an insurmountable obstacle if love is at stake. But it isn't. And, he tells himself, as they find a table and sit down to drink their coffees and eat their sandwiches, she probably sees it in much the same light. A preposterous incident. High spirits. A holiday fling under cover of darkness. And that lethal grappa leading them on. They both got carried away, dug in their spurs and the moment galloped off with them. But now that they are heading back home it is time to rein in and take stock. It seems sensible, to Owen, to take the initiative and dispel any misunderstandings quickly, before they become ingrained. Besides, it would be prudent to have their tête-à-tête before they overnight in a hotel, to avoid any awkward embarrassment.

'Naomi?'

'Yes?'

'I'm going to quit the market.' He waits to see how she takes his announcement. She sips her coffee, blows the steam off the cup, and appraises him with her queer eyes. 'I've stayed long enough. It wasn't intended to be permanent. Just a summer job. Filling in.' He sounds as if he is making excuses.

She runs an index finger back and forth along her neck chain, as if easing a tight collar, then stops abruptly. 'I've been thinking the same. Time to move on. A fresh start. A new beginning.'

He smiles over at her. Showered, in fresh clothes, with her make-up newly applied, she looks altogether more self-assured. He wonders if he has been worrying unduly. The café is busy. Animated conversations conducted in Italian, co-ordinated with frenzied gesticulations, fly from customer to customer, the clatter of trays, the hiss of steam, the

260

ring of a till, all reach him like surround-sound. 'That's a great idea. A change will do you good,' he says approvingly. But he is not thinking of her benefit. It is Catherine and Bria who interrupt the train of his thoughts. His hair has grown too, bleached to wheat-gold by the sun. He rakes his flop of fringe off his face. His skin glows with wind burn. What she asks next brings him back with a jolt.

'Where shall we go, Owen?'

Despite not having started on his sandwich, he wipes his mouth with a paper serviette as fastidiously as if it is covered with grease. 'We?' he queries hesitantly.

'You and me.' She is pulling at the chain again and he can see where it is cutting into the base of her neck, the indented lines pinking.

'Naomi, I'm going by myself,' he corrects her. She tilts her head, a childlike confusion in her eyes. 'What happened last night, by the lake . . . well, it shouldn't have. We were both a bit drunk. If we're honest with ourselves and . . . and each other, it meant . . . nothing.' He rubs at his brow with the flat of his hand. The temperature between them has suddenly dropped. He feels it penetrate like an icy blast.

'Nothing?' she echoes, staring at him, her face still as a millpond.

'God no, Naomi, that came out all wrong. It was . . . nice, of course. Just not . . . not appropriate.' He rests his elbows on the table and clasps his hands in an effort to still them. She tugs on the chain as though it is strangling her, and it snaps and drops, landing among the chewed crusts on her plate. 'Oh! It's broken. I'm sorry.' Reflexively he reaches for it,

261

to see if he can fix it. But she shields it with her hands, stopping him, then snatches it up herself. 'Maybe I can mend it.'

'It's not worthwhile. It's only cheap gilt,' she says acerbically. 'Costume jewellery. Throw-away.'

He sighs with regret. 'I'm not handling this terribly well, am I?' Her shrunken eyes give him his answer. 'I don't want to hurt you, especially after you've been through so much. But believe me, we're not suited to one another. You've had horrible luck. Sean, and the pregnancy. And really I do think you should give yourself a chance with someone else, but—'

'But just not you,' she finishes for him.

'Naomi, you can't think it would ever work out with us. For starters, I'm so much younger than you.' Her eyes blaze and he closes his own. With every sentence he is making more of a hash of this. When he reopens them it is with hand-picked words at the forefront of his mind. 'What I'm trying to say is that I'm fond of you. I care what happens to you, but not like that. If I gave the wrong impression, if I misled you, then I promise it wasn't intentional.'

A few links of the gilt chain dangle from her clenched boxer's fists. 'I thought you were different,' she says, reassessing him frankly with those preternatural orbs. He squirms under her microscopic inspection. The café doors swing open and a group of teenage girls in bright dresses come chattering in, and make their way towards the self-service queue. Glancing up at them, he wishes that their high spirits were his, that there was nothing more taxing for him to do today than select a lunch. He pushes away his plate, and drains his now lukewarm coffee. 'I've been stupid. I should have

262

understood how susceptible you are at the moment. All I can say is that I am so sorry. Please, don't let this spoil our friendship.'

She tosses the chain on the table. 'Is there someone else? A girlfriend?' she asks with a lift of her brows.

'No, no! Look, trust me, I'm a mess. I need time to sort myself out.'

'Are you lying to me, Owen?'

'No. I'd never do that.' He has a sudden prick of conscience, as he recalls reporting to her that he did not go into Sean's house, that he did not see the baby, Bria. With shaky hands she rifles in her bag for her cigarettes and matches. She knocks the packet a couple of times on the side of the table, her teeth closing around the tallest, pulling it out. On her third attempt to light it, he takes the matches from her, strikes one and holds the steady flame to the trembling tip. She inhales, breathes out the smoke, then waves it away.

'I can wait for you,' she begs.

He shakes his head. 'Please, don't make this any more difficult than it already is. I'm not ready for a relationship,' he says bluntly, accepting that there is no kind way to reject her. What he does not add is that he is not ready for a relationship with her, that he never will be.

'When we get back I shall tell Sean I'm going, give him . . . and you, a few weeks to sort things out. And then I'm leaving.' She opens her mouth to speak but he pre-empts her. 'Nothing will change my mind, Naomi.' For a few minutes they sit facing each other. 'And if you take my advice,' he continues, his tone suddenly inexplicably tender, 'you will move on too. Because . . . because you deserve better than this.'

He has leant forward, addressing her, as the cigarette in her hand burns down. But he is dwelling on the heaviness of Catherine's head cushioned against his beating heart.

17

Monday, 9 August

2 a.m. In Owen's dream he is standing on the empty beach squinting at the sparkling sea. Beside him on the sand is Sarah's coffin. It is small and neat and white as alabaster. The pink petals of the rosebuds it is wreathed in are crimpling and browning in the scalding temperatures. He looks down and traces the letters of her name engraved on the brass plaque. 'S . . . A . . . R . . .' But the sunlight bounces onto it, dazzling him, so that he does not get any further. When he turns back to the water he sees what looks like a porpoise swimming towards him. It ploughs a creamy furrow as it nears, and he realizes that it is not a fish after all, but a mermaid. She has long wavy black hair, and a tail covered in shiny scales. She swims into the shallows, and he sees her hair moving like the purple tentacles of a jellyfish under the crystal water. Then she fountains up, her tail splitting into legs, into gleaming tin legs, her arms reaching for him.

'I am the lady of the lake,' she calls. 'I am your lady of the lake.' Her eyes are shut tight but now they twitch open, one after the other. First blue, then brown. As her slimy wet body envelops him, she coos into his ear, 'Please stop crying, please

264

stop. I have to make you stop.'

And Owen is awake, sitting up in bed, soaked in sweat, his ears pricked. He can hear a voice rasping in the still dark flat. His heart feels as if it is in his mouth, so that it is hard to breathe. He gets up, turns on his bedside light and pulls on his jeans. He tells himself that it is only Naomi sleep-walking again, that all he has to do is guide her, meek as a lamb, back to bed. He has done it before many times. But if this is the case, then why is he so petrified? Why does the primeval terror that has stalked every age of man have him in its clutches? Terror of the unknown, of monsters too ghastly to contemplate, of Merfolk with lips chiselled from ice and bottomless oceans squeezing the air from your lungs, of the blackest of black interminable nights. He steps into the corridor, cocks his head, listens. The drizzling taps wheeze like heavy smokers. He knows this game of hide-and-seek, knows where she hides and where he must seek for her. She is scrunched up in the cramped space between the settee and the wall. Always the same spot, naked, digging at the plaster. He pushes aside the beads carefully, stills the swinging strands with his hands. For a moment he waits. Trapeziums of moonlight fall through the open windows onto the floor, illuminating a settee armrest, the rug, a corner of the coffee table. The fridge in the galley kitchen hums a single note. There is the faint aroma of burnt toast on the air. She is clawing the wall, the sound frantic, like a trapped animal trying to dig its way out.

'Stop the baby crying. Please, stop the baby crying. It makes my head hurt so. Make it be quiet, Miss Elstob. Make it shush. Baby's hot. Poor baby. Baby

265

can't sleep, she's hot. Poor, poor baby. I shan't scream. I shan't. I'll keep the scream in my head, splitting in my head.' Her voice is light and childlike.

Two of her nails are bleeding a little, he sees, when he takes her back to bed. And the name 'Mara', carved into the wall, is no longer indistinct, for now the plaster is stained with blood. In the morning she tells him that she needs another week before she will be ready to come back to the market. He looks in on her before he sets off for work, and is pleased to see that she is sleeping peacefully. As he steps onto the street the heat seems to crackle up from the pavement.

London has become a coastal resort, but without the sea. Beachwear is *de rigueur*. Calamine lotion vies with suntan oil for record sales. Bodies of every shape and size litter the yellowed grass of parched parks, enjoying the latest craze, sunbathing. Sunburn and prickly heat are the most common complaints in the chemists. Ice cream and cold drink vendors in white coats wield more power than men in suits. Barbecues have replaced meat and two veg for the evening meal. Fractious residents pull their mattresses onto patios and balconies, and sleep under the stars like desert kings. The government is advising people to put bricks in their toilet cisterns, to share baths, to use the leftover water on their dying gardens. The traffic snake's true colours are unrecognizable, dulled down by layers of choking dust. Biblical plagues of ladybirds and aphids have been unleashed. And in the market the most popular T-shirt has the slogan, 'Save Water, Bath With A Friend' printed on it.

On his way into the market, Owen thanks Enrico for arranging their stay in his father's cottage, and

266

tells him what a lovely week they had there. For the duration of their exchange, Enrico struts like a cockerel, delighted at the compliments, unaware of the dark ramblings harassing Owen's mind. While he prattles, Owen relives their last night and recalls the part he had to play in the unfortunate turn of events. He makes his excuses, not wanting to be reminded about what has passed between him and Naomi. 'We'll talk more later. I can see Sean getting impatient, so I'd best go.'

'I'm disappointed,' Sean tells Owen, when he is given the news that he is quitting the market. 'I'll be sorry to lose you. But I can see you've made up your mind.'

'Naomi should be back next week. At least she says that's what she intends,' Owen says, trying to muster up some enthusiasm for arranging fans of decorative hair slides on the mirrored counter. 'I'll try to hang on till then. I don't want to leave you short-handed.'

'That's good of you.'

Owen is surprised by how well Sean is taking it. He was worried that after their desertion to Tuscany, giving his notice would earn him a prolonged tongue-lashing. But he seems unperturbed, preoccupied, so that Owen ponders if he has really absorbed the information.

'And how is the lovely Naomi, after her Italian retreat?' Sean inquires, drawing the blade of a penknife down the taped seal of a cardboard box.

'She's good,' Owen lies. He is becoming adept at lying. 'She loved Italy, but I think she's glad to be back.'

He nods, snapping shut his penknife. 'That's great. I told you she'd get over it. Sunglasses for the

267

kids. What do you think?' he says desultorily, leaping seamlessly from the topic of abortion to novelty goods. He holds up a miniature pair with Minnie Mouse pirouetting in a spotted frock around the rims.

'Fantastic! The kids'll love 'em.'

'Exactly what I thought,' Sean tells him, pleased. For the next couple of hours they are both occupied with the brisk morning trade. But by lunchtime things have quietened down again, the nigh-on-torturous heat putting punters off. They both feel too hot and sticky to eat, but Owen forays above ground to buy iced lollies and cans of Coke.

'Orange or lime?' he offers on his return.

'Orange,' Sean grins. 'I could do with the vitamin C.' He sits on the stool, Owen leans back on the counter, and like schoolboys they give their sole attention to licking and sucking the sugary ices. Owen becomes aware that he is sucking in time to the beat of disco music. When he is down to the stick, Sean, who made short work of his, begins talking.

'You know, if you could do me a last favour before you take off, I'd be eternally in your debt.'

'Like what?' Owen rejoins easily.

'Oh, not much, not at all. It's only that I need to be away till Thursday. I know it's asking a lot, without Naomi giving you a hand, but d'you think you could cope for a few days alone?' The orange pencil of a moustache fringes his upper lip.

Owen sucks his cold teeth before replying. 'I don't see why not.' He shrugs. 'If it's only a couple of days I can manage.'

'Thanks.' Sean's eyes are over-bright, as if he has not slept and is forcing himself to stay alert.

'Where are you off to?'

'Oh, nowhere interesting. Not off to Italy on my hols, that's for sure.' He picks his Coke up off the counter, and tugs the ring-pull. A hiss and coffee-brown froth bubbles out. He raises it to his lips, and Owen can see the serpentine movement of his throat as he drinks. 'Thirsty weather, eh?' he says when he has almost drained the can.

'Mm . . . Is there some place I can contact you if need be?' Owen pushes.

'I'm on the move, you know. Here and there. But like I said, I'll be back on Thursday.' Owen nods. 'My luck's changing. I can feel it. The Midas touch.' He takes a last swallow, then looks far off, far beyond the concrete walls of the market. 'I don't plan to stay here much longer myself. It was only ever a stopgap. One day soon I'm going to have that picture-perfect house for Catherine, with a paddock for Bria to keep a pony in. You wait and see.'

18

Hounslow, 3 a.m. The open windows bring no relief from the stultifying heat. Catherine, in a sleeveless nightdress, shuffles up and down, up and down, like a zombie. Bria fights in her arms, her thin wail filling her ears. The baby is too hot, too hot to rest. The bedside lamp casts overlapping ellipses of light and shadow on the walls. The mesh-patterned wallpaper makes a prison of the room.

'Sh . . . sh . . . shush,' she soothes, circling her fingers gently, massaging her baby's back. 'I know it's hot. I'm sorry. Shush now, shush.'

But in response to her mother's attempts to comfort her, Bria's bleats grow louder, her head rolling fretfully against her shoulders. Catherine has tried her with the bottle but she pushed the teat out of her mouth, coughing the milk down her chin. After each cry she gives a tiny shocked shudder as she gasps in a breath. Her cheeks are rosy, and her brow, when she lays a hand on it, is burning. Tears have started to spill unbidden down Catherine's own cheeks. She is collapsing, one supporting pillar after another giving way within her. 'I don't know what to do,' she sniffles over Bria's jerking head. 'I don't know what to do. I don't know what to do.' Her voice croaks with weariness.

She took her daughter to the doctor yesterday, and last week—twice. She is such a regular there now that the receptionist makes no effort to book her in with the same doctor. There are four at the practice and she has seen all of them. They must be part of a conspiracy because, after a thorough examination of Bria, they each tell her the same thing, that she has a lovely healthy baby.

'How are you feeling lately, Mrs Madigan?' Doctor Newell asked her yesterday. He leant forward and peered intently into her tired eyes. He was the oldest of the general practitioners and didn't make her feel rushed the way the others did. There were photographs in gilded wooden frames arranged on his desk. She had seen them before and had started memorizing details in them. A silver filigree brooch. A rose bush. A floral sunhat. Pearl earrings. A suede jacket. A royal-blue dress. There was a smiling middle-aged woman sitting on a garden chair, a serious young man standing erect in a black graduation gown, clutching a scroll, and the same man a bit older in a family portrait taken in a studio with, presumably, his wife and baby. So, Catherine deduced, Doctor Newell was a grandfather, as well as a father. And they all looked perfect. A perfect family, with perfect children, who grew up and married perfect partners, and had perfect babies. They were the sort of family featured on cereal boxes and in television advertisements.

'Mrs Madigan? I said, how are you feeling?'

'I'm fine. It's the baby I've come about,' she said in a monotone. In her arms an angelic Bria slept soundly. At every appointment, as Catherine stepped into the surgery, her daughter's rigid body relaxed against her, the sea-coloured eyes glazed over, the minute eyelids drooped, and the rosebud mouth stretched in a contented yawn. Seconds later and she was fast asleep, as if she knew here she was safe from her mother's inept care. She frequently had to be woken up to be examined, making Catherine feel an awful fraud.

'You know, babies are very clever at picking up on their mother's distress,' Doctor Newell told her, a kindly twinkle in his dark-brown eyes. He rubbed his hands together and gave her a reassuring fatherly smile. 'If you're unhappy, they're unhappy.' He waited a moment, inviting her confidence. She focused on the ring he wore on his little finger, a gold setting and an agate, was it? A pearly grey swirl in a blue stone, as if there was a spirit trapped inside, a girl sealed under the ice. She took a speedy mental inventory of the monumental causes of her malaise. A mother who left no room for her, a catastrophic marriage to a man she did not love, and an unplanned baby who meant the only exit was effectively blocked off. 'Happy mothers make happy

271

babies, Mrs Madigan,' the doctor reinforced his message. He sang it out jovially like an advertising jingle, and in an instant she was jumping on the big bed with cousin Rosalyn, exchanging slogans from popular adverts. She had been so happy that day, the kind of happiness that is like proved dough, and keeps on swelling till you think you'll burst with it. Happy mothers make happy babies. The doctor's professional opinion was a reminder, if she needed any, that here was yet another of her failings. Her inability to put on a brave face was selfish. Her failure to replace her slough of despondency with stoic cheerfulness, for the sake of her child, earned her another black mark.

She had wanted to breast-feed Bria, despite her mother's insistence, delivered primly, that a bottle was infinitely more tidy and convenient. 'You were bottle fed, Catherine,' she pointed out succinctly when she came to visit her in the hospital. 'I wasn't going to have any of that messy carry-on. With the bottle you can be sure baby is getting everything she needs.' She was standing by the window re-applying her lipstick. She hadn't stopped fussing with her appearance once. Face powder, hair, jewellery, collar, belt, shoes. Adjust, pat, tuck, smooth, align. Anyone would think she was a model about to step onto the catwalk. Catherine wanted to scream at her to stop, to just stop, to come close and look, look at this beautiful baby she had made, at what a miracle she was, to call her by her name, Bria, instead of the androgynous *baby* she kept using.

Her mother's preference had been Jane or Elizabeth or Ann. Or for a boy, James or David or Timothy. Solid, sensible names, she said. When Catherine had whispered their choice of Bria for a girl and Carrick for a boy, her mother had looked askance. 'You don't want baby to be teased at school. Because that's what'll happen if you give it a silly name. You mark my words.'

'They're Irish names, Mother,' she had rejoined defensively, her lips quavering. 'Sean wanted an Irish name.' Her mother had raised one eyebrow and sniffed in disgust, whether at the mention of Sean or their chosen names, she didn't know.

In the maternity ward she watched Catherine's attempts at breast-feeding her granddaughter with an expression akin to horror. 'Quite honestly, I don't know why you're bothering with all that palaver.' She looked away from her daughter's exposed breast, a seed-pearl of milk oozing from the flushed, peaked nipple. 'A formula feed will ensure that baby gets all her vitamins.' She began taking apples, oranges and grapes out of a carrier bag and arranging them on the plate set on the bedside table, where a few evidentiary chocolate-bar wrappers lay scrunched up. 'A nourishing diet is essential to give baby a good start in life.'

'But she'll get everything she needs from me,' Catherine protested, eyes rabbit-pink from all the crying she had done since the birth. Sean had missed it, of course. He had promised to be there, in the delivery room, a modern father, but he was late. The only thing she could predict accurately in her husband was his unreliability. Later, he brought an oversized cerise bear, cheap and garish, and a box of dark chocolate Brazil nuts. She hated dark chocolate and Brazil nuts. The combination, so soon after the trial of labour and birth, made her want to be sick. He told her she was a great girl, altogether, and he held Bria and said that she was a great girl too. 'Pretty as a fairy princess,' he flattered. But she wasn't a fairy princess, she was a real baby who had to be fed and changed and loved and talked to, a baby who needed a father as well as a mother, a father with a steady income to support her. After that he went to the pub, to wet the baby's head, he said with a wink. Only the baby was here with her, not in a filthy smoky pub, where strangers bought him double brandies, and slapped him on the back, congratulating him on becoming a daddy.

She had painful mastitis. Her breasts had become pendulous appendages, throbbing and swollen. The nipple had cracked on her left breast, and a thread of blood had leaked from it. Various nurses made concerted efforts to get her milk flowing, pinching her sore nipples and ramming them in the eagerly rooting mouth, but to no avail. She was persevering but without success.

'Why must you be so stubborn about this?' her mother demanded tersely, as Bria alternately sucked and then wailed at the cruel deprivation she was suffering.

'It's something I want to do,' Catherine retorted, in the voice of the frequently thwarted child, whose shoes she had not long outgrown.

'You train baby much more easily on the bottle,' her mother had countered, as if that was the end of the matter, as if her daughter was a puppy who needed to be housebroken. It had not been a question of perseverance in the end, but of survival. Did she want baby to starve? And so she had given in, bought the tins of SMA powdered milk, filled up the sterilizer, submerged the bottle and teats, and hoped that a full belly would mean a contented baby.

But now, as she paces the floor watching the minute hand approaching 4 a.m., Bria still grizzling and sleepless, exhaustion making her feel faint, she knows it is not nearly that simple. Her daughter's needs are complex, so complex that she does not believe she will ever be clever enough to interpret them. Tonight, or perhaps it is more accurate to say this morning, it is the heat and the consequent nappy rash that is distressing her. In desperation she decides to give Bria a bath, a middle-of-the-night bath. She fills the yellow plastic baby bath with lukewarm water, hefts it onto the bathroom floor, undresses Bria and lifts her carefully into it. Her daughter reacts instantly, her face registering wide-eyed amazement. She ceases fretting and looks about her with interest. Afterwards they slumber for two hours straight, side by side in the double bed. At Bria's first cry Catherine wakes with a start, all the magic fled. She is so tired that her skin doesn't seem to fit, so tired that her head feels far too heavy to lift from the pillow, so tired that the sunlight streaming in at the window jangles on her eyes.

'The most important thing with baby is to have a strict routine.'

Her mother's words haunt her as she stumbles about, with absolutely no idea of what comes next. As she staggers downstairs the post falls on the mat. There is a letter postmarked 'New York', where Rosalyn now lives, that she doesn't open. 'Not now,' she whispers, putting it to one side. She knows it will be full of all the exciting things her cousin is doing. The remaining envelope she does open—a final demand for the electricity. The one for the gas is due imminently. She wonders how it will pan out, her and Bria in this falling-down house, with no hot water, no means of cooking, no fridge, no lights. Each day her world will get smaller. If they don't pay the rent, eventually the bailiffs will come and put them out. Then what? God forbid that they will have to move in with her parents.

Sitting at the kitchen table feeding Bria her bottle, she stares down at the unopened letter from her cousin. The accident on the ice—some days she wonders if it might have been better if she had died—not Rosalyn, though. She deserved to survive. She is one of the bright shining stars they stared up at through the skylight in Wood End. She has gone on to glory, made something of herself, is a gifted photographer. But for Catherine, her bleakest premonitions were realized that day as her frozen legs bicycled in the icy water and she travelled precisely nowhere. Rosalyn, her cousin, was worth the saving, she was not. That's what she saw when she glimpsed the hooded face of death on the far bank. Her cousin dying would destroy so many lives—her parents, her brother, her many friends, even the foundations of Catherine's own family would quake with grief. Burying Rosalyn in the unforgiving soil, leaving her to the worms, would be obscene. The gods themselves would clamour with outrage to see her scintillating torch snuffed out, and heaven would rock with thunder.

But for her, what would they do for her? What would have happened if Catherine had died that day, if it had been she who was sucked under the ice? Nothing. Nothing would have happened. Her mother would have looked very stylish at her funeral, Dinah Hoyle dabbing her dry eyes carefully so as not to smudge her mascara. She would have expended considerable efforts with her outfit.

Elegant, chic, a tower of coiffured hair, not a tress out of place. The mourners would have looked on admiringly—in short, her mother would have been momentous grief in *haute couture*. Her brother would have roared in on his motorbike, mumbled a few meaningless prayers with the rest, and roared gratefully back to his dark, oily garage. Her father would have been the saddest, but even his would have been closet grief. He might have blown a bit more London grime on his crisp white handkerchief, dashed away a stubborn tear or two. But he would have hidden it behind his newspaper as he rode the commuter train to Waterloo, as if feeling the loss of her was something to be ashamed of. And Rosalyn? Well, yes, she would have suffered, alighted on the anniversary from the full diary of her own life to lay flowers on Catherine's grave. But that was all. The breach in the ice would just have healed over, until no one would have been able to tell that a girl had died in that pond, that Catherine Hoyle had ended her life there.

And she did die that day, or something of her did, like a balloon with a slow puncture she has been deflating ever since. It doesn't really matter whether her Don Quixote husband is home or not, because . . . because of her guilty secret. 'I don't love him,' she tells the flaking walls now in an ignominious mutter. 'I don't love your father,' she speaks into Bria's ginger-blonde curls. Then she kisses the small dome of her head, the soft wisps of hair. 'When he's home your daddy drinks and garbles his impossible dreams. He tilts at windmills, your daddy does. He makes a fuss of you, lights up like fireworks starring the night sky, coos and gurgles, cradles you in his arms. But then, my precious, exactly like a fireworks

277

display, after a few oohs and ahs, it's all over. And then it's the drink again. You're cursed in your parents, and I'm truly sorry for it, Bria Madigan.'

But as the words form on her lips, so does another truth. Her daughter is the only part of her that is real, that is flesh and blood, a spark of hope. Though she is also a daily reminder of how far Catherine has slipped, how little time she has left before she disappears under the ice for good. She loves Bria, of course she does. But she misguidedly thought that a child would be a companion for her, a salve for her debilitating loneliness. Yet with her baby's arrival the chasm she is in has widened, until she is certain it will require a miracle to drag her out of it. Being a mother is proving the most isolating experience of her life, only steps distant from being a hermit. She knows it is a dreadful thing to think, unforgivable. But there it is. There is no escaping Bria's constant demands, and yet she is unable to communicate with her really.

She has read that the majority of mothers soon master the complex language of their new babies, distinguishing between different cries and moods. The knowledge simply serves to reinforce Catherine's belief that she isn't a good parent. Not that she would ever do anything to harm her, nor does she resent the broken nights and the lassitude that tails her throughout the days that follow them. But she has seen the faces of other mothers in the rec—proud, aflame with maternal fervour as they clasp their babies to their breasts, or rock them in their prams, or sit in the sunshine cradling them in their laps, studies in supreme contentment. How can Catherine confess to these women, these portraits of Madonna and child, that all she has

278

experienced so far is an all-consuming feeling of inadequacy? And the low self-esteem is seasoned with the constant pricking of her eyes and the constriction of her throat, promising the imminent onset of tears.

Bria is a pretty baby, Catherine can see that. Contrary to popular belief, not all are. In the maternity ward of the West Middlesex Hospital she had seen some hideous infants, red-faced, bald and wrinkled, like ancient gnomes. Bria has inherited her father's winning eyes, the pigment of the irises looking blue or green depending on the light. And she has the palest of fine ginger-blonde curls that gather charmingly at the nape of her neck. She has a cute button nose and a sweet pink bow of a mouth. But perhaps sensing her mother's lack of confidence, she is unsettled, insecure, constantly crying and rarely sleeping.

'Well, this won't do,' she counsels them both. 'Sitting here feeling sorry for ourselves. Fresh air and exercise, just what Doctor Newell would recommend.' A quarter of an hour later she sits on a bench at the rec, rocking the pram, enjoying a rare moment of quiet. It is late morning, and extremely hot. Despite the fine weather, few people are out this afternoon. There is a middle-aged man walking a black Labrador around the circumference of the field, a couple of girls pedalling the paved paths on bikes, a group of boys in the farthest corner from her kicking about a football, and a grey-haired woman, perhaps a doting grandmother, pushing a toddler on the swings.

Catherine would dearly love to talk to someone. She finds herself wondering occasionally if she is losing the power of speech entirely, if she is unlearning it through lack of practice. She supposes this is what it is like for the aged living alone, seeing no one from day to day. When she talks to Bria, her voice seems to rebound spookily off the drab walls of the Hounslow terrace. She feels ridiculous too, as if she is carrying on a conversation with herself. And as Bria's blue-green eyes grow more knowing, it is as though she is becoming increasingly wise to this fake mother.

Catherine grows aware of a woman walking towards her. She has the engaging face of a pixie, short black hair, and a petite slight frame, the flowered smock dress she is wearing stretching over her pregnant belly. Catherine judges that she must be about six months along. She assumes that she is going to stroll by her bench, but then the woman pauses to peep inside her pram.

'Oh, what a lovely baby,' she says, smiling. 'Is it a boy or a girl?'

'A girl,' Catherine answers, feeling as if a vow of silence is being broken.

'How stupid of me. I should have known by the pink bear stitched on the quilt. And besides, she is so sweet. How could she possibly be a boy?' Her voice is husky, perhaps a smoker.

'I know what you mean. In the hospital, seeing the babies all lined up in their cribs, they looked identical, wee hermaphrodites. What . . . what are you hoping to have?' she inquires hesitantly. This is a question she finds tricky to pose. On the one hand it seems too personal, too intimate a matter to take up with a virtual stranger. On the other, she lives in terror of committing the ultimate *faux pas*, that of assuming a woman is pregnant when, most embarrassingly, she is merely plump.

Again the woman smiles at her. And Catherine, who has thus far avoided direct eye contact, meets her gaze bravely. She is struck immediately by the most extraordinary aspect of her large charismatic eyes: the irises are of different colours, one a light radiant blue, the other a soft, intense brown. 'I should like a boy, I think,' she replies thoughtfully. She straightens up and shades her unusual eyes, looking far off. 'Phew, it's hot,' she mutters. Catherine nods. She notices that the ends of her hair are bleached, that the colour has grown out. She is older than she first thought too, giveaway lines around the eyes, the brow, the mouth. 'You're not supposed to say that, are you? That you have a preference for a boy or a girl?'

'What do you mean?' Catherine asks, the thread of the conversation lost for a second.

'Oh, you know . . . the correct answer to that question, whether you want a boy or girl, is that you don't care so long as you have a lovely healthy baby. It's blasphemous to start complaining about the sex, when you should simply be grateful that it hasn't got two heads and a dragon's tail.' She turns back to her, seeming to remember herself. 'At least, that's how my doctor's been with me. Ready to rap me over the knuckles if I start moaning about how much I want a boy.'

'Oh, I get you,' Catherine says in sudden understanding. 'Yes, I came across one or two nurses like that when I had my ultrasound. Where are you going to have your baby?'

'Kingston Hospital. What about you? Where did you deliver yours?'

'West Middlesex.'

'Any good?'

'Not too bad, I suppose. The midwife was pleasant enough, but looking back, it did seem to go on forever—the labour, I mean.'

'Mm . . . I'm dreading it. My name's Mara, by the way.' She offers her hand and Catherine sits forward and shakes it, noticing as she does so her bitten nails. They look endearing in a funny way, childlike. And yet she would have said that Mara was well into her thirties.

'I'm Catherine. Pleased to meet you.' She hopes the newcomer does not detect how pleased she really is, how she is seizing on this scrap of social contact the way a starving man might fall on a loaf of bread.

'Do you mind if I join you for a bit?' Mara asks politely.

And again Catherine has to force herself not to leap up and skip joyously about in thanks. 'Please do.' She taps the seat welcomingly. Mara lowers herself onto the bench, a hand pressing into the small of her back.

'My ankles have started swelling up when I've been on my feet all day. I've only recently given up work and it's such a relief. I was a shop assistant and I can tell you, by the time we shut I was in agony.'

'Is this your first baby?' Catherine says. Privately she speculates that if it is, then she is quite old to be having it.

'Yes, I know. I married late,' she replies, reading her thoughts. 'Honestly, Catherine, I was starting to think that I was destined for spinsterhood, that the right man was never going to show up.' She places her hands over her bump and flexes her ankles. Catherine, catching the gleam of a pretty

282

gold ankle chain, reflects privately that her ankles do not appear in the least puffy. 'But Stewart came along in the end, and actually,' she lowers her eyelids demurely, 'he was worth the wait. He works for a firm of architects. It took ages to fall pregnant but he's so excited now, I can't tell you. He bought this book of names and he sits up in bed most nights and reads them out loud to me.' She places a hand on the sleeve of Catherine's blouse, surprising her, and drops her voice to a confidential whisper. 'Last night just before I turned the light out, he said he thought Peregrine was a smashing name. Can you believe that, Catherine? I shall have to put my foot down, swollen ankle or not. Is this your first, too?'

'Yes.'

'What's your baby's name?'

'Bria. My husband, Sean, chose it. He's from Ireland.' She hopes that the disappointment in her own marriage and in motherhood is not betrayed in her face.

'Oh, that's a lovely name,' Mara says admiringly. 'Now if Stewart came up with something like that I'd be able to stop panicking, but as it is I shall have to be vigilant.' Across the field the man with the dog draws back his arm, readying himself to throw a ball, while at his feet the Labrador prances, tail wagging, barking enthusiastically. In the playground the woman is bundling the toddler into a pushchair. And in her pram Bria stirs and blinks up at the blue sky's plumage of faint white feathery clouds. 'What about your husband, Sean? Is he enjoying fatherhood?'

'Mm . . . I think so. He works in London. Long hours. Often he doesn't make it home. He has a flat he can stay in.' She fiddles with a loose strand of cotton on one of the buttonholes of her cuffs, unravelling some of the stitching.

'Oh dear! That must be lonely for you. How do you cope?' Catherine swallows hard. Beside her, Mara combs her tufts of hair with her bitten fingers and fluffs up her fringe. The tears suddenly rush unbidden into Catherine's eyes, as if someone had turned a faucet on. She is helpless to stop them. 'Oh, you're crying. Whatever's the matter?' asks her new friend, gently, solicitously.

As if a switch has been flicked, Catherine is back in the icy waters of the pond, staring across at Rosalyn, bluish specks of light seeming to race at her from the snowscape around them. She was snatching at the frosty air, battling her way through her terrible story, shouting at Rosalyn, telling her cousin she would hate her if she did not listen to the end of it. And her head hurt with the crushing weight of the bitter cold. And it hurt, too, with the effort of furnishing her impoverished imagination with a cast of characters, and with the mental feat of trying to net an orchestra of sounds and sensations. She had to snare Rosalyn's mind, and hold it back from the brink for just a few seconds more. While across the cracking floor of ice, death loured at her from under his hood, waiting for the moment she would flounder, the moment her voice would fade away, the moment he would gather up Rosalyn and clutch her to his vacuous ribcage. She had so nearly failed then, the way she is now. Only this time *she* is in mortal danger from the ice.

'I'm sorry. I'm so sorry. This is pathetic,' she sobs, reaching for the precautionary clean hanky she had tucked into her skirt pocket before setting out. 'I

284

feel so embarrassed.'

'Don't be,' Mara says congenially. 'You look shattered. Don't forget, I'm pregnant too. I may not have a baby yet, but I know what it's like not to get any sleep and to still be trying to stay on top of things.'

She lays a hand on her shoulder, and Catherine feels the encouraging pressure of those nibbled fingers. And then it all comes tumbling out: the lack of rest; night after night up with Bria; not knowing what to do for the best; fretting that she is ill; Sean never home and then when he is, drinking too much. And the debt too, the mounting debt ever at their backs, the unpaid bills, the final demands, the gambling, falling behind with the rent as well. She stops short of telling Mara that she is living a lie.

In the middle of her outpouring, Bria begins to whimper and then to cry in earnest. Catherine is about to haul herself off the bench and pick up her distressed daughter, when her companion asks if she can have a go. She nods a bit uncertainly. And Mara hoists herself to her feet and gathers the baby up, holding her to her chest, and rubbing her tiny back as if she has been doing this every day for all of her life. Amazingly, her daughter quiets, peering down curiously at her mother over Mara's shoulder.

She is so kind, treating her, Catherine thinks, not as if she has just met her but as if they have been close friends for years. What's more, none of the scandalous things that she confessed seem to have shocked her, not even Sean's drinking which, up till now, she has divulged to no one. Perhaps it is because Mara is older, has more experience of life, of men, that Sean, with all his manifest shortcomings, does not seem to disconcert her in the slightest. And this, despite being married to a man who is clearly a model husband. She feels so much better, so much more hopeful about the future. Mara lives a couple of miles away, she tells her, and she would like to have Catherine over to her house when she feels up to it. But in the meantime, as they are just embarking on their friendship, why not meet again the following morning? They agree a time and before they part Catherine thanks her profusely.

'Nonsense. You've done me as much good as I've done you. It has been so nice to chat to you.' She bends over the pram and chucks Bria under her chin. 'And to have had the pleasure of making your acquaintance too, young lady, and letting you dribble all over my new smock.'

'Oh gosh, I'm so sorry about that,' Catherine apologizes hastily.

'Not at all. This is excellent practice for me.'

They move off in opposite directions, Catherine towards the main road, Mara over the playing fields heading for the passageway that runs behind the care home. After a few yards, Catherine stops pushing the pram, and looks over the green expanse of grass at her retreating back. She is energized and full of optimism. She has made a friend, an empathetic woman, a woman who is going through her first pregnancy, albeit in happier circumstances. She has made her believe that things can improve, that it is worth resisting the advance of the ice.

19

Tuesday, 10 August

The market screams with fool's gold. From every aisle, from every stall, from every corner, a thousand brilliant lances joust with each other. Neon purple scintilla ignite in Owen's vision, making his eyes throb. Fool's gold, iron pyrites, worthless. It is trash. That's what his life has become, just so much trash. That he could ever have been fooled by it! Naomi has been withdrawn since their return from Italy. Her sleep-walking has become a nightly ritual, and the things she speaks of while in this trance-like state eat into him. The sick baby whose crying must be stopped, the man called Walt who has to be punished, the priest who has opened her up to find her black soul stained with coal dust, the purging of her sins in the cold of the sea. He tells himself that they are bad dreams, dark fantasies, that there is no substance to any of it. Nevertheless her eccentric behaviour troubles him.

As if in empathy, there is a recurrence of his own nightmares, so that he makes super-human efforts to stay awake. Now he feels wired with lack of sleep, only the thought that Sean will be back on Thursday keeping him going. Punters file past while the music stamps through his aching head. He is dizzy and dirty, subjugated by the unremitting heat. And always there are more, more tourists, more whores, more of the disappointed, the dejected, all on a pilgrimage to put a sparkle into their lives, all believing that the glitter will rub off on them, that down here they can be rich as royalty. Fool's gold. All of it. A vault of fool's gold. And if you peel back the lid of this tin catacomb and let the sunshine flood in, set the real gold to work, in a wink you will see it for what it is. The cheap gilt will tarnish before you reach the top stair, before you set foot on the pavement.

The flat is empty when he lets himself in at six-thirty. He takes a shower, makes a sandwich and turns on the television. But he soon turns it off again when his mind starts drifting. However, in place of reminiscing destructively about the day Sarah drowned, he is whisked back to the year before the accident, to a fine summer's afternoon spent in their back garden. Mother has filled up the paddling pool and Sarah is sitting in it surrounded by assorted plastic toys, a green miniature watering can, a tiny blue bucket, a family of yellow ducks, a red tugboat. They are all bobbing round her, like planets round the sun. She is wearing bikini pants, tied at the sides, a shell print on periwinkle-blue fabric. His mother is sitting in a deck chair in a floppy straw sunhat and cotton dress, reading a book. She has pulled the skirt above her knees and is sunning her legs. His father is in the shed planting up cuttings. Although Owen is wearing trunks, he has no interest in playing in the pool. It feels babyish to him. Instead he has made a den by draping a gingham tablecloth over the lower branches of a pine tree. He has filled a proper metal bucket with water, and hidden away here he is making mud pies in earthenware flowerpots. He is enjoying himself so much that it feels shameful. There is an art in getting the right consistency, not too wet and sloppy or they will not set, not too dry

288

and crumbly or they will fall apart. Suddenly the cloth is pulled back and sunlight chases out the cool shadows.

'Can I play?' demands Sarah. The rounds of her shoulders are pinked with the sun, and so are her knees.

He holds his arms over his feast of precious pies and frowns. 'You've got the paddling pool. Can't you play there?'

'But I want to play here,' she insists, standing her ground. She is dripping into his den. And when she sits down pine needles adhere to her arms and legs, making a woodland creature of her.

'Oh, all right. You have to be my water-bearer though,' he tells her.

'What does a water-beawer do?' she says, sounding 'w's' for 'r's'. Her blonde hair is damp, hugging her face, and her cheeks are all rosy-pink with the heat.

'You fetch buckets of water for me from the paddling pool.'

She considers this for a moment. Then, 'Why?'

Proudly he opens out his arms and reveals his culinary masterpieces, all three of them, lined up and tastefully decorated with leaves and twigs. 'For me to make pies,' he says in a hushed tone. She gasps in wonder at his magnificent creations. 'I have a bowl and spoon for mixing, see.'

The tiny mouth sets in the familiar stubborn line. 'I want to make the pies. You get the water.'

He sighs. 'Getting the water is a very important job. That's why I'm asking you to do it,' he persuades with cunning.

She mulls this over for a second, head to one side, sucking on a strand of wet hair. 'I want to mix the

289

pies,' she insists infuriatingly.

He is trying his best to keep calm. If he raises his voice, his mother will look up from her book and ask what the matter is. And when Sarah tells her that her brother won't let her mix the mud pies, she will scold him for being mean to his little sister. 'Look, you can collect leaves and twigs for decoration,' he bribes.

The lower lip is wavering now. 'But I want to mix the pies,' she wails.

'Oh very well, you mix the stupid pies!' he bursts out in frustration, earning him the reprimand from his mother that he anticipated. He stomps off, bucket in hand, to fetch more water. When he comes back, Sarah has made a hat of his finest pie and is squashing it into her hair. Her other hand is punching into the dome of another. 'No, no, what are you doing?' he yells, snatching the pies back and working rapidly to repair them. But even as he does so, he knows the game is over, spoilt. Sarah will not follow his instructions. The mud pies will be ruined, the pleasure of perfecting them, gone. For some absurd reason tears rush to his eyes. He climbs to his feet, but his posture is stooped because one of the branches of the tree cuts through his hideout. It is only a bit of fun, mud pies after all, he tells himself. She has not broken one of his model aeroplanes, or scribbled over his school work, or hidden his *Dandy* book. But for some baffling reason this seems to have upset him more than all three put together.

That same evening his mother makes meringues. Owen is her rapt audience of one. He often watches, sits at the kitchen table quietly as his mother transforms into a sorceress. She unscrews the tops of jars, and spoons out flour and sugar and rice, she breaks eggs, she carves up bricks of butter, she chops vegetables and meat, she adjusts the heat of the gas flame, she stirs and thickens and sprinkles. Sometimes she follows recipes. She mouths the spells printed on the pages of a book lying on the kitchen worktop, her gold-framed reading glasses propped halfway down the bridge of her nose. Other days everything she does seems to be instinctive, a pinch of this, a dash of that. And like a conjurer, she completes the trick with a flourish of tea towels and oven gloves, setting down tasty savoury dishes, indulging his sweet tooth with cakes and biscuits, custards and pies, trifles and jellies.

He loves the wizardry of the meringues more than anything. It is like observing a scientific experiment, breaking the eggshell and keeping the golden yolk in a fragment of it, while the clear white falls elastically into the bowl. Then seeing her whip it frenziedly with the egg-beater, the tiny handle spinning like a miniature Ferris wheel. And to start with it is no more that a bubbly milky-yellow froth. There is a moment each time when he is convinced that the trick won't work, that it will fail. He holds his breath tonight and as he does so, it happens. In a trice it changes from a watery goo into stiff white peaks, like Alpine ranges, he thinks to himself.

Sometimes he asks questions. Mostly they start with 'why'. His mother answers every one patiently. He even has ideas about adding things, though he doesn't say. Now she volunteers a rule. Some of his friends collect stamps. Well, he collects 'the rules' with a passion, what you must do and what you must never do. He has started writing them down in a private exercise book he bought from the newsagents.

'You mustn't get any shell into the whites, Owen. If you do, however tiny, no matter how long you beat them they won't whip up.'

Sarah does not seem very interested in cooking, though she likes licking the raw cake-mix from the bowl, sucking it from the spoon and from her fingertips. She sits colouring, or playing with dolls, while Mother cooks. What Owen realizes on the mud pie day, is that he cannot care for the garden the way his father does. He is far keener on making the earth into pies than growing vegetables in it. But he is curious about preparing them, all the different recipes there are, all the spells. And he suspects there are a great deal more that his mother doesn't know about. In geography at school he got to thinking the other day, that just as all the countries in the world are different, so must their food be.

Now he says a touch thickly, 'I love seeing you cook. When I grow up I should like to be a cook like you, Mother.'

His mother is not really listening. 'Would you, dear?' she says vaguely. 'That's nice.'

But his father is. He has come in from the garden and is putting down the basket of vegetables he has collected. 'Boys don't grow up to be cooks. Girls do the cooking.' As he says this last, he crouches down and touches the tip of an index finger to Sarah's nose. Her face breaks into one huge smile and she lifts her arms out to him. Owen is devastated. His cheeks are scorched with shame. He bites his tongue and wishes that he hadn't told. He makes up his mind there and then to tear up his stupid book of rules. But then his mother speaks, unexpectedly, in his defence, in her son's defence.

292

'That's not true, Bill. Some of the most famous chefs in the world are men. I think if Owen wants to be a chef, then that's wonderful.'

Owen does not know who she is referring to but it isn't important. He is blushing, but not with humiliation—with pride. And as his father begins to say something else, his mother butts in, something she seldom does. 'Don't you dare crush his enthusiasm, Bill.' Later she stands behind Owen, kisses him on the top of his head, and holds a warm meringue out for him to bite into. He brings his teeth slowly together. And sweetness, light as air, crumbles and explodes and melts over his taste buds, so that he feels as if he is eating love itself.

This is the surprising memory that comes tumbling out of the cupboard on this hot summer's evening in 1976. Nothing came of it, because it wasn't long after that the clocks stopped, Sarah drowned and it all went horribly wrong. Yet now the oddest little flame of defiance lights within him. Why shouldn't he cook? Why shouldn't he at least learn more about it, see if it was a bit of childish nonsense, or if he did have a penchant, a talent, a gift for cookery? He liked the idea of proving his father wrong. But much more than this, he liked the idea of proving his mother right. After this was over, and it soon would be, after he left London, why not see if he could get work in some restaurants, not only in England, but on the Continent where the Mediterranean food was supposed to be so fresh and flavoursome.

He is preoccupied with this when Naomi pushes her way through the bead curtain. Glancing at his watch, to his surprise he sees that it is after 9 p.m. 'Where have you been?' He tries to sound casual, but his tone is edgy, suspicious.

'For a walk, that's all, Owen. What's the matter with you?' She shrugs, pushing back her mussed hair with her free hand.

In the other hand she is holding a carrier bag, he sees. For a moment he levels his eyes inquisitively at her. He gets up, stretches and then peers into it. He is surprised by its contents, and shoots her a quizzical look. A cushion, one of the settee cushions. He watches as she nonchalantly pulls it out and tosses it down. She enacts this as if it is a normal part of every homecoming.

'Naomi, what are you doing with the cushion?'

She slips past him into the kitchen, making a grab for the kettle, turning the tap at the sink on full and starting to fill it through the spout. Water sprays into her face, up her nose and over the draining board. She giggles, blinks her eyes and pinches her nostrils. She is wearing leggings and a blue, peach and brown flowered smock dress. The ensemble is so markedly out of character that she is unrecognizable. The clothes he is accustomed to seeing her in are all fitted, jeans that hug her slim hips and thighs, T-shirts stretched snugly over her small breasts, short dresses with low-cut bodices. She likes the sort of garments that exaggerate her trim figure, not the blousy, voluminous creation that falls in pleats about her now.

'What on earth are you wearing, Naomi?' He speaks up before considering the rudeness of such a remark. Quickly he adds, 'It's very nice . . . just not your usual style.'

'It was time for a change,' she responds evenly.

She turns the tap off, brings the kettle up and gives it a little shake. The water sloshes about

294

inside. 'Cup of tea?' she suggests.

They sit side by side on the settee sipping from their mugs, Naomi leisurely smoking a cigarette, while beyond the windows the London night closes in. After a bit she puts on a record. The Beatles song, 'Penny Lane', trills from the record player. She sings along with it. He mentions the men who keep showing up at the stall, Blue and his thugs. 'They're rough sorts. Doesn't Sean realize the risk he's taking getting mixed up with them?'

She moulds her lips into a disdainful moue. 'That's up to him. Shall I make us something to eat?' she proposes when the song has finished. She is on her feet and reaching for his empty mug.

'No thanks.' He eyes the vexing cushion, tramlines scored deep between his eyebrows. 'Why did you take the cushion with you when you went out?' he asks.

'Oh, you know.' Her reply is offhand, drifting to him as she opens kitchen cupboards and then slams them shut again. 'Maybe we should eat out, mm? What do you think, Owen? Treat ourselves?'

'No, no, I'd rather not. What were you doing outside with a cushion?' he reiterates stubbornly.

She hesitates. 'Well . . . it . . . it was—' Abruptly, mid-sentence, she jars to a stop. 'This is terrible. We have no food. I'm starving. Well, we'll just have to go out.' She folds her arms. 'Are you coming?'

'The cushion?' he tries again.

She lifts her eyes and sighs heavily. Then her gaze slides back to the record player. 'It always jumps in this bit,' she complains to him as the music stutters in the background. She moves to stand by the windows, peering into a murk festooned with blinking lights. 'It is so pretty, the night, like

295

opening a jewellery box.' A pause, then, 'I'm very hungry.' She snatches up her bag from the dining-table and heads out of the flat.

20

Wednesday, 11 August

Brighton Beach. Sean is sitting on a bench on the promenade, looking south, out to a sea paved with gold. His face is ruddy and wind-kissed, his nose reddened with sunburn and drink. Despite the baking heat he keeps his jacket on. In the inside pocket is a fat envelope stuffed with money. It crackles a bit as he shifts on the seat. He has taken off his tie and undone the top two buttons of his shirt, but this is his only surrender to the soaring temperatures. Around him the British Riviera is in full swing. The pebbled beach has been invaded by leisure seekers, all wanting relief from the scorching sun. The grey-green swell teems with people of all ages, all shapes, all sizes. Bodies spill out of bright swimwear. They paddle, play with beach balls, loll on colourful lilos, duck and dive in the breaking waves. They take on the English Channel, furrowing through it with the crawl, the breaststroke, the sidestroke, the doggy paddle. Families stake their claims with rectangles of bright beach towels, windbreaks, picnic baskets, deck chairs. Dogs bark and run at the elusive surf. The promenade is busy with folk taking their ease, stretching their legs, walking arm in arm, sucking on ice cream cones and lollies.

To his right is the West Pier, the white elephant, the pavilions looking deceptively grand. Sean has strolled past it, seen that it is closed and dilapidated, that it is slowly crumbling away. To the east is the Palace Pier, Mecca of tat, of slot machines and bingo halls, where cheap cuddly toys are displayed in tiers according to their prize-winning status. Sean feels at home there. The sea sighs, the pebbles tumble, the sun-worshippers burn to turkey-red, and laugh and chatter. And the gulls screech and flap. An old couple sit down beside him. They rifle in a bag, then munch contentedly on tongue sandwiches, and swig ginger beer. The woman tears off the crust of one of hers and tosses it towards a gull. There is a brief ugly skirmish, cawing and posturing, during which it is pilfered by a pug dog trotting by on a lead.

Sean does not like gulls. They are scavengers. He recalls flocks of them descending on the fields back home, feasting on the newly planted seeds, jeopardizing the crop. He does not want to spend his life scavenging, scratching a living in the grudging dirt. The sweat is pouring out of him under his showy jacket. His skin prickles. His rash is a source of constant irritation. But today he throws his head back and closes his eyes against the glare. The insides of his eyelids glow like dying embers. There is cash, a wad of cash, cool and crisp, next to his heart. And what had he had to do for it? Little more than take a train ride, book into a hotel, and meet a man on the pier. Who knows where it comes from, the money. Drugs? Prostitution? Extortion? He's smart and doesn't ask. Catherine would say it was dirty money, but to Sean money is the one pure thing, the thing that cannot be sullied. It is inviolate.

297

He has sniffed it and it smells of possibilities. Tomorrow he will pass it on to Blue, and then? Then take his wage, and wait for his turn to come round again. He puts a hand on his chest, over his heart, and presses. A low crackle, making him think of the crackle of new straw as you settle into it.

The crackle races like an electric current through his brain, jostling memory cells. It lights up a scene from his past. A boy alighting on fresh straw, straw that smells sweetly of meadow flowers riffled by river breezes, by the sandy-silt breath of the Shannon. He burrows into it, and curls up in the sty, his back to the great belly of the pig. It vibrates with every grunting snore. He draws the blanket of heat it gives off about him, and lets its muddy shit smell fill his lungs. He has grown fond of this big black pig, whose hair is coarse as wire, whose snuffling snout runs shiny with mucus, the way his brother Emmet's does. He likes the lazy manner of it, how it flicks the flies off with a twitch of its rump, or a flip-flap-swivel of its veined lop-ears. He likes its beady intelligent eyes.

He has given this pig a name, Derry. He knows any day now Derry will be slaughtered, that he will have to help to hold him down, that the knife will be drawn across his taut throat while he is screeching with fear. And that his Da will boast afterwards of a clean kill, a quick kill, that he will have to hold the bowl under the slit neck to catch the spraying blood. He thinks Derry will fight more than most, hopes he will, that his trotters will scuff at the earth for full minutes before the life drains out of him and he goes limp to the world. His Da looks forward each year to killing the pig. Sean senses this, the way his eyes have the veneer of avarice over them when they rest on the brute. Sometimes he brings it treats, an apple, a carrot, a slice of bread and dripping. And they grunt together, his Da approving the spread of his girth, the pig falling on the gourmet morsel in moist, snorting grunts of ecstasy. But there will be nothing clean about the kill when it comes. Sean knows this from past experience. His hands will be red with blood. And there will be blood spattered on his face and soaked into his clothes. The death stink will be weeks in going.

He thinks about the cycle of Derry's life, of him having been not much more than a piglet when he arrived, of fattening him up, of listening to his grumbles and his excited squeals, of how comic he looks when he runs, and the joy of him as he slumps in a mess of mud, and of the way he loves to have you draw a twig back and forth across his rump. Then he wanders into another scene, the star of which is a pie—the pie that Derry ended up in, actually.

Mother baked it. She was a good cook. They had a small range by then. He had taken to spying on her, watching her about her business in the kitchen, when she was all alone. He peeped in at the window over the sink. He marvelled at the locomotion of her, that she never stilled, slicing, chopping, peeling, weighing, washing, scrubbing, stirring. She moved about the kitchen, her long serge skirt swishing like a broom. She squatted on the three-legged stool and poked at the fire. She sucked on her teeth while roses bloomed in her cheeks, and perspiration pearled her nose. And she counted her silvery-grey rosary beads in her rough hands.

'Hail Mary, full of grace, the Lord is with thee; blessed art thou among women.'

Today the window is ajar and he smells her sweat and smoke and the steamy soap suds in the enamel sink. He imagines the place under her skirt, the soft damp place between her thighs, the briny wetness there, how he has come out of it.

'And blessed is the fruit of thy womb, Jesus.'

With one hand she feeds pieces of Derry into the meat mincer clamped to the side of the kitchen table, while with the other she turns the handle. He can see pink and white meat worms come wriggling out of the mincing mouth, as if it is spewing. She swipes away stray strands of greasy black hair that dangle before her eyes, and hunches her beetle-black brows as she seasons the worms in a cream china mixing bowl. Later he watches her rub butter into a snowfall of flour, add a drop of water, and with the wooden rolling pin lean her weight into it, flattening it into shape. His eyes are trained on her, as she spoons the squashed Derry worms into a pie dish, and when she carefully lifts the pastry lid over it, pinching the edges between her fingertips. Lastly she pricks it with a fork and paints it golden yellow, dipping her pastry brush into the beaten froth of a separated egg yolk. The pie bakes slowly, and after an hour he comes back and hides under the window, among the bracken, the juices running into his mouth at the delicious gravy fragrance that wafts to him on the summer air. As he is leaving he falls into a clump of nettles. They feel velvety for a second, and then the velvet changes into metal, painfully grating his lower legs and arms.

The next morning, milking accomplished, he spies on her once more, as she makes up his and Emmet's lunch pieces for school. He sees her cut hunks of bread and wedges of cheese, sees her lay them in the centre of the squares of calico cotton. Then he sees her walk to the larder, open the door, go inside and return bearing the pie. The crust is the colour of the midday sun, and when she cuts into it a squirt of mouth-watering clear brown jelly clings to the silver blade of the knife. She slices a single thick slice, and she folds it into one of the calico squares, then knots them both. She puts the pie back in the larder, and lays the lunch pieces on the dark-wood dresser. After they have spooned up the last smear of their porridge, he and Emmet go to fetch their lunches. Seeing them, she rises quickly and picks both bundles up, one in each hand. Sean knows which contains the slice of pie because he saw her set them down. Now she holds it in her right hand. Her sons stand before her, ready to receive her blessing. Sean stops breathing. His mother looks steadily into his foreign eyes, as she places the bundle in her left hand into his. Then she turns to Emmet and gives him the other, her eyes softening. Outside in the yard the cock crows. 'Hacca croodle oooh,' it goes, 'Hacca croodle oooh.'

All day Sean meditates on the pie, how good it will taste, how the crisp butter pastry will dissolve against your tongue. He visualizes the succulent pink worms, how they will have set together with flecks of white fat into firm flesh. He broods on Emmet opening up his calico square, and his greedy eyes glittering up at the sight of the pie wedge. He envisages him cramming it into his gobbling mouth with its overbite, gulping it down hog fashion, without savouring the flavour, the texture, all the Derry days that have gone into the making of it. His

301

own cheese feels hard and bitter in his mouth, and the bread appears stale and sour, so that it sucks the moisture out of him. And he goes to the toilet and spits out his rejection, ignoring the rumbles of his empty tummy.

That day at school they learn that wolves once roamed free in Ireland, that as the oak forests were cut down and the land cleared, the wolves were driven by starvation to hunt on farmland. They preyed on cattle and sheep, and the farmers hunted them down until the last wolf was extinct. Sean imagines what it was like to be that last wolf, large and grey and lonely, with a bushy tail, long snout and pointy ears, and eyes sharp as unrequited love. He thinks about how he must have searched for another of his kind, that he would have loped about at night, those lone eyes silvered with moonlight, howling his grief. He wants to howl like the last wolf. He wants it so badly that he cannot wait for Sunday to come round. When the house is abed and they all sleep soundly, he creeps out and prowls in the night-shine. He runs light-footed through the black land, till he comes to her. Her face, with the amber harvest moon and cloud shadows flitting over it, is polished tortoiseshell. He strips and sinks into her, and she moans, cold and hard as nails of cut glass raking over his body. He takes a balloon's breath and hauls himself under her, down and down in the darkness. Then he opens his mouth and as she pours into him, he howls the howl of the last wolf.

In Brighton, beside Sean on the bench they come and go, the elderly couple, two young women bickering, a man who dribbles water from a bottle over his panting dog, a family with two children who

302

vine themselves around the ornate iron armrests. He knows it is time to leave, to catch his train. But as he makes his way through the High Street he drags his feet like a recalcitrant schoolboy. He pauses in a doorway to take a nip from his hip flask, and he greets the kick of it as it hops into him, like a dear old friend. The pavements have gone all continental, cafes spilling out onto them, people lounging like dusty cats in the sun. The envelope still crackles. There is twenty thousand pounds in it, a fortune. For a few hours he is a rich man. He will sit down at one of the tables and enjoy an ice-cold lager. If he misses this train he will catch the next . . . or the next. What is there to worry about? What is the rush? After all, he is his own master.

His order is taken by a girl with a white streak in her wispy brown hair, and glasses with square lenses burnished copper by the sun. Perhaps it is the weather, perhaps it is his heartbeat drumming through the money, but he is backward looking this afternoon, glancing over his shoulder at yesterdays. His granda comes to his mind—Da's Da who went to the bad. That was how they all referred to him, Granpops who went to the bad. But Sean met him before he arrived there, when he judged there were still some drops of good left in him. He came to stay at the farm once. Sean's Ma was taken ill and rushed to the hospital in an ambulance.

She was a month off giving birth when it happened. Tiny babies often slipped out of his Ma. Each time she fell, she went to church and prayed to God and Lord Jesus and all the saints, to hold them in. And she prayed some more at home, kneeling before the tiny shrine she had made to Mother Mary, in the kitchen. She rubbed her knees raw with the praying.

But one after the other out they slid, refusing obstinately to stay in the snug red of her. Sean wondered if perhaps they knew what sort of life was waiting for them on the farm, if they preferred to go back to where they came from rather than fetch up here. Anyway, this baby had hung around and grown some, till his Ma's belly was stretched and popping with it. It was spring and she'd been to the fields and picked a bunch of wild flowers, daisies and poppies and tree mallow. She'd put them in a glass jar in Mary's shrine.

'For the thanks,' she said. Then she sank down to her swollen knees, began groaning and didn't get up again. His Da went with her, and Emmet was sent to his cousins. Sean was left to manage the farm and Granpops arrived in his beaten-up old truck, to help keep things running. He was a huge man who smelt of whiskey, tobacco, age-old dirt and sweat. The few occasions Sean had seen him, he was wearing the same clothes, and they looked as if they had not been washed for years. Trousers like tree trunks, they were so creased and besmirched, braces stained with oil, a patched wool shirt grey with ancient food stains that would not do up over the hump of his stomach, and a battered old porkpie hat.

But it was Sean who did all the running, while Granpops sat in the easy chair by the fire, and smoked his pipe and drank his whiskey. When Sean came in from the fields the bottle was half empty, the pipe had been knocked out on the kitchen table, and the fire was dead. He was awful hungry, ready for a plate of stew, or some Colcannon with good mashed tatties and chopped kale and cream, or a slice of blood sausage flavoured with tansy herbs.

But there was nothing, so he started rooting in the cupboards.

'What are you doing, boy?' drawled his granda from under his porkpie hat. And Sean jumped in his weary hide, because he had been sure that Granpops was snoozing. He whipped off his hat and squinted at him with his one good eye. The other was a greenish smear and gave Sean the willies.

'I'm looking for something to eat,' he told him guiltily.

Granpops heaved himself out of the chair and he rootled about with him. They found two tins without labels on, and he clumsily opened them both with a penknife which had dried blood on its blade. Sean fetched spoons and forks, and they sat at the kitchen table eating. Sean had beans, and from his can, Granpops forked apple slices through his smacking fleshy wet lips. They had to be careful not to cut their mouths on the jagged metal edges. Halfway they swapped. Then Sean lit a candle, and his granda had a few more swallows of whiskey and belched. He told stories of how he'd been a sailor and worked his passage across the Atlantic Ocean to America. But he hadn't liked it there. 'The work was too hard and the living poor, you know. Not a fit life for a real man.' So he'd come back home to the green land.

Later, when Sean was going to bed, Granpops said, 'D'you want to come for a ride in my truck, boy?' And Sean nodded, although it seemed a crazy thing to do, drive about aimlessly in the dark. They motored a long way, the truck coughing and spluttering and farting, and Sean being shaken about so much he thought that he might fall to pieces. His granda leant on the wheel, and squinted with his good red-rimmed eye at the dirt track that wound ahead of them. 'D'you know where we're going, boy?' he asked. Sean told him that he didn't. And his granda chuckled at that and laid a grubby finger on his nose, a large nose that began in one direction and ended in another. They came to a barn and there were other cars and trucks parked outside it. As he climbed out, Sean smelt oil, and he burped a whiff of beans and apples. He looked up at steel stars nailed into the inky walls of the night. The moon was the colour of pumpkins and seemed to rock overhead, so that fastening on it made him feel giddy as a rolling cartwheel.

Inside, the barn was lit with oil lanterns, and it was sardine tight with men. The noise of excited voices leapt and juddered and jumped, and Sean saw that money was changing hands. Granpops had forgotten about him, so he squeezed through the mass of bodies to where they all fringed a sawdust space. There, two men were stripped to the waist, circling each other like snorting bulls. To Sean they appeared as David and Goliath. David was stocky with broad shoulders and a bushy brown moustache. And Goliath was tall, with a long neck and a bald head. The next day, thinking back, Sean could not remember who threw the first punch. Only that the barn suddenly erupted, and there was jeering and barracking and shouts of encouragement. The mass of people pushed behind him. There was the reek of sweat and rage, of acrid oil and feverish dreams in his nostrils. The fists flew and the contact cracks caused shivers to run down his spine. A spray of blood specked his cheek. There were grunts and moans as the punches were landed. One of David's eyes swelled up so much that he couldn't open it, but he kept on fighting. Sean had been sure that Goliath would win, but it was David who was the victor, with a sneaky right hook that the giant never saw coming. Back at the farm, Sean had his first taste of whiskey. It was like a hot stinging coal setting his throat on fire.

'Like it?' his granda asked.

It made him feel sick, but he did. He liked it so much that he took another gulp. Granpops rubbed his whiskery chin, and pulled on his web of grey hair. He waggled his nose between his finger and thumb so that Sean could hear the cartilage creak. He plunged his big hand into his pocket and laid five twenty-punt notes on the kitchen table. 'When we set out tonight I only had one of these,' he said. 'But I took a gamble, boy, and I won. Now I have five. Let that be a lesson to you.'

Sean had never seen so much money. 'How did you know that the little man would win?' he slurred, rubbing his tired eyes and feeling his head swirl.

His granda dragged up his shoulders and dropped them heavily. 'I took a chance. Didn't have to lift a finger, but today I'm a rich man.'

The baby, a girl, was stillborn. Sean didn't think he'd mind but he did. He'd lost his little sister before he even had her. They had a proper funeral for her with a mite-sized coffin. And they lowered it into a mite-sized grave, and put a wooden cross on it. His mother called her Molly. He was sad when they put her in it, which was funny because he hadn't known her. No more babies followed Molly. And he only saw his granda a handful of times after that, sitting outside a pub in Kildysart, swigging from a bottle, singing to himself. By then, his Da said that he had gone to the bad altogether.

Sean has finished his lager now, and it feels to him as if his head is bobbing on a cool minty sea. He can still hear the seagulls yawping and scrapping with each other. He pays the bill and leaves. On the way to the station he passes a betting shop. He hesitates for a moment, only a moment, before going inside.

'Didn't have to lift a finger, but today I'm a rich man,' he whispers. And he remembers the gleam in his granda's good eye.

21

Thursday, 12 August

Midday. The thump, thump, thump, of the deadening bass rhythm inside his head makes Owen want to scream. He does not think that he will ever complain about mucky grey skies and drizzling rain again. In the sauna of this unending heat wave these things have become the stuff of fantasies, rare and wondrous as unicorns. A tickling sensation marks the passage of a drop of sweat trickling between his shoulder blades. Sean should be back by now. He had hoped that he would be here to open up with him this morning, that perhaps he could have left him to it and taken the afternoon off. His eyes veer between his wristwatch where the hands keep on revolving, and the flight of stairs, splashed with sunshine from above. They grow as they descend, the new arrivals, shoes, jeans, skirts, tops, and last of all he is able to put a face to them. He is searching for the familiar cheap suit when, with a lurch of his heart, he spots Blue. He is fingering goods with disdain on a neighbouring stall, his minder as always behind him.

The stallholder is transparently nervous, wary of the interest her souvenir cups and plates are garnering from this unlikely quarter. Owen's heart bangs in his chest and the heat drains from him at the mere sight of them. With no more than a slight nudge and shift of his round, dead eyes, the meatloaf indicates to Blue that Owen has seen him. He glances up, turns slowly, and clamps on the parody of a smile. Taking their time, the two stroll towards him. Owen, his back to the counter, stiffens under their scrutiny. He can feel the nerves in his fingers tugging, the tendons alive with anxiety.

'I'd like a little chat, if you don't mind,' Blue says. Owen's brow instantly tightens into a frown. They are hemming him in, a barrier between the stall and the stream of browsers.

'What about?' he inquires, keeping his tone friendly.

Blue gives a predatory smirk. 'Just friendly, nothing to worry about. I'm after a bit of information, that's all.'

He is wearing a flesh-pink shirt, sleeves rolled up, neck open to reveal pallid skin. Under the market lights it resembles a loose second skin. 'Unseasonably hot, isn't it?' There is a newspaper folded on the stool, which Owen has been trawling through for restaurant vacancies. Blue snatches it up and fans himself with it. 'Like a furnace down here. Don't know how you stand it.' He licks his thin lips and pulls at his open shirt. 'You'd think they'd get you poor bastards a bit of air conditioning, eh? You'd like that, wouldn't you? A blast of cold air.' He raises a hand to twiddle the sparkling stud in his earlobe.

'Look, what . . . what exactly d'you want?' Owen stumbles.

The meatloaf sees off two Japanese women who have been sifting through the leather bags at the edge of the counter. 'Sorry, closed, love,' he mumbles through his harelip, arms wide, shepherding them in another direction.

'If it's Sean you're looking for, he's not here,' Owen says with a growing sense of unease.

Blue scratches his pointed chin thoughtfully, and a look passes between him and the meatloaf. 'That's a pity, 'cos you see, it *is* Sean I'm after. Your boss. The Irish. He has my money and he stood me up. D'you happen to know where he is? Think very carefully before you answer, eh?'

Owen tries to swallow but his mouth is dry as sand. 'He . . . uh . . . he said he would be away for a few days. He didn't say where he was going. That's all I know.'

Blue ferrets inside his shirt for a second, creating the impression that he has plunged a hand underneath his skin. He fixes Owen with an interrogative glare, his icy blue eyes unblinking. Then, 'That's a shame,' he remarks. 'A real shame. If he calls you, be sure and tell him I'm on his scent.' His eyes slide to the meatloaf.

Then he is moving off, his minder bringing up the rear.

'See you very soon,' he calls over his shoulder, partnering the farewell with a dismissive wave.

Owen closes up early. Naomi is not in when he gets back to the flat in the afternoon. He makes himself a coffee and sits on the settee, trying to collect his thoughts. He is busy being mature and sensible, when the tears of a small boy who has no more fight in him begin to flow. He lets them come, releasing all the pent-up, confused emotions that have been rampaging through him for weeks now. When he is done he goes to the bathroom and dashes cold water on his face, then dries it, rubbing at it roughly with a towel, determined now to marshal his wits. Sean has got himself into trouble, this much is obvious. He warned him of the dangers of getting entangled with thugs like Blue. But it isn't his problem. All this would have happened if he'd never come here. He will wait to speak to Sean. He is bound to ring. And then he will tell him he is going, that this chaos is of his own making and he will have to manage it himself. And the new beginning he has promised himself, that second chance, well, he is going to take it, to have a go whether his father approves or not.

He returns to the lounge and stands by the window, watching the ant trail on the streets below, glancing about the room. He really does not know what he is doing here with the kitsch bead curtain, the red paper-lantern lampshade, the lopsided Jimi Hendrix poster, and the lava lamp, its dismal orangey-brown blobs sitting like rotten egg yolks at the bottom of the glass funnel. His eyes stray back to the buttery-gold shafts of sunlight that lance through the windows, then to the steam-train trails of aeroplanes criss-crossing the blue sky.

Sean lets himself into the flat half an hour later. If he is surprised to see Owen, sitting on the settee when he should be manning the stall, he does not show it. Neither does he ask where Naomi is. He stands and stares at him speechlessly. He resembles someone who, despite finding himself in the throes

311

of chronic flu, has dragged himself out of bed to a purpose. He looks haggard, his skin has a plastic sheen to it. There are tiny blisters of perspiration spotting his nose and brow. His bloodshot eyes are permanently screwed half shut, as if sensitive to light. His hands are thrust deep into his trouser pockets. Unusually, he wears no jacket. His clothes look crumpled and soiled. Only his hair is neatly combed, greased down, not a strand permitted to spring out of place. It is Owen who breaks the standoff, recounting Blue's visit to the market.

'They're looking for you, Sean,' he winds up.

'I'm sorry for your trouble,' Sean says. 'I'm sorry that you got involved. Are you okay?' His voice is battered, raw, but the sincerity in it is unmistakable.

'I'm fine,' he tells him, though he isn't. 'They didn't touch me.'

Sean moves restlessly about the room, avoiding the windows, his hands fidgeting constantly. One moment he is pulling on his chin, the next, he is fingering his neck where the rash is in full bloom, and an instant later cracking his knuckles. It is Owen who takes control, climbing to his feet, and making his way across the room to sit at the dining-room table. Sean follows his lead and joins him, his eyes filled with a profound melancholy when they find his.

'What have you done?' he asks. Sean bites in air. 'They're not going to let it go.'

He nods. 'I can handle it, Owen. A bit of bad luck, that's all. I just need a little time to get things straight in my head.' He is sitting on the chair with the slash in its arm. He tugs at a tiny flap of yellow plastic, picks at the foam filling.

'Where is Blue's money?' But Owen has guessed

312

the answer.

'I can get it back.'

There are three place settings on the table fashioned out of strips of bamboo. Now Sean starts pleating one of them. 'It . . . it was so easy, you know. A kid could have done it. A train to Brighton, meet a man on the pier, pick up a packet, deliver it to a contact in London.' His tone is soft, mildly self-deprecatory. 'All I had to do was . . . was pass it on. Like that children's game, what is it now?'

'Pass the parcel,' Owen volunteers.

'That's right. That's the one. Pass the parcel.' He pauses to draw a laboured breath, then another. Looking at the bruised shadows under his eyes, Owen is sure that he did not go to bed last night. 'But you see, I thought the music had stopped,' he continues. 'I thought it was my turn to open the parcel.' He gives an ironic smirk. He leans closer. His breath is rank with booze. 'But it's okay. I've got friends I can go to. A bit of a cash-flow problem, that's all. I can sort this all right,' he confides in a stage whisper.

'You're drunk,' Owen points out gently.

'Not as drunk as I'd like to be, I don't mind telling you,' Sean retorts, something of the old twinkle reasserting itself.

'How much money?'

Sean takes a hip flask from his pocket, unscrews the top and takes a swallow. He squeezes his eyes shut, absorbing the heat before opening them. 'Never you mind. I can get it back to them. Give me forty-eight hours and this'll all be forgotten, so.'

'No more gambling, please.'

'There you go again.' Sean lays a hand over his. His skin is very dry, like paper, dry and cold. 'What

313

did I say? The priesthood, that's what you're destined for, you know. Just like Emmet. Sucking on lemons all day, counting sins and telling the world what's wrong with it. From the first I knew you weren't cut out for retail. Am I right?' Owen's stomach churns acidly. Bile rises to the back of his throat and he grits his teeth to prevent himself from gagging. 'No need to reply. I can read it in your face. You'd have been after giving the goods away if you'd had half a chance.'

Crescents of sweat are fast becoming full moons under Sean's arms and over his chest. Buried beneath the facade of his blarney, Owen detects faintly, but distinctly, the acid of raw fear. Sean has returned to monotonously folding and unfolding his mat. His fingers run lightly over the wooden ridges, meticulously counting them, bent on seeing that each pleat contains the same number of bamboo sticks.

'It was going so well and then it all changed. I kept trying to make it better, kept saying to myself, if this one comes in you could do an about turn, go home with cash to spare in your pocket. If not quite a rich man, then at least one who can stand his wife and daughter a weekend in a posh hotel.' Sean pushes the mat impetuously away from him. It rolls over the edge of the table and falls to the floor. He hauls himself to his feet. 'So there it is. I'm going to take a wee holiday by myself instead. A little space to think this through.'

'Sean, you know I'm leaving. I can't stay any longer.' Owen too has risen and they face each other. 'I feel bad—'

'Don't feel bad. I understand. But do me this one last favour.'

'Sean, I can't. I really have got to go.'

'A couple more days, Owen. That's all I'm asking. I'll make it worth your while. So I will.' This last nearly makes Owen laugh outright. Only Sean, plunged into chronic debt to a hood, could have the gall to make such an offer. 'Hold it together for a few more days. I'll be back by Sunday. Have it all ironed out by then, so. I promise you. Just run the stall for me till then.'

Owen sighs. He wants to say 'no'. He wants to tell Sean to bugger off, that from now on he's out for himself. But he can't. Something is holding him back. He hesitates, then, 'You guarantee it.'

'On my life,' Sean says.

'Is there a 'phone number where I can reach you?'

'I'll ring here. Easier that way. I'm going to be on the move, you know. I've spoken to Catherine and she's taking Bria and staying over with her parents till I get back. I've told her to ring you if there's a problem. I hope you don't mind.'

He nods, pleased to hear that Catherine and their baby will be out of harm's way. 'But I'm off on Monday, no matter what.'

'I know. You're a good man, Owen!'

A good man. A tight knot in Owen's stomach begins to loosen at this. Much later, long after Sean has gone, lying in bed, Owen hears Naomi come in. He hears her in the kitchen, the bathroom, the small sounds of her preparing for sleep. Then, apart from the susurration from the dribbling taps, all is quiet. He cannot bring himself to turn off the tiny bedside lamp. It isn't much, this puddle of light, no bigger than the follow spot on an otherwise darkened stage. Nevertheless he huddles under it, face pressed into the pillow. Don't let them come,

315

he begs silently, not tonight. Don't let me hear Sarah's voice. His eyes rake the dimness for the Water Child, until he has satisfied himself that he is not there. He has not come to him all this long hot summer. Perhaps he has abandoned him. Perhaps the next time they crowd him in will be the last. He dreams that they net him in a sweat-soaked sheet, that they pull him through the impenetrable blackness of deep water. He is drowning in a purgatory alive with slimy sea snakes, when her voice wakes him. He gulps in a breath, scrambling up in bed. She is sitting on the floor staring at him, the way she did before.

'You're having a bad dream, Owen.'

'I'm sorry, sorry. Was I making a noise?' he pants.

She surveys him curiously, head crooked. 'Muttering. You were muttering,' she whispers. 'Lots of muttering, that's all.' For a while they both give an ear to the hissing exhalation of the leaking taps. Suddenly she drums her feet on the floorboards, the hollow percussion heightening the tension for him. Then, as suddenly, she stops. She wears a vest top, pants, and nothing else. He can see a packet of cigarettes on the floor and a lighter. She has one between her hands, unlit, sandwiched by her palms. 'We both have bad dreams, don't we?'

'You got in late,' he says inconsequentially.

'I was visiting a friend, a new friend.'

'Oh?' He tells her that Sean won't be back till Sunday, that he has got himself into a bit of difficulty, that he owes some money to Blue. She gives a careless shrug.

'Poor Sean,' she says, her voice going against the grain of the words. 'Poor, poor, Sean.'

'I'm on my way next week.'

316

'I'm so sick of this heat,' she says as if she has not heard. 'I wish I could go down to the lake now, take off my clothes and dive in. I'm imagining the cold smack of it. Do you remember that night that I swam in the lake, Owen? Our last night. The cold black water. It's hard to sleep in this weather. My friend isn't sleeping very well either. She has a baby who can't settle. So we're all awake. You, me, my friend, her baby.' She puts the cigarette back in the packet. 'It's too hot to smoke.'

'Who . . . who is she?' Owen says, his tone querulous. He smoothes a creased fold of sheet over his thigh.

'Shall I tell you?' she continues. 'I've been to see Catherine and Bria.' He stares at her in disbelief, feeling the now accustomed wrench of fear. 'Catherine gets very lonesome, you know. And who would blame her? Shut up alone in that house all day, with only the baby for company.'

'Does she know who you are?' he asks, his voice very low.

She smiles and taps the cigarette packet with a finger before replying.

'Oh no! For Catherine, I am Mara, married to an architect. We're expecting our very own baby soon.'

'Your own baby?' he parrots stupidly. 'But I don't understand how—' He has it then and his jaw slackens. The cushion in the carrier bag, the smock dress.

'For her I make believe, pretend, just like children do. Bria is a peach, fragile as a porcelain doll and just as pretty. There's foxy red in the fair curls and she has her father's eyes. Catherine says she's been having a trying time with her lately, but when I picked her up she was an angel. Very small, very light. When they are so little you have to be careful not to break them, Owen.' He reins in the urge to condemn her actions vehemently, an instinct telling him to tread carefully.

'I told her I wanted a boy. I took care of a baby once. Did I tell you?' He shakes his head. She gets up as she imports this, then comes to sit on the corner of his bed. 'Catherine has a pram with a tiny mattress, the bedding fresh and white and so delicate. Broderie Anglaise on all the borders, like fairies' wings. And a blanket soft as fur, with a pink teddy appliquéd in a corner.'

'Why?' he asks.

'Why what?'

'Why have you been to see her?' He rubs his face as if trying to wake himself up, as if he can't quite take in what she is saying.

Her mouth stretches in a smile. 'I was curious,' she says.

'But surely you realize no good can come of this, only more pain.'

'I wanted to see them for myself. Catherine and Sean's baby, Bria.' There is asperity in her tone.

'And now you have, do you feel better for it?' He is dousing his anxiety, keeping a desperate kind of control. Catherine is a victim in all this, much like himself. And as for Bria, well she is an innocent. The thought of Naomi picking her up, cuddling her, and Catherine not knowing who she is, that this is the woman her husband has been sleeping with, fills him with horror. 'Well?' he prompts.

'I feel like someone who has had an annoying itch for months and months, and now I have scratched it.' She catches her bitten nails on her teeth, tapping them like a dentist.

'So that's it. You've done it. Now you've satisfied your curiosity, you won't see her again.'

'Why are you so worried about it?' There is a shrewdness in her cadence. 'You suddenly seem very concerned about Catherine.'

'I'm concerned about both of you, how this could harm you both. Give me your word you won't go again.' He catches hold of her hand, and when she does not respond squeezes it a touch too forcefully. She squeals and pulls it away as if he has nipped it.

'If it means so much to you. I was getting bored anyway,' she sighs, curling up on the bed beside him. Now she continues speaking in a relentless flat pitch she has not used before. 'So you're quitting the market. Key-rings and purses, buckles and bows. It's all shit, y'know. All this stuff. All crap they make in some hot-house factory in Hong Kong.' Her voice is a distant drone now, a low murmur, her fingers softly striking the headboard. 'I imagine the journey sometimes, Owen. Did you know that?' She does not wait for a reply. 'I sit on that stool, and I look at some trashy trinket winking away under those God-awful lights that leach the life out of you, and I unmake it in my head. First I'm in the box, in a crate in the belly of some great container ship, crammed in with a million other crates. Then I'm being juggled about while an ocean storm batters us and the ship pitches and tosses.' Owen winces involuntarily. But Naomi, lost in her own musings, does not heed his reaction. 'Then I'm being unpacked by some poor kid who gets up at five, works till after dark, and sleeps in a bunk bed, in a room with countless others, a room not so different from this one. After that I'm inside a machine. I'm hot liquid metal inside the cogs and springs of its guts, being stamped into shape. And before that . . . ah, before that, Owen, I'm in the earth, buried. A lump of metal sunk in the grave of a mountainside. And it's quiet there, peaceful. The only sounds you hear are the maggots turning over the crumbs of dirt. All that way. Pulled and pushed and poked and melted and moulded, to be sent halfway round the world. For what? To light up the Irish's stall like a bit of raggedy tinsel. And then we lie to the gullible and tell them all that glitters is gold. Isn't that right, Owen?'

Her head swings round, and she fastens her disarming eyes on his. 'I've come a long way too. Did you guess that? You did, didn't you, Owen?'

22

Friday, 13 August

The heat makes it hard to comfort Bria. It is not the weather for hugging, for cuddling, for swaddling her baby in blankets and getting cosy together. Even the warmth of the bottle seems to distress her. It has been another terrible night spent pacing and rocking and sighing and crying. Sometimes she rocks when she isn't holding her baby, as if it is really her who needs comforting and not Bria. A little after 4 a.m. her daughter finally drops off, the hiccupping sobs slowly lessening, the spaces between them growing longer. By then, though Catherine is overtired, she has her second wind, the blood seeming to whir through her veins. She draws a chair up to the cot and sits quietly contemplating her baby. She is so beautiful that it robs Catherine of her breath. The love she has for her feels like gravity. She is the centre of a whirlpool, the nucleus of her life.

Outside, the main road keeps up its endless dirge. The light that is beginning to filter through the open window is a grey-blue. It reminds her of Isleworth Pool. She misses swimming. She will start going again and she will bring Bria with her. She will teach her daughter to love the water, not to be sucked underneath it. She should be at her parents' house now. Sean told her to go, made her promise to. Well, she lied. Hadn't he lied to her dozens of times? She doesn't want to be lectured by her mother on the do's and don'ts of childcare, on how abysmally she is neglecting the former and enacting the latter. He is in choppy seas, her husband, heading for a tempest. He has done something stupid, something rash, something reckless. She knows it instinctively. Oh, he tried to cover it up, his tone chrome bright. But as she listened it was apparent to her, and she felt anger and pity vying for pole position in her heart.

'There is absolutely nothing to go fretting yourself about, Catherine. I'm totally in control. It's only a matter of bridging the gap, you know.'

And she thought, how wide, how wide is that gap, Sean? Because there comes a point when it's not feasible any more to bridge a gap. Be honest, it's not a gap, it's a crevasse. And you've marooned us in it. But she'd said, 'Are you sure?'

''Course I am, darlin'. I'd prefer it though, if you'd go to your parents. A couple of nights, so. That's all.' She said nothing. 'Catherine? You will go, won't you? Take Bria. Promise me?'

'I promise,' she echoed dully.

'Good girl.' And when he'd called her that, *a good girl*, she'd wanted to scream at him that she wasn't a girl, she was a woman. And she needed a man beside her.

'Where are you going?'

'To see an old friend, that's all. I'll be back before you know it.' Then came a hiatus and just the sound of them both breathing, like divers drawing air through their mouthpieces.

'Does she have a telephone number, your old friend?'

'Catherine, what are you thinking of? Don't be silly. This is strictly business. Ring Owen if you need anything. At the flat or at the market, okay?'

'Okay.'

'And, Catherine?'

'Yes?'

'Kiss Bria for me. Tell her that her daddy loves her more than she will ever know.'

Catherine has read that the orchestra played music while the *Titanic* went down. She reflects that it was an insane thing to do. Surely they would have been more usefully employed bending their wits to surviving. But what if it was hopeless, truly hopeless and they each knew it, deep down, a fact chiselled in the gathering icebergs? They had a choice, they could all go to pieces, gibbering and squawking with panic, or they could carry on as normal, keep their dignity and show some courage. She will not go to her parents. Bria stirs in her sleep. Her closed eyelids have a lavender hue on them. There is a milk blister on her rosebud lips. Her cheeks are flushed. Her curls are spread against the cot

322

mattress. It seems beyond credulity that such a wondrous child can have resulted from the debris of her life.

But as the light in the room strengthens, she has the strangest sensation that she is swimming up from the deep, rising to the surface where she will take a life-sustaining breath. Today is special, set apart from all the other days that have gone before, because today she is meeting a friend, Mara, at the recreation ground. She has only known her a week, and in that short space her outlook has altered from irredeemable to hopeful. No, she will not confide in her mother and have her rain reproaches down upon her. Rather, she will tell her new friend about Sean's latest fiasco. She will talk freely, a concept so alien to her that it is like learning another language. And afterwards, as she has done every day this week, she will feel as light as chaff.

*   *   *

'So Owen, when is Naomi coming back, eh?' Enrico greets him as he enters the gloomy fug of the market.

'Soon. The holiday did her the world of good.'

'I knew she would love it there.'

'Yeah, it was great. Really kind of you to arrange that. You've a good family.' His eyes are still adjusting to the gloom and the Italian's face is all shadow, excepting the jumping purple beads and the stringy orange beard.

'Who is more handsome, me or my brother, Lorenzo?' He gives a snort of laughter.

'Impossible to choose between you.' He has placed a hand on Owen's shoulder, hampering his

323

progress. 'Him and your father, they've done a wonderful job restoring the cottage.'

'But there is no money there and the tourist season is too short. He'll leave eventually, the way I did. Hey, did you see Teodora?' he laughs and catches hold of his St Christopher medallion. 'The ghost of the lake?'

Owen's jaw tightens as he visualizes the drunken intercourse with Naomi on the banks of the reservoir. It takes him a second to compose himself. He knows the expected retort should be some humorous quip, but he cannot deliver it. 'I'm afraid not,' he says feebly, rubbing a hand clammy with perspiration on the back pocket of his jeans. 'No spooks turned up while we were there.'

He shrugs. 'Well then, did you swim in the lake?'

'I can't swim.' Enrico lifts an eyebrow.

'But it was hot? Hotter than here, I bet?'

'Yes, it was very hot.' He sucks in his lower lip, then, 'Naomi swam.'

'Ah, of course she did.'

'She should be back next week, then you can ask her all about it yourself. Look, I'd better go and open up.'

Enrico grins and stands aside. Then, as he passes, 'So you're the man now, eh, Owen? You're the man.'

Later on, Owen stares down at his own reflection in the mirrored counter looking for *the man*, but only seeing the choppy blond hair and anxious eyes of a boy. His features are partially concealed by dozens of pairs of shimmering hair grips. He has the sudden urge to swipe them onto the floor, to stamp on them. Because of his own troubled dreams and Naomi's worrying confession, he has had little

324

sleep. Now, as he replays her words in the busy warren of the market, far from dispelling his alarm, they only seem to intensify it.

'I wanted to see them for myself. Catherine and Sean's baby, Bria.'

He feels he should be doing something—but what? All these secrets and no one to turn to, no one to share them with, to lessen his load of cares. The conditions in this hell hole are inhuman, he decides. It feels as if there is no circulation, no ventilation, as if they are all struggling to breathe the same tiny condensed mass of stuffy foul air. In the heat the odours of unwashed bodies, of sweat and incense, leather and rubber, seem as pungent as putrid meat. He wishes Sean was here. As soon as he gets back he will tell him what Naomi has been doing. Then he can deal with it. Last night's revelations have filled him with ominous portents, and persuaded him irrefutably that she is far from well. As for her assurances that she will not continue in this ludicrous charade, he doubts their sincerity. Still, he comforts himself, there is no risk to mother and baby today. They are not in Hounslow. Sean said that they are staying with Catherine's parents, beyond Naomi's reach. Besides, it isn't his problem, it is theirs. What is any of this to him? In a matter of days he will be gone. In a couple of months he probably won't even be able to remember their names, Naomi, Sean . . . Catherine . . . Catherine and Bria.

The morning inches by, the confines of the market as claustrophobic as a dungeon. He waves away a customer. 'I told you, we haven't got any in that colour. The next aisle. They have them, love.' He is starting to sound like Sean.

He leans heavily on the counter, arms braced, hands splayed for support, his head sagging. His homing-pigeon thoughts keep finding their way back to Catherine and Bria. Sensations claim him, the way Catherine's tears damped his shirt, the snug fit of Bria in his arms. Covering his face with a hand, he blinks back tears. Then, he rolls his head and lets his eyes rove the concrete ceiling. Muzzy pokers of white light arrow off the fluorescent tubes. Right on cue Gary Glitter starts hollering that he is the leader of the gang. He needs to pull himself together. This is his overactive imagination. He is fabricating something sinister where there is only understandable inquisitiveness, and yes, perhaps resentment. But that is all. If Sean phones, he will tell him everything. If not, then, when he sees him on Sunday. There is certainly no need to panic about it.

'Anyone serving?' comes an American voice from behind him. More from habit than self-control, in the instant it takes for Clark Kent to become Superman, he is the convivial salesman, hurrying to hook down a handbag that the customer is pointing at. She is a large, loud woman with a tired, bleach-blonde perm, a slack-skinned face, and restless desirous eyes. 'Oh, don't you just love this bag, Ada?' With a wave of her hand she conjures a thinner version of herself. He launches into his sales pitch, his spiel packed with effusive flattery, and vows of the best possible deal ever. In fact, it is a steal at the price he is going to give her. He has just tucked away the notes she gave him when he spots Blue striding towards him, his face distorted with wrath.

326

Mara is in control. She is fond of Naomi but she lacks the necessary purpose. She has tried cohabiting, a half-and-half arrangement. But experience has taught her that it doesn't work. The problem is that Naomi lets The Blind Ones take advantage of her. She doesn't stand up to them, doesn't take them on. She wants the ruthless streak. Mara is the ruthless streak. In fact, Naomi owes her everything. If she didn't step in from time to time and take the upper hand, Naomi would still be procrastinating, and nothing would ever be accomplished. Mara is on the train to Hounslow where she will meet their new friend, Catherine. Opposite her is a woman with a bawling baby. The woman looks at her bump and gives her a sisterly smile. Mara strokes it complacently. Her baby, when it comes, won't cry. She will have a special baby, not like the squalling red-faced infant floundering just feet from her. The shrill lament feels as if it is trapped in her head, an angry wasp repeatedly stinging her thoughts, injecting its poison into her reason. What she does not understand is why no one else in the carriage seems to bother about it. Are they Blind Ones too, pretending, pretending, day and night, acting out their charades? Miss Elstob has deaf ears when it comes to baby's yelling.

'That baby's sick with the fever, Miss,' she tells her. 'All burning up, you feel her brow. See if it's not.'

'Mind your own business, Mara, and don't be cute with me,' Miss says, cuffing her about the ears until the blood throbs inside them, and they feel thick and hot as drop scones fresh off the griddle.

327

But today she wakes with the conviction that something is about to happen, something out of the ordinary, something that will forever scatter the regimented days of her existence. It's not as if there is a clue, though. In the bedroom are the same six beds all with blanketed humps inside them. She can see through the window that the sun is in its usual place in the sky. Baby is crying in the cot beside her, and she can hear Miss Elstob downstairs banging about in the kitchen. It is the school holidays, and the house is as crowded as ever. It is so jam packed that you can't help tripping over children and bumping into them. She dreams of being alone, all alone, of having a place where you can hear your own thoughts without them being chopped up like firewood. In the coal cupboard she can hear them loud as a cannon some nights, her thoughts. But it's not a good place, that cupboard. It's filthy. And while the voice is cracking in her head, she is getting filthy too. The coal dust gets into her cuts and turns them blue. So when she comes out she is black and blue.

But it's been a while since they chucked her in there. She's been good. And if it wasn't for baby howling away like a banshee, she might stay that way. Not long after breakfast the house gets empty. All the children ran out of it, and so does Miss Elstob. It is on account of something bad occurring that they rush out of doors. In house seven, one of the biggest boys, big as a man he is, a bully called Arthur Datcher, has lost his temper. A fight started between him and the house mother, Miss Lister. She is an evil cow too, with a goitre on her neck that makes it look as if she's swallowed an egg that won't go down. He shouted at her, and she shouted back and slapped him round the solid block of his face. The boy who brought the news said Arthur puffed himself up then, like a big old turkey, and his face went all purple. They were washing the breakfast things when he seized up a fork. He didn't hold it like a fork, the boy said. He held it like a knife. And then he sort of turned round very slowly in the corner, where he was standing. His nostrils got big as cherries and he stared at Miss Lister, and stared and stared. He pawed the ground with his foot like a bull. He was pop-eyed and dribbling. But she just went on shouting until she was almost hoarse. Then suddenly he charged. He threw himself at her, directly at her, stabbing with the fork. She took a fall and well, the fork went into her cheek.

'Gah! He speared it like it was a tomato,' the boy said. 'It's dreadful bad, and Mother's squawking and rolling all about.' Then he told them that an ambulance was coming and the police, and that Arthur was being taken away, and that they should come and see. After he dashed off, all Mara could hear was the clomping of shoes on the wooden floor, and Miss Elstob's boots too. And they all ran to take a peep for themselves.

Mara doesn't know how long they'll be, but for now the house is hollow as a shell. Her voice when she speaks has a bit of an echo. She hasn't been in a cave but she's been told caves have echoes too. Baby is upstairs in the cot and still crying. The cry has got thinner though, as if baby is losing its voice, like Miss Lister did. Mara looks all round and waves her hands in the space. There is so much of it to push about. She picks up Miss Elstob's pinny and ties it on. It's a bit too long for her, like an evening dress but the wrong material.

329

'I'm going to make believe that this is my house, that I'm Mother. And that baby is my baby,' she announces to no one. Then she goes upstairs and tells baby, 'Because I'm Mother, my job is to make you stop crying.'

Baby looks up at her with slitty eyes crusted with dried ooze. Thick green snot cakes her nose so that she huffs and snorts to breathe. Her mouth is pushed wide open to make room for all the yells to come squalling out. And her face is apple red and fat as a grapefruit. Her brown hair is sticking down as if it has been glued on. 'Poor baby,' says Mara. 'Mother's here now to take care of you.' She picks baby up, and she is all hot and wriggly, stinking of wee, with a sodden nappy heavy and dropping off. She carries baby downstairs to the bathroom, pulls off her nightshirt and nappy, and lays her on a towel on the floor. There are two baths in here, a small one for babies, and a large one for the big children. The baby bath is a white enamel tub resting on tall fluted metal legs. Because it's high up you can stand when you bathe baby. There are two shiny silver taps at the end of it nearest the wall. And there is a soap dish made of white china screwed above them, with a big tablet of soap in it. Mara only runs the cold tap, puts it on full so that the water comes crashing out. It's like a waterfall. She's seen one of those on a walk. And it's so fast that the bath is full up before she knows it.

'Now Mother is going to take away all your hotness,' she explains to baby. 'This is like water medicine, and when I pull you out you will be all well again. And you'll stop crying and go to sleep. Then I can go to sleep too.'

But baby just makes yammering noises and kicks

330

thin legs and thrashes thin arms. So Mara scoops her up and holds her over the icy bath. It is quite difficult because baby is like an eel, bending this way and that, and trying to look sideways at what is under her. 'One, two, three,' Mara counts and she begins to lower baby. When baby's bottom and back touch the icy water, she jumps like a frog. She is slippery with sweat, and Mara has to hold on tight to avoid dropping her. Now baby is struggling so much that she has to push her down, push her into the water, down, down to the bottom of the bath and hold her there. She is much stronger than Mara realized, so that she has to use all her brawn to keep her under. Even so, baby looks very pretty beneath the water with her brown hair waving like weed, and tiny silver air bubbles sticking to her face as if shiny beads have been stitched into her skin, and her eyes all wide with the crusts washing away.

That is the instant when the door bursts open and Miss Elstob is standing there. For a second she is made of stone. Then her thin body cracks like a whip. She grabs Mara by the hair and sends her spinning across the room. Then she plunges her scrawny arms in the water and yanks baby out, all dripping silver and wobbly, the loveliest quiet baby Mara has ever seen.

She lays baby on the towel and presses her tiny ribcage. And now Miss Elstob is sort of screaming in air, her forehead a tangle of wrinkles. Lots of faces pile up on top of each other in the doorway, because the children are all back. And just like the boy described Arthur, they are pop-eyed, all their mouths slack and fish-flapping. Curled up and holding her broken head together, Mara sees that baby is being sick, silver sick, water sick. And that the sick is not just being coughed out of her mouth, but out of her nose too, along with the watery snot. Then baby is whining in breaths, the sound like a bow scraped quickly over a violin. Mother wraps her up in the towel, and gives her to one of the older girls to hold.

'Get a blanket for her, double quick. We'll take her to the sick bay,' she orders. When she turns on Mara, she is white with rage. And seeing this whiteness, Mara knows that it is much more awful than any red anger you can imagine. It is what comes after the red. It is so scalding that all the colour is burnt away.

'What were you doing to the baby?' she says in a radio-hiss voice.

'I was making her cool, making her all cool,' Mara whimpers. ''Cos baby was sick with the fever.'

Mother pulls out some of her hair dragging her to the coal cupboard, so that her scalp is bleeding when the door is slammed shut, dripping down her cheeks when the key is turned. She hugs her head and imagines that she is mending it, pasting chunks of her skull back together. Her hands are sticky with blood. She can hear the children calling her names through the door.

'Baby killer.' 'Mad Mara.' 'Mara's a murderer.' 'She's gone and drowned the baby.'

She throws lumps of coal at them to show them that she doesn't care, and they bang on the wood. Then she digs, and piece by piece begins burying herself under the coal mound. When she sucks her fingers she can taste coal dust and blood all mixed up. She wanted to be Mother, that's all, to be Mother and for baby to be hers. Then Owen won't go. He'll stay to help her look after baby, and they'll be a family, Mother, Father and baby. She loves Owen and he loves her back. He mustn't ever leave her and go with someone else, the way Walt did. He mustn't grow bored of her and want to throw her away. She thinks about her thighs locking him inside her, and her body wet and sleek with the lake. She thinks about the crying baby and how she gets confused sometimes, so that it seems the crying is coming from her, that she is the cry baby. She thinks about Mother, not the house mother but her real one, the one who left her behind and died.

She closes her eyes and sees lipstick edging Mother's front teeth, pearly pink, and her headscarf fluttering in the wind, and the sun shivering on her sunglasses, and golden buttons on the uniform of the soldier, and the salt taste of the sea on her tongue, the way it carried her in its swingeing grey-green arms, how it beat the badness out of her, broke up the coal in her and turned the nasty dust to gleaming white sand. The last thing she hears before the black rubs her out, is the high-pitched whistling scream of the train as it roars into a station. Or is it baby's piercing cries hacking at her head again, making it ache so?

*   *   *

Raw terror grips Owen. His heart bucks, his senses sharpen, nausea takes hold. He might run if he thought that his legs would carry him, if he thought that he stood a chance. Knowing it is risky to turn your back on an attacking dog, he faces them, Blue and his thug. His back is to the counter, his arms propping him up. There is no browsing today. They bullet through the shoppers and stall-holders, shoving aside anyone that makes the mistake of obstructing them. They wear dark trousers, long-sleeved shirts, ties—but no jackets. Blue hops agilely up on the stool, his minder flanking him.

'You heard from Sean?' Blue asks without preamble, his blue eyes like lasers burning into Owen's.

'No,' Owen lies. 'I told you yesterday.'

Blue loosens his tie. The blue and gold stripes remind Owen of his old school uniform tie. 'That was yesterday. This is today. A lot can change in twenty-four hours,' he says in a tone of barely concealed threat. He undoes his top button.

'He went off at the start of the week, said he'd be back by Thursday. Like I said before. But he hasn't showed yet.'

Blue winces and draws a finger delicately over his effeminate mouth. 'What's your name?' he says softly, the finger still sliding over his lips.

'Owen.' His legs are trembling so that he has to concentrate on keeping them braced.

'Well, Owen, your boss has my money. A great deal of money, as it happens. And I want it back. Understand?' He lowers his hand and picks a speck of dust off one of his trouser legs.

Owen nods. 'I'm sorry. I don't know anything about that. I only work for him part time.' His high voice and the rapid pace of his words betray his dread.

'Are you smart, Owen?' Blue asks.

'I don't know what you mean.'

'Are you smart?' he repeats obdurately. Owen shrugs. 'Because you're not telling me what I want to hear, and that's plain idiotic.' He grinds his teeth. The minder sees off a couple of customers.

'If I had any information, if I knew Sean's whereabouts, I'd pass it on to you.' He flicks his tongue over his dry lips, swallows, then clears his throat.

Blue takes a thoughtful breath, surveying him head to toe, then blinks slowly. 'You're trying my patience, kid.'

Owen manufactures a fretful sigh and scratches the back of his head. 'What do you want me to say? I've told you the truth.'

'Oh I hope so, for your sake, Owen. I do hope so.'

'Honestly, I wish I could be more—' But he never finishes the sentence. At a sign from Blue, the minder lunges forwards and lands a punch directly in his solar plexus. Owen folds like a hairpin, every atom of breath knocked out of him. He is trying to hoop air back into his collapsed lungs, but he is winded and they will not inflate. The blurred shapes of his own shoes rush at his eyes. He is suffocating, dark stars zooming towards him. He totters, nearly overbalances, feels a hand bunching the collar of his shirt, hoisting him up like a puppet. He is going to pass out. In a second the stars will meld together and become one glittering black moon, obliterating all else. Then a merciful vein of air seeps into him. Slowly, and with a scalpel thrust of pain, his lungs begin to swell. Immediately, he is seized by a spasm of violent coughing, his breath cannoning out of him with pumice-stone friction. The hand unhooks him and he stumbles. Tears are coursing down his cheeks as he gulps in oxygen and spits it out, a wicked spur jabbing his diaphragm. The present reasserts itself. Faces bear down on him, immutable eyes hold his.

'Jogged your memory?' Blue says. Owen gabbles,

335

unable to latch onto any words. He works his mouth for a moment but all he manages is some more gibberish. Blue slips a hanky from his trouser pocket and unfolds it carefully. He makes much of blotting his brow and wiping his hands on it. After he has tucked it away he rubs his palms, once, twice, on his trouser legs.

Then, 'You tell Sean that bright people don't miss appointments with Blue. You tell him we'll be back, and so will he with the money, or else. You tell him no one ever cheats me and gets away with it.' His tone is sugary as candyfloss one instant, the screechy discord of a stuck pig the next. He pats his butterscotch curls into place, momentarily glimpsing his reflection in the mirrored counter. Then, carefully, he examines his fingernails, head tilted ruminatively.

'I've broken a nail. Damn!' he mutters, peeved. 'You make sure that you pass on my message, all right, sonny?'

Owen nods dumbly. He has begun trembling with shock. And then they are making their way towards the stairs, Blue taking them two at a time. Eyes of neighbouring stallholders are averted. They know Blue by reputation and that is sufficient impetus to ensure that they do not get involved. It takes several minutes for Owen to gather his wits and think coherently. He swipes the tears from his face and counts his breathing in and out, until his heartbeat calms. Then, working through the pain that radiates from his core, the pain that makes every inhalation slew through him, he begins methodically packing up the stall. The music jangles and bumps, the lights strike his eyes like paper pellets, as he goes about determinedly filling cardboard boxes and tidying

336

them into the under-counter cupboard. His camel's back is broken. Not another straw will it take. He will leave the keys in the flat and go—now. If this means that he is running away, that he is taking the coward's route, so be it. He has one aim fuelled by terror, to escape London, to get far away from Blue and his cronies, from Naomi, Sean and this rat-hole of a market. He padlocks the stall doors, his eyes sweeping over the scintillating maze one last time. Then, he turns towards the sunlit stairs.

'Owen, you must come quickly. There's a call from Sean's wife. She's asking for you.' Spinning round, he comes face to face with Cat, short for Catalina. She is a tall, dark-haired Hispanic woman with the stall nearest the toilets. 'She's hysterical. I think it may be something to do with their baby.' And then he is racing down the aisles, dodging customers, heads turning in his direction. Finding his way across the jostling market to the telephone, he feels like a pinball hitting one obstacle after another.

'Here, watch your step!' someone yells after him. And another of the punters swears and makes an obscene gesture at his retreating back.

'For fuck's sake, who do you think you are, pushing me out of the way?' Owen has a fleeting impression of a luminous pink miniskirt, a sequinned top and large eyes outlined with kohl. 'Bastard!' she screams after him. Cat ushers him through the swing doors and into a concrete cell. With a jut of her chin she indicates the 'phone dangling from its cord.

'If you need me, holler,' she tells him and vanishes. Four narrow toilet cubicles line one wall. Opposite them is a basin, and set a few feet beyond it, the payphone. He steps up to it, and warily picks up the receiver as though he is drawing a primed gun from its holster.

'Catherine, Catherine it's Owen. What's the—' But she interrupts him with a rush of hysterical words that he struggles to follow. 'Who has taken her? Who has taken Bria?' But he knows, he knows who has her. And in that moment he knows, too, that her life is imperilled.

He listens to a repeat of the previous night's narrative told from another perspective, that of a parent in fear for her baby's life. A volley of words, the smell of uric acid hitting the back of his throat, and the name, Mara. A friend, a pregnant woman she met at the rec. Catherine was going to go to her parents. Sean told her to. But in the end she couldn't face it. And now . . . The floor and walls seem to shudder to the muffled beat of the music, an interminable drum roll. Only this story has a new chapter to it, one where Mara goes back to Catherine's house, and they talk. And she is so nice, so kind that she trusts her implicitly. She says Catherine should have a rest, that she will mind Bria for her while she sleeps. And she is tired, very tired, and the caring eyes keep reassuring her till she assents. Mara is downstairs with her baby. She can hear her singing a lullaby. And she falls asleep. God forgive her, she falls asleep. And when she awakes, Bria has disappeared. The woman has taken her, taken her baby. A razor-edged silence comes then, like the poise of a guillotine blade seconds before it falls. The beat blunders on. Then suddenly Catherine's curdling screams leap from the receiver into the squalid surroundings.

'Listen to me, Catherine. I know who has Bria,' he

338

tells her firmly, his eyes on a metal mesh bin in the corner of the room where blood is slowly soaking through a shiny white sanitary bag.

'Where is she? Where is my baby, Owen? Where? Tell me where to find her!'

He is visited by a second of fright. He drops the phone, follows it swinging from its cord, casting a shadow that crawls over the concrete floor and walls. 'Owen, Owen,' comes the muted tinny shriek, as if travelling universes to find him. He forces himself to take hold of it again. He tries to speak but his lips refuse to respond. The door gapes open with a slap of cooler air. A big man with a shaved head, and a raised milky-green scar meandering lizard-like across one cheek, stands stolidly taking in the tableau that greets him. The look in his close-set ash-grey eyes is blasé as they jerk away from him. He steps into one of the cubicles, and seconds later Owen hears his stream of piss striking the enamel toilet bowl.

The words come unstuck at last. 'Mara is really Naomi, Catherine. It's Naomi. She has your baby. She has Bria.'

'Naomi? Why would she—' A pause as one thought leads to another. Then, 'Where? Where? Where, Owen?' Catherine's voice is a heavy boot striking him, making him flinch with pain. The man lumbers out of the stall, doing up his flies. He gives a knowing sneer, then without comment he melts back into the market. 'Where?' she echoes again, her tone altered now, hollow and pitiable. 'Tell me where? Please?'

'I don't know for sure. Maybe the flat in Covent Garden. She won't harm her. I promise you. She'll be looking after her. I can't explain now but you have to believe me. You haven't told anyone else, have you, Catherine?' He has visions of police cars surrounding the Hounslow terrace, of it all escalating rapidly. And if Naomi feels trapped, cornered . . .

'No. You're the only one. I don't know where Sean is. I haven't rung my parents. I wanted to speak to you first.'

'Don't alert the police yet, Catherine. It's very important. You stay where you are. I'm going to find Bria now. And I'm going to bring her home, safe and well. I'll ring as soon as I have news. Wait by the phone.'

Catherine's voice is light as goose down. 'Bring her back!' she begs. 'Bring her back, Owen!' And all at once he is transported down the ladder of years to a bar of golden windswept sand. He is staring down at Sarah. Her skin is misty blue, like the wings of advancing night staining a blanket of snow. There is grit in her dripping curls, tiny bits of shining grit. Her eyes are shut, the heavy lids shaded purplish-grey. Her lips are slightly open so that Owen can see her tiny front teeth. His father is standing in his sodden, wrinkled clothes, his big hands at his sides fumbling in the air. Sunlight slaps his balding wet scalp, making it gleam. Salty sea tears scroll down his cheeks and mingle with his own. His mother is kneeling by the side of Sarah's body, clutching her withered starfish hand. She lifts her head. Her eyes lock with her husband's, his father's.

'Bring her back!' she hisses. 'Bring her back!' The present reclaims him. In it another child is lost and another mother hisses, 'Bring her back!'

'I'll bring her back,' he tells Catherine. 'I'll call the moment I have news.'

340

He hangs up, flicks his face with water from the corner basin, and rushes out. It seems wholly inappropriate that it is such a beautiful day, that the Londoners he shoulders past have sunflower faces upturned to the skies. They are clothed in gay cotton prints, sit at street cafés letting the hours slip through their fingers, while he strives to bring back a missing baby. His hand is shaking as he opens the door that fronts onto the street. When, gasping for breath, he reaches the third floor, he has the key at the ready. The flat door is locked from the inside.

'Naomi? Naomi? It's me, Owen.' With a closed fist he raps smartly. 'Come on, Naomi, let me in.' He is an actor giving the performance of his life, his tone amicable, easygoing. He puts his ear against the wood and listens for the sounds of a baby. Nothing. Then Naomi's voice returns to him.

'Are you alone?'

'Yes, yes,' he attests jovially. 'I'm by myself.' With relief he hears the bolt being slid back, and the door edges open a few inches. She has been crying. The whites of her eyes are a watery pink. Her mascara has run, staining her face with sooty streaks. Both of her eyelids are shadowed with black. Her scruffy hair is tangled. She is wearing yet another smock dress, a busy viscose print with a fussy lace collar. Her cushion belly is being flattened in the narrow crack.

'May I come in?' he asks quietly. She cranes her neck and peers beyond him. He shakes his head. 'It's just me, Naomi.' She snivels and wipes her nose with the back of her hand. Briefly she locks eyes with him, as if checking for traces of a lie behind his contracting pupils. At last she stands back, letting the door swing open. He steps

341

through, and instantly she slams it behind him, relocks it. She shuffles past him. Both bedroom doors are ajar and he scans them hastily, searching for Bria. But he sees no evidence of her. Emerging through the bead curtain, he finds the lounge flooded with brutal light. From the street below comes the usual road rumble. Nothing is amiss. All the furniture is as he left it this morning. There is no addition to it—no baby.

'I am very tired,' Naomi mutters dazedly, sinking down onto the settee. Again she rubs at her nose with the back of her hand. 'I need to sleep now.' Unconsciously she pats her dented cushion womb. Owen crouches down and rests a hand on her bent knees. For a moment she stares blankly at it, then looks up, finding his face.

'Naomi, where's the baby?' With protracted blinks she closes her eyes.

'The baby?' she mimics in mild puzzlement.

'Yes, the baby. Bria. What have you done with the baby?' He intones this cordially, as if he is asking the whereabouts of a lost coat, or a pair of shoes.

'Oh, the baby's dead,' she breathes, smiling, happy to be of assistance. She leans her head to one side, her eyes now wide and staring. She gives an expansive sigh, yawns and picks at her scalp with her stubby fingers. 'I had to get rid of it. My baby's dead.' She leans closer to him. 'Come to bed, Owen.'

'Where's Bria, Naomi?' She is wearing grey leggings and no shoes. He notices red pumps peeping out from under the fringe of throws. She worries at a tiny hole on her peaked knees. Her brow puckers into its one crooked frown line.

'But it's all right because I got another one. Bria.

342

Bria. It's a nice name, isn't it?' she says to herself. 'Now we can be a family, Owen. A proper family. I'll be Mother. You'll be Father. And Bria will be Baby.'

Fleetingly he thinks of Catherine, Bria's true mother, staring at the 'phone. And he thinks of Sean, her father, God knows where, doing God knows what. He lifts his voice a notch. 'That's right, Naomi. So where is our baby? Where is Bria?' Now she is trying to push the tip of her little finger through the hole. 'Listen to me. She's very small. She needs looking after. Her mother is so worried about her. And that's why you have to tell me where she is. So that I can take her home.'

Her vacant eyes find his. 'I'm the Mother,' she says. 'This is our home.'

'Yes, yes!' Impatience colours his timbre and he takes a beat to control his rising pitch. 'So tell me where you left her, where you left our baby.'

She seems to consider this carefully, her hands palpating her feather-filled belly unconsciously. Then her racoon eyes suddenly cloud over. 'I was very sad,' she says under her breath. 'But no one cared about me, no one listened to me. They put me in the coal cupboard and it was very dark and dirty in there.'

Owen's stomach suddenly cramps and it dawns on him that he has eaten nothing all day. It feels tender too, the flesh bruised and sore. He scrapes back his hair, frustration and a sickening consternation warring inside him. 'Where is Bria?' She stares at him, a stubborn adolescent. In the silence that ensues he becomes aware of the lisping of the leaking bath taps, a sound he has grown so accustomed to that it takes a minute for it to register on his sense of hearing. Then, listlessly, Naomi straightens up and indicates the bead curtain with a nod of her head. 'Bria is in the bath, Owen. I put her in the bath,' she says angelically. 'She was bad, very bad, and she wouldn't stop crying, so I put her in the bath to make her all cool and quiet again.'

He climbs to his feet unsteadily, feeling as if he has no skeleton to prop him up. His hands cover his mouth. He turns back to Naomi. She is staring fixedly at the wall, at the lopsided Jimi Hendrix poster, her mouth moving in a haunting rhyme. His hands fall away. 'Dear God, Naomi, what have you done?' But she makes no reply. He moves like a machine through the clicking beads, hesitating before the closed bathroom door. He feels the paralysing horror of the small boy on the beach, the overriding impulse to run. With a man's courage he pushes down on the handle of the door and nudges it open. He sees the toilet, the basin, the small cabinet hanging above it, the mirrored front cracked, the bath. There is a green blanket in the bath, a sodden blanket lying in thick folds. The taps are dribbling, slowly filling the tub.

He steps to the bath's edge and forces himself to look down. He is holding his breath as he leans over. His spread fingers start exploring the fat pleats of woolly fabric, pockets of water trapped like miniature rock pools within it. Now he is patting it carefully, his hands travelling swiftly across its rugged landscape. He touches something satiny as soap, a tiny foot. He scrabbles at the drenched shroud, peeling back the heavy layers to reveal a baby. Bria. She is lying on her back in inches of icy water. She is lifeless, her skin waxen, her lips a bluish hue. With a light touch he probes

344

the small torso, dares to lay the flat of his hand against the saturated pink baby-grow. Through the towelling material he feels a flyaway tick, the rapid tremble of a heartbeat. She is alive! He slips his hand under the baby's body, cups her head and carefully lifts her up. Hugging her close, he hurries to his bedroom.

Bria's head falls on his shoulder and the ghost of a whimper escapes her mouth. There is a bib still tied at her neck, with a nursery-rhyme cow leaping a golden bracket of moon. It is blotted with the watery yellow of infant bile. Her eyes are shut fast, her fine hair is plastered to her head, and she is icy as death. He lays her on the bed and strips the clothes from her. Last is her nappy, laden with water. He rummages in the wardrobe and pulls out a navy cotton sweatshirt. Somewhere he has read that the most efficient way to restore heat to a baby is to hold it next to your own skin. He rips off his T-shirt, enveloping her with the heat of his own body. 'Bria . . . Bria . . . come back,' he whispers, clasping her close, willing life back into her, gently rubbing the tiny limbs to restore the circulation. When at last he feels her stir he lays her on the bed, and swaddles her in the sweatshirt. Supporting her in the arc of his bent arm, he sees her eyes start, then the lids droop again. He is going to ring Catherine, but as he emerges from his bedroom, Naomi appears in the beaded doorway, barring his way.

'Where are you going, Owen?'

He daren't risk Bria's life further by delaying with this mad woman another second. He steps to the flat door, slides the bolt and opens it.

Naomi's head lolls to one side. Her hair is virtually

black now. Her lapidary eyes are unfocused. 'Owen?'

'Out. I'm going out.'

'Are you taking our baby?' she asks.

'Yes.'

'Don't be long.' As he descends the stairs he hears her call after him, 'Because we're a family now. We have to stay together, no matter what.'

*   *   *

Catherine has stared at the 'phone so long now, that like a word uttered over and over, it has grown surreal, an unfamiliar object. It feels as if time has slowed to a standstill. She sits in the husk of a house that is not a home. She has put all her faith in a man she has only met once. She does not know why. Her baby's life depends on him, and him alone. She should have rung her parents, contacted the police. And yet something compelled her to turn to Owen, to charge him with bringing her back. Bria is dead, her reason tells her so. Her baby is dead. She must accept this. But her heart prays, please, please.

She gazes round the hall, her senses heightened. The front door is painted yellow, mustard yellow. Beneath this epidermis lie many other shades, she is sure, past lives layered one over the other. The walls are papered, a pattern of cream lozenges on brown lozenges on beige lozenges. Looking at it makes her feel woozy. The floor is lino, muddy green hexagons. The early evening light is unkind to the ill-used house. It exposes the pram, the empty pram in all its hopelessness. This morning it had a baby in it. This evening it is empty.

Catherine knows about death. She knows you may

be larking in the snow one minute, and being sucked under the ice the next. She knows that it has a small voice, small but determined. Death is easy. Death is a slip. It trips you up when you least expect it. She thought it didn't matter, that none of it mattered. The dreadful days she has slogged through made her pine to be back in the ice, to let it have her. She felt the clamp of the frozen jaws and welcomed it. She thought there was nothing much worth salvaging in her life. Then Bria came.

And so she waits poised on the edge of a second, knowing she may fall either way. Her hearing is sensitive. Voices slur through bricks and mortar, music pounds, traffic keeps up a dreary debate, a bus's brakes grind and wheeze, a horn sounds, engines turn over like cement mixers. Then one slows approaching number 17, stops, a door slams, footsteps approach. She has the sudden insane desire to drop to the lino floor, clasp her hands over her head, to take cover before the bomb blast. Knocking. Someone has come knocking at her door.

'Catherine? Catherine?' More knocks. 'It's Owen. I've got Bria. I've . . . I've brought her back. I've brought her back, Catherine.' She is not sure if she can get up, if her legs will support her. 'Catherine? She's okay. Catherine?'

She climbs to her feet in increments, like a frail old woman, and feels her way along the wall, leans into it, lets it press the kinks out of her. She rolls onto the door, presses her face up to the frosted glass panel set in its top half. She can see him on the other side of it, his features glimpsed through the pane of ice. Fair hair, blue eyes, red hair, green eyes, undulate. He stoops so that he is level with

347

her. Their lips would be touching but for the glass. She stares at her reflection in him, and he stares back at his, in her, Water Children, kindred spirits. A mother who has lost her child. A child who has lost his mother. They surface and breathe in unison. In the division of a second, something comes of nothing. And the splinter of ice lodged in both their hearts begins to melt.

'Catherine, it's all right. You can open the door.' His lips brush the pane as he speaks. He waits. Bria squirms in his arms. She is warm now and hungry. Catherine thinks, I am going to faint. But she doesn't. She lays her hand on the door knob, turns it and pulls. The door judders open. Arms that are not hers levitate by themselves, they rise and reach. And the breath snags in her throat so that she keeps having to tear it out of her. He puts the baby in the arms that are not hers, and the breath rips, and the cry comes.

'Ah! Bria!'

Later, he thinks about the paradox, that the baby held *her*, and not the other way round. He sees the buttercup light that spilled into the hall as she opened the door, sees it giving her red hair the lustre of gold. He thinks about her dreamy green eyes, their soft setting of light-brown lashes and brows. He recalls the way his body relaxed as he watched her ministering to her baby. He had not known that he was all angles and ridges until then. They communicated in broken sentences, a phrase, a gesture, a dialogue of action. She rang her father and told him that she was worried that Bria was ill. He came to collect them, and said he would take her to the doctor. She agreed to stay with them for the time being. Before Owen left she took his hand

and held it a long moment, then she gave him her parents' telephone number.

Heading back into London, he thinks about the leaking tap, how the water was rising speedily, how little time there was left. He thinks about how easy it is to drown, how a little girl on a sunny day can wander into the blue of the sea, and be snatched and dragged to her death in seconds. For a time he strolls the city streets. He watches young women in bright summer cottons laughing and chattering, tossing their heads, linking their arms, running for a bus, climbing into a cab, pedalling a bike. What would Sarah be like now? What kind of a woman would she have grown into? He did not realize that the pang of missing someone you never knew could be so acute. Would they have argued, joked, teased, laughed? Would they have had nicknames for each other? Would she have leant on him and he on her? Would entwined stretches of their lives have been like a three-legged race? Would her brother have meant as much to her, as her absence meant to him? He does not go back to the flat. He boards another train, overground. He is journeying west, his destination North Devon, an outing to the seaside. He is on a pilgrimage to Saunton Sands, to revisit the sea that took his sister. He is going to turn back the pages of his life and bookmark his last day spent with Sarah.

23

Nothing much had changed on the farm. In fact, Sean thought, it was rather like journeying back in

Doctor Who's TARDIS. His father was dead and buried. A brain tumour had reduced a man built like an ox with the most robust of constitutions, to dust. Emmet, the second son, the favoured one, the child who fit snugly into the rural scene, had assumed the mantle of authority as his birthright. And to fortify his position he had taken himself a wife, Grania Quinn. She was the fourth daughter of good solid stock. Her jaw line was well defined. Her eyebrows were raven black and bold. And she had a light furring of hair across her upper lip that looked like a moustache in the midday sun. Her wide hips had effortlessly delivered him two strapping sons, Colum and Hugh, proving the merit of his choice. His mother still presided over the kitchen, only now they had a stove, electricity, an inside privy, and running water, hot and cold.

Emmet had greeted his sudden arrival with deep-rooted suspicion, which even the bottle of Jameson's Whiskey had done little to assuage. He still feared being usurped by his older brother, his eyes contracting to pencil-thin lines, his lips pulling like a drawstring purse when he saw him toiling up the lane. Inwardly Sean crowed at his wariness. But as his fatigued eyes took in the slopes of tussocky pasture, the cows ambling aimlessly about beset with flies, he admitted to himself the full extent of his loathing for this mean, grudging soil. Emmet could have it and welcome. He had never wanted it, not any part of it; not his mother sucked of all goodness until her weathered skin was wrinkled like a prune's and her hands were rubbed raw; not his father who had lumbered about, arrogant in his ruthless, unyielding assertion of right and wrong, dealing out his farmyard justice with a peeled birch cane; not his brother who smugly attended church with his family every Sunday morning, and who masturbated away the afternoons in the outside toilet, poring over pictures of naked women he had found under the leaves of an unlit bonfire on the Boyles' neighbouring farm.

Sean had talked up his London success over a supper of stew and potatoes, his fast-growing retail business, his beautiful wife, Catherine, his model baby daughter, Bria, while Emmet's brood goggled at him curiously, and Emmet's wife busied herself cruising the table, topping up her family's fast-emptying bowls. The spoons had scraped the china like chalk squeaking discord on a blackboard. His nephews' Adam's apples had yo-yoed madly in their feeding frenzy. And his mother, an animal's unquestioning tolerance in her empty eyes, had chewed and chewed with her bad teeth on a chunk of bread soaked in milk. Every so often she had eyed this man who had grown in her womb, as if he had fallen from Mars. Emmet, at the head of the table, had sipped his whiskey sourly from a greasy tumbler, spooned his food unthinkingly into his mouth, and glowered at his older brother at the opposite end of the table with close-set eyes. If he had been a cat his tail would have been twitching, and a low premonitory growl would have emanated through the nicotine-stained enamel of his overbite.

They'd made up a bed for Sean on the settee in the small room off the kitchen, the one that his mother optimistically liked to call the parlour. The family was settled at the other end of the house, beyond the right-angle in the tail of the single-storey building. Sean sat and waited. He listened as the distant sounds of the house quietened, a door closing, something grating, his brother's gruff bark, and then there were only the creaks of the ancient farm's bones, the dyspeptic gurgles of pipes and the sonorous tick of the mantel clock. At just gone midnight the nocturnal cradle song stole into the comparative hush, the breeze hefting the window experimentally, the hoot of an owl, the click of claws behind the wainscot, the plaintive lowing of a cow, and yes, he could just detect it, the a cappella chorus floating to him on the unfurling spinnakers of river mist.

He had brought the book and he fingered it now in the squint of lamplight. The grey cover was worn and tattered, and the pages had grown flimsy as tissue paper with constant handling. He leafed through it, pausing at the diagrams, those fantastical diagrams that had fired his young mind. He sniffed in the frowsty odour, more welcome to him than the bouquet of a fine wine. Who would have thought the absurd little man in the old-fashioned pantaloon bathing trunks, and the hat that looked like a pilot's helmet, would have taken him step by step to heaven? With infinite patience he had taught him how he might seduce an Eve who was the nonpareil of womanly perfection. Again he heard her call to her lover. In answer he took up the book, pushed the packet of prescription sleeping pills, Mogadon, twenty in all, to the bottom of his trouser pocket, slipped the bottle of Armagnac under his arm and set off.

As he started down the hill, he felt a charge of adrenalin course round his body at the prospect of the reunion. All these years, he had not forgotten and neither had she. He recalled the welts on his bare buttocks, his thighs, his back, how they stung

352

after his father's savage beatings. He halted for a moment, wincing as he recollected the exquisite pain. For days it had been as if his skin was covered in a swarm of wasps, biting him over and over. It had bled, to begin with a weak, watery sort of blood mixed with pus, that gradually thickened to a deep crimson goo. Then this too had hardened, and small scabs had formed that had caught on the fabric of his clothes, occasionally being knocked off with friction and weeping anew. And afterwards the itching as the healing commenced. Somehow all of it was connected with her. The humiliation of having to strip before this red-faced Da, the man who had set himself up to be Sean's judge and jury. And the submission, bearing the torture without crying out, humbled by the feelings of self-purification that had invested him later.

It was a cool, damp night, the haze of mizzle moonlit, so that it seemed he was walking through a fairy landscape draped with lengths of spangled organza. Over his head was a pauper's night sky, with here and there cloud rags worried by eddies of wind. The moon was as yellow as the thick cream which rose like a sun in the still-warm milk pails of his boyhood. The sight of it recovered the smells of the milking shed for him; the immaculate astringency of the sluggishly breaking day; the sweetness of the straw crunch interspersed with the ripe steam of the beasts' breaths; the splat of dung that exuded the comfortable waft of the earth's entrails; the taste of his own inhalations, still vinegary with the stagnancy of sleep; the 'siss, siss' of the bluish-white line of milk darting into the snowy broth; and the invasive chill that made him lean in closer to the heat of the coarsely haired

353

flank, while the dumb creature patiently tolerated his fumbling, stiff fingers pulling on her udder.

But now as he reaches his mistress his face is saturated, the burn of his eyes delivered into a healing witch-hazel bath. Oh no, he does not imagine the leap of her as he tumbles out from the now heavier curtain of drizzle. He sags on the small apron of beach in his jeans and soggy fisherman's sweater, in his socks and his shoes, feeling overdressed in her presence, wondering if she can really recognize him after so much of her has flowed on past to the sea.

'I didn't bring my bike,' he mutters bashfully, as if to prod her memory. Mist vapours cling to her black surface, like a slinky diaphanous evening gown, affording slashed glimpses of her sable flesh. His heart is so full that there is no room for words. But the most incredible thing about her is that it doesn't matter, that she reads his deepest thoughts as though they are her own. He treads down to where she varnishes the shingle and the pebbles, flirting with the wet tickle of her. And he sits, clumsily, falling on his bottom at the last, jarring his coccyx painfully on the unyielding jags of the stones. His shoes are dipping in her and she is seeping, soothing as balm, into his nylon socks, tempting him. He leans forwards, and without unlacing them shoehorns them off, hurling them as far out as he can, hearing, gratified, her splashes of reception. She toys with one of them for a second, makes a raft of it and gives it safe passage, before wrecking it with a sudden surge and greedy suck.

He uncorks the brandy, holds the bottle to his lips and drinks a long draught, so that it barely touches his mouth, so that it is a moment before he experiences the resurgent slam of it, jabbing hotly into the soft membrane of his throat. Then he sets the bottle down among the grit, silt and stones. Next he rummages in his pocket, produces the envelope and carefully prises it open. He jiggles the white tablets out into the tremulous palm of his hand, drops his head and licks them off it, four, two, one, three, and again until they are all gone. As he chews his mother looms out of the mist. She is masticating her softened white bread like one of their cows chewing cud, mindlessly. She swallows, her toothless mouth yawning wide, and fat white maggots of script wiggle out of the cracked corners.

'Wicked . . . unnatural boy . . . naked . . . no shame . . . as God was his witness . . . diving off the rocks . . . the Shannon . . . an evil spirit in him . . . the Father says it's Satan's doing . . . whip the sin from him . . . cavorting with the devil in the river . . . a water demon.'

When his taste buds start humming with the bitterness, and the impulse to spew up all the wretchedness threatens to overwhelm him, he reaches fast for the bottle. He gulps and his throat, anaesthetized to the scorch, feels nothing but a woolly abrasion. He gives it a shake. Over half gone. He places it carefully back down, pulls off his wet socks and climbs to his feet. He undresses, his baggy, soggy cable-knit first, making a shorn sheep of him, then his granddad T-shirt. While the drizzle smacks the crucifix set of his shoulders and runs in little rivulets down his belly, he wrestles with his belt buckle. He blinks back raindrops or they might be tears, and contemplates all the buckles he has ever sold in the market, visualizes a mountain of them glittering in the sun like a pile of factory waste. The belt comes apart as if by its own volition, and he unzips his flies. His jeans fall in elaborate circus flounces around his bare feet. He wears no pants and once he has stepped out of them, more tricky to accomplish than he has envisaged, he is naked and has nowhere to hide. The crab pinch of the riverside stones is at him then, but they seem to be hurting some other man on some other shore. He is . . . what? He breathes . . . he breathes . . . he breathes the way the cows breathe in the milking shed in the early morning greyness, with will and effort, a wilful, effortful soughing.

He will dance for her, dance for her in the rain. He has the spider bite in his blood and he will dance the venom out of his heart, dance the tarantella. And so he begins, slowly, slowly, step and step and twist and fall, and lift his arms and arch his back, and roll his head, and clap and whirl and duck and spin. Bend like a blade of grass torn from its roots by the keen trawl of the north wind. Faster and faster he goes, immune to the daggers that pierce the soles of his feet. He is like Hans Christian Andersen's little mermaid, only a merman, treading on the points of nails or sharp knives, but like her he bears the agony willingly for his lady. He kneels down and begs her forgiveness for leaving, for his failed dreams, for Catherine who lay like an iron clod under him, for Bria who he loves dearly but not enough, for letting the hounds and horses run away with him, for chancing his luck with a mad blue buck who has trodden him down to the muck of his being.

'For all this and more, Shannon forgive me.' His confession, heavy with tears, falls and trickles between the stones, then subsides into the silt of her.

He staggers up, stoops for his bottle, drains the last drop and sends it spinning through the night to plant the crystal seed of itself in her belly. It is his harbinger, going before its master to bring her news of his coming. Again he offers her the gyre of his body, spinning arms outspread, the way he did as a boy. When at last he pauses, breathless and giddy, he is showered clean so that he is ready for her.

'Holy Mary, Mother of God, pray for us sinners, now and at the hour of our death.' He hesitates, in that instant knowing he is unworthy, raising his heavy head in the certain knowledge of her rejection. But when, black arms braceleted with bangles of moonshine, she beckons, her desire, he understands with a start, is as great as his. And as he wades into her icy embrace, collapsing into the polish of her mystery, she slides in eager response over him. He can wait no more. She senses it and opens her currents to him. He plunges then, plunges into her and she cushions his fall in the finest watered silk.

In her perfection is his absolution. He is as fine now as the virgin boy who came to her in his innocence. He has let life inveigle him away from her. He deserted his only true love, his Shannon. But now he will make amends for his betrayal, he vows, as he swims into her depths. He will give himself wholly to her, forsaking all others, forevermore. She succours him and then bids him lay his weary head on her dusky bosom. 'I am so tired, so very tired.' She knows his thoughts and lisps back to him in the parlance of the river.

'Lie with me, Sean. Give your will over to the flow

of me. And let me take you with me to my mother, the sea. For there a bed has been made ready.'

24

He is not sure what he expected—a great outpouring of grief, a fit of uncontrollable rage, to be so overcome by his phobia that he cannot bring himself to walk on the beach. But it is none of these things. The hot weather means that Saunton Sands is busy. He perches on a sand dune and spends an afternoon spying on other families, families whose perfect day is not going to end in tragedy. The scene has the bright certainty of a child's painting, the broad brushstrokes of the blue sky, the even bluer white-capped sea, the sun bright as a warrior's shield, the miles of sand the colour of sawdust. And dotted about in this collage are flags of pure colour, beachwear and picnic paraphernalia. It is a pleasure to see. There is a refreshing salty breeze tousling his hair. The rough and tumble of the waves and the plaintive cawing of gulls fill his ears—a holiday atmosphere.

He shades his eyes and plays 'X marks the spot'. But he cannot remember where it is, where the Abingdons pitched camp all those years ago, where Sarah drowned. And incongruously, this does not make him sad, but happy. So much sand has shifted since that dark day, so much that it looks like a different beach, washed clean. He stays in a nearby hotel for a few nights, and then for a week or so he drifts, staying in bed and breakfasts, moving from town to town. He outfits himself cheaply in beach gear, T-shirts and shorts. He rings the number Catherine has given him twice but there is no reply. He needs an update on Bria's condition, wants to hear that she has made a full recovery, that Catherine is coping, that Sean is back and his problems are sorted. He feels a degree of compunction about Naomi too. She is mentally disturbed, he is certain of it now. But perhaps she can be persuaded to seek psychiatric help. In truth though, he probably would not go back to the flat but for his photograph album, and his framed photograph. The clothes and few items he took with him to London, he can easily survive without, but his photographs are priceless.

There are not many of them. They do not begin to fill the worn blue leather album. But their rarity serves only to increase their value. Among his favourites are a shot of Sarah running in a rose garden. She wears a plaid dress with a round white collar. She is looking back at the camera laughing, her blonde curls flying. She has a daisy pinned in them, and she is surrounded by huge roses in full bloom, yellow, peach, cream and pink. There is a shot of them both on a slide. He is crouched at the top, arms wide, gripping her little hands. She is lying on the slide itself, pointing her feet and insisting that he let her go. In another they are sitting together in the stone-arched window of a castle, looking suitably awed. There is a family shot of them all together, outside a tent on a camping holiday. His mother is sitting in a fold-out chair with Sarah settled in her lap, and Owen and his father are standing to either side of them, striking masculine poses. The one of him and his father that he likes the best is of them flanking a huge train wreathed in clouds of steam. He can still remember the scorching smutty smell of it.

But his most highly prized photograph is the framed picture of him and his mother, just the two of them, bundled up in coats, scarves, gloves and hats, proudly showing off the snowman they have built. His mother is leaning over him, her arms criss-crossed over his chest, her rosy cheek next to his. He is holding a carrot to his nose, in mock imitation of the masterpiece they have created. And they are both having a fit of giggles.

He recalls the building of this snowman with the clarity of yesterday. Sarah had a cold and consequently wasn't allowed to play outdoors. She was crayoning by the fireside. His father was browsing through seed catalogues. His mother was baking and the house was spiced with the mouth-watering aroma of warm gingerbread. Outside was a winter wonderland carpeted with glistening white snow, irresistibly tempting for a young boy.

'Father, would . . . would you help me build a snowman?' he ventured tentatively.

'Not just now, Owen. P'rhaps when I've finished my tea.'

'But it'll be too late by then,' he worried.

'Maybe tomorrow. We'll see.'

He was unsurprised by the response, but this didn't make him feel any less crestfallen. He resigned himself to reading *The Shooting Star*, his latest Tintin adventure, and was about to fetch it when his mother appeared at the lounge door.

'You old killjoy, Bill.' This last delivered hands on hips, to his father. Then, turning to Owen, 'I'll build a snowman with you,' she said, her brown eyes shining impishly.

'Really?'

'Of course. It'll be the best snowman ever. Better get togged up because it looks freezing out there.'

She brought two chips of coal for the eyes, a carrot and string beans for the nose and mouth. 'Plus,' she whispered like a naughty schoolgirl, 'one of Father's old trilby hats, and that knitted scarf Granny made him that he won't wear. You get the twig broom from the shed just to finish him off.'

They'd worked at it until their cheeks were afire and their noses were red as a clown's. His hands in their gloves were numb with cold, but he felt hot as toast under his duffel coat. While he was bent over patting the last few handfuls of snow onto their snowman's plump girth, his mother pushed a handful under his collar. He squealed and jumped with the chill of it, and then set about making the biggest snowball he could.

'No, no, no!' she shrieked as he chased her round the garden. 'Have mercy, Owen.' But he threw it all the same and it landed with a thump on her back. As she brushed off snow crumbs, she was breathless with laughter. 'You little tinker,' she said affectionately. The light had a blue tint to it by then and she looked so lovely, her pale skin enriched by it. Sarah and his father waved at them through the window, as if trying to remind them both that they existed. And he thought that they looked rather jealous of the fun they were having. That was when his father got his camera and snapped the shot of them cheek to cheek, him with his orange carrot nose. Then they went indoors and ate hot gingerbread, and drank cocoa with nutmeg grated into the froth.

When, days later, she saw him patrolling the

361

snowman as it melted in the sun, she came outside and asked why he looked so sad. He faced her, his eyes welling up, his mouth a tight slash. 'I can't bear for it to disappear, Mother, to see what we made destroyed bit by bit. It's awful.'

She put her arm about his shoulder and considered for a moment. 'Think of it like this, Owen,' she said. 'He isn't a snowman at all, he is a water child locked in that big frozen body. The sun is releasing him, letting him escape. Look. Don't you see him in that puddle, the silver light dancing on the surface? Can't you feel how happy he is to be free?' And she squeezed his shoulder. The following year there was only a smattering of snow, not nearly enough for a snowman. Sarah wasn't waving at the window. His mother was nowhere to be seen. And the Water Child was the only light that stopped the darkness from swallowing him.

Towards the end of August he tries Catherine's number again from a call box. Her father answers. Owen recognizes the ponderous voice. He asks who is calling.

'It's Owen Abingdon. We met at Catherine's house in Hounslow a couple of weeks ago, when Bria wasn't too well.'

'Ah yes, one moment, please.'

A pause, then, 'Owen? Is that you?' There is relief in her tone.

'Yes. I've rung before but I must have missed you. Are you okay?'

'Not really.'

'Is Bria all right?' he asks anxiously.

'She's fine. Doing really well. It's something else. I don't want to tell you over the 'phone. Can you meet me?' They agree a rendezvous the following

362

afternoon in a café close to Covent Garden.

'One more thing. Owen, I rang the flat. I had to talk to you. I thought it was you who answered. I didn't say much. "Owen, it's Catherine." Just that, I think. And then I realized it wasn't you at the other end of the line, it was her. Naomi. I hung up straight away.'

'It's okay. I'll deal with it. Don't worry about it,' he told her.

'But Owen—'

'Catherine, it's all right. I'll look after you.' He reflects on those words the next day, as the train he is travelling in nears London. He has to remind himself that she is married, that it is not his job to care for her. It is beginning to feel as if Britain's climate has altered permanently, as if its population will never again be able to bemoan drab rainy skies. Hot-water bottles, toasting crumpets over the fire, bed socks and umbrellas, plastic fold-up rain bonnets, all these seem relegated to the past. They have become relics of a temperate age, consigned to annals of history alongside the ice age. The ventilation windows adjacent to his seat are jammed. After a third attempt to yank them open Owen resigns himself to stewing.

'Phew! It's too hot for comfort,' the man sitting opposite him comments. He is middle-aged, rotund, with a short boxed beard and thinning walnut-brown hair. And, Owen is to discover, he is garrulous. He puffs his cheeks up, then gusts air out, making his sparse fringe riffle. 'How anyone can work in this heat . . . I don't know.'

'Rain must come soon,' Owen says without much faith.

The man pushes the sleeves of his blue and white

striped shirt up and undoes another front button, exposing inches of chest hair. 'I tell you what, it makes you want to join a nudist colony.' Owen smiles politely. 'Round where I live the tarmac is actually melting. Melting! Can you believe that? The other day my daughter was sunbathing in the garden listening to her records. Five of the 45s warped in the sunshine. Ruined, they were. Pubs running out of lager. It's like the end of the world.'

'Let's hope not.'

'People passing out on the underground with heat exhaustion. Farmland turned to dustbowls. I heard the reservoirs have run dry. Fires everywhere. Here, have you heard they've appointed a Minister for Drought, Dennis Howell? They're calling him The Rainmaker. What d'you think his chances are, eh? 'Cos I tell you what, we need someone to perform a bloody miracle and fast.'

The Rainmaker. Owen reflects on this as he makes his way to the café to meet Catherine. There is an old film with Burt Lancaster and Katharine Hepburn called *The Rainmaker*, he recollects now. Burt's character, Starbuck, was a conman, he thinks wryly, wondering if Dennis Howell is any fitter for the job. He is early. They are meeting at 4 p.m., so with a quarter of an hour to spare he orders an ice-cold Cresta Soda. As soon as it becomes vacant he pounces on the table nearest the pedestal fan. After they have talked, he plans to call in at the flat, to see Naomi and retrieve his photographs and his few possessions, before setting off for good.

She looks beautiful when she arrives, in a cheesecloth dress, flowers embroidered on the yoke. Her hair brushes his hand as she sits down. It is loose, held back with sunglasses worn like an

Alice band. There are gold sleeper earrings piercing her earlobes. She orders the same as him when the waitress comes round.

'How are you?' Owen begins. 'How's Bria?'

'We're both fine.' But her eyes are sorrowful as she says this. She touches his hand for a second. 'It's so good to see you again, Owen.' The waitress sets down the drink and a glass. He sees that her fingers are trembling as she pours it. She looks up and her eyes find his. 'Sean's dead,' she says simply.

There is a momentary pause while he takes in this terrible news. 'Oh God, no! I'm so sorry, Catherine!' His initial assumption is that somehow or other Blue got to him, but this is dispelled an instant later when she tells him that it was suicide.

'He drowned himself, Owen. He drowned himself near his childhood home, in the Shannon River. He took sleeping pills and booze and went for a midnight swim. I went to Ireland for the funeral.' He cups his mouth and takes a few juddering breaths. But at least he knows that Blue did not catch up with him, that in the end he was quicker than the horses and the dogs he bet on, that he outfoxed them all.

'It's been awful. My cousin Rosalyn was here. She came over for the service. I went to the place where it happened, a secluded shelf of shingle beach and the huge greenness of that river pushing past it,' Catherine tells him. 'His mother said that he used to go there to bathe, that as a boy he taught himself to swim in that very spot in the Shannon River.'

He nods and a night audience with drunken Sean revisits him. My mistress, my green mistress. He should be shaking imagining it, the River, how it flowed through Sean's life, then over it. 'My mistress, my green mistress.'

'My green mistress? What's that?'

'Something he said one night. I just wonder . . . if he meant, well, his river.'

Catherine nods, sips from her glass, then sets it down. 'His mother said it wasn't right, what he did as a boy. Teaching himself to swim like that. She said that it wasn't natural, that it was shameful. A man in the village saw him, saw Sean diving from rocks into the River Shannon, and he told her. His father whipped him, Owen. His father whipped him for swimming in the river.'

'That's horrible,' Owen whispers.

'He was cremated. Did I tell you that?' Her eyes look distant.

'No.'

'They gave me a pot with his ashes in it. I asked his mother if she wanted to keep it, but she said no, that he'd caused enough trouble. She said it so dispassionately, as if she really did not care. So . . . so—' She breaks off and unconsciously draws the letter 'S' on the table with the tip of her little finger. Then a small sound as her breath jars. 'So I took it to the Shannon, to the shingle beach, to the place where he drowned. I went by myself. I clambered onto the rocks that he must have dived from. And . . . and I took the lid off the pot and sprinkled his ashes in the river, watched them float away on the swell. Because, well, because I think he loved it there. He must have loved the river to choose to end his life in it. Was that silly of me, Owen?'

'No. It wasn't silly. It was the right thing to do. He would have been pleased.' Owen covers her hand with his. It is small, cool and smooth. Her free hand rummages in her shoulder bag and she lifts out a

366

book, a battered grey book. It is no bigger than a paperback novel and half the thickness. Threads have frayed from its binding, and there are a few discoloured patches here and there. Its spine has been concertinaed with much use. She places it with care between them.

There is a pause while they both drop their heads and look at it. They might be praying. In a café slotted in among so many others, people meet, talk, argue, laugh, crockery chinks, cups steam, machines hiss, tills jingle and voices rise and fall. And Owen and Catherine sit reverently and stare at an undistinguished grey book. It might have come from a jumble sale, or a charity shop. It might have lain on the dusty shelf of a second-hand book shop for lifetimes. Or it might have been found by a ten-year-old Irish boy rifling surreptitiously through his aunt's trunk one Christmas, a boy who hunched over its well-thumbed pages by candlelight, and dreamt of having mastery over the green mistress who ordered all their lives. Now the Water Children sense its powers. Owen knows that when he lifts the cover, he will be opening a door onto another world, a water world, that he will need to grow fins to enter it.

'They found it by the river. He had tucked it under his clothes. But it was wet and so it got a bit damp. The pages are ribbed, see, but you can still read them. And make out the diagrams clearly too. It's a book teaching you how to swim. It's very dated. Ancient, almost. And some of the pictures are so funny.' She smiles, and Owen imagines Sean, the boy, poring over them, his heart racketing in his bony chest as he risked unleashing his imagination.

'I can't swim,' Owen confesses, noting how the

passage of air from the pedestal fan stirs her hair. He lays his hand on the swimming bible and swears to tell the truth. 'My sister drowned. Sarah. She was nearly five. We went to the seaside and my mother told me not to leave her but . . .'

'Go on,' she urges. And he tells her all of it.

When he finishes they sit in silence, their thoughts perfectly synchronized, swimming through a sea of grief. Then it is Catherine's turn. Owen walks with her through the snow. He lets his eyes be mesmerized by its stark monochrome colours. He shares the sense of purpose as they trudge, and the wonder that the ice island holds when they stumble on it. He sees cousin Rosalyn, skating on the ice, her red beret like a bead of blood in the large whiteness. And he sees the two girls sinking into a web of cracks.

'I thought it was Rosalyn who was crippled that day, but it was me. It was me, Owen. And I have been dying ever since. If it wasn't for Bria . . .' But she does not have to complete the sentence. He knows, knows that neither of them are tethered to the jetty of their lives, that all it will take is one rogue wave and they will be driftwood forever. They look through the book at the posturing man demonstrating swimming strokes. Catherine casts her green eyes up and sees a healing breath of laughter making Owen's lips quiver. He traces one of the diagrams with a tremulous finger and she sees a tenuous curiosity light his eyes. He takes it in, this half man, half fish, this merman, setting him a challenge.

'Owen, there's something you should know.'

'Yes?' He has a sudden twinge of concern at what she may be about to divulge.

'I . . . I only hope that it doesn't shock you.' He runs a finger up and down the condensation on the side of his glass, his breath bated. 'I didn't love Sean. And I don't believe he loved me either. I shouldn't have married him. My parents had persuaded me to go to secretarial college. I hated it there. I felt so boxed in, living with them, training for a job I didn't want. Marriage offered me a way out.' She takes a swallow of her drink and pushes her lips together before continuing. 'I think he had his reasons for marrying me, too. He thought having a middle-class English woman for a wife was the benchmark of respectability. He was so ambitious, wanting to improve his lot. But it all went wrong.' She inhales shakily. 'Bria wasn't planned. If it hadn't been for her I think we would have parted within weeks of the wedding. There, so now you know.'

He smiles at her reassuringly. 'I guessed it wasn't working out.'

'I'm going to start over, begin again, get it right.'

'So am I,' Owen says. Their eyes meet and hold, and for long seconds neither speaks. There is no need.

Then, 'I have to pick up Sean's things from the flat. It's the landlord's furniture so there shouldn't be very much,' she says. 'But I wondered if you'd help me.'

'Look, I'll pack them up for you. As soon as they're ready I'll call. You can come by and we'll load them straight into a car. That way you don't have to cope with seeing Naomi. How's that sound?'

She nods, looking relieved. She tells him that she is catching a train from Waterloo, hurrying back to Bria who is being minded by her parents. They walk

369

together, the heat making them dawdle. The commuters have caught their trains. The streets have thinned. The traffic still grinds, but it is more like whinging than grumbling. The dust of the day is settling. The low sun makes the windows of tall buildings twinkle as if festooned with fairy lights. They reach the bridge, Waterloo Bridge, and Owen hesitates. The Thames eyes him blackly, a sardonic humour in its heavy drag. Catherine takes his hand and he learns to walk on water, one step, two steps, three steps, four. He wobbles a bit, but not so that you would notice. She wraps the stone of his resistant hand in the quietly determined paper of hers—and wins.

They pause in the middle of the bridge, the Water Children, poised above the sleek inky river decked in its reflected finery. They blink in unison. The Houses of Parliament stare them down. Important matters of government are decided here, but none as important as what is being decided on Waterloo Bridge this second. Big Ben courteously slows down time.

'I can teach you to swim,' says Catherine, looking up at Owen. 'I'm a strong swimmer. We can go to a swimming pool together and I can teach you.' He remembers the lessons with his father, the humiliation of them, floundering in the water, gulping for air, his father glancing up at the clock, begrudging the wasted minutes. His eyes veer to Big Ben. But Big Ben refuses to be hurried. Take my time, he says. Help yourself. Plenty more where this comes from. 'You'll be safe with me. I promise.'

And Owen knows that this is a certainty, that with Catherine there he will not drown, that the paper of her resolve will make a sailboat of him and keep him afloat. The rocks of his resistant hands cup her face. He leans and she stretches, and their lips meet with a salt-sweet tenderness that only spirits of the water can impart.

The woman who has been following them is standing by the riverside in the shadow cast by a tree. She has two profiles, two faces. One, blue eyed, is glacial, clinical, calculating. The other, brown eyed, is a conundrum, fathomless. And both are trained on the couple kissing on the bridge. Owen and Catherine . . . Owen and Judy . . . Walt and Judy. The names jostle in her head. He betrayed her with Judy. She saw them, fire lit, saw them embracing, saw that he wanted her, wanted to take her right there and then. Crouched in the tent, she observed them sleeping, while music washed over them, making the canvas quake.

There isn't much time, not if she is going to catch Leonard Cohen. To have come all this way and then not hear him sing? She must hurry if she does not want to miss him. He will perform 'Suzanne' for her, only for her, for Mara and no one else. In his poetry is her history. He knows the danger in her sea currents, the way she shelves steeply, and he sees the answers in her deadly depths. For she is the lady of the lake, and in the mirror of it her other self is revealed.

*   *   *

As Owen ascends the stairs to the flat his trepidation grows. He is not sure what he hopes for, that Naomi will not be there, that if she is, she will be repentant, approachable. He cannot insist she has treatment, only advise. Still, perhaps in this interim period

371

while he has been absent, she has done some soul-searching, and reached the same conclusion as him. It is as he passes the first-floor landing that he hears the music, together with the trilling of the 'phone. But it is not until he is taking the last flight of stairs that he can place it. 'Suzanne', the Leonard Cohen ballad. It is one of her favourite records and he takes it as a good omen. The ringing stops as he approaches the door. The caller, whoever it was, has hung up. He has his key ready but it is ajar. When he examines it he sees splintered wood, that the lock is broken. He thinks immediately of Blue and proceeds cautiously, prodding the door open.

25

Catherine watches his receding back as he crosses the bridge, a tall young man with untidy fair hair, shy blue eyes, and the hint of an iron determination growing in the line of his mouth. She can still feel him on her lips, taste him. Something wondrous has happened to time. All the seconds, all the minutes, all the hours, are overlapping, so that she is no longer sure any accurate measure of them is possible. Surely she has known Owen all her life. And yet if the calendar is to be believed, they have only met a few times. She glances across at Big Ben, at the implacable face, to see if he has any explanation. But he is giving nothing away. If the kiss was a colour, then that colour has bled into the seconds before and after it, dyeing them. The outline of her, so sharp and distinct all her life, has suddenly blurred. And the outline of him, please tell her that she has not made a mistake, that has fogged too. She no longer knows where she ends, but she thinks it is in Owen.

It is while she is grappling with this that she notices a variation in the river. There is a strange silvery light playing on the face of the water. Can it be true that the reflected bleached hue of this everlasting summer is fading? Slowly she raises her eyes to the sky and the breath flutters into her at what she sees there. A bank of oyster grey, of gorgeous oyster grey massing on the horizon. A mirage or real? Other people are stopping on the bridge and pointing now. She overhears someone say it, their voice hushed with veneration. 'Rain clouds. I think it is.' Distantly there comes a rumble of thunder. This nimbostratus cloud has become such a rare phenomenon that she has the urge to rub her eyes to be certain of what she sees. Can it be, can it really be that rain is coming? That at last rain is coming? That the long hot summer of 1976 is over?

She turns towards the train station but every step that brings her closer to it, takes her further away from Owen. The silver light skimming on the water beckons irresistibly. As she stares at it over the bridge railings she glimpses a man sitting by the river. He is facing away from her, wearing a black hood. And now he is turning, slowly turning and raising his head. She tears her gaze away, her growing recognition too appalling to contemplate. When she glances back he is nowhere to be seen. Then comes the still small voice in her head. 'If you catch your train you will never see Owen again.' For an instant she is hypnotized by the flickering light. And now she can smell rain, honeyed rain,

373

percolating through the air. Distantly a jag of brilliance flashes in the sky. 'If you catch your train you will never see Owen again.' She hears the solid thud of his heart through the cotton of his shirt as she weeps into his chest, feels his broad shoulders carrying her. She sees him standing on her doorstep, backlit with blinding sunshine, Bria alive and safe in his arms. She feels his hands cupping her face, his lips on hers, him in her and her in him. Their separateness unravels, and the river glides on by beneath them. By the third time she hears the voice she is belting across the bridge, dodging bemused spectators, her panting breaths knifing into her lungs. At her back the approaching storm snarls.

26

For an instant Owen makes no move, only listens, teasing apart the sounds that reach him. The lyrics of the song 'Suzanne', the backing chords of the guitar, the husky sigh of the leaking taps, the murmur of traffic.

'Naomi?' Intending not to startle her, his tone is deliberately soft. 'Naomi? It's Owen.' Her bedroom door is closed. He knocks softly. 'Naomi?' He tries the handle with gentle pressure and finds it locked. In his room the contents of the wardrobe and drawers lie ripped and scattered over the bed and floor. The cardboard boxes of stock for the market have been torn open and gilt key-rings, costume jewellery, bags and purses litter the floor. Now he becomes aware of another noise, louder than the rest, the pounding of his own heart. But his framed photograph is where he left it and he retrieves it. He leaves his room, and parts the bead curtain before stepping through it. Cupboards have been emptied in the galley kitchen, but the lounge is relatively unscathed. Cushions lie on the floor, along with a couple of ashtrays spilling over with cigarette stubs. There is a vase of dead browning carnations in murky water on the small dining table. The record is going round and round on its turntable, the whine of the song emitting from the record player's built-in speaker.

Behind him the beads clatter. A shriek rends the air. Owen wheels round as Naomi launches herself at him. She clutches a carving knife, stabbing frenziedly. Instinctively his hands shoot up, palms outwards in self-defence. The framed photograph crashes to the floor. Arms flaying, he knocks the vase, sending it flying. It shatters. Shrivelled flowers scatter. Slimy water puddles over the photograph of the snowman. Light jewels it. The flash of a face contorted with malice comes at him. A smear of heavy make-up. The blur of a flowered smock. The knife thrusting. He feels the blade slash. The soft flesh of his hand bursts open. He grabs her wrist, tries to turn the weapon away from him. His grasp slips on his own blood. Her strength is staggering. They arm wrestle, knocking the lava lamp over, the telephone. His shoes and her bare feet trample the shards of the glass. His heart is pumping, the tip of the knife only inches from it. He knows he is about to die.

An arm sweeps aside the bead curtain. Catherine screams . . . Naomi's head snaps round . . . Owen twists her wrist . . . the angle of the blade shifts . . . he skids on the wet slick . . . Naomi's head snaps round . . . he skids on the wet slick . . . Owen twists her wrist

375

. . . the angle of the blade shifts . . . Catherine screams . . . they fall in an elegant arc. The knife roots in her soft belly. Naomi gives a breathy grunt. Time stops.

There is an indeterminate interval. Then Catherine's face swims above Owen, the red hair dangling down. Did a strand of it touch his face? He thinks it did. He thinks amid all the other sensations, he can isolate that one. The tickle of her red hair. He feels the warm blood pumping between the sandwich of his body and Naomi's. He is not sure if he is dying, not sure which of them the knife has skewered. Catherine is calling his name. Then she is gone and he can hear her reeling off an address. It is the address of a flat in Covent Garden. It is where he has been living with Naomi and Sean all this long, hot summer. He inhales the chalky taint of powdery make-up. Naomi's eyelids, half open, waver. Her lips are parted, bluish and dry as asbestos. Her pallor is lead-white. Her mouth is froth-full of blood.

'Naomi?' he says.

She lifts her neck in one final supreme effort of will, her bloodied lips moving against his ear make her faltering reply. 'Ma . . . Mara.' As the song finishes, the first fat drops of rain strike the windows.

27

They are standing in the garden examining the sky. This became Bill's habit in June, when the extreme temperatures began reaping horticultural casualties. Ruth joined him, and now this sky-watching ritual

376

is well established. He is squinting at a distant grey mash of gathering clouds, his brow furrowing.

'Do you think it could be rain?' he asks optimistically.

'I wouldn't like to say,' Ruth replies. They have been fooled before. Clouds materialize and then evanesce without a single drop of moisture falling. Her brow is lined too. But it is not the promise of rain that is absorbing her, although she does grant that there is a queer silvery quality to the light this evening. It is their conversation of minutes ago that is fraying her thoughts and unravelling her composure. Bill mentioned, almost casually, almost in passing, that he has been unable to get hold of Owen since he returned from his holiday in Italy and dropped the car off. Again, in isolation this comment would not have been a source of undue concern. Their son lives in London where there is life at night. He is in the heart of theatre land. It is probable, likely even, that when Bill rang he was out and about watching a show, or eating at a restaurant. No, it is his elaboration that is unsettling her.

'Someone answered the 'phone all right. On each occasion. And I rung three times in all, Ruth. I could hear them breathing down the line and some music playing in the background. I asked if Owen was there. I said, it's Bill Abingdon here, Owen's father, and can I speak to him. Not a word of answer. The first time I wondered if I'd dialled the wrong number, so I hung up and had another go. I even tried his flatmates' names, Sean, and the one we met, the woman who stayed here overnight, Naomi. Not a sausage. Bizarre. Still, I should think there's a plausible explanation.'

377

And now Naomi's image keeps hatching in her reverie, the perplexing eyes of different colours, the way they glazed over periodically, the messy tired hair that looked as if it had been repeatedly dyed. As she gazes at the sky and prays for her husband's sake that rain is imminent, her maternal instinct tells her that there is something odd about this woman, something menacing.

She hoods her eyes with a hand and peers and peers. All in all, Ruth has had a strange day. Days have become monotonous for her, one very like another. But this one she has *felt*, and this in itself is remarkable. Because she has not *felt* anything very much for years, it seems. There is an expression that seems apt when describing the all-pervasive mood of this particular day, *the calm before the storm*— except that, increasingly, she is not calm.

This morning she went to visit Sarah's grave, the grassy hump frizzled to tired brown straw. And there was nothing unusual about this. She goes most days, keeps it tidy, takes flowers. Only the flowers have been a problem of late with this intolerable heat. You'd have thought, being married to a gardener, that he would have managed to come up with something. But no, the gardens he worked in, and their own, have become wastelands, the plants so dehydrated you imagine that you hear them crying out for water as you stroll past the beds. She'd finally settled for shop-bought carnations, pale pink as it happens, and then immediately regretted her purchase. She hates carnations, well, certainly the modern varieties. The old-fashioned sort are passable, she supposes. They are larger and at least they have a scent. But the ones everyone has nowadays are small fussy flowers, with absolutely no fragrance whatsoever. What she especially dislikes about them are the very things that make them so popular, the longevity of the cut blossoms, the way weeks after they have past their best the eye can be tricked into believing that there is still life in them.

She asked Bill to stop at the supermarket on the way home. When she emerged with cardboard boxes and no groceries he was perturbed. 'Whatever are those for?' he wanted to know. She gave him a wan smile in reply. When they got home she made a bee-line for Sarah's room and began sorting through her things. Bill hovered uneasily outside the door. 'What are you doing, love?' he asked at last, peeping in. By then she had filled one box and made a start on the other.

'I'm going through Sarah's things, sorting out some bits and pieces for the Church sale, and some for Oxfam.' He looked stricken when she glanced up.

'Is that a . . . a good idea?' he said hesitantly, stroking the bald crown of his head, where the line of his Frankenstein scar could still be clearly detected.

She smiled to herself wistfully. 'After fifteen years, ooh, I think so. We'll have a memory box for her treasures, our treasures, but not a memory room.' He helped her for a while. Then, sensing that what she craved most was to be left alone, he busied himself filling his watering cans with the used bath water they saved each day for the purpose. What struck her suddenly, as she folded small items of clothing, was the sudden revelation that she had to earn Sarah's love, that every glorious day she spent with her was a labour, not of love, but for love. And here was the difference between her son and her daughter, Owen and Sarah. Owen's love for her was unconditional. She was overcome with a choking sensation, and deep inside her chest there was a stab of pain. She took a sharp intake of breath at the realization. She had taken her son's rare devotion, the more mature accepting love, entirely for granted. She thought about the shop-bought carnations, the way they duped you into believing they still had life in them, when in fact they were long dead.

Now she leaves Bill cloud gazing, comes indoors and tries her son's 'phone number twice, but no one answers. Throughout the evening the calm that is not calm, persists. She finds that she cannot settle to an episode of *Dad's Army*, that she is up and down fussing constantly. So that when the doorbell rings, she is ready for it.

It is Bill who seems entirely flabbergasted to find two uniformed policemen standing on their doorstep.

'Mr and Mrs Abingdon, I wonder if we could come inside and have a word with you,' asks the taller of the two. She is aware of her heart suddenly, aware that it is starting to beat extremely fast. They wait for her to sit down, wait for Bill to lower himself into a seat beside her. They take their caps off respectfully. 'It's about your son, Owen.' She is keening, a high shrill note. It is too late, she thinks. He is dead. My son is dead. I have woken up too late.

The rain that started to fall as they left Wantage is cascading down by the time they reach London. Ruth stares out of the car window and she sees that there are people dancing in the streets, dancing in the deluge sheeting down from dark grey skies.

380

They are tearing open their clothes and letting the rain wash the dust of this ceaseless summer away. Her son's injuries are not thought to be life threatening. This is what the police told her, that he was attacked with a knife, that his hand was badly cut, that he is receiving treatment at hospital. She can hear the raindrops hammering down on the car's roof. She can see the gutters running with shining life-giving water.

28

Sitting in the hospital corridor, his hand bound up so that it resembles a white boxing glove, Owen feels like what he is tonight, a little boy. A mobile of busy people turn around him, receptionists, nurses, doctors, patients, relatives. Rush, rush, rush. Everyone is occupied. Everyone seems to know what to do, everyone except him. His hand throbs and his shirt is soaked with blood, hers, whoever she was, and his. Two policemen stand nearby talking in subdued voices, waiting for the cut in his hand to be stitched up, waiting until they say that the young man is sufficiently well to go to the station and make a statement. After the paramedics pronounced Naomi dead, they took Owen in an ambulance to the hospital, with a police escort. Catherine was driven away to make her witness statement. She told him that she'd come back as soon as she could, but for now he is alone.

The lights shrill down on him, making his eyes hurt. And the pattern on the lino floor also bothers him because it isn't symmetrical. They are not equilateral triangles. They are all made up of varying angles. All those angles and none of them appearing the same. It makes him feel insecure somehow. He closes his eyes and he is on the beach all by himself. Looking about him, he can see that there is a whole desert of sand here, dunes of it. And instinctively he knows if he crests one hill there will be another, and another, and another after that. He turns his back on the sand. But this is worse, much worse. The sea stretches before him for eternity. And he has to fish Sarah out, but he doesn't know where to start. He ought to run roaring at the surf and demand that it regurgitates her, spits her back into life. But he knows the waves will only shake with mocking laughter at this.

'D'you want a cuppa, son?' one of the policemen asks. He shakes his head. He *wants* his mother. There is some kind of commotion at the far end of the corridor, raised voices, a row. Nothing out of the ordinary. This is casualty late at night. Owen turns his head robotically towards the rumpus. Who is flying down the corridor, crashing into the placid nurse, sending her papers fluttering to the ground, knocking over a chair, jogging the man by the coffee machine, making him drop his cup? Who is this creating a scene? It is a mother who has lost her son. She has been searching for him for fifteen years. There is no room for English reserve here. Ruth does not care about the nurse hurrying after her calling, 'Miss, Miss. You're not allowed to . . .' Nor does she care about the man with the coffee splattered over his shirt who is swearing at her, or the fact that an orderly has bustled off to alert security. The cotton dress she is wearing, a pink and white patchwork print, is saturated. It immodestly hugs the contours of her body. Her brown hair is loose and dripping. Her sandals squelch as she sprints down the corridor. She is bowling people like skittles out of her path.

'Owen! Owen!' And the small boy hunched alone on the sand hears his name, hears the desperation in it. His head comes up instantly. Then he is on his feet waving his bandaged hand, tears gushing down his cheeks. Her arms strait-jacket wetly around him.

'My son!' And he is shaking with shock and relief, and mumbling incoherently. His father is here now, too, in the background, nodding at the policemen and looking rather sheepish.

'I'm sorry,' Owen says.

'No . . . I'm sorry,' she whispers back.

EPILOGUE

The seagull breasts the evening air with the grace of a glider. The setting sun has given a golden blush to its plumage, and made an eagle of the scavenger. Its eyes swivel tirelessly over sea and land. It spies many things winking in the blue goblet of the bay. There is a secluded cottage built of Cornish stone. A path leading from it meanders across a shoulder of meadowland speckled with wild flowers. It winds down a cliff-face fretted with bracken, chequered with boulders and slabs of rock. The gull anchors on pockets of sea kale, dainty white scurvy grass, and cushions of fluffy pink thrift. Finally, the neck of the path splays out onto a harp of golden-brown sand. Here the armadillo rocks that burrow below the tide line are blanketed with banks of blue-grey mussels, and sequinned with crushed shells.

A balding man sits on a towel in the shade reading a newspaper. A young couple stroll together on the sand, arms linked. He is fair haired, blue eyed, while she is a redhead with pale-green eyes the colour of grapes. A short way from them a tall, willowy, middle-aged woman walks a little girl through the sparkling aquamarine shallows. All five wear bright bathing costumes, scarlet, rich blues and primrose yellow. The girl has a mop of gingery curls tucked beneath an orange sunhat. And when she looks up the gull spies her vivid blue-green eyes. She squeals in delight as the running wavelets break about her feet and ankles. The willowy woman glances at her watch, and then she bends and whispers something to the child. For a few minutes while she collects up their belongings, she leaves her under the watchful eyes of the young couple.

The sun's rays fire the shoulder-length red hair. The gull screeches at the flash of lucent copper, and all of them raise their heads at the cry. The girl sits in the skittish water. She cocks her head and listens to the waves burbling their secrets into the sand. Digging, she finds a pearly shell. She shakes it in the surf, washing the sand grains off it. She likes the taste of sea salt, likes it when it dries to a fine white dust on her skin. She clambers up and toddles a few steps forward. She has no fear of the sea, for she is a water baby. She has been swimming with her mother since the age of two. She likes to draw the mermaids she has seen in her storybook, mermaids with fishtails instead of legs. She uses all the blues and greens and greys to colour them in. In her last picture she drew a small flesh-pink baby in the arms of a mermaid. And when her mother asked who it was, she answered, 'It's me, Mummy, can't you see?'

The tall woman is back. There is a serene expression on her face as she holds out her hand to the child. The girl goes willingly enough, because she knows that the sea will be here tomorrow, waiting for her. She stands patiently while she is towel dried, and they both tug on sandals. They collect the balding man with his newspaper and all three trudge over the sand. They pause once to look back and smile at the couple, and at the waves. Then they climb the cliff path hand in hand. After they have gone the young couple wade into the sea until they are waist deep. Then they climb onto a large rock, its plateau top well clear of the lapping water. They sit and stare out at the felt-tipped line of the horizon. They can see a sailboat and a distant

386

ship, a tanker, he thinks. Gazing upwards at the giddy azure sky, they tail the seagull still eyeing them curiously.

That amber eye has grown wise on wonders, on the moon and the sun at either ends of the corridor of the sky, on storms that make flotsam of mighty ships, on the rigours of an unforgiving sun, on doomed sailors, and pods of whales singing their eerie songs. And now he spies one more. Beside the couple sunning themselves on the rock, sits a child, a Water Child, an enchanted silver jitterbug of pure light. He is no stranger to the seagull. It has seen him before and it will see him again. Together, the man, and the woman, and the Water Child slip into the sea. They swim in triplicate. The couple take huge breaths and dive, opening their eyes on a marvel, a salt-stung vista. A world of flaxen sand. The sponged shapes of rocks in aubergine and maroon, bisque and oatmeal. Forests of glassy brown weed. Pastures of apple-green moss, peopled with prickly sea urchins. Rose-pink and violet anemones. Varnished apricot crabs. Shoals of tiny fish that sparkle like puffs of glitter. The blue fists of the sea pummel them, sparring with them, goading the swimmers on that little bit further. So that it is the Water Child who has to halt them with a starry burst of brilliance, making them know that this is his element, not theirs, that they must turn back now. They see him wriggle away, joyous to be free, like a silver eel slicing into the deep blue. Then they surface, suck in air gratefully, and strike out confidently for the shore. But the seagull, beguiled by the astonishing silvery foxtrot, bolstered by the thermals, tracks the Water Child out into the sorcery of the Atlantic Ocean.

LEGEND OF LAKE VAGLI

The legend of the lake springs from seeds of truth. The ghost village of Fabbriche di Careggine, featured in *The Water Children* is no myth. Founded in the 13th Century, it was once a bustling community. In 1941 work started on the construction of a dam that would harness the might of the Edron River, providing hydroelectric power for the region. With its completion in 1953 the Edron valley was flooded, drowning the deserted village. But folk tell of one inhabitant who remained in her little cottage, the beautiful Teodora, that Lake Vagli became her watery grave. Feared by the villagers, she was thought to be a witch. It is said that this young, lovely sorceress had worked her charms on Anselmo, a man much older than her who became her husband. When he went foraging for firewood in the treacherous mountains, an icy storm blew up. He stumbled and broke his leg. Teodora awaiting his return did not raise the alarm. She knew that if he had been injured his only hope was rescue. He was discovered frozen to death. When the lake was first drained in 1958, as it is every ten years, they searched for her bones. They dug for them in the mud, but found no trace of the enchantress. She is forever the lady of the lake, a siren haunting the silvery depths.

ACKNOWLEDGEMENTS

My deepest thanks to my incomparable agent, Judith Murdoch, and my exceptional publisher and editor, Patrick Janson-Smith, and to my inspirational editors, Laura Deacon and Susan Opie.